T0283550

RUNNING OUT OF AIR

Running Out of Air

Lilli Sutton

/Il MIRA

/II MIRA™

ISBN-13: 978-0-7783-6818-2

Running Out of Air

Copyright © 2024 by Lilli Sutton

Recycling programs
for this product may
not exist in your area.

Mira
22 Adelaide St. West, 41st Floor
Toronto, Ontario M5H 4E3, Canada
MIRABooks.com

Printed in U.S.A.

To my parents, Eilene and Mark,
for raising me with love, nature and stories

CHAPTER ONE

Sophie took ten breaths before her next step. She counted them because the sound of air rushing in and out of her lungs was the only thing tethering her to reality. Hurricane-force wind slammed into her body, cutting through her down suit and chilling her to the bone. And the wind brought snow—an endless sea of swirling white, beckoning her into disorientation. She lifted a boot-clad foot and planted her crampons in the snow. One step closer.

She had reached the summit already. Now she had to return to Camp Four alive. And she wasn't alone. The rope attached to her climbing harness pulled tight, reminding her that for every step she took, Levi had to take one too.

Sophie turned to look at him, shielding her face from the snow as best she could, thankful for the wind at her back as she took a few short steps to reach him. Fewer breaths in between this time—it didn't matter if her body had already reached its limit. She would push beyond to get Levi to safety.

He stood with his head down, shoulders slumped, swaying in the wind like a sapling. He looked like he would topple over if he took another step, but Sophie placed her hand on his shoulder and tried her best to shout above the wind.

"You have to keep going!"

Levi lifted his head slightly. An oxygen mask covered the lower half of his face, preventing him from responding but feeding precious air into his lungs. And his eyes were covered by clunky, dark sunglasses, which had been necessary that morning, when the sky was clear and bright. She wanted to shake him, slap him, anything to rouse him from his trance. But he had reached a state of exhaustion from which he could only return at a lower altitude. They had been climbing for close to nine hours after weeks of sleepless nights, low oxygen, and not enough food—Sophie knew that her body, like Levi's, was deteriorating. But they had to keep moving. Their lives depended on it.

Sophie turned to face the wind again and saw her sister appear from the snow like an apparition. Yesterday she would have laughed at the idea of Evelyn guiding them down through the storm, but extreme conditions necessitated extraordinary solutions. Evelyn stomped up the short slope, moving much more strongly than Sophie felt capable of.

Evelyn yanked her mask down and moved close to Sophie, shouting to make herself heard above the wind. "The ridge. Can he make it down?"

Sophie stared back at her, unable to respond. She'd made it this far without thinking of the ridge, that knife-edge spine of the mountain, exposed on either side, difficult to traverse that morning even in perfect conditions with the thrill of the summit ahead.

"The ridge, Sophie," Evelyn repeated.

Sophie blinked, forcing herself to register the information. "I don't know," she shouted back.

"Should we bivouac?" Evelyn's expression told Sophie she didn't think it was a good idea. Bivouacking meant spending the night in a glorified sleeping bag, insulated from the elements to some extent but still at the mercy of the death zone. The altitude above eight thousand meters could cause all kinds of problems—heart attacks, strokes, or impaired judgment from an oxygen-starved brain. It was not a place to camp out for long.

Her suggestion snapped Sophie out of her fog. "No way. He won't survive. We have to keep going."

"Okay. But once we're on the ridge, we can't stop."

"I know."

Evelyn nodded once and slipped the oxygen mask back over her face. She walked past Sophie, to Levi, and lifted his head. She took off his sunglasses and forced him to look at her. Sophie watched her sister in silence, willing her to do anything to make attempting the ridge possible. She waited for Evelyn to speak, but she said nothing, only slipped Levi's sunglasses into her jacket pocket—a practical gesture, keeping them safe until he needed them again.

Sophie opened her mouth as Evelyn passed, hoping for reassurance that she thought Levi was up for it, but Evelyn only gestured for them to follow. Sophie took the deepest breath she could, glanced back at Levi, and followed Evelyn's quickly fading form into the snow.

The ridge came up faster than Sophie anticipated. She thought of the ascent, when the skies were clear and she had seen the dizzying drop-off on either side, a free fall to certain death down the mountain. At least now the storm hid the exposure, though the gusting winds made every step more precarious. She stopped to check the short rope between her and Levi's harnesses. Sophie knew it was beyond stupid to cross such a feature while roped together—if Levi fell, he would drag her down, too. But leaving him behind wasn't an option.

She glanced up at him, wishing she could pull away his oxygen mask and see his easy smile again. Levi made eye contact with her now, the familiar soft blue of his eyes drawing her in. He nodded ever so slightly, indicating that he was ready. She squeezed his arm with her bulky gloved hand and turned away, ice axe in hand, ready to tackle the monster before them.

Sophie could just see Evelyn ahead. She must have waited, but soon she began to move, dipping down and then back up again at a snail's pace, following the snaking path along the rocks. Sophie steeled herself and stepped forward, felt the line go tight and then slacken as Levi moved with her. They descended to the ridge this way, slowly, but moving better than Levi had for the past hour. Sophie felt a surge of hope. She dared to imagine that they might reach Camp Four, where warm tents and hot food awaited them. And beyond that—they would get off this nightmarish mountain and go back home, to Switzerland. The Yama Parvat summit would skyrocket her career; she'd have sponsors to rely on again. She could return to guiding, no more working in a coffee shop.

It happened so fast—one second Sophie was examining a potential foothold and the next she was yanked off her feet, a few moments of being airborne before she collided with the snow, hard, knocking the breath from her lungs. She was sliding on her back, pelted with falling snow, disoriented, no sense of up or down. And Levi—she couldn't see him, couldn't fathom anything beyond the snow and her speed and death looming, the inevitable drop-off of a cliff or plunging into a crevasse, never to be seen again.

She flipped over onto her stomach and drove her ice axe into the snow with as much force as possible. She struck once, twice, three times before it caught and she scrambled to dig into the snow with her crampons, her upper body screaming with effort to hold on, waiting for what came next—the incredible jolt when Levi's body hit the end of the line, something close to two hundred pounds with all his gear. She braced and miraculously that little ice axe held their combined weight against the jolt, and Sophie screamed, a horrible, inhuman sound that surprised her—she didn't know what caused it, equal parts relief and despair, surprise and sorrow, for she had caught them but there was no way back up to the ridge. The slope was too steep, almost sheer, and she couldn't even make out the ridge above them. Everything was white, and the snow stung her exposed cheeks, and she wished desperately that she had an oxygen mask, because there wasn't enough air to fuel her cries.

Then she remembered her sister. "Evelyn!" she screamed, again and again, feeling her throat turn raw. She knew, even as she yelled, that the odds of Evelyn spotting them were non-existent. They had slid too far, and if Evelyn was smart, she wouldn't even look back until she crossed the ridge, lest she lose her own balance and fall. Maybe she already had, and she was stranded on the other side, calling for Sophie.

Sophie resisted the urge to duck her head and look at Levi. She knew he had caused the fall, had collapsed, or maybe even fainted. The rope tension hadn't released; he hung below her like a deadweight, sapping what little energy she had. But she wouldn't let go. No matter what. She would hold on until the last possible second, until the muscles in her shoulders or arms or fingers gave out and they resumed their fall, to whatever cold and lonely fate awaited them below. She would die with him. She would not let him go alone. After everything they'd been through—the whirlwind last nine months—she couldn't stand the thought of losing him when he hadn't even wanted to come.

If she could take it all back, give up climbing forever and return to her quiet life in Switzerland, she would. But their survival depended on someone else, someone she hadn't trusted in years.

With all her strength, Sophie closed her eyes and called Evelyn's name one last time.

CHAPTER TWO

January 2018,
Yorkville, New York

Evelyn Wright turned off the stove and set aside the pot of water that had just reached a boil. Her appetite, as usual, deserted her as suddenly as it had arrived. The bubbles dissipated as the water cooled and Evelyn left the kitchen, turning off the light behind her.

She found herself in her bedroom, at her desk, which was where she spent most of her time. Her workspace was neat, governed by a precise system of organization that only she knew the rules behind. When Evelyn was deep in a case, Miles would sometimes find a stray document on the coffee table and tread lightly into the room, placing the paper gingerly on the edge of the desk, because he knew, by attempting to file the document himself, he would wreck the entire system.

She didn't want to work, not at 9:00 p.m. on a Saturday, but there was a mechanical process to her labor. Her hands found the edges of her laptop; her fingers lifted the screen and she squinted against the sudden light. She had a habit of leaving most of the lights in the apartment off, remaining in darkness whenever she could, which she knew was not good for her vision. And yet, it felt necessary to live in darkness when the overwhelming noise and color of Yorkville confronted her each morning as she left the building. She still wasn't used to the city even after living there for six years. She still craved, daily, the relative solitude of the ski town where she had grown up. In New York she couldn't escape to a grove of aspen trees whenever the world became overwhelming, which was why, almost weekly now, she asked Miles when they could move upstate. He would smile and say, "When my art becomes something passive instead of active." She didn't quite understand what that meant, but she had enough of an idea. Often, he spent his days trekking up and down the streets of the city, stopping by galleries and small museums, trying to sell his collection. A year or so ago they'd thought he'd made it, after the inclusion of three of his pieces in an exhibit at a prestigious gallery. But his art had fallen by the wayside again, forgotten by the general public. His agent had moved on to other clients, leaving Miles alone to champion his art.

She admired that he hadn't given up, but sometimes she wished that he would take the mural-painting jobs he was occasionally offered, or seek a teaching position. She could picture him in front of a classroom of students, his charming smile putting them at ease as he shared his unique use of light and color. He could teach landscape painting, curate another generation of artists who translated the wilderness to a canvas.

But he would never go for it. He wanted recognition for his artistic prowess, not for beautifying a city or mentoring the next great painter. And deep down, Evelyn couldn't blame him. If she possessed such a singular capability, to render a moment of the natural world into eternity, she wouldn't want to waste it either. She just hoped he wasn't an artist who only achieved recognition late in life, or after death. He deserved it now.

She pushed aside her thoughts of Miles. Her current case was a complicated one, familial homicide with a defendant who seemed nonchalant about murdering his father. Not in self-defense—he'd completed the act in the middle of the night, while his father was asleep. And now he'd gone silent, refusing to provide any context for his actions.

Evelyn felt a kind of abstract despair as she read and reread the facts of the case. When she'd announced that she was going to study criminal law, Sophie had laughed in her face, then said, "Oh, you're serious?" After that, it was a never-ending barrage of questions—*why do you care so much about other people, what about the planet, you said you would study environmental law.* Evelyn could not recall saying that—Sophie had a habit of projecting her own assumptions onto Evelyn, that Evelyn would behave, in any situation, exactly as Sophie did. Which had never been true.

Her mother, on the other hand, had been proud, which should have been all the approval Evelyn needed. But sometimes, lying awake at night, she thought of her father, conjuring the few fuzzy features that she still remembered: his dark hair, his deep voice, his rough hands that lifted her onto his shoulders, where she could see the entire world. Would he be proud? She didn't know him well enough to say. And after all he was dead, had died from cirrhosis five years after he had left, which had been three years after Sophie was born. Evelyn was six when her father disappeared without a trace, her mother offering only vague explanations. *He didn't fit into this life anymore.* In early adulthood Evelyn gathered that he left because he was overwhelmed by two young children. If Sophie had never been born, perhaps he would have stayed. Evelyn was manageable, even as a child, capable of containing herself. Sophie had been a whirlwind.

Evelyn exhaled and realized her gaze had drifted to the wall as her mind spiraled back to the past. She opened a Word file and began typing. A moment later, her phone rang, and she looked at it with surprise. Miles rarely called, and it was late for her mother to reach out. The name *James Haverford* was displayed on the screen. Her friend, a fellow mountaineer. She set aside the stack of papers, rerouting her attention once again.

"Hello, James?"

"Evelyn! How are you?"

"Good, good," she replied, sinking further into her chair. "What's got you calling at this hour?"

"Oh," he said, as if just realizing the time difference. James lived in Colorado, where it was currently a more reasonable time for a phone call. "I can never remember that you're off in the city now. Even after all these years."

Evelyn smiled to herself and waited for him to go on, his gruff voice a welcome escape from the dark cave of her bedroom.

"You may have heard the news already," he continued, "but I'm trying to stay ahead of the curve. I've been given notice that Nepal is granting permits to climb Yama Parvat."

Evelyn sat up now, rapt. She listened as James explained the situation. She knew about the mountain—a giant in the Annapurna range, off-limits to climbers because some religious residents of Nepal believed it was home to Yama, a deity of death. The physical challenge of conquering a peak stood in opposition to those spiritual beliefs, or other sacred significance. She registered her own surprise at the idea of climbers suddenly being welcomed to Yama Parvat's slopes.

The mountain had largely been ignored until thirteen years ago, when geographers had resurveyed the mountain and found the peak to be just above eight thousand meters, which led some of the most prominent climbers in the world to petition the Nepal government for permits. There were only fourteen other mountains above eight thousand meters in the world, including Everest, Annapurna I, and K2, all situated in the Himalayan and Karakoram ranges in Asia. To summit an eight-thousand-meter mountain is to enter the death zone, an altitude so high that there is not enough oxygen to sustain human life. That exact allure, the possibility of a brand-new brush with death, captured the imaginations of thousands.

But Nepal wouldn't budge. So, Yama Parvat remained an unattainable trophy for the mountaineering community. Evelyn had been only fifteen at the time the mountain was resurveyed, invested enough in climbing to read the news, but not experienced enough to truly understand. As she grew older and learned more, she came to see Yama Parvat for what it was: the last great question, a towering challenge that would grant worldwide recognition to whoever claimed it. She scoured online forums and joined debates about which routes to take and if it would be possible to climb the mountain undetected. But in those thirteen long years, Nepal had maintained its stance. There were other mountains like Yama Parvat, smaller, but off-limits, protected for their sacred nature. By extension, the local populations were also protected. The Sherpa guides who assisted foreign climbers up the mountains of the Himalayas were often underpaid, especially considering the difficult physical labor and incredible dangers they faced.

While he talked, she searched for Yama Parvat on her laptop, but there were no new articles.

"Why hasn't it been announced?" she asked when James paused.

"I don't know all the details. Some agreement between Nepal, the native communities, and the major climbing organizations. I heard local companies want to scout the mountain for future treks or even commercial expeditions. So we'll work with Sherpa guides who are more familiar with the area. Anyway, once the permits are set, there will be an official announcement. And then all hell will break loose." She could hear the smile in his voice. "I'm surprised no one has leaked the news yet. Anyway, I'll get to the point. There's a spot on the American team for you, if you want it. Me, Phil, and Danielle."

Evelyn let out a weighted breath. "Huh. Exclusive." The offer excited her, even as she wondered what had changed— why the sacred mountain had now been deemed acceptable to climb. Money, she guessed. Expeditions and tourism required a lot of cash.

"Yeah, well." James cleared his throat. "There are thirty other people I could invite, but I don't trust every person I've ever climbed with. This is an unprecedented situation for all of us. I can't look at a list and say, 'hey, Bill and Bob did a first ascent of an eight-thousander two years ago.' You know? And so I followed my instincts. I've climbed with Phil and Danielle for years, and I know they can also hold their own. You've made almost every summit attempt on an eight-thousander so far. That's no small thing."

Almost. The word made Evelyn wince. Last year, James had invited her to climb Lhotse with a few other American mountaineers—Phil and Danielle included—and she hadn't made the summit. She had turned around one thousand feet from the top, exhausted and disoriented. For weeks back home she had wondered, *If Sophie was with me, would I have made it?*

But James must not be worried about that attempt if he was inviting her again, on an even more important expedition. She swallowed her wounded pride. "I'll come," she said. "Thank you." Exhilaration coursed through her body at the thought of returning to Nepal, on an even grander stage. Yama Parvat might not be the tallest mountain, but it still towered above most in the world, and it was unclimbed. As the idea sank in, Evelyn's heart sped up. She had to stop herself from getting up and running outside and declaring to the world that she'd been invited on the climb of a lifetime.

"Excellent!" James's voice brought her back to reality. "Nothing is set in stone yet, but I expect we'll arrive in Nepal in late March and be on the mountain in early April. I'll send you the details I have so far." He paused. "Could I get you out to Colorado in a few weeks to start training?"

She bit her lip, unable to answer him. Her eyes drifted to the neat stacks of paper on her desk. When she'd climbed Lhotse, she'd had to leave her old firm. "No way," her boss had said. "I can't let you disappear for three months." That afternoon, she'd handed in her letter of resignation.

Evelyn liked her current firm much more, though. The other lawyers were pleasant, and her boss was nice—she seemed to understand Evelyn's passion, had sat and listened to Evelyn's stories of mountaineering on her first day of work. She didn't want to leave. But she'd found that few firms were willing to hire a lawyer who would reliably vanish for several months of the year to Nepal or China or Pakistan, unreachable except at Base Camp, and sometimes not even then. "You should be a schoolteacher," Miles had told her once. "Summers off." She had laughed because the idea of her teaching children—of any age—was absurd. Now, she longed for a job that only expected her presence for part of the year.

"I'll try," she said to James. "I can't promise anything. But I'll start training here." Her eyes wandered to her gym bag, pushed halfway under the bed. She hadn't been to the gym in a few weeks, too busy with work. Her daily walks to the coffee shop and the corner store weren't exactly keeping her in mountaineering shape.

"I trust you," James said. "Look, just do what you can. I do want us to at least have a couple of weekends together. Can you manage that?"

"Of course," she replied, although she doubted her ability to even do that, because here she was, working on the weekend, before James's call had interrupted.

"Great. Listen, I won't keep you any longer, but I can't tell you how glad I am that you're on board. I think we have a really solid chance of making the summit. Like I said, I'll shoot you an email with what logistical details I have so far."

"Wait," Evelyn said, surprised by her own voice, as if her heart knew to ask the question before her brain. "The other teams, do you know who they are? Is there a chance…" She trailed off, cleared her throat. "Will Sophie be there?"

James didn't answer for a moment, then exhaled. "Truthfully, I don't know. She won't be on the American team, obviously, not for lack of ability but because…look, I didn't want to cause any tension. You've climbed a big mountain more recently than she has."

"I'm not offended on her behalf."

"Of course," James said quickly. "I'll be honest, Evelyn, it would be a dream to have both of you on my team. But I know that's not possible." He paused. "I don't think a Swiss team is applying for a permit. I've heard whispers that George

Bennett is putting together a multinational team, but nothing concrete."

"It's okay. I was just wondering. I don't care if she's there." Evelyn paused. "We just haven't been in touch."

"Families are tough," James said, and she could tell he wanted the conversation to end. She said goodbye and set down her phone, sitting in the darkness once again. The case files seemed even less appealing now. On Monday she would march into her boss's office and ask for a sabbatical. She had only been working at the firm for seven months and expected to hear a "no." But she had to try.

Evelyn heard the front door open and lifted her head to check the clock: 11:32 p.m. She had lost track of time, buried in her work, and now her vision swam when she looked anywhere that wasn't a page full of words. She didn't call Miles's name, but listened to his footsteps, the sound of his keys hitting the counter, his hand pushing open their bedroom door. He stopped.

"Look at you," he said. "A creature of the darkness."

She smiled. One of her favorite things about Miles was the way he adapted to her way of living, never asking her to turn on a light. He would go to the farthest room if he wanted the warmth of a lamp, but in Evelyn's presence, he submitted to the darkness, let it come over them like a blanket. He didn't need to always see her, and for that she was grateful.

Now, as the low light of her laptop screen glowed against her face, it was Miles whom she struggled to see. "I have news," she said.

He listened from the doorway as she explained the opportunity to climb Yama Parvat. How she would probably be gone for most of the spring and early summer, but how it was worth it, for the chance of a first ascent. He listened, and when she was done speaking, he remained silent for a while, thinking. Calculated as ever.

"Will Sophie be there?"

Evelyn blinked. She hadn't expected the question, at least not until after some form of congratulations. "I don't know. It's not like I called her up to ask."

He lifted his hands just a bit, defensively, and took a seat on the bed, turning to face her. "So, a climb like this—it's big. Weeks of training, months on the mountain. What about work? You have a job. An important one."

She stared at him, perplexed by the lack of support. "I'm going to ask for a sabbatical."

"I can't imagine they'll give you one, right? You haven't been there long enough."

She watched him carefully. "I know."

He covered his face with his hands for a moment. "Evelyn. We need your income right now. I've got no money to spare."

"Is that my problem?" she replied, and immediately felt a tinge of regret. He was right, but she couldn't resist the urge to argue her position. "The expedition will almost certainly be completely sponsored. I won't have to pay a dime. We can afford rent until the end of the lease."

"And then what?"

"We'll get out of the city. Forever."

"Which is what you want, not me." He shook his head. "You'll be without a paycheck for months. I've told you, you can't have it both ways. If you want a nontraditional lifestyle, you need a nontraditional job."

She stayed quiet, admonished. She couldn't argue with him, not when he spoke from experience. Miles's two passions, painting and white-water kayaking, funded each other—he would win a slalom competition and use the money to sup-port a few months of painting. Then, when a painting or two sold, he would take time to train for his next competition. In his eyes it was a circular, balanced life. But it was not without instability. Evelyn craved the opposite, something to come back to after the mountains. She closed her eyes.

"Evelyn," he said, softer. "I won't tell you not to go. The opportunity isn't lost on me. But when you return, we need a plan. A way of keeping our heads above water. Because soon enough, we'll drown."

She looked at him, surprised by their role reversal. Usually, she was the more practical one, grounded in finances and lo-gistics, while Miles drifted through life, content to take each day as it came. He woke up every morning as a blank slate; she a full to-do list, with highlights and scratch marks and Wite-Out.

She nodded, confirming that she knew their bank accounts would be dry at the end of summer. His expression didn't change, but something passed through his eyes, some small stirring. "Come here," he said, and she did, letting him wrap his arms around her. He smelled like cinnamon, the distinctly crisp January air, and a hint of cigarette smoke. Not his, she knew he didn't smoke, but no doubt he'd walked through clouds of it on the streets. "Congratulations," he murmured into her hair. "A first ascent. I know how much that would mean to you."

Evelyn wondered how he knew when she couldn't put it into words herself. *I'll miss him this summer*, she decided, be-cause she knew she had a choice—to disappear into the wild mountains and forget the last two years of her life, or to re-member.

She would not forget.

★ ★ ★

The first night in Colorado, Evelyn thought of Miles.

He had ridden in the cab to the airport with her, kissed her on the cheek after he unloaded her suitcase. He'd told her to call him, as often as she could. She'd searched his face for a sign that he understood the magnitude of her returning back home but found only indifference, or perhaps acceptance was more accurate. He didn't seem to share the near-constant guilt Evelyn struggled with, the past intertwining with the present constantly in her thoughts, no separation between the man she loved and the worst thing she'd ever done.

She was spending the first night at her childhood home, which in retrospect was not the best idea for someone wanting to escape the past. Standing in the living room, she still felt the burning absence of the three framed photos from Sophie's wedding: one that included the extended family, one of just Sophie and their mother, and—worst of all to think about—the one of Sophie and Miles, kissing, at the end of their wedding ceremony. The physical removal of them had changed little—when she glanced at the mantel above the fireplace, Evelyn still saw her sister, beaming in white, resting her head on their mother's shoulder. It always struck Evelyn how young Sophie looked in that photo. In a different dress, she could have been sixteen, headed off to prom. Five years made little difference—her sister had been young, still was young. And now she was in a different country, living a life that Evelyn could not begin to imagine. How strange it had all turned out.

A kettle whistled in the kitchen. Evelyn winced at the sharp sound but couldn't tear her gaze from the mantel. A different photo had been placed there, in a simple wooden frame— Sophie at age eight, on skis, her dark blond hair dusted with snow, grinning up at the camera. There was an unspoken rule about always having an equal number of pictures of each child displayed in the house. There were solo images of Evelyn, too—rock climbing, law school graduation, at Camp Four on Lhotse, the night before her failed summit attempt. It surprised her that the photo was of Sophie at such a young age. She turned away and came face-to-face with her mother.

"Oh," she said, "I'm sorry. I didn't mean to surprise you."

"You didn't," Evelyn said, thankful for the diversion. She accepted the mug of steaming liquid.

"Tea. Chamomile. It was all I had, sorry. You probably won't have trouble sleeping with the time difference."

Evelyn resisted the urge to shrug and took a sip of the tea. "Maybe. I have enough on my mind to keep me awake for days."

They regarded each other for a moment. Evelyn thought she looked tired. Her hair was in a ponytail, but stray pieces framed the top of her head like a frazzled halo. She had stopped dyeing it, Evelyn noticed, the shade now muddy brown like a river with silver strands like fish flashing through the water. There were more lines on her face, on her forehead, and around the corners of her eyes. She looked more than tired, Evelyn realized. She looked old. The last twenty-odd years of serving as the sole provider for her family had worn her down.

"I spoke to Sophie the other day."

Evelyn braced herself. Whenever the topic of Sophie arose, an argument was likely to follow. Sometimes her mother just liked to provide life updates, to filter back news of her sister's life in Switzerland. But something in her expression told Evelyn that this information held more weight. She raised an eyebrow, urging her on.

"I'm guessing you don't know this. She's been invited to climb Yama Parvat. With Levi."

Evelyn's stomach dropped. She almost asked her mother to repeat herself. A cold surge of fear swept through her, raising the hair on her arms. Seeing Sophie at Thanksgiving two years ago had been bad enough. She couldn't spend multiple months in isolation with her. "You...you're sure?" she managed to stammer. "By who?"

"George Bennett, she said. The multinational team, they're calling it. She's excited. Ready to be back on a big mountain."

Evelyn stared at the floor, letting her eyes trace patterns in the woodwork. "I didn't know." She felt sick with anxiety, her pulse moving uncomfortably fast. Even though the possibility of Sophie climbing had lingered in her mind since that first conversation with James, she hadn't really believed it. Sophie had been out of the major mountaineering scene for years now. Why did George think she was capable of Yama Parvat?

"Maybe you should...well. Maybe you should put some thought into what you'll say to her."

"I can't," she started to say, and then stopped, looking up and squaring her shoulders. "I can't spend energy worrying about her. The expedition is going to be incredibly difficult." Maybe she could convince her mother, if not herself.

Her mother's eyes widened for a moment, then she shook her head. "You're a strong girl, Evelyn. You'll be fine." *Girl*. After everything, she was still a child. Her mother turned away, crossed the room to an armchair, and sat down, slowly, as if she were a much older woman. Silence permeated the room for a moment, and then she spoke. "I watched your sister wither away to nothing for a year in this house." Evelyn opened her mouth to speak, but she held up her hand. "I don't care what happened, or why. It's in the past. I know that you and Miles are happy together. And Sophie is doing much better now. She might be open to—to hearing your side of the story when you're together again."

Evelyn shook her head. "I can't. It would be too painful. For both of us." She couldn't meet her mother's eyes. "I did something unforgivable. I know that. So why bother asking for forgiveness?"

To her surprise, her mother stood up. "Okay. That's all I wanted to say. I should go to bed. I have an early morning tomorrow." She paused. "I'll leave breakfast for you. But I'll be out before dawn. I'll see you in a few days for dinner." She smiled, and Evelyn knew it was a gift, a way of saying, *We'll leave the subject alone.* For now, at least.

She said good-night and lingered in the living room until she finished her tea, replaying the short conversation in her mind. She realized that she had been anticipating another argument that ended in tears. Evelyn let out a breath and felt some of the tension leave her body. She placed her mug in the dishwasher and looked at her phone for a moment, scrolling through the texts from her teammates. She'd agreed to meet James and the others early the next morning, at James's house, to discuss their plans for the next several weeks.

Her finger hovered over the button to turn her phone on silent, but she hesitated. Maybe her mother was right, and now was the time to reach out to Sophie, to bridge the chasm between them. They had dreamed of Yama Parvat for years. Without giving herself more time to think, she opened Sophie's contact and typed a message.

Mom said you've been invited to Yama Parvat, too. Congratulations. Are you excited?

The message felt stilted, hollow, like something she would send to an acquaintance rather than someone who used to be her best friend. Evelyn told herself to forget it and hit Send. She'd reached out. That was all she could do for now.

Upstairs, in her childhood bedroom, she stood in the dark for a moment before turning on the light. She had seen it earlier that afternoon, when she'd dumped her luggage after arriving, but it struck her that the room was unchanged. She knew her mother did yoga in the living room, even though Evelyn had told her to feel free to turn the space into a home gym, a library—whatever she wanted. But the room remained exactly as it had when she'd walked out the door to attend Colorado College, cluttered with familiar furniture, posters torn from issues of *National Geographic* thumbtacked to the walls. Sophie, about to begin her sophomore year of high school, had cried when Evelyn left. Minutes before, she had held Evelyn's hand and whispered, "You can do anything. Absolutely anything." Now, Evelyn realized how true those words were—*you can do anything*—because apparently *anything* included having an affair with your sister's husband.

CHAPTER THREE

February 2015,
Yorkville, New York

If only Evelyn hadn't found it so difficult to find love. She was in her final months of Columbia Law School, with a one-bedroom apartment on the Upper East Side. New York was loud and dirty and complicated, but she liked it because it was different from Breckenridge in every way possible. She missed Colorado, but she had found herself in the city, honed her voice and sharpened her mind until she could create a winning defense for any perpetrator, no matter how vile. Sometimes she wondered if she should have become a therapist instead, tried to fix the darkness in those strangers instead of helping them get off easy in court. Graduation, a few months away, was barreling toward her, and just beyond that loomed the intangible totality of the rest of her life. It scared her most when the clock ticked past 2:00 a.m. and she still couldn't sleep, couldn't slow her racing thoughts. Evelyn had confessed her anxiety once to Sophie, who signed Evelyn up for a daily email newsletter called *Inner Zen*. The emails contained tips on meditation and mindful breathing. Evelyn deleted them for weeks but eventually gave in and started meditating for twenty minutes every morning, and it seemed to help. There was only one thing missing.

She hadn't had a true relationship since freshman year of college, *undergraduate*, and that had only lasted six months before he broke things off—*You're too busy. You spend too much time at the gym*. Funny, since he played on the soccer team. But she shrugged it off, relatively unfazed. What followed over the next six years was a series of unsuccessful dates with increasingly long dry spells in between. And now, in New York, the dating scene seemed hopeless. Everyone was constantly on the go and had little time for more than a few messages on a dating app or a quick drink at an expensive bar. It was a waste of time, she told herself. But still.

Her mother tried to give her dating advice, which was embarrassing, and so did Sophie, which was infuriating. Her younger sister flirted with a string of boyfriends in high school and seemed to have seduced every man in a fifty-mile radius of her college campus. She seemed less self-conscious than Evelyn, able to connect with new people more easily. Sophie's relationships were short, too, but she found the most interesting people—a study abroad student from Norway, a guy who grew up on an isolated ranch in Montana, and of course her latest (and longest), kayaker extraordinaire, talented painter, and quite a bit older than Sophie—Miles. Before Evelyn had met him, she'd received pictures from Sophie—the two of them standing on top of a mountain, squinting into the camera in the bright sun, or standing on the bank of a river in life jackets, ready to run rapids. Something Sophie had only done a handful of times before but seemed to love now that Miles had come into her life. Evelyn thought Miles was handsome, in a rugged way—not quite her type, she only liked the scraggly look in the outdoors, not at home. Still, she could see why Sophie was attracted to him. Hand him a trident and he'd make a decent Poseidon.

Evelyn hadn't been surprised when Sophie had called her after Miles's proposal. She never expected her sister to have a relationship that ticked all the traditional boxes—dating for several years, then a long engagement to plan the wedding. Sophie had always dived headfirst into whatever felt right at the moment. But she was young, her brain still stuck in the stage between adolescence and adulthood. At twenty-one, Evelyn had been so absorbed with schoolwork that she'd hardly given a thought to relationships. When Evelyn thought of the type of men she'd been attracted to at that age—frat guys, climbing gym bros— she was thankful that none of those relationships had lasted. She was concerned that Sophie had made the leap so young, but then again, she'd prioritized her romantic connections as much as anything else. Sophie had probably dated triple the number of men that Evelyn had. If she didn't have a good grasp of what she wanted from a relationship now, when would she?

Four years later, Evelyn felt more herself than ever before, but what she wanted in a partner still felt largely unknowable. Maybe one day she would wake up and understand herself well enough to love someone else, but lasting, mutually fulfilling relationships still sounded like a fairy tale.

Evelyn kept quiet on the phone, allowed Sophie to fill the line with her breathless excitement, but after she hung up, she wondered if she should have expressed her doubt. That said, the response would almost certainly have been: "Can't you just be happy for me?"

Alone in her apartment, in the cool evening light, Evelyn turned the wedding invitation over in her hands. It was silly to think, but she couldn't help it—had she made a wrong turn somewhere along the way, paid attention to the wrong things? Her younger sister was secure enough to get married—at twenty-one years old. Even if Evelyn didn't want to be married yet, it was the principle. Evelyn could clearly trace the pattern that had arisen over the years—anything Evelyn wanted, so had Sophie. First it was skiing, then rock climbing, then mountain climbing. If Evelyn succeeded at an activity, Sophie was right beside her. That kind of matched skill and teamwork was invaluable on a mountain, but for once, Evelyn wished to have something only for herself, and for it to come as easily to her as everything seemed to come to Sophie. Pretend as she might, she wasn't always happy alone.

While she spent her time crafting defenses and rushing around the city, a part of her was keenly aware of a voice whispering in her subconscious: *if you don't slow down, this will be your life forever.* Nearly all her law school friends were single, too absorbed in their future careers to make time for romantic relationships. Sometimes she saw herself reflected in them, in their single-minded drive to achieve lofty goals. But Evelyn always seemed to be worrying about something more—returning to the mountains, keeping up with Sophie. Deep down she knew she wasn't jealous of Sophie because of Miles, but because of Sophie's entire life—how, without really trying, she'd settled into a path that led her to the mountains, to security, to love.

Her flight left the next morning. There was snow on the ground when she stepped off the plane in Denver, and even more in Breckenridge—as she drove the winding roads to the ski resort, she feared hitting a patch of black ice and spinning out into a snowbank. The fear intensified each time she drove past abandoned cars on the side of the road, victims of a recent blizzard. But her rented SUV didn't slide and she made it home, to the brown condo building nestled into the mountainside.

Sophie sat cross-legged on the living room floor, going over the seating arrangements with their mother. She looked up when Evelyn entered, stamping snow off her boots, and beamed.

"Well, look who's arrived. The *real* love of my life."

And how could Evelyn feel anything but grateful in the face of that kind of love? Evelyn set her suitcase aside and went to hug her sister, and they stood for a long time in silence, holding each other because their visits had become rare. Sophie was the first to let go. She stepped back to let Evelyn hug their mother.

"We should have planned this out weeks ago," Sophie said, returning to her seat on the floor, "but somehow it got lost in the shuffle. Plus I've had people drop out. I guess I can't blame them. Breck isn't the easiest place to get to in February."

"Excuses," Evelyn said. "I got here just fine." She waited as her mother and sister argued over where to seat a difficult member of the extended family, and then caught Sophie's eye. "How's Wyoming?"

Sophie's hands flew to her cheeks. "It's incredible," she said, eyes wide. "Guiding in the Tetons...it's like, a total dream come true. I can't get enough of those mountains. You'll have to come out again in a few months. Oh, of course, to prep for K2." She paused. "Miles loves it too. We're within a few hours of plenty of rivers."

Evelyn couldn't bring herself to smile in return. How young Sophie seemed, to be stepping into a commitment she might not fully understand. She cleared her throat, and Sophie's excited expression dropped.

"I'm going to make tea," their mother said, standing up. "Do either of you want anything?"

"I'll have some," Sophie replied.

Evelyn waved her hand. "No, thanks. I had coffee when I landed." She watched their mother retreat into the kitchen before looking at Sophie again.

"Say it."

"What?" But Evelyn couldn't play dumb, not with Sophie. She sighed, running her hands over her thighs as she spoke. "I just hope you've really thought about this."

"I have. God, I don't need your judgment too. I thought you'd be on my side." She tilted her head, indicating the doorway to the kitchen. "She is so mad at me. She's not over it yet."

It took Evelyn a second to fill in the blanks. "Dropping out? Or the wedding?"

Sophie rolled her eyes, as if the answer should have been obvious. "Both. She thinks I'm throwing my life away to chase after a man. I keep telling her, at least I'm not pregnant. She thinks it's a huge mistake, but I'm the happiest I've ever been. I get to climb every day for a living instead of sitting in a classroom listening to a professor drone on about something I don't actually care about." She paused. "I'm not like you. I don't want a career. I just want to make enough money to keep climbing. And right now, I'm doing that, *by climbing*. I can't imagine anything better."

Evelyn ignored the subtle jab, unsure if Sophie had intended to hurt her feelings. "You were so close. Don't you think one more year would have been worth it?"

Sophie shrugged. "It was a waste of money. It's not like I had a scholarship."

Evelyn blinked. That dig felt intentional; she had received a full-ride scholarship to Colorado College for her undergrad. She shifted, allowing her eyes to drift down to the seating chart, pretending to study it. "And moving in with Miles? The wedding?"

"It just makes sense. Neither of us wanted to stay in Washington. And we know we're going to stay together, so why not get married?"

Sophie's naivety surprised Evelyn sometimes, the way her sister had an innate knack for human connections but failed to see the big picture. Evelyn could think of plenty of reasons to not get married at twenty-one, but she held her tongue. Instead, she said, "Where's Miles?"

"Still in Wyoming," Sophie replied. She detected a hint of sadness in her sister's voice. "He was supposed to drive here with me, but the pipe under our kitchen sink cracked, so he had to stay to fix that. He'll get here on Thursday."

It surprised her again, to hear of the problems in her sister's life. A cracked pipe in the house she partially owned. Evelyn couldn't imagine owning a property for years, not until she finally moved out of the city. If she was honest, she was bothered by Sophie's life bounding forward while her own appeared more stagnant. She had the sensation of being stuck at the base of a mountain, watching Sophie speed toward the summit without her. Evelyn reminded herself that she was about to graduate from law school, begin a new career, and that in a few months she would once again be on equal ground with Sophie, as they set off to climb K2 and Broad Peak. She glanced around the room, at the fire burning away in the fireplace and the scattered family photographs, and yawned.

"Go to bed," Sophie said. "We'll catch up more tomorrow."

"We should ski," Evelyn offered. "Or snowshoe or something active. I want to be on the mountain as much as possible while I'm here."

Sophie smiled. "Sure. I can't stop thinking about K2. I feel like we'll never be ready."

She stood up and stretched, feeling all the places in her body where the airplane seat had cramped her muscles, and another yawn escaped her mouth. "I thought I'd make it longer." She looked at Sophie for a long moment, thinking of all the times she had braided Sophie's hair before bed when they were kids. Were they too old for that now? Evelyn said good-night to her mother in the kitchen and went upstairs.

K2, the savage mountain. They had dreamed up the plan on Thanksgiving, the last time she had seen Sophie, when they were feeling grandiose and brave; Sophie had called it Evelyn's graduation present. Last year they summited Everest together. But on Everest they'd been part of a group with other experienced American climbers, and the mountain's puzzle had been solved thousands of times already; their route required no guesswork. Not a walk in the park by any means, but they'd had a straightforward experience with clear weather. K2 was notoriously more difficult. Broad Peak would come after, a bonus summit if they had enough energy left. And Evelyn knew that Sophie would be in better shape—she climbed for a living, while Evelyn was mostly deskbound, though she went on daily runs and made time for the gym when she could. She thought about that as she drifted off to sleep, if she was being too judgmental of Sophie, for following a dream they both shared. The only difference between her and Sophie was fear. Evelyn was afraid of relying on her own determination to make a living, without any sense of security. She knew she wasn't strong enough to follow a nontraditional path. Becoming a lawyer had been a test, a way to prove to herself that she was capable of accomplishing even the most difficult goals. But maybe it had all been a way to avoid chasing what she truly wanted. She sunk into envy and sleep.

On Saturday evening, after the wedding ceremony, Evelyn was pleasantly drunk. The ceremony had been, admittedly, beautiful—on the edge of a clearing that bordered woods, thick stands of lodgepole pines, branches heavy with snow, and mountains all around them. Below, in the valley, Breckenridge slowly lit up as daylight faded away. And then, after Sophie and Miles were wed and kissed, it began to snow from the heavy gray clouds that had lingered overhead all day. Each guest held a candle as they walked single file back to the lodge, a large building adorned with big brown logs and huge glass windows. The bottom of Evelyn's dress was soaked with snow, but she didn't mind. She was the maid of honor, and throughout the ceremony her speech tumbled through her mind, what she would say during dinner, how to convey the forces of her love to a room of friends, family, and strangers.

"Sophie," she said into the microphone, into the hushed room. "You mean so much to me. You're my little sister, my climbing partner, my balance, and my security in this difficult and often tragic world. I've tried to think of a thousand ways to summarize what you mean to me, but I think it's easier to paint a picture.

"When I was eighteen and you were fifteen, we climbed our first 14er, Little Bear Peak. Your idea, of course. I asked if we could do something easier and you said, 'That's no fun.' So we camped overnight in the wilderness and you woke me up at 4:00 a.m. and we started up. You wanted it to be just like the Himalayan climbs you knew we would one day do, only without the snow." Evelyn searched for Sophie's face in the dim room and saw that she was smiling, because she knew the story.

"We made it to the summit a few hours later. There's this section you have to climb through, the hourglass, and you raced right up it and I was shaking when we got to the top. But the view was so beautiful. And then I saw you looking at the traverse to Blanca Peak.

"It's this mile-long exposed ridge of rocky towers that takes you from one peak to the other. I told you no. Clouds had rolled in and I thought it might start to rain. I was worried enough about making it back down the hourglass, not to mention exhausted and hungry. But your mind was made up. You told me I could come with you or wait for you on Little Bear. I didn't want to be shown up by my younger sister, so of course I came.

"I'd never dealt with exposure like that before. A sheer drop on either side and all these choices we had to make. Climbing is like solving a puzzle. There are all these pieces of rock and you have to assemble the pieces to see the path. We were halfway across when it started to rain. The rock got wet and my grip kept slipping. I wanted to turn around, go back the way we came, but you never showed any fear.

"We went a little farther and I started crying. I'd never been that afraid before. The wind was picking up and the clouds had moved in low over the mountain and I thought I was going to die. I never even gave you a second thought." Laughter trickled through the crowd. "I knew you'd survive. I clung to some rock and curled up and cried. It took you a few minutes, but you realized I wasn't behind you. And instead of continuing without me, you came back.

"You sat with me, I don't remember how long. Thirty

minutes or maybe an hour, but you sat with me, and held my hand, and let me cry. You didn't make fun of me or act annoyed. And when the rain passed and I had calmed down, you said we could keep going or go back, together. I chose to keep going.

"We made it to Blanca Peak and I'm so glad we did. The clouds moved away and the sky was so blue and I felt like I was on top of the world. But I learned an important lesson that day. That even though you're younger than me, and less experienced, you're braver and stronger."

Evelyn took a breath and surveyed the room before her eyes met Sophie's again. "And you have the biggest heart. I hope that in Miles you have found a partner who will always value your strength, your resilience. Who will encourage you to keep searching for new heights. Who listens to your wildest dreams. I can't think of anything more you would need. I love you more than anything, and I'm so happy for you."

She stepped away from the mic. Seconds later she was enveloped in her sister's arms, feeling Sophie's tears dampen the sleeve of her dress. She hugged her sister back.

Evelyn hadn't spent much time with Miles in the days before the wedding. He had arrived on Thursday, as promised, but then he and Sophie were busy—last minute decorations at the lodge and meetings with vendors, the rehearsal and dinner on Friday, which Evelyn had also attended—but it had been a busy whirlwind of an evening. So when he approached her after dinner, a glass of champagne in his hand, she took the opportunity to congratulate him.

"Thanks," he said. "Your speech—wow. I have a lot to live up to."

She appraised him for a moment. He had taken his suit

jacket off and wore just a white button-up with the sleeves rolled up, and a baby blue tie to match the bridesmaids' dresses. Evelyn's dress. His dark, wavy hair was combed back, and his beard neatly trimmed. He looked like a different man from the one Evelyn usually saw in photos, with hair down to his shoulders and an untamed beard. Someone who lived for being outdoors and cared little for personal grooming. She had spent a lot of time around those types of people and didn't mind in the slightest, though she herself usually preferred to look neat and polished. She respected that he had the decency to clean up for his wedding. He looked good, she thought, and wondered what she would think of him if she met him in New York one day, a stranger on a city street, not the man who had married her little sister.

She swallowed, her gaze traveling from his exposed forearms back to his face. "You'll do fine, I'm sure," she replied. "Sophie is crazy about you."

"Yeah." He leaned against the wall, looking out over Evelyn's shoulder as if he was talking to someone else, a smile flitting across his lips, as if he knew what she had been thinking. "I'm pretty lucky." He took a sip of champagne and glanced back to her. "What about you? No plus-one?"

Evelyn's cheeks felt hot. "I'm sure Sophie has told you how my dating life in the city is going." She paused. "Besides, I'm busy. What little free time I do have, I want it to be my own."

"Isn't that everyone's excuse? Not enough time in the day. You certainly have enough time to climb mountains."

"Are you suggesting I give that up?"

"No. But Sophie and I have managed to maintain our respective pursuits *and* our relationship."

"Good for you," Evelyn replied. She didn't like his tone. The only other time she'd met Miles, he'd been pleasant enough, but that had been months ago. Perhaps he was just more comfortable now, stepping into his new role in their family. She wondered how much Sophie had told him about her—her unintentional singleness, her doubts about her career. But even she hadn't told Sophie the latter—maybe Sophie knew her that well, could tell when Evelyn was wavering. Or maybe Miles could sense it himself, maybe he saw through her facade of confidence to what she really was: afraid. She looked at Miles, practically a stranger. He was two years older than her and married to her younger sister. She turned the fact over in her mind again and felt, for the first time, only concern, no resentment. She should have tried harder to stop the wedding, to at least talk Sophie into a longer engagement. Sophie and Miles had only been together for a year. How well did she really know him?

Did he speak to Sophie with this same flippancy toward her dreams?

"I know that guiding kayaking trips isn't as demanding as law school," Miles said, smiling, but she had trouble smiling back. "Anyway. I'm jealous of your place in the city. I think I'd have more opportunities if I lived there. With my art. It's hard to find interested galleries in our one-horse town."

"And you think the exponentially larger amount of competition in New York would make that easier?"

His eyes narrowed for just a moment. "My art is good, Evelyn. Some people don't believe in themselves, in their work, but I do. I get better with each painting I finish. And one day I'll be able to quit guiding and live full time off my art." He lowered his voice. "And I don't think that will happen in Wyoming."

She blinked. Why was he telling her this? She glanced over his shoulder and spotted Sophie, who was looking vaguely in their direction. She motioned her sister over, eager to get out of the conversation, and to her relief Sophie headed their way. She slipped under Miles's arm, resting her head against his chest. Safe with him. Maybe Evelyn had misunderstood what he said. They seemed so happy together.

"Look at you two," Sophie said, glancing from Miles to Evelyn. "In-laws."

"Soon we'll be having family dinner every Sunday night," Miles said.

Sophie elbowed him. "Funny. I don't think Evelyn has time to fly out to Wyoming every week. Besides, I don't want to share you just yet."

"I'm not sure I trust the repair job I did on that pipe, anyway. We should probably give it a few test runs before we have any guests."

They fell into conversation about the house, and Evelyn stepped away unnoticed. Sophie's comment about sharing Miles perturbed her. Sophie could keep him; Evelyn wanted nothing more to do with his pompous attitude. She could only hope that he was softer around Sophie, less gratingly sure of himself. Maybe it was the alcohol.

She didn't remember much of the rest of the wedding— two more hours, roughly, of conversation and drinks and dancing. She must have spent it alone or sitting at a table with her mother. She drank too much. That night, she woke up gasping for breath. She'd had a dream about Miles, walking toward her on an empty city street, his hand outstretched. When she had lifted her own hand to take his, she'd been wearing a wedding ring.

CHAPTER FOUR

February 2018,
Capitol Peak, Colorado

Evelyn replayed the wedding again and again in her mind as she climbed. Being home always brought her back to that cold February day three years ago. She often wondered what would have happened if she had met Miles first. Would their situation be reversed, in some cruel trick of fate? Would he have left her for Sophie? She would never know the answer, but that didn't make ignoring the question any easier. She believed that she and Miles belonged together, but maybe she'd only gotten the luck of the draw.

Focus on climbing, she reminded herself. Snow was everywhere, but good conditions, a low chance of avalanches. Never zero, but safe enough that James wanted to make a summit attempt. They had punched in the snow coming up the east slopes of nearby Colorado K2 to check the avalanche risk—to be extra safe—and the snow beneath the top layer of powder was compact and solid. Once past K2 the risk would be even lower. So now she followed behind James, with Phil and Danielle behind her, and as much as she fought against it, her mind wandered with every step.

She hadn't liked Miles at first. She liked him even less after the wedding. She sensed an impermanence to the relationship, mostly perpetrated by Miles. Both moving to Wyoming and getting married had been his idea, yet both turned out to be temporary, until something else came along. Something like her. She swallowed and adjusted her grip on the rough gray rock in front of her face. She had to be more careful, pay more attention, overcome the exhaustion. They had started the hike in the wee hours of the morning, trudging through several miles of ditch trail in the dark before reaching the saddle and ascending to K2. They were heading toward the exposed knife-edge ridge of Capitol Peak now. People had died on this mountain, slipped off or put a foot on unsteady rock. But the knife-edge was short, and she was able to walk across behind James, slow and careful, testing her footholds and avoiding the pockets of snow. Some of the rock was slick and her heart caught in her throat a few times, the familiar sensation of instability and live-wire nerves, but she made it. She stepped back with James and watched Phil and Danielle pick their way across.

Beyond the knife-edge they were still exposed. Bare rock mixed with snow and a steep drop on each side made Evelyn shiver. Nothing like the eight-thousanders she'd climbed, sure, but this mountain demanded both respect and her full awareness—of each foothold, each grip, the positioning of her body, and how her body felt—if she was dizzy or tired or sick from altitude. She had never experienced severe altitude sickness until Lhotse, her failed mountain. The difficult decision to turn around on summit day had partially been made by her, partially by James—she had been disoriented and stumbling, slurring her speech and struggling to clip on to the fixed lines. James had insisted she go back to Camp Four with a guide. Once at a lower altitude, her symptoms eased, but the lack of control over her own body still haunted her.

She looked up and realized that James's leg was just a few inches from her face. She needed to rein in her wandering mind. "What is it?" she called up, her voice carrying above the slight wind.

"Looks like loose rock. Worse than usual. I'm not sure why."

Not an encouraging thing to hear. Evelyn peered around him as best she could.

"Watch out," James said, brushing above with his hand, sending a scattering of rock past Evelyn's left side.

"Shit. That looks rotten."

"It'd be fine if there was only one person climbing," he replied. "But not in a group."

She glanced over her shoulder. Phil and Danielle weren't far behind; they'd come off the knife-edge and were working their way to James and Evelyn.

"Let's try the ridge. We're a little off the standard route, but I'm worried about that being rotten too. With the amount of snowmelt up here, I don't want to take any chances."

Evelyn nodded. A good choice. Loose, or rotten, rocks made for dangerous climbing conditions, where chunks of stone could flake off in a person's hand. James's intrinsic ability to feel out mountain conditions had helped him to successfully summit eight of the fourteen mountains that rose above eight thousand meters. Or fifteen, now that Yama Parvat was no longer off-limits. He had ambitions to summit the remaining six traditional mountains, but Yama Parvat might elude them all. She could trust James, though. As a guide, as a leader.

They reversed their order, taking the ridge the rest of the way to the summit. The rock was slick in places and sometimes loose, but they made it, one after the other, Evelyn second last to step onto the summit. She hadn't climbed Capitol Peak before, although she'd been up a fair amount of the Colorado thirteen- and fourteen-thousand-foot mountains as a teenager and as an undergrad. It did not escape her that she had always planned to tackle this mountain, one of the hardest, with Sophie. But everything was that way now. An incomplete plan.

They stayed on the summit for twenty minutes, drinking in the view of the surrounding peaks and high-altitude lakes.

"I can't stop thinking about the ridge on Yama Parvat," Danielle said to Evelyn, taking a moment to flex her fingers before sliding them back into her gloves. "Every night I pull up the satellite photos and just stare. Matthew looks at me like I'm a crazy person." She laughed. Matthew, Danielle's husband, was not a climber himself. Evelyn had met him a few times before and he always stared in silence, eyes wide, as they described various climbing maneuvers. "That ridge is going to be ten times worse."

"And we'll get through it," Evelyn said, glancing back at the knife-edge that they would have to descend in a few minutes. Capitol Peak offered only one route each way.

Danielle nodded. "I'm more concerned about the amount of people climbing. It's going to be so hard to focus." She lowered her voice and stepped closer to Evelyn. "I mean, I trust James with my life. But Wojciech Skalski? He's always going off route. He climbs alpine style. How is he going to lead an expedition?" She shook her head. "And I have a friend who's climbed in Russia. Says the two on that mixed team are impossible to work with. I don't know why George picked them."

Evelyn's ears perked at that last bit of information. It didn't sound like George to pick difficult personalities. Evelyn wondered how Sophie would react to that. She knew that Sophie's experience as a climbing guide had prepared her well for working with all sorts of people, but it was different working together as peers and not as the voice of authority.

"It's fun to speculate," Evelyn replied, "but we'll just have to see how things shake out when we get there."

Danielle regarded her for a moment. "You seem out of it. Something on your mind?"

There was plenty on Evelyn's mind, but she shook her head and told Danielle she was just tired. James signaled for them to descend and Evelyn fell into line. In the past two weeks the team had summited nine mountains together, a veritable list of some of Colorado's meanest—Maroon Bells, Crestone Needle, Snowmass, Little Bear. Some were repeats for Evelyn, but she appreciated every second spent climbing. Even the late night, early starts that James insisted on—there was a purpose. If they made it to a summit push on Yama Parvat, they would likely need to start in the middle of the night. So much of mountaineering was done by headlamp and feel.

Her flight left in one week. Well, the first of several flights—from Denver to New York to Qatar to Nepal, and then on to a smaller airport, to the city of Pokhara. Yama Parvat was nestled in the heart of Nepal, near Annapurna I, Manaslu, and Dhaulagiri I—three of the six remaining eight-thousand-meter peaks that James had yet to climb. He had told her that he was considering staying on in Nepal to attempt them. Evelyn had felt envy surge through her body. She had no idea what would come after Yama Parvat for her.

Fresh off the plane from Denver, Evelyn turned the key in the lock and stepped into her apartment. She paused for a moment, letting the scent of her home wash over her. She kept a diffuser on the kitchen counter, sage and citrus oil, and the familiar smell released some of the tension from her shoulders. The airplane seat had not treated her body kindly.

Her eyes drifted to the stove clock. Tomorrow morning, her flight left JFK for Hamad International Airport—a twelve-hour, overnight flight. No matter how often she traveled internationally, time zones still made her head spin. She reminded herself again to pack Ambien, even though she never managed to sleep on planes, just put herself into a zombie state that made the whole traveling process feel like a fever dream. Still, she'd be equally miserable if she spent the entire flight hyperaware of being trapped in a metal tube, thirty-five thousand feet above the ocean. She could only handle heights when her feet were solidly on the earth.

Evelyn set her keys on the counter and heard the bedroom door open. It was late morning, a Friday, so Miles was home, probably just waking up after a late night with his artist friends. One of them had recently rented an art studio in Crown Heights and Miles had been spending most of his time there, sharing the space in exchange for modest rent. Evelyn knew it was a good deal, less than he'd spend on studio space virtually anywhere else in the city, but it seemed to go hand in hand with hangovers. She set her luggage down and waited.

He emerged into the kitchen with bags beneath his eyes, curls falling to his shoulders. He'd been growing his hair out for a while now, but it surprised her to see him after a few weeks, how scraggly he looked—it was then she realized that she'd anticipated him getting a haircut while she was away. He crossed the room to her and kissed her, his breath sharp with mint toothpaste. He rested his hand on the back of her head and then her left shoulder blade and then traced his fingers down her spine. He let go and stepped back. "I missed you."

"I missed you too."

"Coffee?" he asked, heading toward the pot on the counter. "Leftover from last night, admittedly. But probably still good."

"No, thanks. I'm awake enough." She glanced at the pile of mail on the counter, some of it already opened. "What's all this?"

He took his time answering, poured a cup of coffee, sipped it. "I thought you might be able to tell me."

She lowered her gaze, suddenly cautious, and picked up one of the open letters. It was addressed to her.

Dear Ms. Wright,
The following letter describes your options for continuing insur-
ance coverage following your termination of employment from
J & C Counsel…

She stopped reading and glanced up at him, heat rising in her cheeks.

"You opened my mail?"

He sipped his coffee again, infuriatingly nonchalant. "I thought it was a paycheck. I was desperate because rent is due in a week, and I don't think we have enough money to cover it."

"I set aside money for it. Also, I get direct deposit. Also, don't open my mail."

"Thanks for communicating absolutely none of this to me." He sounded hurt now, and guilt flashed through her. "I mean, hey, a text that says 'I'll cover April rent and also I quit my job' would have sufficed."

"Well, now you know." She took a breath, set the letter aside, and tried to regain control of her frustration. "Look, my boss said that I can most likely have my job back in the summer. They just don't want to keep me as an employee in case I decide to run away to Nepal forever. It was easier to get all the HR stuff in order while I was still in the States."

"You really believe that? You've been gone since early February, and you think that in June you'll be able to walk right in and ask for your job back? There's a thousand other people fresh out of law school, begging for work. And those people aren't going to quit after a few months to go climb a mountain." He shook his head, leaning back against the counter. "We're partners, Evelyn. You can't keep things from me." He paused, the hurt evident in his expression. "Why didn't you tell me?"

"I wasn't trying to keep things from you. I knew you'd worry, exactly like you're doing now. We'll be fine. I budgeted." She paused, wondering if she should tell him the truth, that she was afraid he'd leave if he knew. But she didn't want to beg for his forgiveness. "The entire trip to Nepal is covered by my sponsors. And you know your income isn't exactly reliable either." She reminded herself to breathe as her temper began to flare. "Besides, I worked for years to get where I am today. I'm not that easily replaceable." The thought of donning a blazer and returning to the high-rise office building made her stomach turn, but Miles didn't need to know that. For now.

"Is that true? I don't want to diminish your accomplishments, but..." He trailed off, and the softness of his expression almost made the unfinished sentence worse. He didn't want to offend her by acknowledging the truth: Evelyn was lying. For all the time, money, effort, tears, and missed life experiences she'd sacrificed to make it through law school, so had thousands of others. She was, in fact, replaceable, probably by someone who found more fulfillment in their work. "And what about your loans?" Miles asked.

Evelyn tried not to think about the tens of thousands waiting to be repaid. "I deferred them. Look, I know you don't believe me, but I'm confident that I can get my job back. Otherwise, I wouldn't have gone through with this." It was another lie, and he saw right through it. Absently, she stacked the pile of mail on the counter, watching it grow into a tower of her mistakes. "Miles, please. This is an opportunity I'll never have again. I have to do it."

He shook his head. "It's already done anyway, isn't it?" He stayed quiet for a moment, rubbing his thumb over the mug's handle. "If you want to operate as two separate entities, that's fine. If you don't want to take me into consideration, I mean. I was offered an artist's residency in Vermont. You can break the lease and move upstate like you planned."

Evelyn felt tears spring to her eyes. "Why do you think I wouldn't go to Vermont with you?"

Miles shrugged. "Why should I believe you'd do anything for me, when you won't even tell me you quit your job?"

She drew a breath. "I don't want to lose you. I thought you understood the concept of making sacrifices for something you love."

"I think you're flying too close to the sun." His voice was cold. "You can't be both a lawyer and a mountaineer, at least not now, so early in your career. You need to pick one and stick with it. I worked low-paying jobs for years because I knew they wouldn't care when I disappeared for a race."

"I forgot, you have all the answers," she snapped, no longer able to control her tone. "I guess you're right. I never should have pursued my ambitions. I'll stay home forever and be a good housewife like you want."

"You sound so much like Sophie sometimes." The comment caught them both off guard and they stared at each other. Miles sighed and set the mug down, reaching up to rub his eyes with both hands. "Evelyn, I love you. In part because you're so rational. You care about things like having a stable income and a safe place to live. That's something I've always needed in my life. But I can tell you're not happy here."

"Maybe you should learn to be rational yourself." She turned her back to him, busying herself with wiping down the countertop. "And you're right. I'm not happy here. Being back in Colorado was a wake-up call. I miss being close to nature. I could take the bar in a different state and practice somewhere else. But you love it here, so I'd better stay. Does that sound rational to you?"

She felt his hand on her shoulder, his fingers sinking into the skin above her collarbone. He turned her to face him. "That's why I'm asking you to stay here. Don't go to Nepal. Stay here, and we'll figure this out. The mountain isn't going anywhere."

She resisted the urge to laugh in his face. "This is a once-in-a-lifetime invitation. I'm getting on that flight tomorrow. And I'm going to climb that mountain. And when I come back to New York, that's when we'll figure things out. I'll go to Vermont with you, if that's what you need me to do."

She didn't wait for his response; she slipped past him and picked up her luggage, carrying it to the bedroom. Miles didn't follow her. Thirty minutes later, while she was still unpacking, he entered the room without acknowledging her, stuffed a backpack with clothes, and left again. Evelyn let the guilt wash over her as she filled her laundry basket, struggling to understand why their conversation had turned so antagonistic. He'd confronted her with the letter, but there must have been a path through the conversation that didn't end with Miles storming off. Sometimes when they argued, she forgot the most important part—that they loved each other.

He didn't come back the rest of the day, and when she woke up the next morning, Evelyn tried not to think about how well she had slept without him there. She was just used to it, she told herself, she'd been away for weeks. As she packed the last few items in her suitcase, she thought of Sophie. Dropping out of school, moving to Wyoming—she always suspected that Miles had influenced those choices and had told Sophie as much. She had thought that the six-year age gap between Sophie and Miles had resulted in a lopsided power dynamic, with Miles calling all the shots by default. But now, maybe he was trying to do the same thing to her, to subtly control her decisions. Or maybe he just wanted what was best for her. For them. She knew they were both unhappy in the city, but it was also where they had the most opportunities—for Miles's art, for her career as a lawyer.

She let a shirt fall into her suitcase and lifted her hands to her face, surprised to find tears pooling in her eyes again. She and Miles were headed toward an impasse. He'd given her a chance to turn back and she had barreled straight ahead. Evelyn dropped her hands to her lap and surveyed the clean, minimal bedroom that looked exactly as it had before Miles had moved in. They'd never hung up any of his art, or any art for that matter. No new furniture, nothing to make it his place, too. The reason pierced her like a bullet. This was never his home.

CHAPTER FIVE

July 2015,
K2 Camp Three

"Oh my god, don't go out there."

Sophie shielded her face with her arm as Evelyn stumbled inside and struggled to zip the tent closed, fighting against a wind that seemed determined to rip them right off the mountainside. After another minute, Sophie leaned forward and grabbed part of the tent door, holding the thin flap of material as still as possible as Evelyn tore off her thick glove and managed to zip the door completely. They both fell back, panting, and tried to stabilize the tent as it billowed and snapped in the wind.

"So. Was it worth it to pee?"

Evelyn laughed. "I mean, I survived. What's the alternative? Kidney failure?"

"You could pee in one of these bowls."

"Gross. We eat out of those."

Sophie shrugged, glad that she had no reason to leave the tent. Outside, one of the wildest storms she'd ever encoun-

tered raged. When they'd reached Camp Three and set up
their tent that afternoon, it had been difficult to stand upright. The winds had only grown stronger as evening fell.
Evelyn took off her headlamp and laid it beside her sleeping
bag, adding to the soft white glow of Sophie's headlamp. The
shifting tent walls sent eerie shadows bouncing across her skin.

"So," Evelyn said, propping herself up on her sleeping bag
and turning on her side to face Sophie. "We're in for a long
night. Entertain me."

Sophie rolled her eyes. "How? Nothing new has happened
to me." Almost a month had passed since they'd started the trek
to K2, and they had barely left each other's sides in that time.

"Let's talk about someone else then. What do you think
Miles is up to right now?"

Sophie frowned. Although she was normally happy to hear
Miles's name—it always reminded her that she was connected
to someone else, part of a unit, *married*—she had spent much
of their trip trying not to think about him. They'd gotten
into a few fights before she left for K2, even while Evelyn
was sleeping in the guest room, hushed arguments that were
a continuation of a bigger disagreement. For months now,
Miles had been talking about moving. His discontent started
in the winter. He hated being cooped up in the cabin, snowed
in and unable to leave. The rivers froze over, cutting off a
steady portion of his income. While Sophie was happy to ski
on the mostly deserted roads, Miles languished, working on
a painting for an hour or two and spending the entirety of
the rest of his time, it seemed to Sophie, complaining. At her
encouragement, he started staying with a friend in Jackson for
short stretches of time, whenever the roads were clear enough
to make the thirty-mile drive. Sophie was often away, too,
staying at park lodging on weekends for work. But when they
were together, she heard the same thing from Miles again and

again. He thought they should move to New York, to San Francisco, to Chicago. He thought his time in Wyoming was over. And he was ready for Sophie's to be over, too.

Evelyn's eyebrows rose as she noticed Sophie's expression. "What?"

"Nothing. I don't even know what time it is back home. He's either sleeping, painting, kayaking, or packing up to leave."

She tried to say the last bit as casually as possible, but Evelyn leaned forward, eyebrows rising even higher than before.

"What?" Evelyn repeated.

Sophie sighed, wishing she hadn't phrased it that way. She didn't feel like laying out all the facts for Evelyn, not after an exhausting day of climbing, and not at twenty-one thousand feet of elevation, where breathing and thinking were equally difficult. But she had brought it up for a reason—the months of arguing had set her on edge. She didn't have a person in the world to talk to about it besides Evelyn. And she suspected Evelyn might have overheard them fighting, anyway, because it was hard for Sophie to keep her voice down when she talked to Miles about how his insistence on uprooting their life made her feel. Which was more than a little hurt, and more than a little angry.

She laid out the details for Evelyn, Miles's desire to move, his inability to see how living in a city would entirely disrupt her life, and how little time they spent together these days. "I thought staying with a friend was just an arrangement for the winter, but he stays in Jackson so often now. The cabin, Wyoming, it was all his idea. So why does he want to leave now?" She felt pathetic, with Evelyn's concerns about her dropping out of school and following Miles around fresh in her mind. Evelyn had never said out loud to Sophie that she didn't like Miles, but Sophie had fielded constant skepticism throughout their relationship.

"I feel like you're being very calm about this. I mean, Sophie, it's absurd that he wants to move again already. It's been a year. You've built a life there. Moving to a city would be entirely for his benefit."

Sophie shrugged. A fierce gust of wind shook the tent, distracting her for a moment. "We've had a really good relationship so far. I love the—" she gestured "—*idea* of the life we've tried to build together. I just feel so distant from him right now. We're on separate wavelengths. If he could just sell a few paintings, get some big deal, I think he'd be happy to stay. I keep telling him to build his image as a Western artist, but he doesn't want to be seen that way."

"Sounds like you're the one putting in all the effort," Evelyn said, blowing out a frustrated breath. She paused, as if recalibrating. "Well, I guess not. You're married. But you can't live his life for him, you know? If he really wants to be an artist, he'll make it happen anywhere. If he thinks Wyoming is boring in the winter, too bad. He picked it." Sophie could see her sister's brain working, thinking of solutions.

Sophie nodded, but her mind was already back to Miles, wondering if she should revisit the Western artist conversation when she returned home.

"What if he moved somewhere else in the winter? He could rent in a different city or find an artist residency or something. You'd still have most of the year together."

Evelyn looked pleased with her idea, but Sophie shook her head. "We don't have any extra money for that."

Evelyn's brow furrowed, signaling that she was about to reenter problem-solving mode.

"Let's talk about something else, okay?" Sophie said quickly.

"I'll deal with Miles when I get back home." If all went well, they would summit K2 next week, but they had already agreed to stay longer and attempt neighboring Broad Peak if they succeeded. They had the resources—the food, the guide, the permits—and the time. But it was a long time to spend away from Miles, with close to zero communication. Sophie felt like she'd left behind a looming question mark that over-shadowed everything she did. She didn't actually think Miles would move while she was gone, but she wondered what state their relationship would be in when she returned. Maybe his mind would be made up as another winter approached. She felt helpless, and Sophie hated feeling helpless.

"I'm pretty beat," Evelyn announced. "Let's try to sleep soon."

Sophie agreed, though she knew Evelyn struggled to rest at high altitude and often lay awake for hours after Sophie her-self fell asleep. She reached over to switch off her headlamp. "If only James was here. He'd tell us to shut up and sleep, 'or else.'"

Evelyn laughed. "That 'or else' is such an empty threat."

"Because he knows we'll find out the consequences of our own actions. Remember Everest?"

"Don't remind me," Evelyn groaned. "I'm never getting drunk on a mountain again."

"I thought you were going to die. I've never seen you look so sick," Sophie replied, smiling at her memory of Evelyn, pale as a ghost and vomiting outside their tent the next morning. "I think James regretted inviting us after that."

"Hey. We summited." Evelyn turned off her lamp, too, plunging the tent into complete darkness.

"We sure did. And we'll summit K2."

"Don't forget Broad Peak. The less impressive little sister."

"Hey," Sophie said, reaching through the dark to punch Evelyn's arm. "I resent the implication."

The next morning, they descended to Camp Two, another day of acclimatization. Downclimbing included traversing the black pyramid, a technical array of steep, spiky rock formations that required intense focus. Sophie woke up early and stretched outside the tent, relieved to be greeted by bluebird skies and a gentler wind. A few other climbers had spent the night at Camp Three, and she watched them preparing for their day. Some were headed on toward Camp Four, and some were also descending. Tashi Sherpa, the mountain guide they'd hired to assist them on their climb, organized ropes beside his tent. He would descend before them and work on setting up their Camp Two accommodation again.

Sophie stuck her head back in the tent, eager to begin descending before the black pyramid became crowded with climbers going both up and down. "Almost ready?"

"Yeah," Evelyn replied, though she didn't sound confident. "Sorry. I'm moving slow this morning."

A few minutes later she appeared, appropriately bundled head to toe. She strapped her crampons onto her boots and looked up at Sophie. "Okay. Let's do this."

The sisters entered the spiderweb of ropes offering different paths through the rocks. Sophie took the lead and paused to check the connection of each rope, yanking as hard as she could before clipping on and rappelling. A loose rope would be a death trap. A frayed rope could be, too, but those were much harder to spot. She noticed Evelyn wasn't doing the same—she simply clipped onto whichever rope Sophie was finished with, without checking the strength.

"Hey," Sophie called up. "Double-check the ropes, okay?"

"Why?" Evelyn called down.

Sophie resisted the urge to roll her eyes. Her sister should know better. "Because if the rope is loose, you'll die," Sophie replied.

Evelyn didn't respond right away. "I'm doing my best, okay? My arms feel weak. I don't want to use up all my energy."

Sophie considered her response, wishing that Evelyn had told her sooner that she didn't feel in top shape. They were well into the pyramid, which had taken four hours to ascend. The descent might take just as long. They could have spent a day at Camp Three—less restful than Camp Two, but better than another exhaustive day of climbing. *But Evelyn would have told you if she didn't feel up to it*, Sophie reminded herself. She trusted Evelyn completely; that's what made them a good team.

"Focus on finding good footholds then, okay? Don't put all your weight on the ropes. And clip onto two when you can!" Sophie called up, her voice echoing off the cathedral of rocks. Moving slowly, she watched her sister navigate her path through the pyramid, following many of the same steps as Sophie even though she couldn't see her. Sophie called out good footholds and dangerous spots, working as two pairs of arms and legs and eyes: hers and Evelyn's.

Two hours later they reached the snow gully beneath the black pyramid. Exhausted, mentally and physically, Sophie unclipped from the last line and tried to catch her breath as she waited for Evelyn. She glanced over her shoulder, taking in the staggering view of Broad Peak, among the other nearby mountains, and the wide glacier far below.

Minutes later, Evelyn was by her side. "Man. That was tough."

Sophie nodded, though part of her wondered how much more quickly she could have descended without waiting for

Evelyn. She admonished herself for thinking that way, because Evelyn's weakness had prevented her from climbing recklessly, had kept her safe.

"Thanks for looking out for me."

Sophie smiled. "Of course."

"I'm leading tomorrow," Evelyn said, her voice easy with confidence. Even in moments of weakness, she was good at maintaining an aura of certainty. Maybe that came with being born first—a natural sense of leadership even when following.

"Deal. I can't believe we have to climb that mess again tomorrow."

"Yes, you can. I bet you're planning a different route up already."

"You know me so well," Sophie replied.

But it was Evelyn who saved Sophie's skin on summit day. Climbing into the bottleneck in lead, Sophie couldn't help glancing up every few minutes at the massive serac hanging over the route. Something in her gut told her to turn back, but she ignored it. Pure instinct, probably—it went against all rational thought to walk beneath a gigantic, unstable shelf of ice.

Sophie paused for a minute, catching her breath from the near-vertical climb. They were already in the death zone; the clock was ticking. She looked over her shoulder at Evelyn, who was close behind. Evelyn had recovered from what they realized was a minor bout of altitude sickness the day they descended the black pyramid back to Camp Two. Her climbing had improved now that her body had fully acclimated.

"Everything okay?" Evelyn asked.

Sophie nodded, though her stomach flipped as she gazed past Evelyn, down the sickeningly steep slope they'd just ascended. "I wanted to stop for a minute here, because we can't in the bottleneck." Speaking seemed to steal all the oxygen from her body.

Evelyn's eyes were covered by sunglasses, but her mouth twisted in concern. "If you need O2—"

"No," Sophie replied. "I'm fine."

"Don't let your pride get in the way, is what I was going to say."

Sophie resisted the urge to snipe back. She knew Evelyn meant well. The altitude left Sophie's brain feeling supercharged and fuzzy at the same time. So she held her tongue, nodded, and gestured for them to continue on.

Through the bottleneck, they turned left, traversing a steep, slow path beneath the serac. The sun had burned off the morning clouds and the ice shelf shone clear white, smooth except for the cracks and ridges running across its surface. Sophie tried not to look, focusing on each footstep. Her head pounded and each breath was a hard-fought battle, but they were close. The summit was within reach.

"Sophie, look out!"

Evelyn's cry stopped her in her tracks. She had only an instant to look up, to connect the strange, eerie groan to the crack that followed as a car-sized block of ice, loosened by the warming sun, broke off and careened down.

Sophie stumbled back. The ice block crashed into the lower part of the serac, shattering into smaller pieces and loosing another shower of icy boulders, before smashing into the route, mere yards from where Sophie crouched. She watched in awe and terror, heart in her throat, as the mountain stilled again, as if nothing had ever happened.

Moments later, Evelyn was by her side. "Are you alright?"

Sophie nodded, speechless. She tried to whisper "thank you," but knew Evelyn didn't hear.

"Do you think," Evelyn continued, pausing for breath, "it's safe to keep going?"

In spite of herself, Sophie laughed, and Evelyn laughed too. "Never safe," she managed to say. "But let's."

"Want me to lead?"

"No. Want you to keep looking out for me."

"I can do that," Evelyn replied.

Hours later they made the summit, and for exactly twenty minutes the sisters were alone on what felt like the top of the world. The views of the surrounding mountains were mostly obscured by a sea of clouds, with only the tallest peaks poking through, but the sky overhead was a piercing blue. The world felt infinite to Sophie—an endless list of adventures sprawled out as far as her eyes could see, so many more mountains to climb than her lifetime would allow.

She wondered if Evelyn was thinking the same thing but couldn't bring herself to voice the question. The reality was that their climbs together would always be numbered. Evelyn had graduated law school in May and would take the bar at the end of July, just a few days after returning to New York. If she passed, she would no doubt be working for a firm by the end of the year. Sophie had trouble scraping together enough money for Himalayan climbs, even with her sponsors. She wished that every year could be like this, both of them escaping their regular lives to spend most of a summer with each other. But it wasn't realistic.

"I wish you'd move back to Colorado," Sophie heard herself say.

Evelyn looked at her, surprised. "You know I want to stay in New York. Besides, you're not even in Colorado anymore."

"I know. But you'd be closer, and we'd climb together more often."

Evelyn's expression softened. "Maybe one day. I want the best chance for establishing my career that I can get."

Sophie nodded, but a lump had risen in her throat. She looked up at the distinct sound of crunching snow and heavy breathing that signaled another team about to make the summit.

"Come on," Evelyn said. "Let's let someone else have our spot."

Sophie smiled. "We have another mountain to climb, anyway."

"That's right. You're stuck with me for another two weeks."

Sophie wished they had more time.

CHAPTER SIX

March 2018,
Pokhara, Nepal

"You look miserable."

From her cocoon of blankets, Sophie peered up at Levi's smiling face. She couldn't match his expression. "I hate to break it to you," she said, "but I think I caught a cold."

His smile fell. "You don't sound so good." He set aside a small paper bag and felt her forehead. "You feel warm. But you're also under three blankets."

"I'll survive." She sniffled, throwing off the top layer of blanket and sitting up. Traveling always did her in—she tended to get sick as soon as she got on an airplane. The trips to the Himalayas were always particularly grueling—they had flown from Geneva to Istanbul and then on to Kathmandu, before catching a bumpy flight to the tiny Pokhara airport. Sophie had crashed hard at the hotel when they arrived midafternoon, and spent most of the day sleeping, rousing only for a quick dinner of dumplings and rice before falling into another dreamless sleep. Levi, on the other hand, seemed to have boundless energy. She had never traveled long-distance with him before and was impressed by his high spirits.

"Maybe this will help." He handed the slightly greasy paper bag to her. Sophie opened the bag and a buttery, sugary scent rose to greet her. Inside were gwaramari, little round pieces of fried dough, and jeri, intricate fried disks coated in syrup.

"You're the best," Sophie said, taking a bite of jeri.

"I'll get us something more substantial in a little while." He paused and wolfed down a piece before continuing. "Everyone else got in yesterday. Penelope, George, Ruslan, and Ivan. I talked to them last night. The plan is to meet with the porter agency today and get everything sorted out for tomorrow. Maybe a day trek. Get a good view of Annapurna."

"And then you'll decide that you want to try Annapurna instead."

He smiled again. "Maybe one day." They both glanced toward the door at the sound of a knock. "Are you expecting someone?"

Sophie shook her head but gestured for him to answer. Levi opened the door to reveal Penelope and George. Penelope was slender and elegant, dressed in beige and cream, her light brown hair pulled back into a smooth ponytail. George looked fit and healthy as ever in his down jacket and hiking boots, a hint of stubble on his cheeks.

"My apologies," he said, glancing at Sophie. "We didn't mean to disturb you."

She waved a hand, swinging her legs over the side of the bed. "I'm alright. Just jet-lagged." She wore pajamas and hadn't yet glanced in a mirror; she knew she must look disheveled compared to Penelope's polished appearance.

"Is everything okay?" Levi asked.

"It is," George said, turning back to Levi. "Ruslan and Ivan took off to Phedi for a hike. I'm a bit worried that those two might have their own agenda for this trip. But," he continued, glancing sideways at Penelope, "we wanted to stick together as much as possible."

"Yes," Penelope said, nodding. "We have a responsibility to look out for each other, *oui*?"

Levi glanced at Sophie, checking in with her. She nodded. "Yeah, of course. I can be ready in just a few minutes. I would love to see more of the area."

"Great. We'll be in the lobby. We're expected at the agency around 3:30, so we have plenty of time. Ruslan and Ivan know the time. We'll see if they turn up."

Levi shut the door after they left. "George doesn't seem to have much faith in the Russians."

"Maybe just two particular Russians." She stood up and began rummaging through her luggage, looking for clothes appropriate for a day hike. "George invited them for a reason, right?"

"Yeah, probably that they're fearless. George has the experience, you, me, and Penelope are the youngsters, and the Russians are the muscle. Together, we'll be successful."

"That's beautiful," she replied, pulling on a shirt. "Nothing I love more than harmony on a mountain."

"Come on, no sarcasm. George has such a good feeling about this team. It's kind of inspiring."

"Yeah, and all the other teams who have been training together for weeks will race right past us." Sophie tried to keep the bitterness out of her voice. She would have preferred to get to know her teammates before climbing a massive, uncharted giant with them. As much as she trusted George, the unknowns were hard to look past. In Sophie's mind, a good expedition team meant everyone pulled their weight, and she had no idea what her other teammates expected.

She felt his hand on her arm and glanced at him. He turned her to face him, gently, and kissed her forehead. "I know you're nervous. But it's not like you to be so pessimistic. Can you try to find joy in the fact that we're in Nepal? Climbing mountains with friends?"

She let herself smile, more for his benefit than her own. Although she was more awake now, her stomach churned with anxiety. She could think only of Evelyn. With each passing second, she grew closer to seeing her sister again. She wasn't ready, no matter how hard she tried to pretend.

"Perfection," George announced, stopping to take in the view. Levi and Sophie, following a few feet behind, caught up and fanned out beside him. Penelope had brought up the rear and was taking her time, a trait that Sophie suspected would transfer to the actual expedition—and one she admired. It was difficult not to rush on a mountain sometimes, to tire oneself out well before a day's work was over.

Sophie shielded her eyes from the bright sun. It was a clear day, and below, the Pokhara Valley spread out, Phewa Lake shimmering in the sun. A little farther up the trail, a group of gliders prepared for takeoff. The colorful paragliders looked like wings stripped from birds of paradise. But none of this captured Sophie's attention the way that the mountains in the distance did—the Annapurna range, snow-covered giants rising from the lush valley. She could pick out Annapurna I's distinctive peak, but the others in the range were unfamiliar.

Beside her, George seemed to sense her curiosity. He pointed out the three other peaks that shared the Annapurna name. "And Gangapurna. Tilicho. All good climbs."

"I haven't climbed in this region yet," she admitted.

"You're young. You'll find yourself out here again."

"So, where is Yama Parvat?"

"In that area toward the right. She's a bit unassuming." He paused, tracing the outline of the mountain with his fingertip. It was difficult for Sophie to distinguish.

"I'm sure the view from the top will be just as good as this one."

"That's the spirit."

Beside Sophie, Levi cleared his throat. "George. Something's been on my mind since we arrived."

"Go on."

"I was so excited to come here, to see Nepal and experience a new culture. Being here physically…" He trailed off, as if at a loss for words. "It feels different. Seeing the poverty in town. I can't help but feel like I'm parading around how wealthy I am in front of people who have very little, or nothing at all."

Sophie watched George. She'd had the same conversation with Levi the night before and had tried to reassure him. George's brow furrowed as he listened, and his gaze shifted from Levi back to the view of the mountains. "It's a complicated subject. I could tell you that the Nepal government needs our money, and that some of that money may trickle down to cities like Pokhara and even the remote villages, but who knows if that's true. Pokhara's in a better position than most cities in Nepal. There's a healthy flow of tourism dollars here. And a lot of our dollars go directly to people we've hired." George paused to cough. "Personally, every time I climb, I donate to a charity in that region. One where the money goes directly to the people, for something practical, like health care or education."

Levi nodded slowly, the way he always did when he was in deep thought. "Yeah. That's a good idea. But what about—" he gestured "—the mountain itself?"

Penelope, who had been listening in silence, spoke up. "To me, the mountain is not alive. It cannot think or speak to us. I treat it like a piece of art. Climbing is an art form, *oui*? I would not go to a museum and damage the paintings. Climbing a mountain is an act of beauty. I am not doing something beautiful if I am hurting the mountain or the people that love it."

"I agree," George said. "It's just rock and snow. The sacredness of the mountain? That's not my belief. I'll respect what the locals tell me about it, of course. I'll listen to them. And I'll do my best to leave no trace. But to me, it's the same as an unnamed, uncharted mountain in Antarctica. If someone else wants to impose a sacred deity onto it, that's their choice. I'm just here to climb."

"But then why not—"

"I hate to rush," Sophie interrupted, knowing the conversation would go on for another hour if she stayed quiet, "but shouldn't we head back soon? I don't want to be late to the agency."

"She wants time to *eat* before the agency," Levi said, and though Sophie shot him a look, he wasn't wrong. Her stomach growled at the thought of a warm meal.

There were no protests from George or Penelope. They made their way back down from Sarangkot, and with each step Sophie looked out toward the Annapurnas, where the next few days would lead.

A cool wind whipped through the Pokhara Valley as Sophie and Levi approached the porter agency the next morning, the sidewalks mostly empty at the early hour, few cars rolling down the streets. Smoke rose from chimneys and enticing scents wafted from open restaurant windows as they began the day's cooking. Sophie gazed longingly into each restaurant

they passed; she hadn't had time to eat more than a handful
of granola for breakfast. Levi gently tugged her on. When
Sophie saw the others already gathered outside the building,
she picked up her pace and waved to them as she drew closer.

"Morning!" George called, motioning them over. "We're
just about set."

The sidewalk in front of the agency was covered in massive backpacks, stuffed to the brim with supplies for the next
several weeks. Each team member would also carry a small
backpack with some personal items—clothing, snacks, emergency medical supplies—but the porters were hired to lug the
heaviest necessities to Base Camp. Sophie didn't envy them,
but she knew the money they earned on the journey went a
long way in supporting their families.

A trio of Himalayan climbing guides stood beside the porters, distinguished by their red jackets. Sophie recognized
one of them and changed her course, calling his name as she
drew closer.

"Pemba Choden!"

The man turned to her, blinking for a moment before his
face lit up in a smile. "Sophie?"

"You remember me?" she asked, before glancing back at
Levi. "Levi, this is Pemba Choden. He was our sirdar, our
head guide, on Everest."

"Of course I remember you," Pemba replied. "You and
your sister, the two of you were funny. I have good memories from that trip."

Sophie tensed in anticipation of him asking where Evelyn
was, but he left the subject alone. "I can't believe it's been four
years. Why aren't you at Everest this season?"

The smile left Pemba's face. "One of my friends, he passed
away last year. He fell from near the summit while roped to a

novice climber. I looked for work on Manaslu or Kangchen-junga instead. Then I get a call about the permits for Yama Parvat. I say, 'put me on the list.' And here I am."

"I'm so sorry about your friend."

Pemba nodded, his face expressionless. "I think of him often."

Sophie wished she could say more, but she knew the guides accepted the possibility of death every time they set foot on a mountain, as did everyone else. The difference was that for them, it was work, and for her, it was leisure. She said good-bye to Pemba and the other two guides, who he introduced as Dawa Gaden and Dorjee Norbu.

"Man," Levi said, after they'd stepped away. "I can't imagine losing a friend like that and having to just carry on with work."

"I know," Sophie said. "But so many people would never summit a Himalayan mountain without guides like him." She paused, glancing up at the mountains that loomed above the city. "When we climbed Everest, it was his fifth time summit-ing that mountain. I'm sure he's made more summits since."

"But would that be his way of life if rich people weren't paying him to risk his life?"

"I don't know," Sophie admitted. She fixed her gaze on him. "You're here too, remember? You didn't pay your way here. Your sponsors did."

"I know," Levi replied, lifting his hands as he relented. "I'm still not used to it." He glanced at the label stitched on his jacket sleeve. "Now everyone knows I'm a sellout."

"Everyone here is a sellout, too, me included." On their first climb together in Switzerland, Levi had impressed her with his gentle yet agile way of climbing. His gear had been basic and well-worn, nothing fancy or showy about his style. His understanding of the mountains seemed intuitive, something he was born with, not taught. Sometimes Sophie envied the way he could visualize a line up a rock face and execute it, error-free, on the first attempt.

Levi glanced back at the guides. "I'd love to hear what they think about climbing Yama Parvat. Do you think any of them will set foot on the summit?"

"I'm curious too, but look, we'd better pay attention." She pointed toward George, who was waving them over. "Or we're going to get left behind before the climb even begins."

The trek to Sinuwa was a slog. After a few clear days of travel, torrential rains had met them on the long climb to the village, dampening everyone's spirits. Sophie had noticed a handful of blisters beginning to pop up on her feet where water had soaked into her boots. She put on some drying patches and prayed they would look better in the morning.

In the common room of the small, dry teahouse, she sat drinking ginger tea and listening to George argue with Ruslan and Ivan. That seemed to be a developing theme. For the past few days they had sprinted ahead of the rest of the group, turning up again at the night's destination looking no worse for the wear. But George was livid.

"We cannot abandon each other on the mountain," he insisted, turning his mug of coffee in circles on the table.

Ruslan and Ivan exchanged a look. "You are too slow," Ruslan declared, and they both laughed.

"Really, though, it's…" Penelope trailed off, as she had a habit of doing, trying to find the right words. "It's not, as you say, in the essence of team spirit."

"So, we'll lay the ropes going up. Make things easier for you."

George shook his head. "No. That's the guides' job. We'll

take turns leading as we've discussed. Without everyone's co-operation, this team will fall apart, and we won't make it."

Sophie glanced at Levi. He was seated beside her, watching the conversation with rapt attention. She brushed her hand against his, which rested on her right leg, and leaned closer. "Want to step outside?" she whispered. "I can't listen to this anymore."

A minute later they were on the porch of the teahouse, sheltered from the elements by the roof above. Straight ahead, thick white clouds drifted in the rift between the mountains, promising more rain to come. Lush forest surrounded them, and Sophie was struck by how small she felt.

"Do you ever want to run away to somewhere like this?"

Levi stepped closer to her, resting his arms on the porch railing. "Sure. But I don't think there's a place for me here."

"What do you mean?"

"I'd stick out like a sore thumb."

"Oh. Like I do in Geneva."

He shot her a look. "You look more Swiss than I look Nepalese." He straightened up, regarding her for a moment. "Every inch of the land here is so sacred. I feel bad just for setting foot on it. I can't imagine moving here and trying to feel like this land belonged to me." He paused. "I'm not sure if I can separate the physical elements of a place from the cultural aspects, like George said the other day."

Sophie felt a twinge in her stomach. "Are you having second thoughts about climbing?"

Levi shook his head quickly. "No, no, not at all. It's just…" He lowered his head to his hands, running his fingers through his hair. "I've never done this before. Climbed in the Himalayas. It feels different from climbing in Switzerland. It's how I felt when I went to Bolivia, like I wasn't supposed to be there.

I can't put my finger on it." He raised his head again, gazing out into the forest. Strange birdcalls filled the silence. "What was it like for you, the first time you came here?"

"Oh…well, it wasn't here, exactly," she replied, and Levi nodded. "But you know that, right. Everest was different. I was so young and excited. Base Camp was a party every night. So many teams on the mountain, so many people to meet from all around the world. Like a miniature city. I guess I didn't think much about if any of us had a right to be there. We just were. I mean, I was grateful. I was in awe. But I didn't think about the ethics of it, besides trying not to leave any garbage behind."

Levi listened in silence, tracing the railing with his fingers. "And what about when you came back? For K2 and Broad Peak?"

"It was a quieter experience for sure. I had more time to think about the mountains, to observe them. And it made sense to me then, why they're so important to the cultures and religions that surround them. I mean in a spiritual sense, beyond just how…how magnificent they are. But I still didn't have doubts about the climb itself. I didn't think about it the way you seem to be doing."

"Well, I've had plenty of time to think."

"What were you going to ask George before?"

"Oh," Levi said, tilting his head back as if trying to remember. "Right. I was going to ask that if the mountains are all the same to him, if they're all just rock and ice and a different puzzle to solve, then why come here at all? Why climb the sacred mountains like Yama Parvat?"

A small smile crossed Sophie's lips. "You know what his answer would be."

"Because it's there."

She nodded, and let the silence fall between them again. During their conversation, the sun had slipped behind one of the mountains, and the forest had rapidly descended into the cool evening dusk. More thick clouds had drifted in, but no rain fell yet. The air was heavy with moisture; a cool breeze made the hair on Sophie's arms stand up. She felt a lump rise in her throat and glanced at Levi.

"I don't know what I'm going to do after this trip." He looked at her, imploring her to continue. "About where to live, I mean. I don't know if I want to keep playing the long game in Switzerland. Ten years is a long time. I know I can keep the permit, but…I don't know if it will ever truly feel like home."

"I understand," he said, so quickly that it surprised her. "I love Switzerland. It's a home I can always go back to. But I don't know if it's the best option out there for me. How could I? I've never lived anywhere else."

"I have to go back to the US. After this trip, I think. Finalize the divorce. Change my last name."

"That would be good to take care of." He turned to her, interlacing his fingers with hers. "And then we'll travel the world and if we decide that we like Switzerland best, we'll get married and you'll become a citizen."

She couldn't help but smile. "Listen to you. Proposing marriage right after I talk about my divorce."

"I'm not proposing," he laughed. "You'll know when that's happening."

The thought of getting married again brought a wave of unease. Marriage had gone so poorly for Sophie last time. As much as she knew that Levi was different from Miles in every possible way, she couldn't help seeing marriage as an unnecessary complication. There was no reason to make two independent beings into one unit, so hopelessly tangled by paperwork and promises. Her freedom mattered more than a governmental binding of their love.

Sophie let go of Levi's hands and glanced at the teahouse door. "Do you think they're done arguing?"

"I think that the second we reach Base Camp, those two are going to split off. But we'll have George and Penelope in our corner. We'll be alright."

She followed him back inside, enamored by his unrelenting optimism.

From the teahouse in the forest, they moved on, always toward the mountains, and finally to the Annapurna Base Camp, their first night spent in tents. Already Sophie felt more at peace—the reality of her disconnection from the modern world had started to set in. She hadn't touched her cell phone in days except to take pictures, which meant that she had a lot fewer chances to open her messages and stare at the text from Evelyn she left unanswered.

On the eighth morning, walking through the rocky, snow-dusted landscape, shadowed by the Himalayan giants, part of Sophie wanted to turn back to Annapurna. No one had set foot on Yama Parvat in more than ten years, and no one had ever stood on the summit. There would be more unknown variables than any other mountain she had climbed before. There was some reassurance in that—if she died on Annapurna I, someone could probably point out her mistake. If she died on Yama Parvat—well, how could anyone know what went wrong?

Five hours later they reached Base Camp, a sloping swath of dirt and rock scattered with a few yellow tents. It looked much like the other Base Camps where Sophie had stayed—less rocky than K2 and Everest, thankfully, and less crowded.

She knew which teams were here already—Japan and Poland, who had both made it clear that they would be arriving early. At least her team had beat the Americans. A pit had settled in her stomach since the day Evelyn texted, congratulating her on being invited to climb. Sophie knew right away that her mother had passed along that information, because she'd done the same thing for Sophie—informing her, gently, that Evelyn had a spot on the American team, and then imploring her to find time to speak to her sister. Sophie had said she would think about it, to appease her mother. But she hadn't been thinking about it—training in Switzerland and trekking in Nepal had both been good distractions. At Base Camp, she suspected a feeling of claustrophobia would set in. She was trapped here, awaiting Evelyn's arrival.

Beyond the colorful tents, Sophie's eyes were drawn up, to the massive presence of Yama Parvat that loomed above her. The mountain, snow-covered like all the others, looked unassuming at first—just a large mass, not a distinct shape like K2. Of course, the Annapurnas were different from the Karakoram range, where each mountain peak seemed as sharp as a knife tip. She regarded Yama Parvat for several minutes longer, breathing in the thin air, before she noticed that everyone else around her was also still, reverent, even Ruslan and Ivan. Studying, wondering what it would be like to strap on crampons and start climbing. They would all have to wait a few days. The acclimatization process was essential. If they moved too fast, altitude sickness would likely strike, ruining any attempts at a summit.

"You've made it." Sophie blinked and lowered her gaze from the peak. A man had approached them. She recognized him as Yakumo Yoshiyuki, the leader of the Japanese team, and a respected climber who had made first ascents of peaks in Antarctica and Russia.

George stepped forward to shake his hand. "Indeed. Here we are. Not a bad trek."

He sounded so jolly—it was partially his Yorkshire accent— but Sophie wondered if he was putting on a front, pulling cheer from some stored reserve. He had been simmering for the entire trek to Base Camp, irritated by Ruslan and Ivan.

"We have," Yakumo said, gesturing at the tents, "a general setup, but you're welcome to pitch anywhere. There are a few really wonderful people from Adventure Nepal who are staffing the food and medical tents. I suspect they'll take good care of us."

Sophie made a mental note to stop by the medical tent and ask for some relief for the blisters that still plagued her feet.

Yakumo excused himself, and George turned back to face the small group. "So, we'll pitch—in that area?" He pointed to a barren spot left of the food and medical tents.

"Looks as good as any," Levi replied. They took their supplies from the porters and set off, covering the short distance in silence, and dispersing slightly to begin setting up.

Sophie and Levi pitched their tent together. Most climbers had their own tent at Base Camp; but most would share at the higher camps, even though the tents they carried at high altitude would be even smaller. It helped to have another person close by overnight, both for body heat and in case someone began to suffer a medical emergency. But if the weather took a turn, they could be stuck in the tiny shelters for days. Sophie and Evelyn had experienced their share of boredom and claustrophobia-induced arguments when crammed together, but in the past, Sophie couldn't imagine being stuck in a life-threatening storm with anyone else. She wondered if she would come to feel the same about Levi.

That night, everyone gathered at the long plastic tables in the mess tent for a meal of dal bhat, momos, and roti. The smell, warm and inviting, was a reminder that fresh food would be scarce for the next few weeks. The Adventure Nepal team seemed keen on providing freshly prepared meals as long as there were climbers at Base Camp—they were scouting the mountain, Sophie learned, for future commercialized expeditions. Their presence was reassuring. George had said there would be food at Base Camp, but he hadn't given specifics. Sophie looked at packages containing beef jerky, nuts, dried fruit, crackers, and other snacks arranged in massive piles at the back of the tent and let out a breath of relief. No one would starve on this trip.

It struck her how little she had worried about the logistics of things like food and medical care. That was always Evelyn's jurisdiction, to the point where Sophie rarely had a say. Evelyn would spend days talking on the phone and writing emails, and when they showed up to the mountain, their supply of food would be waiting. Luckily, Sophie never had an issue adjusting to the eight-thousand-calories-a-day diet that mountain climbing required. She would drop a few pounds each trip, sure, but not like Evelyn, who already ate like a bird at home. Her sister often returned from trips looking sickly and malnourished, the outline of her spine clear through a T-shirt. Sophie wondered if the extra stress of her presence would render Evelyn completely unable to eat. She felt an unwelcome surge of worry and focused on folding her napkin into a tiny square, sealing the thought inside.

After dinner, boiling water and a variety of drink options

were provided—coffee, tea, hot chocolate. Sophie chose the latter and a bar of chocolate as well, returning to sit beside Levi.

"Go big or go home," he said, glancing at her snack.

Penelope, seated across the table, stared down at her own mug skeptically. "I have no appetite," she declared. "It will return in three days."

Sophie blinked. "You know that for a fact?"

"*Oui*. It happens as I reach new elevations. I'll adjust here, and then," she said, wiggling her fingers to indicate climbing, "is gone again. Three more days, I am sick. I force myself to eat. I feel worse! There is no solution." She took a sip of coffee and made a face.

"Maybe you just need to work up an appetite." Sophie turned to look at Ivan, who was peering at Penelope over the top of his mug. She couldn't tell if the comment was meant to be suggestive and glanced at Levi, who seemed to have the same question.

"It is enough work putting up with you," Penelope replied. Ivan grinned and took a long drink from his mug.

Sophie appreciated that Penelope had a good attitude, even when she felt sick. That kind of perseverance was necessary on a mountain, where self-pity would only result in failure.

They looked up at the sound of George clearing his throat as he approached the head of the table. "I've been talking to Yakumo and Wojciech," he announced. "Yakumo is planning an ascent up to Camp One tomorrow. The Poles are still acclimating and have offered to take us a short way up the mountain tomorrow. They're doing a different route, which we anticipated. South ridge instead of north. It's totally uncharted, so we'll let them have their fun. The Japanese team, though, they're heading our way and it seems likely they'll be able to pitch Camp One tomorrow."

Ruslan scoffed. "We should have come earlier."

"It's not a race."

"It quite literally is. If we don't summit first, what's the point? Hell, the Poles are smarter than we are. At least if they don't summit first, they'll be the first to carve a new route."

"You are well familiar with the challenges of mountaineering. Anything can happen. So, I wouldn't count on Yakumo's team summiting first, even if they have a head start."

Ruslan snorted. "At least we'll beat the Americans," he muttered.

George gave him a withering glance and then returned his attention to the rest of the table. "I'm thinking that we'll get started around 8:00 a.m. tomorrow, so be up and fed before then. If anyone is feeling off—lightheaded, sick—please come tell me. We'll get you taken care of."

Levi nudged her as George turned away. "Hey. Phone is clear. You first, or me?"

"I'll go," Sophie replied. Base Camp was stocked with a few clunky satellite phones, mostly for the Adventure Nepal staff to communicate with. Tonight, though, they had offered up one of the phones for calls home. A stout, soft-spoken woman showed Sophie how to dial—it was a model she hadn't used before—and she listened to the staticky, far-away rings. It was as if she was holding the phone at arm's length even as it was pressed to her ear. She watched the woman return to fiddling with a set of two-way radios. There was some problem with the connection, Sophie had overheard. No way for the teams to communicate with Base Camp.

"Hello?" Her mother answered on the third ring. She sounded as if she were underwater, but still, she was there, and it was good to hear her voice.

"Mom. It's Sophie. We made it to Base Camp today."

"Oh! Honey, that's wonderful, I'm so glad you're safe. What time is it there? It's just after 9:00 a.m. here. I can never keep Nepal's time zone straight."

"I know. It's offset, remember? I think it's quarter to 7:00 p.m. I don't have my watch on." She spoke softly and twisted in the little plastic chair so that her back was to the rest of the tent. She wanted her conversation to be as private as possible, not knowing when she would speak to her mother again. They had last talked when Sophie had landed in Kathmandu before she flew to Pokhara. "It's exciting to finally be here. How are you?"

Her mother laughed, a sharp burst of static. "Oh, I'm alright. Climbing my own mountains here." She paused. "I spoke to Evelyn yesterday. She was at a teahouse, day three of their hike, I think. She'll catch up to you soon enough."

Sophie tensed. "That's good. I'm glad she's safe too. We haven't...spoken."

"I know. She said the same." Another pause, longer this time, punctuated by a sharp exhale. "I know that I'm useless right now, sitting here on the other side of the world, but I wish I could get you two to talk. Just listen to each other. You're going to be living in the wilderness together for weeks. I can't think of a better time to reconnect. It's all I want. It breaks my heart every day to see my girls like this."

Sophie balled her left hand into a fist and squeezed it. She should have expected this. Instead, she had envisioned a simple conversation, one where she described the mountain, and her mother wished her luck. But Evelyn had wormed her way in yet again. "I don't know, Mom. We'll see. My priority is staying safe and summiting."

Her mother took a long time to respond. "Okay. Call me

again when you can, sweetheart. I'll be around. Stay safe. Use your head. I love you. And I'll be waiting on that summit photo."

"I love you too," Sophie replied, and hung up before handing the phone back to the woman, who was still working on the radios. She rubbed her eyes with the palms of her hands for a moment, although she didn't feel like crying. Her mother's words lingered in her head, pushing her toward Evelyn, encouraging her to make up. But she couldn't fathom where to begin.

Sophie woke before dawn the next morning, her internal clock still shifting. The rush of wind was the first thing she noticed, buffeting against the walls of the tent. Beside her, Levi slept, his breathing rhythmic and soft. She was reluctant to leave his warmth, but she would have to get used to this process each morning, prying herself from the comfort of the tent and stepping out into a harsh, unwelcoming environment.

She leaned forward and opened the door. Overhead, the moon was bright, illuminating the strands of colorful prayer flags snapping in the wind. She could see no people moving around camp. A fine dusting of snow covered the ground. An ethereal, breathtaking landscape. She zipped the door and slid back into her sleeping bag. For another hour, she could pretend to be home, warm in bed.

Home—it surprised her to find she thought of Switzerland, not Colorado.

They spent the next three days trekking up and down, pushing a little farther each time. A snowfield extending down the mountainside near Base Camp made for easy enough climbing early on, but higher up the mountain, the glacier was littered with crevasses, deep cracks in the ice caused by the glacier's slow movement.

Sophie skirted her way around the edge of a jagged crevasse as she followed her team. They were working behind the Japanese team, who were good, considerate climbers. Although the Japanese team had pushed to Camp One already, they had descended back to Base Camp for more acclimatization. Now they were headed up again. Ruslan and Ivan had found equally spirited counterparts on the Japanese team and climbed in front with them, laying ropes and checking footing.

"Let them," George had said. "They're like puppies that need to be worn out."

George and Penelope tended to bring up the rear, slower and more methodical, which left Sophie and Levi midpack. Levi was efficient, threading the ropes through his carabiners with ease and rarely looking back to check on her. Sophie challenged herself to match his energetic strides, even as her energy dwindled.

The acclimatization process was tedious, her least favorite part of climbing. She kept her gaze trained on the ground ahead of her to avoid looking up at the peak, that towering mass of snow and ice that beckoned all of them. They reached their highest point to date, one thousand feet below Camp One, and stopped for the day.

Yakumo circled back to talk to George, who had stopped nearby. "Well, we're pushing on."

George nodded. He had taken off his gloves for a moment to dry the sweat on his hands, and already the skin was bright red. "You're not worried about the radios?"

Yakumo shook his head. "It's only a night. I spoke to the Base Camp team; they expect to have them fixed soon. I'd rather not waste another day."

"Right, then. I think we'll wait until tomorrow."

Sophie nudged Levi aside. "He's being so cautious."

"I know. I wonder why."

She shrugged. "He has more experience than any of us. I guess we should listen."

"Yeah. But at this rate the Polish team will be back home drinking beers and soaking their feet before we even pitch Camp Two."

"George is worried about his lungs," Penelope said. Sophie flinched; she hadn't realized the other woman was behind her. "I'm sorry, I did not mean to interrupt. But I don't want you to think he is not moving us forward for no reason."

"Has he not been feeling well?"

"I do not really know the answer. But he seems worried. Privately, he tells me that this mountain will be hard. Do you see," she said, pointing up, "the ridge? It is very exposed and we must cross it to summit. George thinks if we all end up there at the same time, it could cause trouble." Her lips tightened in a thin smile. "But he fears an avalanche, too. 'Let the other teams run up the mountain and see what happens.'"

"It makes sense," Levi replied. "No reason to take risks in an unknown environment like this."

Sophie nodded to show that she was listening, but she couldn't take her eyes off the ridge overhead. She had seen satellite images of it, the sharp backbone of rock rising to meet the sky, cutting one swath of snow from the summit plateau. Even from far below it looked fearsome; she couldn't imagine trying to cross it in anything but clear, still weather. On a mountain like Everest, which had been summited thousands of times, fixed ropes marked the route for much of the way to the top. Every year, legions of local guides adhered ladders to allow climbers to cross dangerous areas and made sure the ropes were in working order. Though each team on Yama Parvat had hired guides, they would set ropes as they went. On the highest parts of the mountain, where no one had ever set foot, the path to the summit would be a guessing game, and there was no telling how much time and energy might be wasted charting the course. All they knew for certain was that crossing the ridge would be involved, and it looked like a beast.

They descended slowly, collecting ropes as they went. George had decided, finally, that the ropes weren't necessary at this part of the route, which would save time tomorrow. They could climb up to meet the Japanese team at Camp One. Maybe George would change his mind overnight. She doubted it, but there was no harm in hoping.

When they came into view of Base Camp again, Sophie stopped in her tracks, so abruptly that Levi bumped into her. "What?" he asked, sliding an arm around her shoulders and stepping beside her.

She pointed wordlessly. Below, Base Camp was a flurry of activity, small bodies pitching tents and unloading supplies.

"We knew they'd be arriving today," he told her gently.

"I'm not ready," she whispered, so quietly that she suspected he didn't hear. She cleared her throat and stepped forward, forcing herself to continue walking. Overhead, the sky was beginning to fill with clouds, and she could sense a change in the air. "I think it's going to snow," she called over her shoulder to Levi.

He groaned. "Don't say that!" He jogged a few steps to reach her and grabbed her arm, arresting her movement until she turned to face him. "Hey. You okay?"

She shrugged. "I have to be."

"Well." He let go of her arm. "If you need anything, I'm here."

His clumsy response signaled that he was just as uncomfortable with the situation as she was. She offered him a small smile. "Where else would you be? Let me know if you're planning on wandering off."

"Not in a million years. Come on, let's find something to eat."

She nodded and followed him, unzipping her puffer jacket as she went. She tended to run hot while climbing, but she also suspected that the dampness on her skin came from nerves. Levi stopped by the tent to remove his crampons, which she did as well. There was a good bit of commotion by the mess tent—everyone was hungry, she suspected; it was well past noon and every single person had been on the move today.

"Are you ready?"

She nodded. They set off the short distance to the mess tent, which smelled heavenly inside, the air rich with spices. The Adventure Nepal staff were cooking rildok and puri. Sophie scanned the makeshift building—no sign of Evelyn, or any of the Americans for that matter. There were a few new faces—the Canadian team, she guessed, who had arrived today too. She spotted Wojciech in a serious conversation with Pemba and edged closer while Levi took a seat at the table. Wojciech glanced at her and beckoned her over.

"The weather is turning," he said. "Satellite shows a good amount of snow tonight, maybe a blizzard. Tell your team, get the word out."

"The Japanese team is at Camp One," Sophie replied.

Pemba frowned. "We should bring them down."

Wojciech shrugged. "Maybe not. They can survive a blizzard at that elevation."

Pemba shook his head, adamant. "No. We do not know

how much snow will come. We cannot lose an entire team because of carelessness."

Wojciech raised his shoulders again and turned away, bringing Sophie with him. "I know Yakumo. He won't want to lose a night because of some snow. But I suppose it'll be us climbing to get them. Can't send the new arrivals."

"What was that about?" Levi asked as Sophie sat down.

"Snow. Bad forecast tonight, I guess. We're supposed to go retrieve Yakumo's team. Or warn them, at least. Wojciech thinks they won't come back down."

Levi considered this. "The radios still aren't working?"

Sophie shrugged. "I don't think so. Yakumo didn't seem too concerned earlier."

He grimaced. "It's a huge risk to take, climbing when we know a storm is coming."

And I'm sure it'll push us back another day, she thought. George would almost certainly delay their plans if the forecast rang true, and she couldn't blame him. But she had been counting on leaving Base Camp behind while the Americans acclimated. Staggered schedules, so she could spend as little time around Evelyn as possible. And now that possibility had all but vanished.

After lunch she left the tent alone. Levi had stayed behind to talk to George and Penelope; she wanted a few minutes of peace before gearing up again to climb to Camp One. They hadn't yet decided who was going—perhaps it would just be Pemba and Dorjee, or guides from the other teams. But she wanted to be prepared.

She stopped in her tracks when she saw Evelyn—standing outside a red tent, alone, looking up at Yama Parvat. She was angled slightly away from Sophie, but she was unmistakable—

her lean frame, the cascade of dark brown hair down her back. At once Sophie felt both compelled to go to her and to leave, to turn away and pretend she hadn't seen her. But it was too late. Evelyn turned, as if to head to the mess tent, and noticed Sophie. They weren't close, but they weren't far away, either, at least in the grand scheme of things—the insurmountable mental distance between them over the last two years reduced to a few dozen feet. Neither of them moved for a small eternity. Then Sophie lifted her hand, almost involuntarily, the smallest greeting she could offer. And Evelyn turned away.

CHAPTER SEVEN

May 2015,
near Kelly, Wyoming

Evelyn slammed the passenger door shut as she stepped onto the dirt driveway and took in the cabin.

It photographed better than it looked in person. In the pictures she had seen, it appeared ramshackle in a whimsical way, nestled among the trees like a storybook home for wandering animals. But in reality, it looked like a family of raccoons might have actually taken up residence. The porch sagged, several shingles had fallen off the roof, and the worn brown siding gave the impression of a shed rather than a cabin. And though Evelyn technically stood in a forest, surrounded by trees, the cabin itself was in a cleared lot composed of dirt and a little bit of grass holding on for dear life. Miles's beat-up truck was parked unceremoniously in the middle of the yard.

"What do you think?" Sophie asked, circling around from the driver's side of her '01 SUV.

Evelyn struggled to form a positive spin. "It's rustic," she managed to say. "I didn't realize it was on a clear lot."

"It's nice. We have a good view of the stars at night."

"I bet," Evelyn said, searching for something else nice to say. "It's so quiet here."

"Yeah," Sophie replied, nodding. "You can't hear any cars from the road. The downside is the lack of cell service and internet."

Evelyn grimaced. She didn't like being cut off from the world unless she was climbing. But that's where they were headed: to K2 and then Broad Peak, both in the Karakoram range on the China-Pakistan border. Evelyn had agreed to fly to Wyoming to see the cabin and plan some final logistics with Sophie, although flying out of New York would have been much easier. But she knew how much Wyoming meant to Sophie, and she didn't mind a break from the city.

Evelyn wondered, sometimes, what her life would look like if Sophie hadn't followed in her footsteps. If she alone had enjoyed climbing, had met James, had scaled bigger and grander mountains. If Sophie had some other talent, music or baking, a different universe of passion. Evelyn might have remained anchored in Colorado, sharing the mountains with found family instead of her sister. She would tell Sophie stories about her expeditions and Sophie would listen in awe. Evelyn would have a different partner in the mountains, someone else she trusted with her life. She didn't necessarily wish for that version of reality, but her brain conjured it up sometimes anyway. She thought about it briefly as Sophie opened the SUV's tailgate and lifted out the first of several suitcases that contained thousands of dollars of highly specialized climbing gear, mostly gifted from sponsors. Would she have had the courage to plan this trip alone?

"I know the cabin doesn't look great on the outside," Sophie said, pulling Evelyn's mind back to the present. She joined Sophie and removed a suitcase. "It's got rustic charm. It grows on you."

"I don't mean to sound rude, but why don't you sell it and buy something a little nicer?"

Sophie set down the suitcase and pulled a hair elastic off her wrist, deftly tying her dirty-blond hair into a bun. "It's complicated. Miles has a weird attachment to this place, since that old guy he knew in Washington sold it to him for dirt cheap. He's always like, 'That guy believed in me. I can't disappoint him.'" Sophie's tone indicated to Evelyn that Sophie did not feel particularly reverent about the old guy in Washington. "Also," she continued, "land around here takes months, sometimes years, to sell. We're trying to save up so we can at least rent somewhere decent while we wait. But that's probably a couple years away."

Evelyn nodded. At least Sophie was financially responsible. "Okay. Let's see the inside."

They hauled the suitcases up the front steps of the porch and through the door. The main section of the dimly lit cabin was a large, open room—a small kitchen to the left and a living room to the right, with a couple of worn-looking couches and chairs. A handful of easels with half-finished paintings were situated in the back corner of the living room, behind a table. There was a small loft above the living room, although it appeared to be piled full of boxes and bins.

Miles turned around from the refrigerator, a hand towel slung over his left shoulder. "Hi, Evelyn. I didn't hear you pull up. I would have helped with your luggage."

"Good news," Sophie replied, as Evelyn lifted a hand in greeting. "There's plenty more in the car."

"I'll grab them. Listen for the timer, okay? The chicken is almost done."

Sophie led Evelyn down a hallway and pushed open a door. "Your room. The bed probably isn't very comfortable, sorry. We got it off Craigslist. But there's a bunch more blankets in the hall closet if you need them. You probably won't. We don't have AC."

Not even window units, Evelyn noticed. But the windows were open, ushering in a light breeze. The whole house smelled like a sunbaked forest. She set her suitcase on the floor and sat on the bed, suddenly exhausted from her day of traveling.

An incessant beeping started up and they both turned their heads. "The chicken," Sophie said, rolling her eyes. "Miles makes an entire roast chicken almost every week. So that we always have leftovers. He thinks I'll starve to death if he doesn't stock the house with prepared meals."

"Well, you probably would."

"Ugh. I don't want to hear it." Sophie disappeared from the room and was replaced a moment later by Miles, a suitcase in one hand and a duffel bag in the other.

"I'll take that," Evelyn said, jumping up and grabbing the duffel bag. "You can put the suitcase anywhere."

He set it beside the growing pile of luggage. "This is an impressive amount of stuff. Sophie's been packing too. I forgot what preparing for a big expedition looks like."

"Yeah, well," Evelyn replied. "We haven't been on one since Everest."

"And you're going just by yourselves this time. Are you nervous?"

Evelyn shook her head. "I think we're ready to spread our wings. Besides, I'll have the world's best guide at my side."

Miles offered a hint of a smile. "She'd be happy to hear you say that."

"Don't tell her. Can't let her get too cocky."

Sophie reappeared in the doorway. "Don't tell me what?"

"Nothing," Miles said, shooting Evelyn a conspiratorial grin. Evelyn wondered if she had judged him too harshly at the wedding. He seemed more at ease here. Maybe the formality of the wedding had made him uncomfortable, or he had had too much to drink. Either way, she felt herself soften toward him a bit, although he still wasn't who she wanted to spend time with. She refocused her attention on Sophie.

"Did the chicken survive?"

"Yes. Me, not so much." Sophie extended her right arm to reveal a large red splotch. "Minor burn."

The smile dropped from Miles's face. "Sophie. You need to learn to take things out of the oven."

His exasperated tone didn't seem to faze Sophie. "I won't have to worry about ovens for the next two months. I'm putting any learning on hold."

Miles still looked annoyed, and Evelyn had a sudden urge to leave the room before an argument unfolded between them. Evelyn didn't know if she'd be able to hold her tongue. "Can we take a walk, Sophie? I know you mentioned trails." Tired as she was, she wanted to get out of the house.

"The ones on the property are nothing special. There are better ones we can drive to, if you're up for it."

"You two have fun," Miles said. "I have to go get ready for dinner with that potential client. I know it's early, but do you guys want to eat now?"

Evelyn shook her head. She'd grabbed a sandwich at the airport, and besides, she wanted to get Sophie alone so they could catch up. "I'm okay. Thanks. A hike is all I need."

★ ★ ★

Later that afternoon, Evelyn and Sophie sat on the shore of Lower Slide Lake, taking in the blue-green water, the mountains swathed in firs, white spruce, and pines, and the stillness. It always amazed Evelyn how much calmer she felt in nature. She could skate by unaware of her activated nervous system when she was in the city, the constant noise and light overwhelming her, but she always felt at a distance from her own body. It was a relief to come back to herself, to feel the warmth of the spring sun.

"I'm so excited for K2," she said. "I can't wait to be unreachable for two months."

"Why?" Sophie asked, leaning forward to rub her ankle. "You're done with school. What's stressing you out?"

"I still have to pass the bar, remember? It's not like I'm home free," she added. The allure of seeing the Karakoram range, those endless, shining towers of imposing granite, had motivated her through the final days of school—a brief pause before real life resumed.

"Don't worry," Sophie said. "The K2 curse will get us, and you'll never have to think about your career again."

Neither of them had yet acknowledged the K2 curse—that so many women who summited the mountain either died on the way back down or met their end on a different mountain, for no apparent reason.

"It's meaningless. How could you possibly correlate successfully climbing K2 with dying on a different mountain?"

"Maybe it's a ploy to keep women off the mountain. They want a boys' club on K2."

"Horrible. And speaking of men," Evelyn continued, glancing at her sister, "how are you and Miles? How's married life?"

"We're good," Sophie replied. She sounded nonchalant.

"We're both so busy, we hardly see each other sometimes. But we're both independent, so it works for us."

"You? Independent?"

Sophie rolled her eyes. "I can be independent *and* have a partner. Plenty of people do it. That's what drew me to Miles in the first place, remember? He doesn't care if I disappear to climb for two months because he does the same thing with kayaking. He gets it."

"He seems more invested in his art these days," she said, thinking of the numerous paintings in the living room.

Sophie shrugged. "Maybe. He's had a couple of pieces commissioned recently. He still guides single-day kayak trips in the summer. But he hasn't competed in a while." She looked preoccupied, her eyes squinting against the rich late-afternoon light that turned the edges of her blond hair to gold. "Why don't you like Miles?"

Evelyn blinked. She hadn't been expecting the question. She cleared her throat and focused on the flashes of light reflecting off the lake water.

"I don't dislike him. I just don't think he's good enough for you. I still can't forgive him for convincing you to drop out of school and move to Wyoming."

"But I'm happy here."

"I'm not finished," Evelyn said, shooting Sophie a glance. "I don't like how he talks to you sometimes. Or about you. Like you wouldn't survive without him. Like you're too dumb to feed yourself. And at the wedding—"

"What about the wedding?"

"He made it sound like he didn't want to stay in Wyoming for much longer. After everything you gave up to move here. I feel like you settled for less than you deserve."

Sophie hesitated, then shook her head. "What did I give

up? A degree that I didn't really want and a worse job?" She chewed her lip for a moment before looking back at Evelyn, the directness of her gaze impressive. "I'm happy here. I'm happy with Miles. That's enough for me."

Evelyn nodded. "You're right," she replied, although Sophie's response had done nothing to change her own feelings. "Look, I just want you to be happy. So, as long as you're happy…"

"I am," Sophie said firmly.

Without speaking they stood up and retraced their steps to the car. Evelyn stole a couple of glances back at the lake, her heart in her throat. She was almost a lawyer, for god's sake, and she was unsuccessful at the one argument that should have been easiest: convincing Sophie that her relationship with Miles was unfulfilling. It was too late anyway. They were already married. Evelyn chastised herself for not trying harder to talk Sophie out of marrying Miles in the first place.

Sophie's assurance now sowed seeds of doubt for Evelyn. Maybe she was looking at the relationship with blinders on, too caught up in her role of the overprotective big sister. Maybe she needed to take Sophie's words at face value and stop worrying about something she couldn't control. The familiar envy crept back in. Sophie seemed to have it so easy. Meeting Miles, the Teton job, a house—all the pieces of her life fit seamlessly together. She never had to force her dreams to come true: they simply did. Evelyn had spent the last seven years of her life nose-deep in books, running between classes and meetings, filling her brain to the brim with knowledge of the law. Perhaps fulfillment was just around the corner. At the end of July she would take the bar, pass—of course she would pass—and find a firm. A spark of hope flamed up, burning back her jealousy. Her life was about to change. Evelyn lifted her face to the fading sun and decided not to worry.

★ ★ ★

That night, she woke up to hushed, angry voices outside her room. It took Evelyn a moment to remember where she was—those weren't strangers arguing in her apartment building hallway, but Sophie and Miles. She crept from bed and pressed her ear against the door, but their voices were muffled. She made out a few words: *move, city, regret,* and then her own name, spoken by Sophie. The voices fell silent, and moments later a door across the hallway slammed shut. Evelyn retreated back to bed, her mind racing.

But the next morning, she didn't have the courage to ask what was wrong.

CHAPTER EIGHT

April 2018,
Yama Parvat Base Camp, Nepal

Evelyn hadn't anticipated seeing Sophie so soon. Now she realized how delusional that was, expecting to avoid someone at Base Camp. It was like any other camp, stuck with the same people for weeks on end. Inevitably you'd end up in a group together, forced to make crafts and talk about your feelings.

Sophie still stood a short distance away. She looked like she wasn't going to come closer. Good. Sophie raised her hand. A wave? A question? Out of instinct, Evelyn turned away, pretending not to see. She regretted it instantly but when she looked up, Sophie had already turned and was striding in the opposite direction. From the set of her shoulders, Evelyn knew she was upset. She didn't have the energy to go after her, not so publicly. Speaking to Sophie could wait.

Evelyn crawled into her tent and fell back on her sleeping pad. Her head pounded, a side effect of reaching fourteen thousand feet of elevation. She *had* planned on it, talking to

Sophie. She had been working up the courage with every step toward Yama Parvat. They had hiked in with the Canadians, who were nice enough, but Evelyn had taken a personal vow to say as little as possible on the trip. *Moving meditation*, she called it in her head, which sounded like something a suburban mom going through a midlife crisis would shell out thousands of dollars to attend.

She knew that the hardest part of talking to Sophie would be conjuring up an apology that sounded authentic. Her mind blanked every time she imagined apologizing—she hadn't gotten past *I'm sorry*. She suspected that every day she stayed with Miles drove the knife a little deeper. But now Evelyn worried about the state of their relationship. He hadn't come home before her flight, had only texted her *have a safe trip*, which she hadn't seen until she landed in Qatar, because he hadn't sent it until after her plane had taken off. Had that been intentional, or did he forget the time? She had tried calling him from Kathmandu to no avail. She didn't have the urge to try again from Base Camp. Besides, she suspected he wouldn't answer. He had always been unreliable with his phone. She would just have to wait two months and then find out if he still lived in her apartment or if he was gone. But, against her better judgment, Evelyn still loved him. She still wanted to believe that after everything she and Miles had been through, he might decide their relationship was worth fixing.

"Evelyn? Is this you?"

She sat up and opened her tent, squinting into the bright light. James stood outside, with Phil and Danielle close behind him.

"It's grub time. Come on."

She left her tent reluctantly. Her appetite had deserted her for much of the trip already; she had managed a few meals here and there but had mostly sustained herself on nuts and dried fruit. She knew she would have to force herself to eat now that they had reached Yama Parvat, but high altitudes always made her queasy. She followed her teammates in the direction of the big tent, noting the thin clouds covering most of the sky.

"Has anyone mentioned snow?" she asked.

James glanced at her as they walked. "Yeah. I saw Wojciech a few minutes ago and he told me the forecast looks bad to-night. Apparently, the Adventure Nepal staff are asking for volunteers to head up to Camp One and warn the Japanese team. I guess they're having some issues with communication. The radios still aren't functioning. Jeez, you'd think they'd get that sorted out."

"Hey," Phil said. "The magic of a first ascent. Nothing works and no one knows how to fix it."

James nodded. Evelyn knew that he and Phil had made first ascents of two smaller—but no less dangerous—mountains in Pakistan. She envied that this experience was nothing new for them, at least in the sense of facing the unknown.

They entered the dark tent and Evelyn blinked, waiting for her eyes to adjust. There were a few people sitting around— a man and woman, a couple of burly men engrossed in con-versation, and a trio of men seated near the back. Uniformed members of Adventure Nepal milled about in the rear, clean-ing up after lunch. They were late, Evelyn realized, but there were still a few large containers of hot food on a table. Well— probably not hot anymore, but it made no difference to Ev-elyn. She could make herself eat anything if she had to, even frozen beans and Spam, which she and Sophie had resorted to on past trips.

As her eyes adjusted, she looked more closely at the man and woman sitting together. She recognized him from the photos her mother had shared. Physically, he looked completely different from Miles—wiry, almost, and unassuming. Short hair, probably, though he wore a hat so she couldn't tell for sure. She wondered if he would recognize her, if Sophie had ever shown him a picture. She glanced again at the woman next to Levi, but it wasn't Sophie. *One of their teammates*, Evelyn thought, but it still surprised her that Sophie was absent. Evelyn grabbed a plate and a scoop of white rice before turning to the snack area, rows of boxes containing what kept her alive on a mountain—nuts, dried fruit, jerky. She took a few packages and walked slowly back to the table. The rest of her team had seated themselves, and to her dismay, the only seats left were at the end of the table, where Levi sat. She took a chair diagonal from him and when she looked up, he shot her a friendly smile. Then, in an instant, a look of recognition crossed his face. He set down his fork.

"You're Evelyn."

So, he had heard about her, enough so that he was looking at her as if she were a mythical creature, descending from the Himalayas to wreak havoc on his girlfriend's life. She nodded. "That's me."

"Levi," he said, extending a hand across the table. She shook it. "I'm—well, you probably already know."

"I do." His smile didn't put Evelyn more at ease. He was friendly, but she worried that at any moment Sophie might walk through the door and see them seated across from each other—what would she think? She could only imagine that Sophie might have more of a jealous streak now.

The woman seated beside Levi had watched their introduction with a bemused look on her face. "Penelope," she said, keeping her arms crossed over her chest. "With Levi and

Sophie and George and—" she twisted in her seat "—those two oafs."

"A bit harsh, don't you think?" Levi said, but it was obvious to Evelyn that he felt the same.

"I didn't mean to interrupt," Evelyn offered, feeling like the new kid at school who sat at the wrong lunch table.

"Oh, you didn't interrupt," Levi replied. "It's nice to meet you. Truly. I've been curious."

"I'm sure you've heard plenty about me." She took a bite of rice and struggled to swallow it, combating the anxiety in her chest.

"A bit. But Sophie…she'll come around."

Evelyn thought of Sophie's tentative wave. "I think I might have missed my chance already." She noticed the look on Penelope's face, her wry smile. "What?"

"I think you're both being too, eh, optimistic. I do not think she likes you very much." Penelope took her plate and stood up. "Excuse me. I need to rest."

Levi watched her walk away and then looked back at Evelyn. "Well, she's not sugarcoating things today."

Evelyn winced, wondering how much of her personal life had become gossip over the last two years. Maybe Penelope would go straight to Sophie and tell her that her dreaded sister was currently schmoozing with her boyfriend. "It's okay. I guess my reputation precedes me." Evelyn forced a smile. She'd tried to lighten the mood, but Levi was looking at her expectantly, as if he wanted her to wrap up the conversation. But a thought struck her—*he must know how Sophie feels*. If she was going to make amends with Sophie, she might have to go through Levi first. Evelyn cleared her throat. "It's just—well, I don't know how to start apologizing."

"I'm afraid I can't help you with that. But I'm sure you'll figure it out. It was nice to meet you, but I should probably also go see what the plan is."

She nodded in acknowledgment and watched Levi leave the tent, disappointed that she hadn't made more of the opportunity. At least he was willing to talk to her. She looked back down at her plate, barely touched, and forced down another bite. Wasting food always made her feel guilty.

"Hey, Evelyn?"

She looked up to see Lowell Hall. She hadn't spent much time with the Canadians, except for today. The two teams had started the trek at different times, the Americans always a few hours ahead, leaving the teahouses earlier in the morning and often asleep when the Canadians arrived. But this morning they had all trekked to Base Camp together. Now Lowell towered over her, even from the opposite side of the table. She thought he looked like he'd just strolled out of the woods—bulky, bearded, kind brown eyes. All he was missing was an axe slung over his shoulder.

"Yes?"

"I'm trying to get some interviews rolling, and I wondered if I could speak to you."

He wasn't just here to climb Yama Parvat; he was also writing an exclusive article on the expedition for *Summit* magazine. Evelyn had seen his work pop up in various climbing publications and on news websites before. She took a moment to consider his question, to gauge if she felt like opening up to a near stranger. The answer was no, but it would pass the time.

"Yes. If I reserve the right to answer 'no comment' to every question."

Lowell stared at her for a moment, then grinned. "Thanks for having a sense of humor about this. I've gotten some snappy responses today." He glanced over at the closed doors.

"Can you spare some time now? I've got this dodgy record-ing setup in my tent."

"I bet you say that to all the girls," Evelyn said, and Low-ell's face reddened. She hadn't meant to embarrass him. "Yes, now's fine. Just give me a second."

She threw her trash away in one of the bins that would later be packed out and then emerged behind him out into the swirling snow. Base Camp had been reduced to stillness, although the lights were on in the kitchen, mess, and comms tents. Squinting against the snow, she followed Lowell to a bright blue tent on the outskirts, walking beneath the omi-nous outline of Yama Parvat.

CHAPTER NINE

February 2015,
Breckenridge, Colorado

Sophie took a sip of champagne and observed the event hall. Darkness had fallen outside the large glass windows that lined the building, and the snow-covered ground reflected the lights from inside, casting an eerie yellow glow. She sat alone at a table by design, wanting a moment for herself amid the wedding chaos. She had listened to the speeches, eaten dinner, and made the rounds with Miles. Now, as she watched their friends and family members mingle, talking loudly and laughing, Sophie had never wanted to be invisible more. She felt outlandish in her A-line white dress. She had insisted on simple—not a speck of lace or sparkle on the entire thing—but she'd never been designated like this before, as the special person in the room.

Miles and Evelyn, in conversation by one of the windows, caught her eye. For a moment, the sight of them talking warmed her heart. She wanted Evelyn to like Miles—to love him, even, to think of him as family. After all, they were.

But Evelyn hadn't tried to disguise her lack of enthusiasm about the wedding, or even about the relationship itself. She brought up the six-year age gap between Sophie and Miles often. Even when Evelyn hid her emotions with words, her body language usually betrayed her. And now, she stood at an angle from Miles, arms folded across her chest, looking like she had a plethora of opinions to unleash.

With a resigned sigh, Sophie set her glass down and marched across the room, dodging wedding guests who wanted to compliment her dress or her hair or the ceremony or wish her luck. She knew they meant luck *in life*, but what she needed now was luck in ending the conversation between Evelyn and Miles before Evelyn said something regrettable.

Evelyn noticed Sophie approach and waved her over. Sophie slipped beneath Miles's arm, casting her gaze between them. Evelyn looked visibly more relaxed now.

"Look at you two," Sophie said, glancing from Miles to Evelyn. "In-laws."

"Soon we'll be having family dinner every Sunday night," Miles said.

Sophie elbowed him. "Funny. I don't think Evelyn has time to fly out to Wyoming every week. Besides, I don't want to share you just yet."

"I'm not sure I trust the repair job I did on that pipe, anyway. We should probably give it a few test runs before we have any guests."

"With how much you cook, you'll have it fully tested in a week. Besides, didn't your parents say they wanted to come visit soon?"

"In the spring," Miles said. "I don't want them to deal with all the snow."

"So, June?" Sophie asked. She glanced away for a second

and noticed that Evelyn had disappeared. "Oh. I was going to thank Evelyn for her speech again."

"She thinks very highly of you," Miles replied. "I always thought you looked up to her, since she's your older sister. But after talking to her, I think it might be the other way around."

Sophie shrugged. "Maybe it's not looking up. Maybe it's mutual respect. I think we're on the same level, you know? Our lives are very different, but we want the same thing."

"Are you really going to climb K2 and Broad Peak this summer?"

Sophie took a step back. "Why wouldn't we?"

"She just seems busy," Miles said with a shrug. "Like you said. Your lives are very different."

"We have our permits already. We've started getting sponsor equipment and money." Sophie narrowed her eyes at him. "Did she say something?"

Miles lifted his hands, deflecting her suspicion. "No. No, I'm just impressed that she's able to make it work."

Sophie searched the room, eventually locating Evelyn in conversation with their mother and one of their uncles. If Uncle Bill was present, they probably weren't gossiping about her. But Sophie knew, without ever hearing them say it, that Evelyn and her mother were on a united front about her life choices.

"I should make more rounds," Sophie said, kissing Miles and then stepping away. She wandered in her family's direction, stopping for short conversations with guests as she drifted closer. Uncle Bill had wandered on—now Evelyn and her mother were standing closer. Evelyn gestured as she spoke, but Sophie couldn't see her face. She decided not to wait any longer for one of them to notice her.

Stepping between them, she said, "I see Mom is more exciting to talk to than me."

Evelyn flushed. "Oh, I…" She trailed off. "I didn't want to interrupt."

"I'm kidding. It was me who interrupted."

"I can't get over how beautiful your dress is," their mother interjected, running her hand down Sophie's right sleeve.

Sophie tilted her head in her direction, allowing herself to smile. Maybe she was being paranoid. "Thanks, Mom. I'm glad you helped me pick it out."

"I'm still sorry I couldn't come dress shopping," Evelyn said. "I was so busy with—"

"Law school," Sophie said, finishing the sentence for her, thinking back to her conversation with Miles. "It's okay. As long as you make it to K2."

"I wouldn't dream of missing it."

Beside Sophie, their mother shook her head. "Where did you two come from? This adventurous gene. It's a mystery."

"I think you're to blame, for teaching us to ski," Evelyn said.

"Skiing is hardly the same as spending months in a different country, with no communication, climbing a mountain where a thousand different things could go wrong." She shivered. "Oh. I'm going to get an ulcer from worrying."

Sophie leaned against her. "Mom. You raised us to be strong and capable. We'll come back home safe."

"Besides," Evelyn said, winking at Sophie. "At least we don't ski down the mountains, right? Some people do that. Come to think of it, I bet we could fit our skis on the plane. First ski descent of K2?"

"Absolutely not," their mother replied, taking a step back. "I'm going to refresh my drink. Anyone else?"

"Can you bring me a glass of Riesling?" Sophie asked.

Their mother made a face before turning away. Sophie exhaled. She had received a lecture that morning: *don't drink too much or you won't remember your own wedding.*

"I'm just glad the wedding is almost over."

Evelyn's brow furrowed. "Really? Why?"

"It's just the stress of it all," Sophie replied. "I just want to be married already, you know?"

"You are," Evelyn helpfully pointed out.

"Sure, but I want to be home. In Wyoming. Guiding climbs and training for K2 and Broad Peak. Just me and Miles. Without any prying friends and family."

Evelyn nodded. "You're sick of us. I understand."

"Not you," Sophie said. "I don't see you nearly enough. The thought of this summer is what's kept me going these past few months. Through all the wedding planning stress, through dealing with the cabin all winter, through all the worrying about money I've done. I knew that, at some point, I'd get to spend two months on a mountain with you, with no one else around."

Evelyn shifted. "You didn't go into debt for the wedding, right? I know you're tight on money—"

"No," Sophie replied, resisting the urge to roll her eyes. "I told you, Mom covered a lot of it. And Miles's parents. It's just everything else. Being alive is expensive." Evelyn looked like she had more to say, so Sophie pushed on. "Just promise me that we'll always find a way back to the mountains together."

"Of course," Evelyn replied, without hesitation, like Sophie had asked her to pick something up at the grocery store. But Sophie knew why her response came easily—the mountains were an integral part of their relationship, intertwined with most of their significant life experiences. Though college had taken them to different coasts, climbing had brought them back together.

"What do other siblings do?" Sophie asked. "The ones who don't share an extremely dangerous hobby."

Evelyn laughed. "They probably never have anything to talk about. They probably also aren't going to put their mother in an early grave due to excessive stress." Evelyn glanced over Sophie's shoulder and then looked back at her sister, a conspiratorial expression on her face. "Speaking of which, she's headed right for you with a glass of water. So let's go get that wine."

Through the crowded room, Sophie followed her, wondering why she ever doubted Evelyn at all.

CHAPTER TEN

April 2018,
Yama Parvat Base Camp, Nepal

Sophie looked up when she heard the door unzip. She had been rereading the one worn paperback she had shoved in her backpack, *Annapurna*, enraptured by Maurice Herzog's description of reaching the summit—*above us there was nothing!*—and the radical fulfillment he experienced in that moment. Her proximity to Annapurna and the task of climbing an uncharted peak made the account of the mountain's first ascent even more relevant. The book was a small luxury, the only entertainment Sophie afforded herself on the mountain. Levi had lamented not being able to bring his wood-carving tools, his favorite hobby, but every ounce of pack weight mattered. He'd brought a worn deck of cards instead and played solitaire beside Sophie while she read, or played other games with anyone willing during the evening in the mess tent, sociable as ever. He'd even cracked the ice with Ruslan and Ivan, got them to teach him how to play durak. Levi entered the tent and collapsed on the sleeping pad beside hers. "I'm beat. Has anyone stopped by?"

She set down the book. "What do you mean?"

"George or one of the other team leaders. I don't know who's climbing, or when."

"Me either. I'm just camping out in here for now, trying to rest." She paused. "I saw Evelyn. I tried to say hello to her, but she turned her back on me. Can you believe that?"

He raised his eyebrows. "Are you certain she saw you?"

"Oh, she saw me."

"Huh. Well, I spoke to her. I think she wants to talk to you."

"You talked to her?" Sophie straightened up, glaring at him. "Why?"

"Hey, it's okay. I was eating and she sat near me. I recognized her and introduced myself, and we chatted for two minutes, tops. It's nothing to be upset about." He observed her for a moment. "Really, you can't let her mere existence get to you like this or you'll never climb this mountain."

"I don't need you to tell me how to feel." Her own harshness surprised her; she had never spoken to him like this. "Please, just don't do what you always do and go making friends with everyone. I'd prefer if you didn't talk to her anymore."

He tilted his head and reached for her hand. Reluctantly, she let him take it. "I don't know if you're worried about us becoming close because of what happened—with— But don't, okay? I'm just trying to be pleasant."

She let go of his hand. "Are you implying that I think she's going to steal you away? God, Levi. I'm not a child. It's not jealousy. I just—I hate her. I don't want you around her because I can't reconcile the person she used to be with who she's become. I need to keep my distance. And I need you to as well." She looked away, embarrassed that she was unable to explain her feelings more articulately, to draw on all the years when Evelyn was her hero, her best friend, the greatest older sister in the world, and the moment when all that had collapsed, the beginning of the darkest year of her life. She'd thought she wouldn't make it out alive. But she had never said it out loud before—*I hate her*—and wasn't sure if it was true. Her feelings about Evelyn swirled inside a black void that she didn't dare enter beyond the very surface.

He watched her for a moment. "Look, I'm not trying to tell you what to do. I just think—I mean, when are you going to have this opportunity again? You're family, Sophie. I know how much it hurts you to be estranged from her. It's been two years. Why not try to mend the bridge?"

"It's not my problem to fix."

Levi reached to take her hand again and Sophie flinched involuntarily. Levi blew a breath through his lips and looked away, his jaw firmly set. "I'm telling you, she's willing to fix it. Now you're acting like a child."

"Why do you care so much?" Sophie asked.

"Because…" He drew a breath, glancing back toward her. "It's frustrating that you expect me to avoid her. And because I think you're going to regret it if you leave here without speaking to her." He held up a hand when Sophie tried to speak. "What if something happens and you haven't forgiven her? You know the reality of how dangerous this climb is." He paused. "Beyond that, think about the future. In two months you'll go back to separate continents, and then what?"

"You sound like my mother," Sophie scoffed. The thought made tears spring to her eyes and she looked down, hoping Levi wouldn't notice. "I don't need you to pressure me to do this."

Levi touched her shoulder. After a moment, he said, "I'm

not trying to pressure you. I'm just telling you that I don't understand it, letting this resentment rule your life."

Her head shot up. "If I have to explain to you again what happened—"

"Hey, no, that's not what I'm saying. I know—what happened. It's not that I don't understand how painful that must have been. But it happened two years ago. We have a lot more life left to live, if we're lucky. Just maybe, it's time to move on?" He paused and then patted her shoulder once. "Let's take a walk. Go find George and see what the plan is. We can't keep going in circles."

"Okay," she said, because she didn't have the energy to prolong the argument, to explain that two years ago felt as fresh as yesterday.

The sky had turned overcast. Tiny snow flurries, almost imperceptible, zipped through the air, carried by the wind that rattled the sides of the tents and snapped the lines of prayer flags that zigzagged through camp. Their conversation had distracted her from the noise. She was used to constant wind on the mountains, but this was something different. Weather was coming.

Beside Levi, she scanned the area. "I don't see him."

"Let's check the mess tent."

Sophie remembered, steps away from the tent, that Levi had last spoken to Evelyn while she was eating. Not much time had passed. She steeled herself to meet her sister's gaze again, but when her eyes adjusted to the dimmer light, she saw that Evelyn was not inside. Only a few people were—George, Wojciech, and James, the American team leader. He had been instrumental in helping her and Evelyn train for Denali, their first summit above six thousand meters. And then he had accompanied them up Mount Everest, their first eight-thousand-meter peak, the tallest mountain on Earth. She knew James well, yet they hadn't spoken since Sophie went home to Colorado and fell out of touch with the mountaineering world.

She made eye contact with him and smiled, and he grinned and lifted a hand to wave. That reassured her, although she expected nothing but professionalism from someone who had climbed as much as he had. He had probably dealt with worse interpersonal conflicts on teams.

Sophie circled around the table to George's side, Levi trailing behind her. "Any plan yet?" she asked.

George turned to her. "Roughly. We're trying to be fair here. Wojciech and I will climb again. And one from each of our teams. Pemba Choden too. And James is insisting on coming along. Do you want to go?" When she hesitated, he continued. "Look, it doesn't matter to me. Penelope doesn't feel strong enough. I don't want to wrangle Ruslan and Ivan. So, it's one of you two, unless you're both strongly opposed."

"I'll go," Sophie said quickly. Better to stay busy. Plus she suspected Levi might be more tired than he let on; he had never climbed in the Himalayas before and though he was skilled, there was something additionally taxing about these mountains, the extreme scale. She didn't want to be stuck in a tent worrying about him all evening.

"Great. We want to leave in thirty minutes, so gear up. We might get stuck in the snow. We'll carry tents in case we have to spend the night at Camp One. It won't be fun, but we'll see what we can do to convince Yakumo to come down."

Half an hour later she met with George, Wojciech, his teammate Maja, James, and Pemba outside of the mess tent. The wind had kicked up even more, swirling the flakes in the air around them. Pemba spoke to George in a low voice, gesturing with his hands. When he stopped, George nodded and turned his attention to the group.

"Let's start. We have no time to waste."

The group headed through Base Camp to the snowfield that led up the side of the mountain. Sophie calculated the time in her head—three hours up to Camp One, two and a half if they really pushed it. Then the conversation with Yakumo—would he even want to come back down? She imagined the Japanese team tucked into their tents, sleeping through the snowstorm. Then the same amount of time back down, or longer, if the storm continued to worsen and visibility decreased. It would be well after dark by the time they reached Base Camp again. Sophie gritted her teeth, trying to tamp down the fear that rose when she considered the facts of their situation. Mountain climbing was dangerous on a good day; they were choosing to go in objectively unsafe conditions. If something happened—she didn't like thinking that way, but she imagined Levi calling her mother from Base Camp to break the bad news. The image stuck in her mind no matter how hard she tried to push it away.

But Sophie had volunteered; there was no backing out now. She would want someone to do the same, theoretically, if she was stranded during a storm with nonfunctioning radios. It was an unspoken code of mountaineering: look out for each other. Protect each other from the dangers as much as possible. She just didn't like sacrificing her own safety in the process.

It took all Sophie's focus to follow George's path through the snow. Her boots sunk through the top layer, requiring more effort with each step. As they moved farther up the snowfield, into the glacier ice, crevasses began to appear all around, an earth with many mouths. One wrong step could be fatal.

When the terrain became easier to traverse, she caught up to George. "What did Pemba say to you?"

"He thinks we're having bad luck because there hasn't been a puja yet. We're supposed to have one tomorrow morning, but he suspects the Lama won't come because of the weather. So, another day cursed." She could tell he was amused by the idea, although it made perfect sense to Sophie. She was ashamed, too, for forgetting about the puja ceremony entirely, one of her favorite parts of climbing in the Himalayas. In the States or in Switzerland, the trips felt incomplete, lacking a blessing. She missed the feeling of rice raining over her shoulders, tossed by the other climbers in celebration.

"We'll have to hope he's not right," she replied, shouting to make herself heard. The visibility was still decent, but if the snow picked up, they'd be climbing blind. They reached roughly one thousand feet below Camp One, the highest point any member of her team had reached thus far, and continued following the bamboo poles sticking out of the snow that marked the route. Sophie could feel fatigue worming its way into her muscles. Even her lungs were exhausted, desperate for more oxygen. She reminded herself that she was climbing twice as much as usual on an acclimatization day, that it was normal for her body to be so tired. Still, with each step it became harder to lift the heavy crampons. As the path up the glacier grew ever-steeper, she switched from flat footing to a hybrid step, kicking straight into the slope with her right foot and stepping sideways, flat, with her left. She kept her head down and focused on the ice and snow beneath her feet, waiting for the signal that they had reached Camp One.

She didn't know how much time passed before the trio in front of her—George, James, and Pemba—stopped. They fanned out, and she caught up to them, surveying the wide swath of snowfield in front of them. Her heart sank before she even heard George acknowledge the problem.

"They're not here."

"You're sure this is the right place?" James asked.

They all looked at Pemba, who nodded. "Positive. This is the agreed-upon location. Look," he said, pointing at a red flag across the snowfield, barely visible above the snow. "It's been marked on a previous trip up."

"What's the issue?" Wojciech asked. He had been climbing behind Sophie with Maja and had just caught up. He stepped around the group and then turned back, his mouth open in surprise.

"Christ," George muttered, cradling his head in his hands. "We'll have to keep looking."

"We're losing daylight. It's dangerous," James interjected.

"I'm bloody well aware that it's dangerous," George replied. Sophie had never seen him so heated. "But we certainly didn't pass them on the way up. So, they're either farther ahead, or they've all fallen off the mountain. We can still find them if it's one of those options."

"The storm—" Pemba said, but George cut him off.

"I'm aware. We're also losing daylight. One hour, okay? One hour to search, and then we'll descend."

If anyone agreed verbally, she didn't hear. Sophie stepped aside as they spread out, moving methodically across the snow-field. Ahead, large rocky formations loomed, turning white as the snow continued to fall. Somewhere between those rocks, the route to the summit continued. Sophie couldn't imagine why Yakumo would have pushed on past this seemingly perfect campsite, but she hoped that he had. The alternative was too grim to entertain.

An hour passed. It was nearly dark. They had covered the snowfield and a little beyond, snaking up the narrow couloir between the rocks but stopping as the route grew steeper. Now, clustered together, illuminated by headlamps, George admitted defeat.

"Maybe we'll get some answers tomorrow. Thank you for your efforts."

The trip back down was somber, no sound for company besides the wind singing over the rocks. Sophie felt exhaustion in every inch of her overextended muscles, and fear, too—of the conditions, of her slowness, of her inability to react in case of disaster. She hated climbing scared. She resented George for pushing them to search for Yakumo, resented Yakumo for disappearing.

"Stop!" someone shouted behind her. Sophie turned, throwing an arm across her face to shield herself from the falling snow. She made out James, several feet behind her. He stood on the edge of a large crevasse, pointing at something. It ran parallel to the climbing route, but the group had given it a wide berth. Sophie glanced at George, who gestured to James; Sophie walked back in his direction, her body angled into the wind.

When the group gathered around, James pointed again. "Look. Is that a body?"

It was difficult to see. Sophie squinted, following the path of his hand, and saw nothing except distant snow and ice—a faint undulation in the ground, perhaps, but probably nothing more than a rock buried beneath the snow.

"Why on earth would they have gone to that side?" George said.

James turned to him, letting his hand fall. "I don't know. Maybe they wanted to see what was over there," he replied, with a tone of exasperation.

"Sightseeing?"

James shook his head. "I'm going to take a look."

George opened his mouth and then closed it. He waved his hand. "Be my guest. We're already here."

"Thanks for the permission, old friend." James turned his back to them and set off around the edge of the crevasse, growing smaller as he headed into the distance.

Sophie realized how long it would take him to reach the other side and began to pace in small circles, aware that she needed to keep her blood flowing or risk frostbite.

"Can barely see him," George muttered, more to himself than to the group. "This was a stupid idea."

"You don't think they're over there?" Wojciech asked.

"No. And I don't think—holy shit. He's gone."

Sophie blinked. She had been staring at James while George talked and hadn't understood what her own eyes had seen, the sudden disappearance of the orange backpack that her gaze had followed.

No one said anything for a long minute. They watched the distant crevasse edge as if James might reappear at any second. Sophie willed him to, against all probability. But the mountain remained still and silent except for the wind.

George let loose a string of expletives under his breath and set off without looking back. The others struggled to keep pace with him as they looped around the edge of the crevasse. As they drew closer to the spot, George began shouting James's name, and the others joined in, a small chorus of barely audible voices. George halted abruptly.

"Did you hear that?"

They listened again, and for a long moment only heard the reply of the wind. But then a faint shout echoed up from the crevasse, from the depths of the icy earth.

The group set off again, following George's lead, playing

call and reply until they located where James seemed to be caught. George slung off his backpack but Sophie stopped him.

"I'll go," she said, tossing her backpack onto the snow. She knew they needed to set up an elaborate pulley system if they were going to rescue James. But more urgently, they needed to know his exact location, and Sophie weighed less than George. It was safer for her to approach the edge. After taking a few steps, she crouched down, crawling forward and eventually shimmying on her stomach until she was close enough to peer in. She looked down at the strange blue walls of the chasm. Her heart lifted when she noticed James stranded on a small ledge far below, clinging to his ice axe.

"We'll get you out," she shouted down, and he gazed up at her, his face cast in shadow.

"I'll warn you now," he called up. "I'm in bad shape."

Sophie carefully retreated from the edge and went to help the rest of the group with the pulley system. When it was time, she tossed the rope down to James, who caught it in his free hand.

The process of hauling James out was slow and laborious. Sophie had been through many rescue courses in her life, had even taught a few herself. But she had never done the real thing, relied on her strength and a pulley system when someone's life was on the line. The snow picked up, swirling around the group in mysterious gusts as the wind rose and fell. Sophie's chest felt like it was going to burst and her muscles ached with fatigue.

"Alright. Hang in. This should do it." George reset the hauling prusik on the line and gestured for Maja and Sophie to pull again. Pemba and Wojciech moved to the crevasse to help James as he reached the surface. Sophie and Maja leaned back, pulling against the rope with all their strength, and

James's hand appeared at the lip, followed by his head. Maja let out a whoop and Sophie exhaled with relief, almost a laugh, every muscle in her body shaking now.

Pemba and Wojciech pulled James up and helped him to his feet. George, Maja, and Sophie stayed where they were, all hesitant to get closer lest another disaster strike. As James and his human crutches approached, Sophie inhaled a sharp breath. James's face was bloodied, an injury on his forehead that extended down his left cheek. He limped, and his left arm hung at a strange angle.

"Boy. I'm glad to see you." James paused for breath, leaning against the men holding him upright.

"I'm glad to see you too, mate. What the hell happened?" George asked.

James shook his head, as though even thinking caused him pain. "The edge caved in. I was closer than I should have been, trying to get around faster. The ice wasn't stable. And I took a hard fucking fall, man. I think my arm is broken. Don't know about my leg. Head is—"

"Save it for the doctor. I'm just glad you're alive. Let's get back before something worse happens."

Sophie and Maja worked quickly to disassemble and pack up the anchor and pulley system. *The edge caved in.* James's words played on repeat in her head. Just a few minutes ago, she had leaned over that same edge. What if the ice hadn't held? She could have fallen to that same fate, or worse. James had gotten lucky, landing on the ledge. Crevasses could be hundreds of feet deep. Sophie had to shut out reality to climb sometimes, but now the full force of it hit her. With a slightly different sequence of events, she might have ended up stuck hundreds of feet below the earth's surface, sentenced to an icy grave.

But I'm alive, she reminded herself. *And James is alive. That's all that matters.*

Sophie suspected he'd be unable to continue the expedition if his arm really was broken. She didn't think he would exaggerate an injury. She wondered what it meant for the American team—if they would pack up and follow their leader home. She doubted it, but the selfish part of her hoped for such an easy solution—that Evelyn would disappear as quickly as she had arrived.

It took another two hours to descend to Base Camp, their pace slowed by James. The neon tents were visible even through the darkness and falling snow, and the mess tent was lit up like a beacon. Pemba and George helped James to the medical station. Sophie stopped by her tent, hoping to find Levi there, but it was empty. She shed a layer, zipped back into the waterproof hard-shell pants and jacket, and headed to the mess tent like a zombie, desperate for warmth and food.

As soon as she stepped into the tent, she realized that she was the first from the mission to arrive. All conversation stopped immediately as heads turned toward her. She blinked, considering how to break the news. It would be worse to sugarcoat the truth.

"We couldn't find them," she said. "We climbed to Camp One and they weren't there. We searched farther up the standard route and found nothing."

Blank stares. How else to respond to such news? The disappearance of an entire team was about the worst possible way to start an expedition. She opened her mouth again to speak, to tell them about James, but didn't know how to break the news of two misfortunes in a row.

"Will there be another search party tomorrow?" someone asked, and Sophie shrugged. It wasn't her responsibility to decide. A flurry of movement caught her eye—Levi waving to her. Thankful for the excuse to step out of the spotlight, she claimed the empty seat next to him and pulled off her gloves, sliding her frozen hands into his.

"They're really just…gone?"

She nodded. "Maybe they went on to Camp Two. Maybe they got lost. Visibility wasn't awful, but—who knows? We couldn't keep looking. I'm exhausted." She felt tears spring to her eyes and pulled her hands back to wipe them away. "The whole thing was a disaster. James slipped into a crevasse and we had to pull him out. That's why it took so long. He's injured. He should be with the doctor now. I don't think he'll climb again this trip. I'm just glad he's alive."

He regarded her for a moment. "That's awful. I'm so sorry, Sophie. We've been worried about you guys, watching the weather pick up here."

She shrugged. "We survived."

She felt someone nudge her and glanced to her right. "One less team to compete against for the summit, right?" It was Ruslan, grinning and holding a can of beer aloft. He touched the can to Ivan's, seated across the table. Sophie shot him a look of disgust. She hadn't even noticed his presence at first, but here he was, celebrating the possible death of five climbers.

Penelope, seated next to Ivan across from Levi, looked equally revolted. "If you're going to be pigs, don't drag the rest of us through your mud." The comment only solicited a laugh from Ruslan and Ivan, so she rolled her eyes as she turned back to Sophie and Levi. "Will you look again tomorrow? What is the plan?"

"I've done my part," Sophie replied, glancing at the door as Wojciech and Maja entered. "I don't think I can push myself that much, not after the rescue. Maybe someone else will go."

"You shouldn't go again," Levi said. "It's supposed to keep snowing through tomorrow. They've been checking satellite images, and it doesn't look good."

"Well, there you go," Sophie said, pushing her chair away from the table. "It's in Yakumo's hands now." She wanted to get away from the conversation, even for just a minute. She couldn't push away the lingering feeling of guilt, even though they had collectively failed to find the Japanese team. In her head, a scene played on loop: five bodies slowly covered with snow. Some remote part of the mountain, a misstep off the route that led to disaster. She wanted so badly to be wrong.

She filled a bowl with that night's meal of tofu curry. She hadn't lost her appetite yet, a small grace. Although not even eating was simple on the mountain, with the amount of food she needed to consume each day.

Does Yakumo's team have enough food? Are they still alive to eat?

"Are you okay?" Levi asked as she sat down.

Sophie realized the worry must be visible on her face and tried to rearrange her expression. "Never been better," she replied. "Hungry, tired, you know. I'm fine." If they had been alone in their tent, she might have told him the truth, but here, surrounded by people who might overhear, she wanted to paint a brighter picture. She didn't care if he sensed the lie. She ate greedily, focusing on the food to shut out the sounds of conversations. She had plenty of practice in going inward, ignoring the outside world to get through a difficult situation. She hadn't imagined that this trip would share similarities to the year after Miles and Evelyn's affair, but here she was, in survival mode already. She had often guessed that some fundamental part of her had broken two years ago, when two of the people she loved the most had betrayed her. Never mind that she and Miles fought daily, that the cabin in Wyoming was basically a shack, that she spent all her time working. That had been her life, and she would have fought viciously to protect it if given the chance. But instead, it was stolen from under her nose, no choice given. Maybe that was the problem—she didn't like feeling powerless.

Her spoon scraped the bottom of the empty bowl. "I'm going to bed," she announced, for the benefit of anyone who was listening.

"I'll come with you," Levi said, and as they stood up, he grabbed her bowl, stacking it on top of his, and when he caught up to her at the front of the mess tent, they stepped out together into what was now a blizzard. He stayed close, and quiet, and she loved him for that.

CHAPTER ELEVEN

June 2017,
Geneva, Switzerland

When Sophie had first arrived in Switzerland, she had been a shell of herself. Or rather, the essence of herself had been compacted into something hard and small, buried deep within the center, while her body slowly withered away until she felt paper-thin—pale, her muscles weak, dark bags beneath her eyes. She couldn't stand to feel the sun on her skin.

When Zoe spotted her at the airport, she drew a sharp breath and said, "My god."

Sophie blinked at her. "What?"

"Nothing," Zoe said quickly. "You just look different. Tired. Here, let me help you with your bag."

Sophie didn't protest. She handed her suitcase to Zoe, but Zoe didn't take it; instead, she pulled Sophie into a hug.

"I missed you," she mumbled into Sophie's hair.

"I missed you too," Sophie replied, because it was the polite thing to do. Truthfully, she hadn't missed anyone for the last year except herself, her former personality and her former life, which now seemed fuzzy and intangible. She couldn't remember how she used to get up each morning and worry about things like a grocery list and what gear was needed for the day's climb. Even mountaineering no longer felt like a passion. Instead, she remembered her summit days as if she had been told the stories by an old friend—vividly, but with a sense of removal. *She* had not strapped crampons to her boots and sipped lukewarm broth at 3:00 a.m. in a tiny tent two years ago, on the slopes of K2, her sister's body pressed up against hers for warmth as a storm raged outside. They had feared for their lives that night, sharing furtive glances, afraid to speak the truth: *we could die on this mountain.* Of course they both knew that. There was no way to escape death on a mountain; years ago, they had walked past the frozen, eerily preserved bodies on Everest, which reminded them that with each second, they flirted with death. The unspoken thing between them: they both loved it, exerting control in such unfathomably dangerous situations, reaching the top of a mountain when all odds were stacked against them.

But those days belonged to a different life. Sophie could hardly get out of bed most days now, let alone spend weeks on a mountainside, acclimating and pushing and retreating and huddling in a tent, trying to convince herself that it would all be worth it. She pushed the memories aside. She had made it to Switzerland, and that was enough for now.

She let go of Zoe and stepped back, glancing at the other passengers streaming past on both sides. "I'm here now. Let's go."

Zoe lived in a stately old apartment building overlooking Lake Geneva, part of the Rhône, which was fed by glaciers. Sophie thought it was the most beautiful city she had ever seen, but maybe it was just because for the last year, her surroundings had consisted of her childhood bedroom. Zoe indulged her and took her for a tour of the neighborhood that evening, pointing out historic buildings and the best cafés. Sophie stayed quiet, taking it all in, until she stopped walking so abruptly that Zoe bumped into her. Sophie turned to her friend, her eyes wide, an unsettling expression on a person already so thin and weary.

"Do you think this was a mistake? Was I crazy to come here?"

Zoe blinked, and then her demeanor softened. "Oh, Sophie, no. You did the right thing. I'm so happy to have you here. I can't imagine...what you've been going through. There's no way I would have been able to stay."

Sophie felt Zoe's hand rest on her shoulder. The sun had begun to set, and the sky above was a gentle blue, the wisps of clouds slowly turning pink. She was in Switzerland, for an indefinite amount of time, had only bought a one-way ticket to allow her future self to decide when to return. She'd never spent a long period of time in another country where she wasn't on an expedition—sure, she had spent almost three months in Nepal, but save for the start and end of the trip, she lived on Everest, waking each morning to snow and rock and her sister's face. She hadn't traveled for pleasure, to see the world except for from the summit of a mountain. She stepped away from Zoe, letting Zoe's hand slip off her shoulder, looking down at the calm water that reflected the changing sky.

"You're right," she replied. "I was always meant to end up here." She felt silly, saying it out loud, but lately she'd been trying to convince herself that it was true—that her life, careening wildly off its formerly straightforward train tracks, was a matter of divine providence, some greater force guiding her into a deeply troubled time to teach her a lesson. She just hadn't figured out what the lesson was yet. And though it had been easy, as a kid, to believe that everything happened for a reason, she was finding it harder to believe now that other people were involved.

Zoe's apartment was inspired by her college years in Sweden, white walls and streamlined decor. "Only the essentials," Zoe said, hanging her tote bag on a single peg, perfectly placed on the wall near the door. Sophie's blue suitcase stuck out like a sore thumb, even pressed up against the wall. There was only one bedroom, but Zoe had offered her the couch, for as long as she needed it. It went unspoken that Sophie would never be able to afford an apartment on her own—her bank account had all but run dry, and she didn't have a visa, which would make finding work more difficult. She was overwhelmed by Zoe's generosity. The plan was to look for work as a climbing guide, but those jobs were scarce, and as the weeks passed, Sophie found that she still didn't miss climbing; not even the Alps drew her attention.

Somewhere in those days Sophie checked her email for the first time since arriving in Switzerland. She scrolled through the various coupons and newsletters, looking for what, she wasn't sure. At the bottom of her inbox sat a chain of emails from one of her sponsors, Black Diamond—sent by one of their marketing specialists, asking if she had any plans to climb this year. Sophie had responded a few months ago to say that she was taking some time off. Now another summer would pass without any summits.

She scrolled back to the top of her inbox. An email with no subject caught her attention. She opened it and read: Sophie, Switzerland? What the hell? Call me.

From Miles. He'd sent it from his professional email, GreeneArt, and the signature at the bottom of the message contrasted sharply with the tone of his words. Sophie closed the email app and set her phone aside, hot anger rising in her chest. She knew why he was upset—her fleeing to Switzerland meant another lengthy delay on their divorce—but who had told him? She could only suspect that he had heard from Evelyn.

Too bad. Calling him was the last thing in the world Sophie was going to do.

In the evenings, she took long walks through Geneva, exploring the busy streets and the shaded parks. She had yet to have a single interaction with a person that wasn't in a store, with Zoe, or one of Zoe's friends. But she liked that—the solitude, the lack of care or responsibility. She was free to drift and pay Zoe a meager sum of rent each month, and already she had begun to feel more like herself again. She knew it was a privilege—to escape from her life, to run away to a European country and pretend that her problems didn't exist—but it also felt like a gift, the other side of misfortune.

Her cell phone rang when she reached Parc La Grange. She paused beneath one of the large cedar trees, using the shade to look at the screen. Her mother. They hadn't spoken in weeks, giving each other space since Sophie's unceremonious exit from the States. She drew a breath, steeling herself, and answered.

"Mom?"

"Sophie! It's good to hear your voice."

A bell rang and Sophie stepped off the path as a bike whizzed by. She wandered down into an open field, feeling the soft give of the grass beneath her shoes. She could see a narrow strip of Lake Geneva in the distance.

"Yours too," she replied, the truth. She missed her more than she cared to admit. Her mother had spent the last year doting on Sophie, bringing her food and tidying up her room while Sophie cried in bed. At the time, it had felt almost demeaning, how readily she accepted Sophie's inability to care for herself. Now, she wondered if she would ever experience love as plainly and efficiently again.

"I was worried about you when you left so…abruptly. But I thought I should give you space. Then I thought, what if she thinks I'm upset at her?" She laughed, her voice clear and bright through the phone. "Anyway, Sophie, I just called to tell you how much I miss you. And that I can send you a check in the mail."

"I miss you too," Sophie said, surprised by how much the words caught in her throat. She didn't want to cry here, in broad daylight, surrounded by children playing in the grass and couples picnicking. She walked to the edge of the field, plopped down in the cool shade beneath a tree. "You don't need to give me any money. I'm managing. Switzerland has been great. It's amazing to see Zoe again, like no time passed at all. I mean, she's so generous. I feel bad for cluttering up her living room. But if it bothers her, she's great at hiding it."

"I'm sure she doesn't mind. You two were so funny as kids. It's hard to picture you both grown up, in another country." She seemed to permanently view Sophie as a twelve-year-old, strong-willed and preternaturally excited about life. Even if that wasn't true for Sophie anymore, she had good reason to remember Zoe that way. They had met at ski camp, Zoe visiting American relatives in Colorado for the summer. They had kept in touch as pen pals over the years, until cell phones made the task easier, and considerably less special. "Have you visited the Alps yet?"

"No, not yet. Zoe doesn't climb. And I haven't made any friends here yet." She paused. "I've been meaning to look into a guiding service. Book a couple of trips. It would be fun to see more of the scenery." A white lie. She had been thinking of renting a car or getting a train ticket to see more of the country but climbing wasn't on her list. Still, she wasn't ready for the questions if she admitted that.

"You'll have to send me some pictures."

"Sure."

A silence passed between them. Sophie tilted her head back and watched the tree branches sway in the breeze, creating little patterns of sunlight and shadow across her face. The air felt light and warm, rich with the sweetness of midsummer.

Her mother cleared her throat, anchoring her back to reality. Sophie tensed, expectant. "I...well, I spoke to Evelyn the other day."

Sophie resisted the urge to throw her phone as far as she could. Of course she had called with an agenda. Never just to "say hi." She closed her eyes and took a deep breath. No point in snapping, although she had never wanted to more.

"I don't want to hear about Evelyn."

She exhaled, and Sophie could hear the weight of the sadness in that breath. "Right. I know. I just thought you might want to know how she's doing."

"She's fucking my husband. I'm sure she's doing wonderful." As soon as she said it, she regretted it. She never cursed in front of, or to, her mother. That was always Evelyn, the older child, bolder. Sophie usually demurred and kept her strong emotions to herself. But the sheer audacity to call, to reach her thousands of miles away on a beautiful afternoon and remind her that Evelyn existed, was too much.

"She's—Sophie, really." She sighed. "She's actually *not*

doing well. She called me crying the other day and said how much she wants to talk to you."

"Maybe she could have thought about the consequences before she ruined my life."

Silence. Then, "Okay, sweetheart, I can tell that now isn't the right time. I'm sorry. I shouldn't have brought it up." A pause, as if she was waiting for Sophie to tell her that it was okay, that it didn't really matter. "Honey, I'm glad you're having a good time in Geneva. We'll talk soon, okay? And not about…Evelyn. Or what happened. I just want you to be happy. Okay? I love you. Send me pictures."

"I love you too," Sophie replied, and hung up. She really did want her daughters to make up and be friends again. Sophie couldn't fathom that she thought it would be that simple, that she could call Evelyn up and say *No, really, it's fine, all forgiven and forgotten. Let's be best friends again and climb mountains and when we grow old, we'll buy two houses, side by side with a view of the ocean.* At that moment, she would be happy to never see Evelyn again in her life.

Sophie found the job at the coffee shop about a month after she arrived in Geneva. She'd explored many of the local shops but kept coming back to Mistral, which was situated on a corner three blocks from Zoe's apartment. The interior was painted forest green and decorated with simple wooden furniture, and she spent hours drinking kaffe-crème and browsing job listings on Zoe's laptop. She suspected Zoe only let her borrow it for the exact purpose of job hunting—Sophie had her cell phone, but it was difficult to format a résumé on the tiny screen. She felt guilty whenever she realized she'd been browsing mountaineering forums for nearly two hours, trying to stay abreast of the news, instead of scrolling through the job boards. But she'd applied to what felt like a million jobs without so much as a single email telling her they were thinking it over. To most employers, she was completely undesirable—an American who only spoke English and had not lived in the country nearly long enough for a permit. She hid that fact, when she could, but many of the jobs asked the same question: *Do you now or in the future require sponsorship to continue working in Switzerland?*

So it was with relief that she spotted, one day, the Help Wanted sign on Mistral's door. The manager, Mila, played it cool throughout the interview, her face expressionless as Sophie answered her questions, but broke into a smile as she set aside Sophie's application.

"I'd like to offer you the job. I'm glad you applied. I need someone else above the age of eighteen around here."

Sophie fell into an easy routine, thankful to have a real excuse to leave Zoe's apartment—no more aimless wandering around Geneva, at least in the mornings. But besides her friendly-but-professional relationship with Mila, she didn't make much headway with the rest of her coworkers or the legions of customers. The Swiss were, as Zoe had told her many times, reserved. Occasionally a tourist wandered in and was happy to chat with Sophie for a few minutes after she delivered their coffee, but often, her only interaction with customers was a few words and a curt nod.

So, that was why she was startled when one day, as she handed a cup of kaffe-crème across the counter, the man on the other side said, "I like your tattoo. Is that—by chance— is that K2?"

Sophie looked up in surprise. No one outside of the climbing community had ever recognized the mountain tattooed on her body. To the uninitiated, it looked like any mountain, but K2's pyramidal shape was something of a symbol among mountaineers. She often forgot it was there, the black-and-white picture nestled on her right forearm. She tried not to think of the identical tattoo on Evelyn's left arm. She appraised the man for a moment. She had seen him in the shop a few times before—brown hair and blue eyes, lean, like a runner—but couldn't remember anything specific about him, if he always visited at the same time or always ordered the same drink.

"It is," she said. She wanted to say, *I climbed it two years ago with my sister and it was the most beautiful and terrifying experience of my life*, but she held her tongue, wary of monopolizing his time.

But he lingered. "I've done a lot of climbing," he said. "But never anything like K2. Wow."

She couldn't help smiling. "You're assuming that I've climbed it?"

He flushed, embarrassed. "No, well, I—I guess I did. Have you?"

Sophie nodded, shrugged, also feeling embarrassed to admit to the greatest physical feat of her life while standing in a coffee shop, wearing an ugly apron and acutely aware of the growing line of customers. "Yes. Two years ago."

"Modest," he replied, and laughed, and Sophie thought that she could listen to that laugh many more times and not get sick of it.

Someone said her name, and she glanced over her shoulder, at one of the cashiers motioning frantically to the growing list of receipts tacked to the ticket holder. She looked back at him apologetically. "I should go."

"Yeah, of course." He regarded her a moment longer, unabashedly studying her face. "Listen, I—I'd like to talk to you more, about climbing K2. I haven't met many people who have done that. I'll be…" He gestured vaguely around at the open tables. "I'm going to drink this here."

She understood his clumsy proposal. "I'm off in half an hour. I'll find you."

He smiled and turned away. Sophie went back to work at a furious pace, trying to stay on top of the unusual rush of early-afternoon customers. She realized that she didn't even know his name and chided herself for falling back into the same habits—getting momentarily seduced by a handsome stranger and agreeing to something she didn't necessarily want to do. She spied him through the crowd—sitting at a back table, typing at a laptop. At least he wasn't just staring at her. He seemed nice. And she desperately needed a Swiss friend who wasn't already one of Zoe's. Throughout the rest of her shift, she convinced herself that this was the smart thing to do—put herself out there, make friends. By the time she took off her apron and approached his table, she was feeling something close to confident.

"Hi again," she said, sliding into the seat across from him. "I realized I don't even know your name."

"Nor I yours," he replied, looking up from his laptop. "Damn, and you're not wearing the name tag anymore. I was going to cheat."

"So you looked at the name tag, but not at the name?"

He tilted his head, admonished. "No. Lack of foresight. Can I take a guess?" He paused, waiting for her to nod. "Is it something stereotypically American? Jessica? Sarah?"

She shook her head, laughing.

"Okay. I give up."

"Sophie," she said, "and I won't even make you suffer the indignity of asking if you're called Michael or Justin. What's your name?"

"Justin," he said flatly, but his eyes betrayed the joke. "It's Levi. Rouanet."

"Wright. My last name." Funny, that the first time she'd lied to him had been so early on. But she still felt like a Wright, at heart, tied more closely to her family than to Miles. She contemplated, briefly, if it would be worth changing her last name to something entirely different, whenever she went back to the States, to forge her own path as the sole member of a new family. She set the idea aside, to ponder later whether it would be too cruel to her mother.

"Ah. So, you're always right? I'm sure you've heard that one before."

"About a billion times."

He shrugged. "I didn't want to talk about your name, anyway. But I recognize it. And now I really do believe that you've climbed K2. Among others."

She flushed. "I suppose I make the news sometimes."

He raised an eyebrow and began typing on his laptop. She shifted in her seat, uncomfortable with the idea of him searching for her name, seeing the pictures of her on mountaintops. It felt oddly intimate, even if he was also a climber. She was a different person in those photos, though it was hard to tell beneath all the layers of clothing—thinner, strung out on pure adrenaline, living on a kind of desperate, instinctual energy that she felt nowhere else. She had once heard an old mountaineer call it "being close to the marrow of life," which of course implied the breaking of bones to get there.

"'Evelyn Wright,'" Levi said, "'and her sister, Sophie Greene, formerly Wright, summited K2 at 10:36 a.m. on July 2.'" He glanced up at her, plain curiosity on his face. "*Formerly Wright?*"

"I was married. Am. Technically."

He pushed the laptop aside, all his focus on her again. She felt his gaze travel over her bare fingers, connecting the dots. "You're married? Go on."

"I'd rather not." She suddenly wished she had brought a coffee or a bottle of water over to the table, something to distract herself with. "It's complicated. Messy. The reason I'm alone in Switzerland."

"I get it," he said. "Not a stranger story." And Sophie was thankful that he didn't pry, that he understood the necessity of a private past. "But I have to ask," he continued, and she tensed again, "did you come here to climb, or work in a coffee shop?"

She let out a breath. "Neither. I came to stay with a very generous friend. I—well—I haven't climbed in a long time. The last year or so of my life has been a nightmare. Only recently has it started to feel like I've begun to wake up."

Levi regarded her for a moment, serious, before he closed his laptop and leaned back in his chair. She thought he was going to leave, that she'd gone too far, hinted too strongly at how disturbed her mental health had been. Maybe he was no longer interested in spending any time with a married, depressed, *former* mountaineer. But he simply stretched, and scooted forward again, his attention on her.

"I don't want to overstep," he said, "but it seems like a great tragedy that someone like you, and I quote, 'hasn't climbed in a long time.'"

"It's not..." She trailed off, trying to find the words. "It's not for lack of want. It's just that everything has felt insurmountable for a while. It's hard to find the energy to climb a mountain when getting out of bed feels just as daunting." There. She'd said to him what she had admitted to no one else: that her passion was gone, her drive. And with it had gone the rest of her energy—at times, even her will to live. She looked down at the table in embarrassment. "I'm better now, for the most part. I've seen how beautiful the Alps are and pictured myself climbing. I've been meaning to look into a tour group."

He waved a hand, unfazed by her confession. "No need. When are your days off?"

"Tuesdays, Sundays, and afternoons."

He considered for a moment. "I'm doing some climbing with a couple of friends this weekend. We were going to go on Saturday, but I can see if they can do Sunday instead— if you'd like to come. We're climbing the Riffelhorn. Have you heard of it?" When she shook her head, he continued. "It's not big, but it's fun. My friends, they're more into rock climbing, most of them, and I figure it's good practice regardless. Are you in?"

She could think of no reason to say no, besides that he was a stranger. But she liked him already—conversation came easy, and he was undaunted by both her honesty and her secrets. She nodded. "Yes, if you can do Sunday. But don't change your plans just for me."

He regarded her for a moment, and she thought she saw the hint of a smile on his face. "Of course, I would never." He glanced down at his watch and seemed to start. "Sorry, I have to get back to the office. Can I have your number? Or email, if you're old-fashioned."

He said it so casually that it was almost reassuring—he was offering nothing more than friendship. She told him her phone number, watched as he typed it in. He handed his phone over for her to check, and she thought how easily they could become strangers once more, lost to each other forever. She could disappear back to America without ever speaking to him again. But part of her knew, already, that their lives would continue to intertwine.

★ ★ ★

Sophie met Levi and two of his friends in the early-morning hours on Sunday. They introduced themselves but seemed generally uninterested in her presence, which made her wonder if she wasn't the first woman Levi had invited along on a climb. The thought didn't bother her. The opportunity to climb shone before her, a bright light blocking out all other distractions.

The streetlights cast a warm glow on the streets of Geneva as Sophie slid into the back seat of the car beside Levi. She tried to stay awake but at some point, she shut her eyes and when she opened them again the sun had risen. The view of the Alps astounded her. The little car inched steadily higher, bringing them closer to the mountains and to the heavens.

"We're almost to Zermatt," Levi said, noticing that she was awake. "We'll take the Gornergrat to the Rotenboden station, and then it's just a walk to the Riffelhorn."

She nodded, the words meaningless in her half-awake daze. He had told her, via text, the route they would take to the Riffelhorn, but now that it was happening, she was struck with the wonder of the scenery and how easy it was to *do* things again, to say yes and be swept off on a new adventure. How had she ever let herself stop living? She didn't have time to answer before they reached the station.

They departed the train at Rotenboden, Sophie still in awe of the scenery. The fresh air hit her in a cold wave as she stepped off the train, but the sun shone above, promising another mild summer day. She shouldered her backpack and sidestepped a group of hikers, who were stretching in the wide dirt area off to the side. Levi caught up to her and pointed to a peak in the distance.

"The Matterhorn. Isn't it beautiful?"

She nodded. "I recognize it. Have you climbed it?"

He ducked his head, smiling. "Not yet. I've been waiting for the right person to take along."

"I told you, it's been a long time," she said, but he was already turning away.

"That changes today," he said over his shoulder, pointing to a mass of rock in the near distance. "That's the Riffelhorn. A bit less exciting, but still a blast."

He called to his friends and they set off, a short fifteen-minute walk to reach the Riffelhorn and then a somewhat exposed traverse around to the southern face.

"They're doing the Kante route," Levi said, nodding at his friends as they donned appropriate shoes. "We'll keep our boots on and go for Eck. It's a little less technical."

Sophie nodded, her gaze drifting to the Matterhorn as Levi readied their equipment. She tried to imagine herself standing on the summit and failed. The sharp pyramid of rock and snow looked like a more dramatic version of K2. She glanced back at Levi as he handed rope to her and reminded herself to focus. Just as her muscles had weakened and turned soft over the last year, so had her mind, her ability to concentrate. She had to enter a certain headspace to climb, almost like meditation, leaving all other thoughts behind. She wasn't the type who could write her grocery list while attempting a route. But her thoughts ran freely these days, scrambling over each other like a pack of dogs.

"Ready?" Levi asked, after she had clipped onto the ropes.

She squinted up at him, backlit by the bright sun. He wore a smile, his cheeks red from the wind and the cold. He looked ready for anything, and so she nodded, putting her trust in the hands of a stranger.

★ ★ ★

They reached the top a little over an hour later, steps behind Levi's friends, who cheered and made a show of clapping everyone's backs. Sophie stepped away from the ledge, smiling, proud of herself for once. It wasn't the most technical route, but her muscles ached with a welcome fatigue. The blustering wind did its best to whip her hair free from her ponytail. She shielded her eyes from the sun and turned to Levi.

"Nice work," he said. She had followed behind him up the rock face and had been impressed with his relaxed way of moving, the casual fluidity with which he moved between footholds. She wanted to climb with him again but couldn't bring herself to say it, in case he didn't feel the same. Perhaps she had been too slow, too hesitant. She no longer had the same faith in her abilities.

Back in Geneva, the car pulled to the curb in front of Zoe's apartment building. Levi got out to take her backpack from the trunk and handed it to her as he stepped up beside her on the sidewalk.

"Thank you," she said, "a real gentleman."

He grinned. "I try."

"Really, though," she said, glancing back at the car, trying to gauge how long his friends were willing to wait. "Thanks for bringing me along today. I needed this." She didn't elaborate on what she meant, confident that Levi would understand.

He nodded, his expression growing more serious. "I'm glad you came along. And," he said, "if it's not too much to ask, I'd like to take you out sometime. On a more traditional date."

"Was this a date?"

"I don't know if we can call it one with those two along,"

he conceded, nodding at the car. "But maybe if dinner goes well, I'll consider a climbing date."

"High stakes."

"I'll call you," he said.

She stood on the curb, watching as he retreated to the car, lifting a hand in a wave as the car pulled away onto the road. Normally, at the beginning of a relationship, Sophie wanted to tell the world about that person, call all her friends to discuss her latest love interest in detail. But there was something different about Levi—or maybe it was Sophie who had changed. She didn't want another soul to know about him, wanted him all to herself, for as long as her time in Switzerland would last. She hadn't meant to fall for anyone. But her life hadn't gone to plan for the last year, so what was one more complication?

CHAPTER TWELVE

April 2018,
Yama Parvat Base Camp, Nepal

Lowell stooped to unzip the door of his tent and waved Evelyn in. She brought in a burst of snow as she entered; he quickly zipped the door behind them to keep in the warmth. Seeing the crossword puzzle books spread out across the floor, the pile of dirty clothes, Evelyn felt as if she had stepped into his *bed*, not just his bedroom.

"Sorry about the mess," he said, following her gaze. "I tried to get the comms tent to let me set up a corner for interviews, but they said there was no space. It's not easy luring people back to my tent, you know?"

"I can imagine," Evelyn replied, although now that she had settled on the floor, she was thankful to be out of the snow and in someone's company. The interview would distract her from worrying about Sophie and the others searching for the Japanese team. She was surprised that James had gone, but then again, he lived by a strict code of ethics on the mountain. "Help others as you would want to be helped." That ingrained attitude of selflessness must be why Sophie had offered to help search.

Lowell fumbled around for a moment, producing a notebook, a pen, and a small recording device from his backpack. He made eye contact with Evelyn, checking to see if she was ready, and she nodded. He clicked on the device and sat back.

"Alright. So, just to remind you, this interview is for an article in *Summit* magazine. Can you state your name and which team you're climbing with?"

"Evelyn Wright. I'm climbing on the American team."

"Thanks. So. I'll start with the question I've been asking everyone. How does it feel to be on Yama Parvat?"

"Oh…" Evelyn let her gaze travel to the ceiling of the tent, watched it billow and fold in the wind. "Unexplainable, but that's a cop-out." Lowell smiled and waited for her to go on. "It feels like my entire mountaineering career has led to this moment. My whole life, even. Since I was young, I dreamed about the world's tallest and most challenging mountains. My sister and I—" Evelyn caught herself, surprised at how quickly Sophie had come up. She took a breath and tried again. "We always used to talk about how we'd summit all the eight-thousand-meter mountains first and then all the most dangerous smaller mountains. I realize now how naive we were, but it was nice to dream. I remember us talking about Yama Parvat years ago, before we knew it would be possible." She paused again, trying to recalibrate before memories of Sophie took over the interview. "Anyway. It feels like the culmination of a dream and a lot of hard work."

Lowell waited a moment, to make sure she was finished. "I've talked to a lot of people about the sacrifices they've made to come here. You're a lawyer, right? How do you navigate making time to climb with such a demanding job?"

Evelyn smiled and looked down at her hands. "I quit."

"Wow."

"Yeah. That's my tip. Don't let anything stand in the way of your passion, even being a rational adult who plans for the future." She grimaced, thinking of the conversation with Miles.

"You're not alone. I've met plenty of other people who have left their jobs for their dreams. But a lawyer—there's a lot of time and effort invested to get there."

Evelyn shrugged. "I know. And I hope it's something that I can return to. I just couldn't pass up the opportunity to climb Yama Parvat. Just to see it, even." She paused. "When James Haverford invites you to join his team, you don't say no."

Lowell nodded. "I talked to James earlier today. He's a cool guy. So humble. You've done expeditions together before, right?"

"Yes. On Denali and Everest. You're right, he's humble, for all that he's accomplished. I'm thankful that he's taken time to mentor me. I wouldn't be sitting here right now without him. Obviously, because of the invitation, but also because of the training he gave me early on."

Lowell wrote something down and clicked his pen. "The person you've shared the most summits with is your sister, Sophie Greene. She's here at Yama Parvat, too, but you're on separate teams. How does that feel?" He saw the look on her face and raised his eyebrows.

"I—I don't know—" Evelyn fumbled for her words. "Can we stop for a minute?"

Lowell reached over and switched off the recorder. "Off the record?"

She blinked at him, confused.

"I meant, if you want to talk to me about it, you can. It's not some big secret. People are used to seeing you together. I imagine it's strange for you, that's all."

"I climbed Lhotse without her last year," Evelyn said. She longed to get out of the cramped tent and back into the fresh air, no matter how cold. "We can move on. Back to the interview."

"We're done, actually," Lowell said. "Those were my only questions for now." He watched her for a moment, saw her glancing at the door. "Evelyn, you can go if you want to, but I just wanted to say again that I'm here if you want to talk. I think I might understand some of what you're feeling."

"You do?" The pull to retreat to her own tent was still there, but he had sparked her curiosity.

"You might know this. I had a good climbing partner, my best friend, Pablo Pedrero. We met in high school. He spent his childhood in Mexico and was just crazy about the mountains in Canada. I grew up in Calgary and was like, casually outdoorsy, but he was rabid about it. So, we tried some routes, and damn, he was good. I could hardly keep up. But he was never competitive. We just helped each other." He paused, took a breath. "One summer in college we took off to the Yukon. We lived in a shack at a dog sledding operation and worked until we had enough money to attempt Mount Logan. I mean, we were just dumb kids. Cheap gear, not enough food, way too high of expectations. But we did it. We climbed Canada's highest mountain."

When he paused, she interjected. "You don't have to tell me what happened. I know." Hearing the name had refreshed her memory, the article she had read about Pablo, who had fallen to his death on Kangchenjunga three years ago. His body had never been recovered.

He nodded and looked relieved. "I thought I would never come back from that. It seems impossible, you know? To go from sharing every step, every damn cold night in your tent, every victory with someone to just having them disappear. I know your sister isn't dead," he added quickly. "But still. It must feel isolating."

"It's my own fault. Besides, we're both here. That's about as good of a resolution as we could have hoped for." She didn't know if she believed her own words. There was nothing good about being stuck at Base Camp, worrying about Sophie as she searched for the missing team, but unable to greet her when she returned. Not unable—but. She had dug her own grave the first time she had kissed Miles, and kept going, tunneling straight through the earth to emerge in some backward version of the world.

Lowell cleared his throat, reminding her of his presence. "It's not my place to say. I admit I don't know the details. But don't worry, I'm not going to tell you to just make up and be friends again."

Evelyn studied him for a minute, allowing silence to pass between them. She couldn't tell if she liked him. He seemed honest and forthcoming, which was a breath of fresh air after Miles's usual caginess. But Lowell had gotten something right—the trip felt isolating. So had last year on Lhotse, even with other friends there. Every night she crawled into a tent alone and curled up in a fetal position inside her sleeping bag to keep warm. Everyone did. But she wasn't used to being everyone, because before there had been Sophie, and they lay side by side, shoulders touching, and talked until one of them fell asleep. Almost always Sophie fell asleep first, and Evelyn lay awake for another hour, letting the darkness wash over her as she thought about tomorrow, what time they would wake up and what they would eat and how far they would go. Evelyn wasn't the spiritual one, that was all Sophie's territory, but sometimes she believed that they were created to be two halves of a perfect whole, a team that worked in seamless unity. Maybe Sophie had it easy, maybe the universe dropped good things into her lap, but at least on a mountain Evelyn could tamp down her jealousy and appreciate what a perfect partnership they made. Some small part of that universe had shattered when Miles had stepped into Evelyn's life. It was easier to blame him, but she knew the part that she had played.

"Storm's picking up," Lowell said, breaking the silence. Evelyn listened for a moment to the wind buffeting the tent. "I keep waiting for us to get called on part two of the rescue mission. The worrying is driving me insane."

"Me too. I'd hate to be out in this weather. I keep thinking they'll be back any minute, and then they're just…still gone." Evelyn shifted, her back protesting from how long she'd been sitting cross-legged. "I haven't even checked the time."

"A little after six," he offered. "At least, last time I checked, which was when we started our interview. It must be closer to seven now." He let out a long breath. "Anyway. You like crossword puzzles? I have some sudoku, but I'm terrible at it."

Evelyn tilted her head, wondering if she'd misheard him. "Is this an interview question?"

Lowell smiled and shook his head. "No, this is still off the record. I figured you might not want to walk back to your tent in this weather. Of course, if you do, I won't keep you. Mind if I…" He trailed off, gesturing past her, and she glanced over her shoulder to see a stack of puzzle books in the corner of the tent. He hadn't been kidding.

Just a few minutes ago, Evelyn had been eager to leave, but now that they'd moved past talking about Sophie, she admitted to herself that she enjoyed Lowell's company. She didn't fear the slog across Base Camp to reach her tent, but as she pictured herself sitting alone for the rest of the evening, she knew worry would consume her. Here, at least, she had the presence of another person. She decided she would stay until the search team returned to Base Camp.

"I'm bad at it too. Sudoku. I wish I was better with numbers."

"Well," he said, handing her a crossword book, "if you're not good with numbers, then you must be good with words, eh?"

Not necessarily, she thought, but accepted the book and a pen without complaint.

"I'm not the most exciting company," he said, looking sheepish. "This is my routine every night. I do crossword puzzles until I go cross-eyed, and then I sleep."

"That's about as much excitement as I need," Evelyn said, and she meant it. They settled into silence, accompanied only by the sound of the wind and the occasional scratch of a pen, or turning of a page. Neither of them asked each other for help with clues, but when Evelyn announced that her fingers were freezing, Lowell produced a few hand warmers and tossed them her way. She activated two and shoved one into each glove, appreciative of the instant heat that made its way over her palms and down to her fingertips. She was overwhelmed by the simplicity of the moment—the snow, the silence, the kind company of a relative stranger.

"Hear that?"

She blinked and realized that she had been staring at her gloved hands. She lifted her head and listened, heard voices, faint but growing closer.

Lowell opened the door and poked his head out. He withdrew a moment later. "It's them. I can't tell how many people. It's dark, but I saw the headlamps."

"Good. Should we go out?"

He shook his head. "I think the situation is handled. We'll be called if there's anything we can do."

Evelyn nodded. "They made it back down. That's what matters."

They fell back into silence. It was easy for Evelyn to stay inside and let other people handle the team's arrival. Rushing to help was more Sophie's domain; Evelyn was content to keep her head down and focus on herself. Selfish, maybe, but one had to be when overexertion could prove fatal. Teamwork mattered to an extent, but at the end of the day, you had to be capable of saving yourself.

Evelyn wasn't sure how much time passed before she looked over and saw that Lowell had fallen asleep. He lay on his stomach, arms folded, a crossword book in front of his face and a pen by his side. Glasses still on. She wondered if she should wake him, but she knew personally how hard it could be to find sleep on a mountain, especially in a storm. The blizzard outside did not make the walk to her tent appealing. She lowered to her stomach on the sleeping pad, stretching out her cramped legs, and turned to a new page in the book. She would leave after this puzzle, she told herself, and then realized she was too optimistic. *After you run out of clues you know,* she thought. But after only a few words her vision blurred and she lowered her head to rest in her hand, felt the warmth from her palm reach her cheek, and fell asleep.

When Evelyn woke up, the sun had risen. She was briefly disoriented by the blue tent instead of the familiar red of her own, but then she remembered the night before. She hadn't meant to fall asleep and wondered if Lowell minded. He was still sleeping but had made his way inside the sleeping bag at some point and had taken off his glasses. She sat up and rubbed a sore muscle in her neck before unzipping the door slowly, trying not to wake Lowell. The light from outside briefly blinded her; she blinked furiously until her vision adjusted. The wind seemed to have retreated but there was snow everywhere, covering the rocky ground and most of the tents. A fresh foot of powder, maybe. The American team was supposed to stay at Base Camp all day, so it wouldn't affect their plans. She wondered if they might even stay longer, since James had gone up to Camp One without acclimating.

She heard movement behind her and turned, almost bumping her face into Lowell's as he sat up and peered over her shoulder at the blanket of snow. "Making a quick exit?"

"Sorry," she replied, feeling herself flush. "I didn't mean to fall asleep."

Lowell shrugged. "It's fine. Could have used my sleeping pad, though." He paused, considering the snow. "Lucky they fetched the Japanese team."

"Yeah. I'm sure there's more snow at higher altitude." She paused, feeling the growl in her stomach. "Are you hungry?"

"Yes, but not enough to get out of this sleeping bag yet."

"I think I need to eat. Like I said, I'm not the best at having an appetite."

He nodded, eyes half-closed as he slipped back into his sleeping bag. "Enjoy. A winter wonderland."

She smiled to herself as she left the tent. He was kind. Funny. She needed to spend less time around him.

She walked quickly across camp, hoping that no one saw her hurried exit. They would assume the worst, immediately. She didn't really care what anyone thought except for her own team, didn't want them to think that she was distracted or wasn't taking the expedition seriously. She made it to her own tent and changed into new clothes, trying to shake the feeling that she'd done something wrong.

The mess tent was somewhat lively, more than half of the chairs taken. She grabbed an assortment of offerings from the back—dried fruit, Nepali breads, thin pancakes—and was about to sit down when she caught someone waving to her from the corner of her eye. She looked: Levi. Her heart sank for a moment—she had clearly seen him; she couldn't ignore him now. But then another thought seized her. Had something happened to Sophie? She pushed her chair in and made her way to a seat across from him, noting Sophie's absence. Instead, Penelope was by his side again.

"Good morning," she said as she sat down.

"Sorry, I won't keep you long. I wanted to let you know about Sophie."

Her heart skipped a beat. "Is she okay?"

He raised a hand quickly, as if to deflect her concern. "She's fine, she's okay. Just really worn out. Could barely stand up this morning."

"Oh." *That was the news?* "Well, thanks for telling me. I'm glad she's okay. That must have been exhausting. But worth it, to bring Yakumo's team down."

Levi blinked at her. "You haven't heard?"

"What?" He was going to give her a heart attack, making vague statements like this.

"They couldn't find the Japanese team. They weren't at the Camp One location. They searched farther, but the team is missing. No sign of them anywhere."

She set down her fork. "Oh my god. Really? Just...vanished?"

He nodded. "There's a possibility, of course, that they could be somewhere else. But it seems unlikely. I mean, you saw how much snow we got down here. It could be worse farther up the mountain. Windier, at the very least."

"I saw the headlamps last night. I thought... I just assumed they were successful. I didn't get out to check."

"I didn't either," Penelope interjected. "I was sound asleep. This morning, I woke up, and George told me, 'Yakumo is gone.' I couldn't believe it."

Evelyn felt a tap on her shoulder and glanced up as Phil and Danielle passed by, waving at her. She lifted a hand back, wondering if she was the only one out of the loop. "Will anyone go to look today, now that the storm is over?"

Levi shrugged. "Maybe. No talk of it yet. We," he said, indicating himself and Penelope, "were supposed to go to Camp One today, but George and Sophie are in no shape for that. So, for now, we're stuck."

"Us too. I mean, we just arrived yesterday. Acclimatization and all that." Levi gave her a funny look. She pushed her plate aside. "What?"

"It just occurred to me that you should probably talk to your team," he said. His caginess bothered her and she raised her eyebrows, imploring him to continue. "It's not my place to say anything," he said, as if he hadn't been the one to hint at something more. "James was injured yesterday. He's in bad shape, according to Sophie."

Evelyn sat back in her seat, her thoughts traveling at light speed. She shot a glance over at Phil and Danielle; they were seated near each other, eating and talking. She felt a flash of anger and wondered why no one had told her. Then she remembered where she'd spent the night. They'd probably looked for her and found her tent empty.

"Thanks for telling me."

"Sorry I had to."

His tone wasn't smug, but she wondered what he thought—
it would seem strange, to an outsider, that she hadn't been privy
to such important news. "Like I said. I didn't leave my tent last
night. It's my fault." She wanted to leave the conversation but
couldn't bring herself to stand, to walk over to Phil and Danielle and hear the details of James's condition. If he was out of
commission, their summit bid might be over before it started.

Levi cleared his throat, as if eager to change the subject.
"There's talk of a puja today if the Lama made it through
the storm."

"You'll have to wake Sophie up for that. She loves the ceremonies."

He nodded. "I know. I think she's told me about all the ones
you experienced together in the Himalayas." He paused, gaze
shifting to the door as George entered.

"I'm going to check in with him," Penelope said, slipping
out of her seat.

Levi made no move to stand up. "Do you need to go?"
Evelyn asked him.

He shook his head. "I'll wait for him to get settled. Honestly, and I don't mean this in a self-pitying way, I think I'm
the least important member of the team. They're all better
athletes than me. I think I just made a good impression on
George in the Alps. He liked my personality, maybe, but
George, Penelope, Sophie—they're out of my league. Ruslan and Ivan, too. They're total powerhouses. I don't know
how I'm going to keep up."

She wasn't sure how to respond to his confession. "Have
you told George? If someone on my team was anxious about
keeping up, I would want to know. It affects everyone."

She was worried that she had sounded harsh, but he didn't
seem to be offended. "No, I haven't. Right now, it's all hy-

pothetical concerns. I'll see how I feel after Camp One." He paused. "Honestly, I'm more nervous about telling Sophie. Not that she'll judge me, but I could see her trying to get both of us to quit."

Evelyn blinked. She wondered how much climbing he had done with Sophie, or if she was just a different person with him. Sophie didn't quit climbing. Other things, sure—she hadn't finished college, she often gave up on extracurriculars in high school, and she constantly got distracted midway through chores, leaving half a sink of dirty dishes for Evelyn to begrudgingly finish. But on a mountain, Sophie was all business, determined to finish at any cost. Even though they worked as an inseparable team, there had been times when Evelyn suspected that if she were to call out, Sophie would have pushed on, alone.

She decided to change the subject, uncomfortable with Levi revealing too much about his abilities to her, lest she become the only one who knew that he "couldn't keep up" should something happen to him. It was a dark thought, but she wasn't about to spill his concerns to George herself. "Do you think," she said, before she really knew where the sentence was headed, "that Sophie would talk to me?"

He stared at her. "Like, today?"

She shrugged. "Sometime soon. Today or tomorrow, ideally."

"I can suggest it to her," he said. "But I don't think she's too happy about us talking."

"You told her?"

"I mentioned that we had met. She reacted poorly. So…" He trailed off, shaking his head. "Maybe I shouldn't say anything. Maybe you should approach her."

"You're probably right." She paused, listening to the sounds of conversation around her, the clinking of forks. If she closed her eyes, she could pretend she was back home in a New York restaurant, seated across from Miles, not Levi, though the cold air and the dull drone of the space heaters were hard to ignore. "Things have been—difficult—lately, between me and Miles," she blurted out, because there was no one else in the world to tell. She knew that Levi probably didn't care; he was a world removed from her relationship with Miles and, therefore, Sophie's relationship with Miles. But he was the closest thing she had to Sophie right now, and there were few consequences to sharing the information. Miles was back in New York, and if Levi told Sophie—what difference would it make?

Levi leaned forward in his chair, regarding her with trepidation. "I don't know if you should tell Sophie that."

"Why?"

"Because I think she's finally come to terms with it. Well, that might be an exaggeration. She sees you as her sister who is dating her ex-husband. She's wrapped her head around it. If you tell her it's not working out, she's going to see all that pain as having been for nothing."

"I didn't think of it that way." She paused. "But we haven't broken up. We had a fight before I left. He wasn't exactly thrilled about me coming here. I haven't had a chance to talk to him since we arrived."

Levi raised his eyebrows. "Look, I've heard plenty of bad things about the guy. Maybe it's better if we don't get into the details. Just try to catch Sophie when you can. Maybe she'll want to talk to you. Now, if you'll excuse me, I should probably check in with my team."

She watched as he made his way to the end of the table closest to the door. She appreciated his candor but had hoped for a different answer—that Sophie was eager to talk to her, had been planning on starting a conversation. Evelyn knew that she couldn't keep stalling. If James was seriously hurt and their team couldn't attempt the summit, she might have to leave Yama Parvat in the next few days, and she didn't know when she would have a chance to see Sophie again. She knew they wouldn't end up celebrating Thanksgiving or Christmas together anytime soon. If they made it off the mountain without talking, the river of hurt rushing between them might become uncrossable.

Evelyn picked up her still-full plate and walked slowly down to where Phil and Danielle were seated, dreading the inevitable conversation. As she sat, Phil gazed at her, brow furrowed.

"What do you know?"

She hesitated. "That James was injured last night. That he's in bad shape."

Her teammates exchanged glances. "Good. We tried to tell you last night but your tent was empty."

"I was taking a walk."

"In a snowstorm?"

"I had a lot on my mind."

Danielle nodded, accepting Evelyn's excuse. "We saw him this morning. He was taken to the doctor pretty quickly last night. And he's okay, nothing he won't heal from. He has a concussion, a broken left arm, and some bad bruising. But he'll be alright."

Evelyn exhaled, though it wasn't a sigh of relief. "Is he leaving the mountain?"

"Not yet," Phil said, fiddling with his mug of instant coffee. "At least a week, to see how the concussion comes along. But knowing James, he'll want to stick around until someone summits."

"So we can keep climbing? The three of us, I mean?"

Danielle snorted, pushing a strand of black curls behind her ear. "I think James would have rather died in that crevasse than not see us make a summit attempt."

"You're right," Evelyn conceded, though she was thankful for her teammate's reassurance.

"You can probably see James if you want to," Phil said. "He's laid up in a cushy cot in the medical tent. Although," he continued, shooting a glance at Danielle, "he told us he'd rather sleep in his tent."

"That doesn't surprise me. He probably hates all the doting." Evelyn looked at her plate and realized she still hadn't eaten anything. She took a few quick bites of the now-cold pancakes and wrapped the dried fruit in a napkin, tucking it in her pocket for later. She said goodbye to Phil and Danielle and minutes later found herself outside beneath a brilliant blue sky. A sharp wind blew through Base Camp, raising ghostly waves of snowflakes that stung Evelyn's cheeks like a million tiny needles. She circled around the mess tent to the much smaller medical tent, knocking twice on the canvas door.

When no one answered, she stuck her head through the door, blinking in the sudden darkness. "Hello?"

"Come in," said an unfamiliar voice. She stepped inside, securing the door behind her, appreciative of the well-heated tent after the bitter cold outside. The doctor was seated at his desk, filling out paperwork. A nurse sat cross-legged on the floor in front of the desk, reading a book. She looked up at Evelyn after a moment, appraising her.

"You're here to see James," she said, and stood up, tucking the book under her arm. "I'll let him know." She slipped behind what looked like a solid wall, though Evelyn realized it must hide a small room, some simulation of privacy for patients. A minute later, the nurse reappeared, nodding at Evelyn. "You can see him."

Evelyn thanked her and ducked behind the canvas flap. James was seated upright on a cot, his left arm in a cast, his face partially bandaged. He saw her expression and grinned.

"It looks worse than it feels. Trust me."

Evelyn found herself frozen for a moment, filled with uncertainty. "I'm sorry," she managed to say, although it didn't feel like enough.

"Me too. Pretty unlucky. I must have dealt out some bad karma at some point." He gestured at a folding chair beside the cot. "Sit. Keep me company in my misery."

She did as he said, angling the chair to face the cot as best she could in the cramped space. "I'm sorry I didn't come with Phil and Danielle this morning. I didn't know."

"Yeah, I was surprised when they said they couldn't find you. We don't need more people going missing."

"I was just taking a walk," Evelyn said, her face hot, tired of lying. She had chosen the worst possible night to sleep in someone else's tent. "I was worried about you. And Sophie. And everyone else climbing."

"I get it. It's hard to sit around and twiddle your thumbs when it feels like you could be helping. That's why I went. Which was a stupid decision, in retrospect. I should have known better."

"What happened?"

"You don't know?" He paused, turning his gaze to the ceiling for a moment, as if he didn't want to repeat it again. "I was too close to the edge of a crevasse. It caved in." He shrugged his right shoulder and looked at Evelyn again. "A combination of bad choices and bad luck. I just didn't want to stop looking for Yakumo yet. It seemed like everyone else had given up. He's an old friend of mine."

"We'll find him," she said, though she knew the words were empty of real promise. "Phil and Danielle said you're staying around for a bit?"

James smiled. "Yeah. Can't get rid of me this easily. I'll stay until someone summits if I can. Hopefully the three of you. I've run logistics from Base Camp on Everest before; I'd be happy to do it again here. If I don't step on any toes." He paused, considering her for a moment. "You'd make a good leader, Evelyn. Phil and Danielle told me they'd be happy to defer to your judgment. Unprompted. I promise I didn't force them to say that."

Evelyn tried to laugh but only managed a weak smile. She thought of her disastrous attempt at being a guide several years ago. "That's a big task. Can we not just be a democratic trio?"

"You can, for a long time if you're lucky. But eventually there will come a moment when you all disagree and someone has to make the decision, even when there's no good option. That's a leader. Bring some of that no-nonsense lawyer energy to the fold."

Evelyn grimaced. "James, I climb to get away from the lawyer energy."

He laughed. "Fair enough. Look, I'll be around for advice if you need it, but I'm not going to micromanage."

"Okay, then I need advice. What should we do today?"

"I'm disappointed in you," he said, shaking his head, though there was a small smile on his lips. "Wait until tomorrow. That fresh snow might cause some avalanches. If the three of you are feeling really good, you can wander around a little but don't do anything that could be described as climbing."

He yawned, as if exhaustion had caught up to him. "I will be doing something that could be described as sleeping."

Evelyn stood up, folded the metal chair, and placed it back against the wall. "Thanks, James. I'll see you around. Let me know if I can bring you anything."

"Nurse Devna's got that covered, but thanks. I'm sure I'll be back in my own tent in a few days, anyway."

Evelyn waved goodbye and slipped out of the makeshift room, nodding to the nurse and doctor as she left the medical tent. The sharp sting of Himalayan cold struck her again as she stepped outside. She looked at Base Camp, which was mostly still, save for the colorful tents shaking in the wind.

She checked her watch. It had been about twenty minutes since she left her teammates at the mess tent. When she ducked back inside, they were still at the table, talking over their empty plates. Their attention landed on her when she sat down across from them.

"How is he?" Danielle asked.

"Probably the same as when you saw him this morning. He's fine, I'd say. Handling it well."

"He's James. He'd handle anything well," Phil said.

"He encouraged us to wander around a bit. Are either of you up for it?"

They both nodded. "It would be good to get some blood flowing," Danielle said.

Fifteen minutes later, they met outside the mess tent, dressed for a light hike in the ten-degree temperature. Evelyn spent the rest of the morning and part of the afternoon exploring the area with her teammates. They stayed off the glacier, for the most part, not wanting to bother with crampons. The rocky area around and below Base Camp provided plenty of opportunities for a workout, especially with the snow, although most of it had melted after the sun rose. Evelyn slipped more than once on a slick rock and shed layers as the air temperature rose, filling her backpack with excess clothes. They watched porters pass on the naturally formed road below, carrying heavy loads of goods to somewhere deeper in the mountains. Overhead, the massive peaks of the Annapurna range reached to meet the sky. Evelyn had to remind herself to focus on the ground below; her neck hurt after mere minutes of gazing at the mountains, envisioning routes up all of them. Perhaps she wouldn't go home after Yama Parvat. She could stay here forever, become a creature of the Himalayas, as elusive and legendary as the snow leopard. It was better to imagine than returning to New York.

She was the first to see the commotion when they reached camp. Phil and Danielle were deep in conversation but noticed when she stopped and pointed.

"What?" Phil asked.

"Is that—look, is that Yakumo's team?" She didn't believe it even as she said it, but close to the mess tent stood a cluster of bodies in navy down suits, which only the Japanese team wore. Someone in the group was talking animatedly, waving their hands. Several other people milled about, some pacing, some staring in what Evelyn assumed was also disbelief at the reappearance of the Japanese team. She had her answer moments later as they got closer. Yakumo was the one speaking, with a vigor as if describing a yeti encounter. But as they drew even closer, she realized he spoke in anger, not excitement.

"He looks upset," she said to her teammates in a low voice. She slowed down, approaching the crowd carefully, to avoid bumping into Sophie. She didn't see her sister, but spotted Lowell, and sidled up beside him. He noticed her and leaned closer, speaking without turning his head from the action before them.

"Hey. Yakumo is so pissed off."

"Why? What happened?" When she saw his look of confusion, she continued. "I've been hiking for a few hours."

He nodded. "Well, Yakumo's team just showed up like thirty minutes ago. Sauntered into camp like they were never missing. Everyone freaked out and asked where they were, why they didn't come down when the storm started. He said they found a better spot for Camp One, sort of wrapped around behind some rocks, off the planned route, more protected from exposure. And now he's livid that the other teams tried to look. Thinks we need to trust each other more. Look out for our own teams and that's it." Lowell shrugged. "I don't know if anyone else agrees."

Evelyn's gaze drifted from Yakumo back to the crowd. Her heart skipped a beat when she noticed Sophie standing almost diagonal from her. Sophie was looking at her, not her face, exactly, because they didn't make eye contact, but vaguely around her. She could feel the heat of her sister's gaze. A second passed and Sophie stepped closer to Levi, who stood beside her, and said something to him. He put his arm around her, and she leaned into his embrace. Evelyn tried to imagine what she felt—perhaps she was also angry, for the wasted search effort and Yakumo's thanklessness, or perhaps she was simply relieved. Sophie had never been one to hold a grudge, not until Evelyn had tested the very limits of her forgiveness.

Yakumo's voice rose, cutting through the crowd. She redirected her attention to him. He seemed to be speaking mostly to Wojciech and George. "I'm glad we agree. We're all experienced mountaineers and it is a waste of time and energy to look for a team of competent, safe climbers. Thank you.

This discussion is finished." He turned and said something in Japanese to his team, who followed him away from the crowd. Wojciech threw up his hands and faced George, their conversation too quiet to hear, although she suspected they were *not*, in fact, in agreement with Yakumo.

Beside her, Lowell exhaled. "Wow, I can't wait to interview Yakumo. This is turning into a circus. Have you eaten?"

She shook her head, aware that it was past lunchtime but not hungry. "I'll go with you."

"Thanks. I slept in, you know, just got up a little while ago."

She walked with him to the mess tent, past Sophie and Levi, wondering if she should say something. But even a simple hello still felt impossible.

Once they were inside and seated with plates of food, she glanced at Lowell across the table. "So. You've heard about James by now?"

Lowell nodded. "I talked to him this morning. He's in good spirits."

"I know. Very Zen about the whole thing." She took a bite of rice and swallowed. "He wants me to lead the team now."

"Really? That's great, Evelyn."

She exhaled and leaned back in her seat. "I don't know. Phil has way more experience than me. And it's only two other people. Not much of a team to lead."

Lowell regarded her for a moment. "He knows that Phil has more experience. He sees this as a good opportunity for you."

"He said that?"

"No, but that's the logical conclusion. He's not throwing you to the wolves. You have two supportive teammates and you'll probably be on the same schedule as us. Andrew will help you if you need it. Which you won't, because you're capable of doing this alone."

"Thanks for the pep talk," she replied, letting his words sink in. "I know it's only been a day since we arrived, but it feels like a month. I can't wait to get out of Base Camp."

"I hear you. If we get stuck with more weather, you and I can sneak out in the middle of the night and climb this thing alpine style."

"And everyone else can entertain themselves by carrying our frozen bodies down from the ridge." She took a sip of water to hide her smile. For now, they were stuck in the shadow of the mountain. But it was fun to dream.

Later that afternoon, as the sun slipped beyond the peaks, casting the mountains in a rich pink alpenglow, the Lama arrived at Base Camp. The guides had spent the last couple of hours preparing for the puja and readying the Chorten, a rectangular stone structure with a hole in the center for a flagpole. Evelyn had witnessed some of the activity before retreating to her tent, tired and weak from that morning's excursion. Her body was in the throes of adjusting to the altitude, which manifested in nausea and a pounding headache. She had managed to eat a small amount of food at lunch, but it wasn't enough.

She and Lowell had gone their separate ways after lunch. She wasn't sure that she would spend another night with him, although every time footsteps passed her tent, she half hoped they would pause and it would turn out to be him, extending an invitation for another night of company. But when boots did pause outside her tent, followed by a gentle knock, it wasn't Lowell standing outside, but Phil.

"The puja is starting soon. Grab your sharps."

"Really? It's almost dark."

He shrugged. "The guides say there's no time to waste. They're not happy that we've already been climbing."

"*We* haven't," Evelyn said with emphasis, grabbing her ice axe and crampons before exiting the tent. "Besides, this is for their benefit."

Phil fell into step beside her. "I like the puja. I'll take any blessing I can get."

"I like it too," she said, "but in a 'this is a cool observation of another culture' way. I don't think it actually does anything."

He shook his head. "This mountain is literally named after the god of death. Maybe he doesn't live on this mountain, but with that name I'm not willing to risk it."

Evelyn stayed quiet, surprised at her own negativity. She had always been a skeptic, embracing atheism in adulthood, but she tried not to stray into the territory of disrespect. Sophie had softened her nihilistic tendencies because she believed in all things spiritual and otherworldly. Without Sophie's constant sense of wonder, Evelyn had slipped back into her cynical nature.

Most of the climbers had already gathered around the Chorten; Evelyn and Phil were among the stragglers trickling in. They deposited their sharps in a pile beside the structure and found Danielle. Chairs from the mess tent had been set up a few feet away; they sat as the last few people arrived. One of the guides lit a small juniper fire, the smoke drifting up to meet the growing darkness. The Lama stepped out from one of the supply tents, walking slowly to the Chorten as a hush fell over the camp. He wore a thick robe of deep maroon and carried a handbell and a small drum, which he placed on the table beside the rice and tsampa.

After placing the items, he sat cross-legged on the mat and began chanting in a deep voice, his head slightly bowed as he read from a Tibetan prayer book. Thirty slow minutes passed, the cold air seeping into Evelyn's skin as she sat still, head tilted back, soaking in the rich navy color of the sky. The chanting stopped abruptly as a few guides emerged from the mess tent, carrying teacups that they distributed throughout the seated climbers. It took a few trips, but eventually Evelyn received a cup of milk tea from Mingma, one of the American team guides, and sipped it quickly, thankful for something sweet.

A few minutes passed in silence before the Lama resumed the ceremony. He rang the bell with his left hand and began to toss rice in the air with his right. The lack of wind caused the grains to fall directly back onto his shoulders. At the pujas on her past climbs, the crowds seemed happiest on the windy days, as if the gods were responding by waving the flags and carrying the prayers of the assembled to the mountain peaks. But that was only their own desperation to receive any sign that the climb might be a success. The collective attitude now felt more reverent than festive. The Lama fell silent, allowing the stillness of the night to wash over the gathered.

Mingma instructed the group to stand as the Lama resumed his chanting. The guides passed between the rows of chairs, giving each person a handful of rice. Evelyn cupped the grains in her left hand, waiting until the chanting grew in intensity and everyone threw their rice into the air, three times, in the direction of the flagpole. Evelyn felt the rice rain back down over her shoulders, pushed away from the flagpole—and the mountain—by a soft breeze. As clear a "no" as she had ever heard.

The Lama put away the sutra and symbolic items. This was the least spirited puja Evelyn had ever attended. Usually, there was a more frenzied, joyful energy in the air, a collective swelling of emotion that marked the significance of the journey about to be undertaken. Under the cover of darkness, the magic slipped away. The Lama chanted again for a few minutes, his voice alone filling the crisp night. He made his way to the mat and the team members were ushered toward him, one by one, kneeling before the Lama to receive his blessing.

Evelyn tried to muster an aura of thankfulness as he tied a golden cord around her neck, placing a khata scarf over top. She sensed a robotic rhythm to the Lama's movements. She thought back to what Sophie had taught her about the purpose of the ceremony: to dispel obstacles that prevented people from attaining their worldly and spiritual aspirations. Because the ceremonies were based on karmic merit, there was no such thing as a failure. The thought comforted her. She could read into the stoic mountain all she wanted, but at the end of the day, it was just rock and ice, incapable of deciding fate. She scanned the crowd until she found Lowell and approached him. He had received the blessing before her and looked otherworldly standing in the moonlight, the cream-colored scarf glowing around his neck.

"Feeling blessed?" he asked as she stepped closer.

"Not particularly." She pivoted to watch the rest of the ceremony. "No one seems thrilled to be here."

"We should have waited until the morning. I don't know why they insisted on rushing through tonight. It feels so… somber."

"I think it's because we've already been on the move."

"Yeah, well. First ascent. No one wants to sit around for a puja when a title like that is at stake."

She nodded. They watched in silence for several minutes, the slow shuffling of bodies back and forth on the mat. When the last climber had received the blessing, the Lama stood, gathered his things into a duffel bag, and walked down the hill into Base Camp, to a small shelter that had been staked near the mess tent. Mingma and the other guides began to pack away the remaining items and roll up the mats, although they left the flagpole in the Chorten. Still, no wind blew to move the prayer flags overhead.

"I'm going to talk to a couple of the guides," Lowell said, breaking the silence. "See what they think about the state of the climb. But I'd like to get a quote from you, too, if you have time later."

"From me? About what?"

"James's injury, what it means for your team. How you feel about taking over as expedition leader."

"Oh." Evelyn stared down at her hands for a moment, her black gloves stark against the white snow. "I'm not sure I'll have anything interesting to say about it."

"That's okay. I have no idea what my angle will be for this article yet. I'm just gathering as many interviews as I can. Come by in an hour?"

Evelyn nodded and Lowell waved her off. She walked back to her tent, taking a moment inside the quiet bubble to breathe. She wanted to leave Base Camp so desperately it scared her. She couldn't survive another day wandering aimlessly and avoiding Sophie. As she lay back on her sleeping pad, she made a small resolution. She would find her teammates tomorrow, and make a case for climbing, as if her life depended on it. She was starting to suspect that it might.

CHAPTER THIRTEEN

November 2016,
Breckenridge, Colorado

Evelyn opened her eyes and braced herself. It took her no time to remember that the poster-clad walls of her childhood bedroom weren't a cruel facade from a dream. They were real. She was home for Thanksgiving, and Sophie was sleeping in the room right next door.

Or maybe she wasn't sleeping, because Evelyn hadn't, not until almost dawn. She had tossed and turned all night, questioning her decision to return home. Her mother had insisted, but what did that matter? It was a horrible idea. As much as she wanted Sophie to forgive her, she knew it was too soon. Sophie wasn't going to understand what had happened between her and Miles. Evelyn herself hardly understood, even though it had now been over a year since he first came to stay at her apartment.

Evelyn forced herself out of bed and cracked the blinds at the nearest window, letting the weak autumn morning light filter in. She stared at the landscape outside the condo—muted, desolate, awash in gray and brown.

She pulled on a pair of fleece-lined leggings and a light-weight shirt and stepped into the hallway. Sophie's door was still shut. She made her way down the stairs and smelled coffee. Her mother was already awake, reading the news on her phone as she leaned against the kitchen counter.

"Good morning, Evelyn," she said as she glanced up. "Coffee?"

"Later, thanks. I'm going for a run." Evelyn continued down the hallway, grabbing her down vest from a hook by the door and stepping out into the cold morning air. *Not cold enough*, she thought, wishing yet again that she was on a remote mountain, unreachable. She would have to make do with a ski resort.

A map of the roads and trails around the resort had long ago burned its way into her mind. She turned left away from the condo complex and ran uphill, her breath coming in short, sharp bursts. Her phone buzzed in the pocket of her leggings, but she ignored it. It was probably Miles, asking how things were. Bad. Things were bad.

Evelyn had flown in the day before, as close to Thanksgiving as possible. Her mother had picked her up from the airport, chatting nonstop to fill the void between them. Evelyn hadn't seen her since the summer, when she'd shown up at the apartment unannounced. Since then, they'd maintained a cordial relationship. Her mother rarely asked about Miles, which Evelyn appreciated. If she could pretend he didn't exist, she could ignore some of the pain she'd caused. But she had, from her mother's updates, a strong idea of exactly how hurt Sophie was. Her sister wasn't working. She rarely left the house. For the first time in her life, she was on antidepressants. Evelyn took all this information and locked it away in a black box in her brain. She opened it often, the guilt gnawing at her from the inside out.

That same guilt had carried her home. Her mother hadn't even insisted. She had suggested, gently, that it might be nice to spend the holiday together. Evelyn had time off work anyway, and Sophie was already home. The ski resort didn't open until December 1. Wouldn't it be nice, the three of them in the same room together? Evelyn hadn't given herself time to think before she said yes, because she could have thought of a thousand reasons to say no.

Sophie had known about her relationship with Miles for several months now. They hadn't spoken since July, and Sophie's rage and disappointment had been palpable then. But Evelyn wondered if, with the passage of time, Sophie's feelings might have softened. Even if she wasn't ready to forgive Evelyn, maybe she would listen to her. As irrational as she felt, a small part of her hoped for a path forward and knew she wouldn't find it without seeing Sophie again.

In a perfect world, she could convince Sophie that she and Miles were meant to be together all along. In her most self-indulgent moments, Evelyn told herself that Sophie had only been a detour in Miles's path to her. They made sense together, Miles's spontaneous, freewheeling spirit tempered by Evelyn's need to plan and prepare, though she allowed Miles to draw her out of her shell sometimes. He was the only person who could talk her into attending a late-night comedy show or trying a new hole-in-the-wall restaurant after a long day of working on a case.

The sisters had avoided each other yesterday. Sophie had gone to the grocery store around the time of Evelyn's arrival and returned while Evelyn was unpacking. Evelyn had feigned exhaustion to avoid dinner together and later snuck out for a burrito under the pretense of buying cranberry sauce—a Thanksgiving staple that the rest of her family hated, but Evelyn loved. She had eaten her dinner in the strip mall parking lot and driven back slowly, watching the minutes tick by on the car clock until she was certain Sophie had gone to bed.

Which brought her to now. The immediacy of running took over most of her brain, leaving little room to ruminate. She followed the winding road up past the lodge—memories of Sophie's wedding flooding back—past more condos and chalets, past the storage warehouses. Her end goal was the top of the mountain, the glass-sided building where the lift arrived, but soon she was bent over on the side of the road, hands on her knees, heart hammering against her chest. Nausea swirled in her empty stomach, bringing an unpleasant taste to the back of her mouth. She waited for her breath and heart to slow before straightening up to study the road. It continued snaking up the mountain until it grew tiny, a mere line cutting through the brown grass. She could see her destination but running the rest of the way seemed impossible. She admitted defeat and turned around.

Back at home, the door swung open as Evelyn reached for the handle. There stood Sophie, dressed for a run.

She looked Evelyn up and down. "Same idea."

"Yeah, sorry," Evelyn replied, unprepared. "I should have waited for you."

"No worries," Sophie said, brushing past. "I would have said no."

At 4:00 p.m. they sat down for dinner. Evelyn had spent most of the day in the kitchen. It was a safe bet—Sophie wasn't fond of cooking. But to Evelyn's surprise, Sophie had ventured down to the living room in the afternoon and stayed there, reading a book. Many times, Evelyn had fought the urge to go speak to her. By dinnertime, she wondered what she was afraid of.

Sophie had made no effort to dress up for dinner. She wore a sweatshirt with fraying sleeves, and her hair still wasn't dry from the shower. Evelyn sat across from her, their mother at the head of the table, which was covered with a traditional spread—rolls, mashed potatoes, green beans, roasted vegetables, a turkey breast, Evelyn's cranberry sauce, and a pumpkin pie from a local bakery. More food than the three of them could possibly eat. The sight and scent of the food, the familiar ritual of the holiday, brought a knot to Evelyn's throat. It almost felt normal.

Their mother cleared her throat. "I just wanted to say how much I appreciate you both being here. I'm thankful, every day, to have two wonderful daughters who have grown up to be such incredible women. I'm so proud of you both."

Out of habit, Evelyn caught Sophie's eyes and rolled her own. They always made fun of her Thanksgiving speeches. *Can't we just eat?* Sophie used to say. But now Sophie simply held her gaze, her eyes rimmed in red. Had she been crying? Evelyn shifted in her seat, aware of how much discomfort Sophie probably felt from her presence.

"Do you want to share what you're thankful for?"

Evelyn blinked. She took a deep breath, trying to think of the least troublesome thing to say. "I'm thankful that I'm healthy and strong," she said quickly, though the memory of her failed morning run mocked her. *At least I made it halfway,* she thought.

"Sophie?"

Sophie glanced at their mother, then back at Evelyn. "I'm thankful that a person's true character is always revealed."

"Look, if you don't want me here—"

"Why wouldn't I want you here?" Sophie replied, cutting Evelyn off. She held Evelyn's gaze, silently daring her to answer the question. "Fine. Let's eat."

Evelyn stole a glance at her mother, but she was looking at Sophie. Evelyn knew whose side she was on. She lowered her head, focusing on the plate of food in front of her, though her appetite had already deserted her.

"Thanks for cooking, Mom," she remembered to say.

"You did half the work."

Evelyn looked at Sophie again, but her face was stony as she ate. Evelyn suspected there would be no more cracking through to her interior. Sophie, like Evelyn, was stubborn. If she didn't want to speak, she wouldn't.

Thirty minutes later, Evelyn exhaled in relief when her mother stood up from the table, signaling the end of the meal. No one had spoken—not even a "pass the potatoes," since everything was within reach on the small table. The clinking of silverware had drilled into Evelyn's brain, leaving her with a headache and punctuating just how much she didn't belong. If she hadn't been there, it would have actually been a normal Thanksgiving. Sophie and their mother would have talked, maybe even laughed. Instead, she sat across the table, the elephant in the room, barging in to remind them of the broken state of their family.

"I'll help with dishes," she announced, offering Sophie an out if she wanted to go back upstairs. To her surprise, Sophie returned her gaze.

"I will too. Mom, why don't you go relax? You've been busy all day."

"Oh." She blinked. "Oh, alright. Maybe I'll read a book. I'll be just in the other room, if you girls…need me."

In the kitchen, Evelyn let the sink fill halfway with hot, soapy water and plunged in. Sophie stood to her left, ready to dry the dishes that Evelyn handed to her.

Evelyn took a chance. "This feels like old times. Like when we were kids."

Sophie took a plate. "Has it occurred to you that I don't really want to reminisce?"

Evelyn bit the inside of her cheek. "I'm sorry. I just thought—"

"Thought what?" Sophie's voice dropped to a harsh whisper, barely audible above the running water. "The last time I saw you, you told me you were having an affair. With my husband. Who I am *still married to*." Evelyn opened her mouth to speak, but Sophie shook her head. "It's not even about that, Evelyn, it's…" She trailed off, blinking in frustration, her cheeks growing red. "You realize you're going to be next, right? He's just using you. He didn't want to be in Wyoming anymore. You have an apartment in New York. How convenient. When the excitement wears off, he'll find some other woman who has the next thing he wants. And you can't come crying to me when it happens."

"Sophie…" Evelyn had no idea what to say. Her heart pounded. She wondered if Sophie was right. She hadn't forgotten their conversation on K2 and the numerous phone calls with Sophie after they returned home, when Sophie complained to her about the continued arguments between her and Miles—he didn't want to go through another winter in Wyoming; she was determined to stay. Evelyn knew he wanted to move to a big city, but—didn't he love her, too? Wasn't he happier with her? Tears threatened to spill and Evelyn blinked them away. "I don't know how we ended up here."

She had meant to say something else. Something that captured how backward it all felt, that explained that even she couldn't make sense of her own actions. She didn't want sympathy. She wanted something else: acceptance, understanding, from the one person she could always rely on to grant her that.

Sophie's lip twitched. "I do." She set the dish towel on the counter and closed her eyes. "I need a minute."

Evelyn needed forgiveness. The one thing she couldn't have.

CHAPTER FOURTEEN

April 2018,
Yama Parvat Camp Two, Nepal

The first morning at Camp Two, Sophie woke up to stillness. Almost two weeks had passed since the failed mission to find the Japanese team, days spent working up to Camp One and down, and eventually sleeping at Camp One, before extending the excursions to Camp Two. Now they were perched on the side of the mountain where the route wrapped around to continue up, below a massive ice bridge that would require a ladder to cross. Beneath the team were the Americans and Canadians at Camp One, probably at Yakumo's version, where Sophie's team had also stayed. It was a longer distance from Base Camp, but the area above the couloir provided more shelter from the elements. The Japanese team had moved on to Camp Three, pushing ahead at a determined pace, and the Polish team was somewhere on the other side of the mountain, following the south ridge route. Sophie knew everyone's position because it mattered, because one of the teams—if they were lucky—would be the first to claim the summit of Yama Parvat.

Sophie poured some melted snow water into her bottle and opened a pack of electrolytes, working quickly as her bare fingers turned red in the freezing air. Once the electrolytes were poured in, she slipped her gloves back on and drank, alternating sips of water with bites of a high-calorie granola bar. She sat facing Levi, who snored lightly, face down in his sleeping bag. He was holding his own; she was proud of him, for keeping on despite his lack of Himalayan experience. When she finished her breakfast, she pulled on an extra layer of pants and shirt, donned her boots, and exited the tent, squinting for a minute against the blinding snow.

She spotted Penelope, Ivan, and Ruslan and headed toward them. She was still wary of the Russian duo, who seemed discontent with their pace, eager to catch up to or even overtake the Japanese team. But George had been careful and patient so far.

"Morning," she said as she grew closer. "Where's George?"

"We were just talking about that," Penelope said.

"You went to bed early last night," Ruslan said, half turning to Sophie, his cheeks ruddy in the cold. "He wasn't himself. Looked ready to pass out."

"And you didn't do anything?"

Ruslan raised his hands in defense, glancing between Penelope and Sophie. "Nothing to do. We asked if he was okay, he said he was. Said he needed sleep."

"Was he coughing?"

Penelope hesitated, then nodded. "He ate with us. I thought it was from the food. Do you think…" She trailed off, her brow furrowed. "Should we wake him up?"

"I think so," Sophie said, already walking in the direction

of George's tent. She knew the symptoms of severe altitude sickness by heart, had seen climbers transported off mountains when struck with the illness. She suspected the others knew the signs as well but didn't think to check someone as experienced as George. She tried to ignore the quickening of her heart as she reached his tent.

"George? Are you awake?" She tapped her hand against the shelter and waited. From inside came a faint swishing, the sound of a body moving against the slick fabric of a sleeping bag. "Is it okay if I come in?"

"All right," came the faint response. She unzipped the door and took in the sight of George. He was dressed, sitting up slightly, but looked pale and tired. He lifted a hand in greeting, but she ignored the gesture, crawling in beside him as her stomach turned over with worry.

"I'm going to take your pulse," she said, reaching for his right wrist. "How are you feeling?"

"Not well," he admitted. "Could hardly sleep last night. Head's pounding. You know." His eyes fluttered shut, and Sophie looked at him in alarm. His condition seemed worse than he was willing to acknowledge.

His pulse was in the nineties. Not necessarily a cause for alarm—Sophie knew that heart rates often increased at altitude. But his general condition concerned her. "I'll be back," she said, ducking out and returning to her waiting teammates. Levi had joined them; he tended to wake up as soon as Sophie left each morning.

"How is he?" Penelope asked.

"Not awful, but not good. Said he had trouble sleeping and has a headache. If he was coughing last night, combined with those symptoms, I don't think it's a great sign. He definitely has some altitude sickness."

"Great," Ruslan muttered. They all looked at him; he shrugged in return. "I am just as worried for his health as all of you are. But this complicates things."

"I think we need to take him to Base Camp," Sophie said. "I don't know if he'll agree. But he needs to be looked at by the doctor. Do we have any oxygen?"

Ruslan shook his head. "We were saving that for the last few trips up, remember? No sense in lugging it to this elevation."

"Right. Maybe that was a bad decision." Sophie paused to consider their options. "Well, I don't think we have much time to waste. Levi, want to help me bring him down? You three can stay behind and break camp. The plan was to descend today anyway, right?"

Her teammates nodded, somewhat begrudgingly. Penelope looked at George's tent, her eyes wide. "What will we do if he cannot continue?"

"We'll worry about that later," Sophie said over her shoulder, already returning to her own tent to don her climbing boots and crampons. Levi did the same, adding an additional layer of clothing. They made their way back to George. "We'll have to see if he can walk on his own," Sophie said to Levi. "The descent from this point isn't super technical. We'll have to stay close to support him, but hopefully we won't have to carry him. George?" She peered through the door. His eyes were closed. "George? It's Sophie," she said again, louder, and his eyes snapped open like a frightened animal.

"I'm sorry," he said. "I drifted off. Couldn't sleep last night…" He trailed off and began to cough weakly.

"It's okay," Sophie said, maneuvering around his sleeping mat to prop his body more upright. He was heavy; she looked to Levi for help. "We're going to descend to Base Camp, you, me, and Levi. The others will pack up and come later." She tried to convey the information nonchalantly, to not alarm him with the possibility of a medical emergency. But she suspected he knew—he was far more experienced than anyone else on the team. Still, altitude sickness often clouded judgment. There was no way of knowing the true extent of his illness until the doctor examined him.

Sophie and Levi dressed George in additional layers and tugged on his boots and crampons. Together, they emerged onto the snow-covered slope. As soon as he was on his feet, George doubled over in a frantic fit of coughing, gasping for breath in between. When he lifted his head, his mouth was coated with frothy, pink sputum. Sophie and Levi exchanged worried looks. She felt the eyes of her teammates upon them.

"Can you walk?" Sophie wiped George's mouth with her sleeve and then positioned herself beneath his left arm; Levi did the same on his right.

George took a wheezing breath. "I think," he said, and paused, as if he didn't have a concluding thought. "I'll try," he said. "Can't breathe much."

"I know," Sophie replied, exchanging another glance with Levi. They had more than a thousand feet to descend to reach Camp One, and another two thousand to Base Camp. "Let's try. One foot in front of the other."

They set off, trying to ignore the sound of George's rapid breath. They made slow progress, moving as a unit, a footstep at a time. Sophie kept her head down, focusing on the ground, away from the looming peaks overhead. The mountain of death, whose sides they stood on. She hoped fiercely that the name did not ring true.

George stopped abruptly, coughing so hard his body shook, as if he were trying to expel something lodged deep in his chest. He coughed until he could no longer breathe and then vomited onto the snowy ground, more pink foam traced with red. Sophie's own stomach heaved and she looked away, listening as George wheezed.

"Can you keep going?" Levi asked. No verbal response, but George must have nodded. "Sophie. Let's walk again."

She didn't know how much time had passed, but every time she looked up, the sun seemed to be marching across the sky at a furious pace while they dragged their feet along the ground. The air grew hotter as the sun's rays reflected off the dazzling snow, creating an oven of the field as they descended. A small, silent eternity passed, interrupted only by George's worsening breath, the drag and rattle of his lungs. Then she looked up again and saw it: the bright cluster of tents.

"We're almost there," she whispered, as much to herself as to the others. Levi glanced at her, a quick acknowledgment that he too saw the first finish line. But George seemed to be in a trance, all his energy concentrated on simply moving forward.

When they came closer, someone at Camp One looked up and spotted them. The figure moved their hands to their mouth, cupping them, and Sophie knew they were shouting, but they were still too far away to hear. It was agonizing to inch closer, watching figures emerge from the tents below, unable to communicate.

Levi halted, so Sophie did too. He removed his arm from George's shoulders and tried calling back. "We need help!" He glanced at Sophie. "Worth a shot."

"We just need to get down there," she replied, moving again as soon as Levi was ready.

They must have heard him, or at least seen the spectacle of the trio inching its way down the mountain, because by the time they arrived a small cluster had formed. Andrew, the

Canadian team leader, broke out of the crowd and approached them, his eyes widening as he realized who they were carrying. "Oh my god, it's George," he breathed, glancing between Sophie and Levi. "What's going on?"

"He's in bad shape. Coughing up pink foam. I think—"

"Pulmonary edema." Andrew finished the statement. He turned back to the crowd. "Lowell, he has HAPE. Can you grab some oxygen?"

Lowell nodded and stepped back from the crowd. For the first time, Sophie spotted Evelyn; genuine worry was clear on her sister's face. George seemed stable enough, though he hadn't acknowledged Andrew's presence or that of the other climbers. He stared at the ground, breathing heavily.

"Should we help him sit?" Sophie asked Levi.

He nodded. "Andrew, do you have a pad or sleeping bag so we can let him sit down?"

Andrew gave a thumbs-up and headed to the tents, moving as quickly as he could in the snow.

Suddenly George leaned over, coughing with a startling force. He gasped for breath, each cough splattering pink foam across the snow. Sophie struggled to hold him upright and lost her grip; Levi too had loosened his while they waited for Andrew and Lowell. George collapsed face-first into the snow, sounding like an unseen force was strangling him to death.

In an instant Sophie was beside him, trying to wrangle his thrashing body so that he lay on his back. Another pair of hands brushed hers, but they weren't Levi's. She looked up—Evelyn. Her sister's gaze was focused on George as she corralled his arms together and held them as best she could as his coughs continued. She looked up at Sophie. "Ready?"

Sophie nodded, unable to speak. Together they rolled George onto his side and then his back, so that he stared up at the sun, glassy-eyed. Sophie found her voice. "He needs to sit up. He can't breathe."

"I know." Together they wrestled him into an upright position. Sophie felt Levi's presence behind her; his hands joined theirs, holding George upright. The coughing began again.

Sophie shifted her position so that she could see George's face. His eyes were no longer blank—they held a terror that Sophie had never seen before. He was drowning from the inside, fighting against the fluid in his lungs. She wanted to look away, cry, hand him over to Levi and Evelyn. But seconds later, Lowell stooped in front of George, sliding the oxygen mask over his face, and checking that the air was flowing from the cylinder. George's coughing eased, though he still looked scared beneath the mask, afraid of his body's betrayal.

Sophie thanked Lowell. He stepped back, watching George carefully.

"Here," Andrew said, stepping beside George and handing a sleeping bag to Levi. He took it and rose to his feet, leaving Evelyn to support George's weight.

"Thanks. I don't know that we should wait around here for long. He's in bad shape." He paused, glancing at Sophie. "Do you think…"

She knew what he was asking: Was she strong enough to continue the descent? She wasn't sure. Adrenaline could probably take her down to Base Camp, but she would be exhausted, probably in poor shape for the next two days. She stood up and shook her head, stepping closer to Andrew, a few feet away from George. "Do you have anyone who can help him down?"

"I will. And—" he turned for a quick scan of the waiting group "—Lowell, you're young and strong. Get over here." Lowell raised a hand in acknowledgment and turned away, presumably to ready himself for the descent. "Everyone else, listen up. You'll stick around up here as planned. Don't head up to Camp Two. Evelyn, agreed?"

Sophie looked at Evelyn with surprise. She knew that the American and Canadian teams were sticking together but hadn't realized that Evelyn had taken over James's leadership role. It was hard to decipher the emotion on Evelyn's face— she gazed up at Andrew and nodded, but her expression remained grim and distant.

"Spend the night and descend tomorrow. I'll stay at Base Camp." He turned back to Levi and Sophie. "What about you two?"

"We'll come down to Base Camp. The rest of our team shouldn't be too far behind us." She pivoted to scan the mountain above them but didn't see the trio. "He's our leader. We can't do much until we know his condition."

Andrew exhaled and lowered his voice. "Well, I wouldn't count on having him around after this. I mean, he'll probably survive, but he needs to go back home. He can't stay on the mountain in this state."

"I know," Sophie replied curtly, because the same thought had repeated itself in her head for the entire descent. "But we don't need to worry about that until we're back down."

Lowell returned, interrupting the conversation. Andrew saluted them and then positioned himself beside George, stooping with Lowell to help the man to his feet. Evelyn stayed close, her hands on George's back until they maneuvered him to his feet, and then stepped back, arms folded as she watched. Sophie tried not to stare, but it was difficult to take her eyes off Evelyn. It had been so long since she had seen her at work—the intense expression on her face, the knit of her brow. It reminded her of when Evelyn studied—all the days they had spent at the kitchen table after dinner, silently doing homework but dreaming of ski trips or hiking trails instead. She felt a strange urge to comfort Evelyn, familiar and foreign all at once, to wrap her in a hug and take away any worry that she felt. Sophie moved closer to Levi, finally tearing her eyes from her sister.

"Should we go with them?" Levi asked.

"Yes. In case anything happens." The image of George a few minutes ago, collapsed in the snow, unable to breathe, flooded her mind. "Now," she said, and took his arm gently, pulling him away from camp. Lowell, George, and Andrew fell in step behind them, and slowly the descent began again, two thousand more feet past crevasses and towering rocks. Sophie paused, once, to look over her shoulder and saw Evelyn watching, arms still crossed. *I should turn back*, Sophie thought, *and say something*. But there were no words to convey what she felt.

"He's stable. We've called in a helicopter for this afternoon. They'll take him to Pokhara and another helicopter will take him to Vayodha Hospital. Then, whenever he's back to normal, he can hop on a flight home."

The doctor paused, looking between Sophie and Levi. After the slow descent yesterday, George had been whisked into the medical tent, taking the cot that James had vacated last week. There had been no updates on George's condition overnight. Sophie and Levi had barely slept; both were awake and dressed at the crack of dawn, in search of the doctor.

"So, there's no chance he'll come back to climb?"

Sophie knew the answer, but was glad Levi asked, for the small part of her that still held out hope.

The doctor shook his head. "No. He'll likely be in critical care for a few days and won't be back to full strength for a couple of weeks. It's not impossible for him to climb again soon, but it would be an unnecessary risk. I've spoken to George; he agrees. He wants to return home."

"When can we see him?" Sophie asked.

"Now, if you want to."

They followed the doctor inside the tent, which was small and cluttered with medical equipment. A large space heater growled in the center, sourcing energy from a solar panel outside. The warmth made Sophie instantly drowsy. The doctor led them past a canvas wall panel to a small room with a cot, where George lay, breathing through an oxygen mask. He was awake and sat up a bit when he noticed Sophie and Levi. He looked at the doctor and gestured to his mask.

"You can remove it for a few minutes," the doctor said. Sophie knew how difficult it was to talk while wearing an oxygen mask.

"I'm happy to see you," George said, after pulling off the mask. "God, what a wrench in the works. Thank you both, for taking care of me."

"We thought about leaving you behind," Sophie replied, testing his sense of humor.

George laughed. "Right. Couldn't blame you then. I was in bad shape. I thought I was going to die." Any signs of laughter disappeared from his face. "Really. I can't thank you enough for acting quickly."

"Of course." Sophie paused. "The doctor tells us you want to head back home."

"I do. I always thought I'd have more of a fighting spirit in these situations, but I'm not twenty-five anymore. When I was coughing up my lungs, all I could think about was having a cup of tea in my garden with my wife and kids. So. I think that's a damn good sign to hurry home and make that a reality."

"We completely understand," Levi said. "I would do the same."

George coughed, though much less forcefully than the day before. "The doctor tells me I cracked a couple of ribs from coughing yesterday. I'd heard of that happening, but—" he gestured to his rib cage "—I never thought I'd have the pleasure of feeling it. I'd better get this mask back on soon. Promise me you'll rally the troops and keep on, alright? We've done well. You've got a summit to make in my name."

"Promise," Sophie said.

"Good. You won't want to miss my grand send-off this afternoon, I'm sure. I've been told the helicopter can't land here, so there's a whole business of lifting me up on this cot. Very dramatic and embarrassing, I'm sure."

"We'll be here," Sophie replied, stifling a laugh. "I'm glad you're okay, George. You've been a great leader."

"I appreciate that." He slipped the mask back on, waving them off as the doctor stepped in to check his oxygen levels.

Sophie blinked rapidly as they emerged into the sharp morning air, momentarily blinded by the snow and sunshine. "He seems no worse for the wear."

"I'd say he's doing about as well as possible, considering the circumstances. Breakfast?"

"Please," Sophie replied, already heading to the mess tent.

She had no trouble scarfing down breakfast. They were the first to arrive, steam rising off the food. As they were finishing up, others trickled in, including Penelope, Ivan, and Ruslan. Sophie and Levi had seen their teammates at Base Camp yesterday afternoon, but not much since then. No one had been in the mood to talk. Sophie waved them over after they had gotten their food.

"We saw George this morning. He's doing okay. They're airlifting him to a hospital this afternoon."

Ruslan whistled low. "Heard he collapsed at Camp One. Guess it's good you carried him down when you did." He paused, his gaze traveling over his teammates. "We should discuss the elephant in the room."

"I know, Ruslan. I've been thinking about it," Sophie replied. Her mind had been running circles around their leaderless team all morning.

"Sophie should lead us," Penelope said.

Sophie shifted in her seat. "I don't know. I don't have that kind of experience."

"None of us have experience leading a first ascent expedition. But who of us made a living guiding climbs? Who has summited the most eight-thousand-meter mountains?" Levi asked.

Sophie shot him a pointed look. "That doesn't matter. That has nothing to do with what makes a good leader."

"You're right," Levi said. "But I'm taking myself out of the running. That leaves you four."

Penelope set down her fork. "Do we need a designated leader? We're a small team. I think we can generally come to agreements."

Ruslan coughed, as if stifling a laugh. "You can't possibly think that. Look, Ivan and I have made many trips together over the past ten years. We have a style that works for us. We travel light and ascend quickly. We've summited without guides many times before."

"We're also…" Ivan trailed off, glancing at Ruslan as if unsure if he should continue. He forged ahead. "We're under a

able as she felt. "It's just that with everything that happened yesterday...I'm not in much of a mood to celebrate."

"No celebrations necessary. I left your present at home," he said, apologetic. "Too big to fit on the plane."

"Then my birthday will happen in June this year. Or May, or whenever this ordeal is over with."

"When it's over with, you won't call it an ordeal. You'll call it something else. Something happier." He paused, fiddling with his empty plate, before reaching into his jacket. "I do have something for you." He pulled out a green envelope and slid it across the table.

The sight of it made Sophie smile. "Green. My mom puts my birthday card in a green envelope every year."

"I know."

"You know?" Sophie blinked, trying to remember if she'd ever told Levi such a small detail. This was their first time celebrating her birthday; she couldn't imagine why it would have come up. A strange expression crossed Levi's face. "What?"

"Your mom told me."

Sophie folded her arms. "When did she tell you?"

Levi exhaled a quick puff of breath. "Okay. Don't get mad."

"No promises."

"She called me back in March," he said. "A few weeks before we came here. She wanted to make sure I knew what day your birthday was."

"And?"

Levi almost smiled. "You know her so well." He paused. "She asked me to convince you to talk to Evelyn, if I could. She thought this was the perfect opportunity to hear each other out. I didn't know what to say. I didn't like keeping this a secret from you, but..."

"But you did," Sophie said, finishing for him. "God. Okay."

She remembered a conversation they'd had recently—Levi asking her if she wanted to hold on to her resentment of Evelyn. Sophie had said Levi sounded like her mother. Now she realized it was her mother's words piped through Levi's mouth. That explained his willingness to speak to Evelyn, too.

"You're mad."

Sophie closed her eyes. "At my mom, yes. The jury is still out on you."

"She was very persuasive," Levi said, his voice quiet. Sophie opened her eyes and watched him for a moment. He was so kind, so willing to accept others for who they were. Except the part of her that struggled not to hate Evelyn.

Sophie grabbed the card from the table and slipped it inside her jacket. "I'm not in the mood to hear anything sappy about how much you love me or how proud of me you are."

"Well," he replied, "I understand. I'm sorry. Really. But that card isn't from me." He studied her for a moment. "You said you weren't in the mood to celebrate. What do you want to do?"

A card from her mother, then—even less appealing. "Sleep," she said, without hesitating.

"Then that's what we'll do."

Sophie woke up hungry. She sat up and stretched, trying to relieve some of the discomfort in her overused muscles. Beside her, Levi was still asleep. Sophie reached for a wool sweater laid over her backpack, then hesitated. She grabbed her jacket instead, slid the green envelope from the interior pocket, and pulled out the card. On the front was a painting of a snowy mountain, brightly colored skiers cutting lines down the slope beneath a rich blue sky, *Wish You Were Here!* written in cheery, looping font. Sophie recognized it as one of the cards sold in the resort's gift shop. Her mother had started a program years ago to have local artists create the merchandise. Sure enough, the artist's signature was on the back of the card. Sophie knew she was stalling and flipped it open, drawing a breath at the sight of the familiar, neat handwriting.

Sophie, of course I wish you were here. But I can't imagine a better place for you to turn twenty-five...

The card went on, a whole page of love. The thought of her mother writing it out over a month ago, then mailing it to Switzerland, of Levi finding the perfect green envelope and slipping the card into its new home, carrying it all the way here without her noticing, made Sophie tear up. She brushed the back of her hand against her eyes before the card got wet and returned it to its envelope.

Levi slept on, oblivious to her surge of emotions. She brushed the hair off his forehead but decided not to wake him and crawled out of the tent after pulling on the sweater, stretching once more in the cold sunshine.

Penelope walked by and stopped. "They're letting us make calls in the comms tent. Just for a little while longer."

"Oh, thanks." Sophie forced a quick smile, hoping she didn't look like she'd just been crying. "How are you doing? Now that the George situation has had some time to settle in."

Penelope frowned and lifted her head up to the sky for a moment, squinting behind her sunglasses. "I want to climb. George wants us to summit. I came all this way. I do not want to turn around because of someone else." Penelope returned her gaze to Sophie. "You are worried about Levi." It wasn't a question.

"Maybe," Sophie admitted. "He's newer to all this. If he doesn't feel safe, then he *isn't* safe."

Penelope nodded. "I can tell how much you love him. I cannot imagine climbing with my husband. We would be at each other's throats."

Sophie glanced at the tent, half expecting Levi to be listening in. Though she was still processing his conversation with her mother, much of her anger had melted away. She knew how convincing her mother could be, and besides, love for her was at the core of their actions. "I have Levi to thank for getting me back into climbing," she said. "He's always been this source of calm for me, which is something I needed. A peaceful relationship, you know?"

Penelope patted her arm. "Hold on tight to that. Excitement, it grows old quickly." She stepped away and waved. "I'll see you later."

Sophie waited a moment longer before ducking back into the tent. She grabbed Levi's leg and shook it gently, waiting for him to stir.

"Good morning, again. Penelope told me the phone is up for grabs. Want to come?"

A few minutes later, they found no line to make a call, just one person holding the large satellite phone to their ear—Evelyn. She was seated in a chair, her back facing them.

Sophie tried to resist the urge to eavesdrop, although the conversation carried in the small space.

"It's been fine besides yesterday... Yeah, we're making good progress... I miss you too. I'll be home before you know it." Another pause, laughter. "New York, Colorado, same thing."

Levi coughed and Evelyn turned in her seat, taking in the sight of them. Sophie nudged him. "Sorry," Levi whispered. "Dry throat."

"I should go, okay? People are waiting to use the phone. I love you." Evelyn paused, shifting the phone to her other ear. "Do you want to talk to Sophie?"

Sophie blinked, caught by surprise.

Evelyn extended the phone to her. "Here you go. It's Mom."

"Right." She took the phone and sat in the chair after Evelyn stepped away. Sophie waited until Evelyn left before speaking into the phone. "Mom? Hi."

"Oh, hi, Sophie, it's so good to hear your voice. How are you? Happy birthday! I've been sitting around all day thinking: I just wish I could tell Sophie happy birthday. I guess my wish was granted."

"Thanks, Mom. I'm okay. I mean, I'm good, but this trip has been hard. George got really sick yesterday, fluid in his lungs. They're airlifting him off the mountain later today. And our group is splitting up and it's just…unlike any other climbing experience I've had. Not that any of them have been alike."

"Just stay safe. Use your brain. You're too smart to get yourself into trouble. I just told Evelyn the same thing."

She ignored the comment about Evelyn. "What time is it in Colorado?"

"Eleven forty-five. I was asleep when Evelyn called, but I saw the number on the phone and thought, it's not every day you get a call from Nepal. And of course, I always assume the worst. But this is a delight, both of my girls on the phone." She paused, then cleared her throat. "Evelyn tells me you still haven't talked."

"Funny you should mention it," Sophie said. "Levi just told me about a phone call he got back in March."

The line was silent, long enough for Sophie to wonder if the call had dropped. "I just thought—I thought, he'll be there and I won't. I might never get to see both of you in the same room again, but he will. Same mountain, at least. You're so stubborn, Sophie, but you trust Levi. I thought he could help nudge you in the right direction."

Sophie could hear the emotion in her voice. The fire in her core cooled slightly, more of the anger dissipating. "I understand. But it's my decision to make, Mom. Please don't use Levi to get what you want." She paused. "Evelyn and I are on different teams, different schedules. She helped with George yesterday, though."

"Oh, yes, she told me about that. I think she's going to come home to Colorado for a while after this trip. She's thinking about doing what you do, leading guided trips. You should give her some tips."

"I don't know if..." Sophie trailed off, biting her tongue. She was disappointed, but not surprised, that her mother was right back to insisting that she should repair her relationship with Evelyn. She still hurt every day, still felt sick to her stomach when she thought of Evelyn and Miles together. The last thing she wanted was to help Evelyn land a job in her own career field, one that Evelyn had already tried and failed in. "I should get going. Levi still needs to make a call."

"Tell him hello for me," her mother replied. "I'm glad he's there with you. I worry about you so much."

Sophie didn't know if that meant *on these climbs* or *in general*, but she didn't ask for clarification. "I'm glad he's here too. He gave me your card."

"Oh, good. I wanted to ask, but I didn't want to ruin the surprise."

"Thank you. It meant a lot to me." Sophie swallowed before her voice choked up. "Okay, Mom, I love you. Bye. I'll talk to you next time I get a chance."

Her mother said goodbye and happy birthday again, and

Sophie pressed the button to hang up. She stood and handed the phone to Levi. "How was it?"

"Fine," she replied, reluctant to get into the details. "Who are you calling?"

"Home. Mom and Dad."

"Okay." She kissed his cheek. "I'll wait outside." A few more people had entered the tent, queuing to use the phone, so she skirted around them. Stepping outside, she nearly bumped into Evelyn, who was standing alone. "Oh, sorry," Sophie said, backing up a few steps.

"It's okay," Evelyn said. "How was Mom?"

Sophie realized that Evelyn must have been waiting for her. "She seems fine," she replied cautiously. "You know, worried as always."

"Yeah." A hint of a smile crossed Evelyn's face. "I think it's worse this time since we're not on the same team. She said, and I quote, that I'm 'climbing with strangers.' As if you and I haven't known James for years. And I was on Lhotse with all three of my teammates last year." When Sophie didn't respond, she pushed on. "I'm sorry about George."

"Me too. It must be devastating for him, but he seems to be taking it well. He's looking forward to seeing his wife and kids." Sophie paused. "Thank you. For helping."

"Of course." She paused. "Happy birthday, Sophie. What a place to spend it."

"Thank you."

"Do you remember when I turned twenty-five? You came to New York and we got drunk at that terrible bar."

Sophie nodded, reluctant to indulge Evelyn's memories of the past. Sophie had been twenty-one, a few months away from marrying Miles. She had felt safe then, in control. An illusion she could never go back to. "Too bad there aren't any cheap bars in the Himalayas."

Evelyn smiled, but her expression quickly fell. She opened her mouth, seemed to hesitate, and then spoke. "Where will you go at the end of summer?"

Sophie regarded her for a moment, wondering how much honesty to answer with. "I don't know," she said finally. "Maybe Switzerland. Maybe Mom's house until I land a guiding job somewhere. I don't want to leave Levi, but I don't know that I want to stay in Switzerland forever. I miss home. I miss Wyoming." Relief washed over her as she said it out loud, for admitting that Switzerland still felt temporary, and better yet for admitting that she missed Wyoming. It had taken her so long to separate them in her mind, Miles and Wyoming, the two so intertwined that the bad parts of Miles seeped into Wyoming and the good parts of Wyoming into Miles. She had no idea where she would live, couldn't imagine anywhere else than the cold, dark cabin in the woods that was always on the verge of falling apart. She wanted badly to ask about the cabin, if Miles had sold it, but didn't dare speak his name in front of Evelyn.

"I'm only asking," Evelyn said, "because I might go back to Mom's."

"She told me. Why?" Sophie suspected she knew the answer. Evelyn's relationship with Miles must be on the fritz; otherwise, she doubted her sister would abandon her high-paying opportunities in New York. But she wanted to hear Evelyn say it, to admit that things between her and Miles weren't working out.

Evelyn cleared her throat. "I won't get my job at my firm back. Realistically, I don't think anywhere will hire me when they see my track record of quitting every summer. As horrible as this sounds," she laughed, "I think I need to cut my losses and realize that law school was an expensive, time-consuming mistake. I don't think I was ever meant to be a lawyer."

She dodged the Miles aspect of the question, but Sophie didn't want to push it. She was still processing the fact that Evelyn had started the conversation, that they had managed to speak to each other without fighting, that Evelyn was *laughing*. Let alone that Evelyn seemed to have given up on the career she had worked so hard for. She rubbed her forehead. "I always thought you'd make a good lawyer."

"I think that I am. It's just not a job conducive to mountain climbing. I should have seen that from the beginning, but I was caught up in the prestige of it all. It makes you feel like somebody, attending Columbia Law School."

"You were always more ambitious than me."

"But I think you were right all along. A nontraditional job makes more sense. I want to try guiding climbs again. Nowhere near Wyoming. I don't want to step on your toes. I think maybe I was too young and immature last time I tried. I could do a better job now." She paused. "I think I didn't give myself enough freedom. I did seven straight years of school, no gap year, hardly a break between graduating and starting a job. It's like I don't even know myself. Maybe I'll go back to being a lawyer someday, but I need to try something else."

Sophie blinked. It amazed her to hear Evelyn sound so insecure, so unsure of herself, to acknowledge that she had been wrong. It went against everything she had ever known about her sister. "Go for it. I don't know if I'll even be back in Wyoming."

"Ready for— Oh, hey, Evelyn."

Sophie turned her head to see Levi behind her, a surprised

expression on his face. "Hi," she said. "Yeah, I'm ready for lunch."

Levi peered around her. "Have you eaten, Evelyn?"

She waved a hand. "No. My stomach isn't up to it right now. But thanks." She turned away, walking in the opposite direction.

Sophie watched Evelyn's retreating back for a moment before gesturing to Levi. They trudged through the snow in silence for a minute before he spoke. "So?"

She shrugged. "She started the conversation. It was fine, I guess. Weird. I don't know why she wants to talk to me."

"Did you want to talk to her?"

She considered the question. "No. But at the same time, I didn't mind. I don't think that one conversation goes very far in repairing our relationship. We spoke. That's it. It's difficult to see her as anything except the person who ruined my life."

"Sophie." He caught her arm and pulled her aside. "Your life isn't ruined. Look around you. You're so lucky to be here. What happened with Evelyn was a nightmare, yes. But it was a small blip in the grand scheme of your life that is to come." He kissed her once, his lips the same temperature as hers: cold.

"I know. I'm speaking from my perspective back then." She stepped away from him, irritated by his incessant positivity, which she usually loved. She was beginning to feel angry at Evelyn, too, for how easily she had started the conversation, for declaring that she was moving back into their mother's house and not addressing Miles.

Were they broken up? Was he moving to Colorado, too? If he came anywhere close to Wyoming, she might as well stay in Switzerland forever. The legal fact of their marriage had become nothing more than a nuisance to her long ago. She'd lost any feelings for Miles as soon as he and Evelyn told her about the affair, though they had started to drift before that, with his many trips to New York—to see Evelyn, she now knew—and constant desire to leave Wyoming, which felt more like home to Sophie with each passing day. At the beginning of their relationship, his laissez-faire attitude had attracted her to him, but over time she understood that he was always scouting for the next opportunity, ready to leave a seemingly stable life behind on a whim. Sophie had thought that she was the same way, but after settling in Wyoming, she liked the routine of living in the cabin. Guiding climbs presented new adventures and challenges each day, but Sophie appreciated having a home base to return to, a quiet place to recharge. For a few months, Miles seemed to feel the same way, but then something shifted.

Sophie's mind still hadn't quieted when the helicopter came, the sky overwhelmed by the sound of the strange, mechanical bird. She watched George's stretcher lift, up, up, until he was safe inside the helicopter and it rose away, disappearing into the blue abyss. A part of her wished that she had hitched a ride, away from the mountain, to a life that made sense. But she would have to travel back in time for that.

CHAPTER FIFTEEN

March 2014,
Seattle, Washington

In March, the first hints of spring trickled into Washington as the sun poked its head out from behind the clouds, and Sophie fell in love.

She had met Miles in the damp chill of February—a new employee at her favorite outdoor gear store, a short conversation at the register, his phone number written carefully on the receipt. She hadn't thought much of it at the time. She was seeing, casually, another climbing guide, sleeping at his apartment some weekends. But they weren't exclusive, so there was no harm in seeing where things went with the green-eyed, quietly intense kayaker behind the counter. And things went well.

After their first night together, Sophie and Miles were nearly inseparable. Nearly—because Sophie had school, no matter how unenthusiastic she was about it, and Miles had work and weekend river running. But they found time, as winter trickled into early spring, for Sophie to slide beneath the heavy flannel sheets in Miles's bed and for him to make them breakfast the next morning. He was a talented chef—*of course he is*, Sophie thought, every time he presented her with brioche French toast and berry compote or eggs Benedict, never mind the fact that he made it all on a two-burner hotplate.

"I'll admit that I eat a lot more yogurt and granola when you're not around," he told her.

"Then I guess I'll have to be around a lot more," she replied.

Sophie started spending more time with him, sometimes driving up to his rented cabin near Darrington on weeknights and staying through Sunday evening. She rescheduled her phone calls with Evelyn on those weekends, but the guilt she felt was minimal compared to how much she liked seeing Miles. She found in him a kindred spirit, someone who understood her obsessive drive. And maybe that should have been a sign, that two obsessives would only light a short-fused fire, that they were too similar not to burn each other out. But late at night, curled up on the couch, surrounded by Miles's paintings of ferocious rivers, swapping stories about climbing and paddling, Sophie couldn't imagine being as happy anywhere else.

They were at a farmer's market when her phone rang. It was lunchtime on the east coast, probably Evelyn's only break in a long day of society meetings and writing papers. Sophie hesitated for a moment and declined the call.

Miles had drifted ahead but stopped to look back at her. "Sophie?"

"Sorry," she replied, typing a quick apology to Evelyn. "My sister called me."

"You always say, 'my sister.' I'm sure she has a name."

Sophie tossed her phone back in her tote bag and lengthened her stride to catch up with him. "It's Evelyn."

They fell into step together, wandering through the crowd, on the hunt for a specific stand that sold the best goat cheese. "What's she like?"

Sophie paused, mulling over how to answer the question, how to summarize a person she knew so well. "She's nothing like me," she said finally, and shot Miles a quick glance. "I mean, don't get me wrong, she's just as good of a climber. But she's so serious, in an 'I want to save the world' kind of way. And she probably will. She's so smart. She can be funny, sometimes, too, when she's not obsessing over some obscure case or law."

"She lives in New York?" He seemed to think for a moment after Sophie nodded. "I'm not sure I could do it. I want to be somewhere wild." He reached over and took Sophie's hand, something he hadn't done before, not in public like this. "You're smart too, Sophie. And driven. Sounds like just not in the same direction." He glanced at her. "I don't think you'd make a very good lawyer."

"Are you kidding? I'd do a great job of getting people off the hook." She heard her phone buzz, probably Evelyn responding, but didn't pull her hand from Miles's grasp to dig through her bag. She knew Evelyn had exams coming up, was under a lot of stress, but Sophie wasn't in the mood to think about someone else's problems. Nor was she in the mood to hear Evelyn's opinion about how much time she was spending with Miles. She had called Evelyn after her first date with him, and Evelyn had asked what the catch was. Sophie remembered her response clearly.

A sharp exhale. "Twenty-six? God, Sophie. He's older than me. Does he know you're only twenty?"

"Yeah," Sophie had said. "He seemed maybe a little bothered by it, but then he said that he doesn't usually go on dates or, you know, get into relationships. So, I guess this is different. Not that we're in a relationship yet."

Evelyn had been silent for a few moments. "Well, just take it slow, okay? I think it's a little weird that he's into someone six years younger than him. It might say something about his maturity level."

So Sophie didn't want to think about Evelyn's judgment now, of her disapproval. They had acted as equals for so long that Sophie resented when Evelyn tried to play the big sister card. If Sophie could make life-or-death decisions on a mountain, she could handle a romantic relationship. The stakes were much lower.

Sophie spent her last weekend at the cabin in mid-April. The climbing season was about to begin, and she would have to be in the Cascades every weekend, and then full time over the summer, living in bunkhouse-style communal housing. It wasn't the worst deal, a free place to sleep on the outskirts of a beautiful national park. Still, they hadn't talked about it much, she and Miles. She foresaw things ending as simply as they began—two unattached people drifting together and then apart, separated by different passions for the natural world. But she was waiting for him to say it first.

On Sunday morning he handed her a plate of blueberry pancakes, her favorite breakfast. She sat in the armchair, Miles on the couch. "Sorry, nothing fancy this morning," he said. "I feel guilty enough for buying the blueberries out of season. And no candles. Happy birthday?" he chuckled softly.

"This is better than any cake."

A moment of silence passed, made sharper by the physical distance. A cloud had lingered over them all weekend. Sophie wondered if they would simply never address it, or if she would have to draw it out of him like pulling teeth. She thought about moving to the couch to sit beside him. But then he set his mostly full plate aside, looked at her, and said, "We should talk."

"Okay." She looked up, plainly, waiting for him to continue.

"I—well, I think the reason why is obvious." He ran a hand through his hair, still messy from bed. "I have—a proposal of sorts, I guess. It might sound crazy."

"Let's hear it." She could no longer guess where the conversation was going.

"I got offered a job in Wyoming for the summer. Guiding river trips. I did it a few years ago and enjoyed it. And then I was thinking, what the hell is keeping me in Washington? Not much. You, maybe. This cabin is a sweet deal. But I have some cash saved up and I thought, maybe if I save all my pennies, at the end of this summer I could buy a place. Just something small. The guiding is good money. Well, I'm sure you know that." She nodded, and he continued. "So here's the thing that might sound crazy. What if you moved with me?"

Sophie blinked. "I have a job here for the summer. And school."

"I know," he said quickly. "But what about just for the summer? See how you like Wyoming. And—" he raised a hand, preempting her interruption "—I have connections at Grand Teton. I already asked my friend there and he said they're short a guide or two. For climbing. And I'm certain they wouldn't say no to someone with experience."

Sophie's eyes traced the dizzying patterns of the rug for a moment. *He wants me to move to Wyoming with him?* She looked at him again and allowed herself to smile. "I thought you were going to break up with me."

"Me too," he said, and then laughed at the look on her face. "Really. I mean, I don't want this to sound like an ultimatum, but that's probably the alternative. I didn't find out about Wyoming until earlier this week. And I thought, shit, there's no way to make this work. But I like you and I like what we have right now, and I started to wonder if there was a way to stay together. And it seemed like maybe we could. In Wyoming." He paused. "I realize I'm asking a lot of you, to uproot your life even if it's just for a few months."

"And what happens at the end of summer, when I have to go back to school?"

"We'll cross that bridge when we get to it."

Sophie leaned back against the chair. She tended to dive headfirst into these situations without thinking. She knew exactly what Evelyn would say when she heard—that she was being irresponsible. That she wasn't thinking about her future. That the relationship would fizzle out and she'd have to find her way back to Washington, a new job, and the motivation to finish school. *Whatever,* Sophie thought, *why do I care what Evelyn thinks?* It was the first time she had disregarded her sister's hypothetical opinion so quickly. Usually, she could recognize that Evelyn was rational and practical and many other things that Sophie was not. But now, she studied Miles's face, the hopeful expression that worked its way across his brow, and she didn't want to think about what her sister would say. She opened her mouth to speak, but he beat her to it.

"You don't have to decide right this second. But I just want to say that I love you."

She blinked, wondering if she had heard right. They had never said those words to each other before, although Sophie was certain she had felt it, standing by his side in the forest or watching him cook breakfast on a cold morning. Love came easily to Sophie; she had fallen in love with nearly everyone she dated, even for a short time, but she sensed that might not be the same for Miles. He looked so nervous now that she realized she must have heard him correctly.

"I love you too," she replied, and set her uneaten breakfast aside, crossing the living room to tuck herself onto the couch beside him. She stayed silent for a minute, half-facing him, her hand resting on his leg. "Is it bad that I already know my decision?"

"I'm all ears."

"I'll come. For the summer, at least. Assuming I pass all my classes and don't have to retake any."

"You could do it online, if you had to," he replied. "Or not. You don't seem to like school that much anyway." He kissed her, briefly, then stood up and retreated to the kitchen to clean up, so she had to twist over the back of the couch to see him.

"It's not that I don't like it. I'm not good at it. I'm not book smart."

"You can be bad at something and still be successful, if you enjoy it. Look, you hate being in class and studying because you would rather be climbing. And guess what? You're good at climbing. So, you have something that you like, and that you're good at, *and* you can make a living from it. So, why not pursue that?"

She didn't have a good answer. Fear, maybe, of not having a fallback. What if she got injured? The risk would never disappear—some people climbed until they were ancient and never got hurt; some were airlifted off a mountainside in their twenties and never walked again. Or worse, lives were cut short. But Sophie knew the risks. Otherwise, there would be no reward, nothing to make scaling a mountain different from a walk in the park. The real answer was a different kind of fear—she didn't want to disappoint her mother or, worse, Evelyn. She sensed all along that they both doubted she would go to college, her mother especially. Evelyn assumed *everyone* went to college; she didn't seem to consider any alternatives. But her mother always looked at her with sad eyes when they discussed Sophie's future—guiding climbs was not a career, she said, it was a job. If you don't have a degree, you'll never have stable income, never have benefits. Sophie didn't care about that, but she worked hard to improve her grades senior year of high school and secretly applied to the University of Washington. Her mother had cried when she saw the acceptance letter. It was the first time Sophie had sacrificed her own desires to make someone else happy; it would not be the last.

"I don't know," she said to Miles. "Leaving school is a huge decision."

He paused in the middle of wiping down the counter to look at her. "I've thought about getting a degree in something that isn't painting. You know what advice is always given to me? 'School is there forever. Kayak while your body lets you.' You're young and strong right now. You won't be forever. Maybe you'll hit forty and you'll have climbed all the mountains you want to, and you can go back to school then."

"That sounds like it would be incredibly difficult."

He shook his head. "What's incredibly difficult is being good enough to coach novices up mountains. And you're doing that. If you transitioned to full time, you'd make a living, easy." He looked at her plainly. "I think you should drop out. Honestly. I do value my degree. It made me a better painter. But you're studying what, natural resources? What's that got to do with climbing?"

"It's natural resource management. Best practices, policy, that sort of thing. I don't know, I thought park management would be an interesting career."

"Or maybe you'll end up managing guests at a ski resort like your mom. How exciting."

She tilted her head, too surprised by his bluntness to feel any anger. "How is that relevant?"

"Just saying there are career alternatives. I know how much you'd love to follow in her footsteps."

He turned his back to her again. Sophie collapsed against the couch, frustrated by his sarcastic tone. He'd never pushed her like this, challenged her choices beyond acknowledging that she didn't seem to enjoy college. She had never mentioned her mother's career in more depth than passing, when she talked about her childhood of skiing the slopes with Evelyn. She knew how Evelyn would react in a situation like this—she'd get angry—but Sophie only felt anxious. Part of her wondered if Miles was right, if she was on track to a meaningless career with a pretty view. She closed her eyes, wishing she had her sister there for advice and decided she would call her on the drive home. Evelyn knew about Miles; her mother didn't, and how was she going to explain that she was moving to Wyoming for the summer with a man she'd only known for a few months? But Evelyn could help her with that, too. She always knew what to say.

Sophie swallowed the lump in her throat and stood up. "I should get going," she said, crossing the room to grab her coat from the hook by the door.

"Your bag is upstairs," Miles replied. "Hey, wait. You don't have to decide anything today. All of this is your choice—Wyoming, school, all of it. I just think you should really consider how you want the next year of your life to look. It's not the end of the world either way. You're young. We both are. We have time to figure out what we want." He paused. "I'd just like to do that together."

"I know." She moved closer, kissed him, felt the warmth of their bodies pressed together. She pulled away slightly. "Tell your friend in Wyoming that I want the job. We'll go from there."

By the end of summer Sophie realized she was irretrievably in love with two things: Miles and the state of Wyoming. The realization came to her while she was away from both, back home in Colorado. She'd taken a few days off at the beginning of the week to visit her mother and Evelyn, who was also home, on break from law school.

They were sitting on the back porch of one of the lodge buildings, sharing a wooden swing and sipping hard cider from their mother's fridge. "This is nice," Evelyn said aloud. The sun set, spreading its fiery reds and oranges across the low-hanging clouds in the distance. Soon the colors would fade to pink and purple, and then night would settle in. It reminded Sophie of a painting Miles had been working on for the last month, of a glacial river at sunset in the mountains. Already the crickets were beginning to raise a chorus. She felt a twinge of nostalgia for all the afternoons they'd spent like this growing up, both off from school for the summer, bored to death on the ghost-town-like property of the ski resort. Their mother worked year-round—the resort held events like work retreats and weddings. But theirs was a quiet existence in the summertime, marked by long days spent trudging up and down the snowless slopes, trying to find the best views. That was until Evelyn, and shortly after, Sophie, discovered the rock-climbing wall at the local recreation center. Summers were never boring again.

"I'm just glad we're together," Sophie said. She was secretly glad for the break, too. Working in the Tetons was the most exhilarating and challenging experience of her life so far. She climbed every day, even on her days off, and her whole body ached with a force that reminded her, every second, that she was alive. The soreness was still fresh today; yesterday, she had summited Torreys Peak and Grays Peak with Evelyn. But it was good to be back home and to knock out two more 14ers. She twisted now, half turning to Evelyn, her heart pounding in her chest. Afraid of what she had to say but knowing that waiting would only make the reveal worse. "I have something to tell you." She hated the way her voice shook and drew a breath to steady herself. "I'm not going back to Washington this fall. I'm staying in Wyoming."

"What about school?"

Sophie hesitated, and Evelyn connected the dots instantly.

"You're dropping out? Sophie. No way."

"Hear me out before you say anything. I love Wyoming. I love my job. I don't love school. And it'll always be there. If I get injured or give up on climbing, I can always go back." She felt like she was parroting Miles's words, but Evelyn wouldn't know that. Sophie had heard the same speech from Miles nearly every day for the last month, as she wavered between staying in Wyoming and going back to school. A week ago, she had decided that he was right.

"That's not how it works. You'd have to reapply. You'll be older than everyone else. It will be harder to make friends and feel included. Do you understand that? You'll feel years behind."

"And right now, I feel like I'm falling behind on the things

I actually care about." She folded her arms over her chest, defensive. Of course Evelyn would use the standard life trajectory to shame her, the one Evelyn had managed to follow flawlessly. "Look. Clearly, I don't care about graduating at twenty-two and having a normal career."

"But you might when you're thirty-five and a freshman again. Couldn't you just take a semester off? You've only been out there three months. What if you feel differently after six?"

"Why put it off? I don't need a degree to climb mountains and that's what I want to do. I can't think of anything I'd enjoy more. Even natural resource management, if I ended up working in a park—it's all paperwork and uniforms. It's not me."

"Sophie. There's more than one kind of job. You could even change majors now. It might take you an extra year or two to graduate, but a degree is important. It might make your life a lot easier." Evelyn's eyes were full of concern, which only made Sophie more annoyed. She had known exactly how this conversation would go; there were no surprises. Silence fell between them, infiltrated only by the chatter of birds and the low rush of the wind through the trees. The sunset colors had already begun to fade from the sky, replaced by the smooth indigo of late evening. Evelyn sighed. "The truth is, I envy you."

"What do you mean?" Sophie had been about to take a sip of her drink, but she lowered the bottle from her lips, turning toward Evelyn.

"You figured it out. Sorry, I sound sarcastic, but I mean it." Evelyn smiled, her gaze drifting to the mountains bathed in purple light. "You're doing what you love, and you seem pretty sure that you can make it work. I wish I had that kind of faith in myself. This last year...it's been hard. Some mornings I wake up and I have no idea what I'm doing. I look out the window at all the buildings and cars and people, and I feel like some animal taken from its native habitat. It all feels so foreign. But it's what I want to do, right? I'm certainly putting myself into a lot of debt for it." She lifted a hand, seeing Sophie's expression. "And before you say anything, no, I will not drop out of law school to be a guide. I tried that once, remember? It was a disaster."

"I was going to say that I thought *you* were the one that was sure of yourself." She did remember Evelyn's first and only attempt at guiding. She'd taken a job sophomore year of college at a company in Colorado that catered to novice hikers, shepherding them up some of the easier peaks. She'd come home in tears after a month and quit because, in her words, "I just can't get through to any of these people." Later, it was revealed that she often forgot she was guiding at all and silently marched up a mountain, only to realize a few minutes later that her group had disappeared. After the fourth complaint from guests, she'd been fired. *Not a people person, that's okay,* their mother had said. Sophie had laughed about it for a week.

"That's rich," Evelyn said, polishing off her drink. "Well, that just goes to show you, no one actually has it figured out and we're all just pretending." She glanced at her sister. "I won't lecture you. I don't necessarily support this and I'm still not convinced it's for the best. But I know that you're stubborn and you're going to do whatever you want to do, because I'm the same way. Our worst trait, or maybe our best."

"The jury is still out on that one."

A moment passed. "And what about Miles?"

Sophie's heart skipped a beat. She knew, even then, that he played too large of a role in her decisions. But she was wild about him, and he had shown her a way to the mountains. She cleared her throat. "I'm in love with him. I know—I know that doesn't mean much. But I'm happier in Wyoming, with him, than I was in Washington. I don't think Seattle was for me. Or maybe I should say that cities aren't for me. I thought I'd love it. People person and all that, you know. But man. I missed these mountains every single day." She realized that she had wandered away from the question and hoped that Evelyn didn't notice. "There aren't many people around where we live but they're all great. On Friday nights we have beers on someone's back porch and watch the moon rise. It's like— everything I've ever wanted."

"Wow. A real cowgirl." Evelyn laughed as she dodged Sophie's elbow jab. "That's great, I'm happy for you, really. I hope someday I find a place that feels like home."

They stayed silent and looked at the stars, still bright even with the lights shining from the lodge building. A few coyotes trickled out of the woods and made their way across the grass, a familiar sight from the sisters' childhood. They trotted across the field, lifting their noses to the wind, so certain of their path. Despite what Evelyn might think, Sophie wished she felt the same.

CHAPTER SIXTEEN

April 2018,
Yama Parvat Base Camp, Nepal

"There was an avalanche last night."

Evelyn almost asked James to repeat himself, desperate to believe that she had misunderstood. But James's face was somber as he stared beyond the gathered team, out into the unforgiving wilderness.

"I thought I heard something," Danielle said. "I thought I was dreaming."

"No," James said grimly. "It was on the southwest side of the mountain. Where Wojciech's team was climbing."

Evelyn realized that her right hand had involuntarily flown to her mouth. She dropped the hand, annoyed by the dramatics of her own gesture, her stomach sick with anticipation.

"Three of the Polish climbers were killed."

"Christ," Phil muttered. Danielle gasped softly.

"Only three? How?" She hadn't intended the question to sound harsh, but James shot her a look.

"They were camped in two groups, apparently. Wojciech, Nina, and Oskar, and the three they lost, Maja, Krzysztof, and Witold. Not far apart, but enough to make a difference." He took a deep breath. "The three who survived descended last night after the avalanche stopped. Which, I'm sure you all know, is goddamn stupid, but they were in a real state when they arrived early this morning. I was up in the mess tent, waiting for breakfast. I can't sleep with this arm. I thought they had altitude sickness when the three of them burst in. But some of the Adventure Nepal staff had heard the avalanche last night. Satellite confirmed it."

"So, what's going to happen now?" Danielle asked.

"There's going to be a meeting later this morning. They radioed word up to the Japanese team. Don't panic," he said, seeing the look on Evelyn's face. "I don't think anyone is going to suggest that you give up the summit altogether. We just need to discuss safety and logistics."

Evelyn wanted to remind him that it was a mountain, and mountains always took lives, but she bit her tongue. He knew that, given his recent brush with death, and she didn't want to appear insensitive. Besides, her mind was less occupied with the avalanche victims than with the fact that she had slept entirely through the avalanche last night, her second solid night of sleep on the mountain. She had retreated to Lowell's tent after sunset and drifted off to the sound of his pencil scratching away at a crossword puzzle. Thankfully, she had woken before dawn to make her way back to her own tent, feeling like the teenager she never was, the one who snuck out to meet a boy.

Evelyn had been in the middle of getting dressed when James had knocked on her door. She had unzipped it expecting to hear a change of plans, that she, Phil, and Danielle should head to Camp Two before breakfast. Instead, he had summoned her to deliver the news.

"Well," he said. "Go eat or occupy yourselves somehow. You can try to make Camp Two this afternoon," he continued, looking at Evelyn. "If you're up for it. You've got plenty of daylight to work with."

They stood for a moment in uncomfortable silence. No one seemed eager to go to breakfast. Evelyn raised a hand to signal goodbye and stepped away, back to her own tent, where she forced down a few granola bars and some dried fruit. She wanted to see Lowell, to discuss the news with him, but she suspected he was somewhere with his own team, learning of the deaths. She wondered if he had slept through the avalanche, too, or had heard it and chosen not to wake her up.

Three hours later, every climber on the mountain assembled in the mess tent, taking up most of the seats at the three tables. Wojciech sat near the front of the tent, Nina and Oskar on his right and three conspicuously empty chairs on his left. The empty space made Evelyn's heart catch in her throat. Though she hadn't spent much time with the Polish climbers, she respected them, as she did everyone else on the mountain.

She took a seat between Phil and Danielle. Lowell sat across the table, and when they made eye contact, she couldn't decipher the look on his face. Pain, maybe. She knew that he was probably thinking about Pablo, who had died on Kangchenjunga. The way that the bodies of the Polish climbers, like his, would probably never be recovered. A recording device, notebook, and pen sat on the table before him.

At the front of the table, Wojciech cleared his throat. "I'll be brief. We all know why we're here." He paused, his chest rising and falling. Even the act of breathing seemed to hurt him. His weathered face, normally cheerful, looked ashen. "Last night I experienced something that has always haunted me. Something I have prayed to be kept safe from. And I was. But." He stopped again, a small eternity passing as he collected himself. The room was deathly silent. "My climbing partners. My teammates, my dear friends. They were not safe." He raised his eyes to the ceiling, as if directing the next part of his speech to the gods. "I'll never understand why I—we," he corrected himself, gesturing to Nina and Oskar, "were spared." His gaze settled on the table again. "I could spend a lifetime questioning the forces of nature, but the truth remains. Three wonderful, talented people lost their lives last night. No errors were made. We carefully chose our camp location. The question we must ask is, where do we go from here?" A few people began to speak at once. Wojciech raised his left hand and the voices dropped. "I want to be clear. I'm not suggesting that any of us abandon our summit attempts. We're certainly not going to. But we'll be changing our approach."

On the other side of Phil, James raised his hand. Wojciech nodded at him. "I think it's clear that we know less about this mountain than we thought we did. I mean, everything beyond Camp Four is totally unclimbed, unmapped. Some of us—of you—are within a week of reaching that point." He glanced at Yakumo. "I think we have to accept that disasters are going to happen, regardless of our best efforts to prevent them. But what steps can we take to minimize our risk?"

"Exactly," Wojciech replied. "We're abandoning the south ridge. We were making good progress, and it would have been a wonderful achievement, but it's not worth risking any more lives."

Andrew spoke next. "Our group," he said, indicating the

areas of the table where both the Canadians and Americans sat, "is quite large. I think it's been working to our advantage. We have plenty of people to help in an emergency, whether that's staying at camp or descending for help. Like when George collapsed." He glanced at Levi and Sophie. "We were able to assist quite efficiently. We could further condense our groups."

"That's my thought as well," Wojciech said. "We can't be strung out all over the mountain. We've had shit luck with our radios. We need more people in reaching distance."

"You're welcome to join the six of us," Yakumo said. "We're ascending to Camp Three tomorrow."

"Yakumo, thank you. We'll talk later, but I think that makes the most sense for us." His gaze drifted to Sophie. "There's five of your team left now? Who's leading?"

"Three," Sophie replied. Evelyn watched her carefully, feeling an unexpected hint of pride for how confident she seemed in a room full of much more experienced climbers. "Ruslan and Ivan have been climbing separately." She nodded toward the Russian duo, seated several chairs down. "We're still trying to get our feet under us after what happened to George. It would be…" She trailed off, as if it was difficult to say what came next. "Beneficial for us to join a larger group."

"Well, I can't speak for everyone, but I say the more, the merrier," Andrew said.

Evelyn flinched involuntarily. She didn't know what Andrew thought, but she suspected that everyone on the mountain knew, at this point, about the sisters who weren't speaking. Sure, that had changed yesterday, but Evelyn suspected her connection to Sophie was tenuous at best. Perhaps Andrew had forgotten. Evelyn looked to Sophie for her reaction.

Her sister nodded slowly. "We'll think about it." Sophie glanced at Levi, seated beside her. As the conversation in the room moved on, she whispered something to Levi. Evelyn was too far away to read her lips.

"Ruslan, Ivan." Wojciech addressed the two men, regaining the attention of the room that had drifted into side conversations. "Care to join an existing team?"

"Respectfully," Ruslan replied, leaning back in his chair, "no. We have our own plans, our own pace. We need T-shirts that say, maybe, Does Not Climb Well with Others." Only one person chuckled, maybe not the reaction that Ruslan was hoping for, but he pushed on. "We all came here to make our own choices, to decide what's best for us. We'll take care of ourselves."

Wojciech seemed annoyed by the answer. "Well, the offer stands." He said nothing else to the room, just spoke to Nina and Oskar in a low voice, and together the trio rose and left the tent.

Danielle turned to Evelyn. "God. That man lost three of his friends last night, missed death by mere inches, and here he is, wrangling all of us through this meeting."

"He's stronger than I'll ever be," Evelyn admitted. She stood up, eager to leave and retreat to privacy, to be alone with her thoughts. Her head reeled. When she had spoken to Sophie yesterday, she had done so because she thought it would be the last time she would see her sister for a long time. Now, she suddenly faced the reality of seeing her every day. She wondered if Sophie would treat her as a teammate or if she would continue to ignore her, still refusing to expel even an ounce of forgiveness.

Evelyn was swept up in the current of bodies slowly leaving the mess tent. Evelyn made it a few steps outside before Dawa stopped her.

"Phone calls in the comms tent," he announced. "Because of the avalanche."

Evelyn thanked him. It made sense—families at home worried so easily whenever bad news came off a mountain. The climbing news sites, and possibly even larger news organizations, would soon publish stories about the avalanche, and even though the articles would all say *Three Polish climbers were killed. No other injuries were reported*, everyone would worry. She changed her trajectory, and made for the comms tent instead.

There was a long line. She fell in behind one of the Canadian climbers and noticed that Sophie was two people ahead of her. She wondered who she would call—home was the obvious choice, but maybe she had a friend somewhere who would worry about the news. Evelyn had also planned on calling their mother. The line inched forward slowly. She couldn't overhear the phone conversations today; the tent was abuzz with voices, everyone surprisingly talkative given the somber nature of the meeting just a few minutes ago.

When Sophie's phone call was over, she stopped by Evelyn on her way out of the tent. "I called Mom."

"I figured," Evelyn replied. "I'll call someone else. I'm sure she's had enough of us these last few days."

A look of recognition crossed Sophie's face. Though it was unspoken, they both knew who Evelyn would call. "Okay. See you around."

Evelyn watched her leave. Sophie's emotions were never difficult to read. Evelyn had been trying to avoid the reality of Miles; she intentionally hadn't mentioned him in their conversation yesterday.

When it was her turn at the phone, she dialed the familiar numbers and held her breath. It rang three times before he answered, and she had just relinquished hope of speaking to him when she heard his voice, low and smooth even over the poor-quality connection.

"Hello?"

"Miles? It's me."

A pause. "Well, good. I thought maybe it was some stranger calling to tell me you'd fallen off the mountain."

She grimaced. "That's the reason I'm calling. My feet are firmly on the mountain, but there was an avalanche last night. It buried a few members of the Polish team. I didn't want you to read about it and worry."

"I'm not worried." *Ouch*, Evelyn thought, remembering how blunt he was capable of being. "About you, I mean. Sorry, I know how that sounded. I saw an article this morning. I knew you were safe."

"Right," she said, a little hurt by his flippancy. "Well, I thought you'd still want to hear from me." She stayed quiet for a moment. "Look, I know the state we left things was confusing."

"It felt pretty clear to me. Evelyn, you getting on the plane was the biggest 'fuck you' imaginable. You left us both with empty bank accounts."

"It's not my sole job to bring in money, Miles. I said I would cover us through the end of our lease, and I budgeted for that. When I get home, we'll have to sit down and go over a new budget together. Maybe find a cheaper apartment. We're both responsible for our living situation. This isn't just on me."

"But you're the one who left—you'll be gone for months, and I have to cover any unexpected expenses in the meantime. You know it's difficult for me to compete right now, and what am I supposed to do if my art isn't selling? I can only do so much."

"I don't have all the answers. Like I said, we have to fig-

ure that out together. But this was a once-in-a-lifetime opportunity for me. Unclimbed peaks don't suddenly spring up
out of nowhere. I'll likely never get a chance like this again."
She paused, still struggling with the idea that he didn't understand. "This was important to me, you should know that.
I've never tried to stop you from traveling to kayak, have I?"

"That's different. You didn't used to have this one-track
mind about climbing, with no room for anything else. You
used to want things—to practice law, to go to dinner with
me, to just—I don't know, build a future together. I'm happy
for you, Evelyn, really. I'm glad you're chasing your dreams.
But I feel a little bit screwed over in the process."

"Wait." The conversation had slipped out of her control.
"This trip just came at a bad time for us. But there are ways
to make this work, so we can both have what we want."

He laughed, a burst of static through the phone. "How?
You quit your job and left me to go climb a mountain. Sounds
like the only real concern is what you want. You keep saying
'together,' but I was the one left to figure it out on my own.
Well, if you want to be selfish, if you want to leave your re-
sponsibilities and me behind, I'm not going to wait around
for you to come back."

Evelyn inhaled a shaky breath, wondering what he could
possibly expect her to say. She hadn't anticipated such a vicious
reaction from him. "Okay. I understand. You won't hear from
me again until after the summit. Then we can—we can talk, I
guess. I—I love you, Miles. Bye." She clicked off the satellite
phone without waiting for his response and sat for a moment,
fighting back tears. She rarely cried, but everything about the
conversation made her want to. She could acknowledge that
things hadn't been perfect with him a few months ago, but

they had been fixable. She would have gone to Vermont with him. He wasn't even going to give her the opportunity.

"Are you finished?"

She turned to see Oskar behind her. "Oh. Yes. Sorry." She handed the phone over and stepped away from the chair, ashamed of hogging the phone from someone who clearly needed it more. Still, she couldn't shake the feeling of shock. What if she never saw Miles again? What if he was already gone by the time she got back? That meant that everything— the grief she put Sophie through, the strained relationship with her mother—would have been for nothing. It was enough to make her head spin.

She spent the next few hours in a daze, alone in her tent, staring at the thin red ceiling and letting her mind go blank, something like meditation. She used to meditate with Sophie on climbs, sit together and see who could go still the longest, sometimes passing whole hours in silence. Sophie almost always won, but Evelyn could hold her own on the right day. Today, she left her body out of necessity, afraid of her own thoughts if she indulged them.

At the tail end of the lunch hour, she emerged and drifted to the mess tent, happy to find it mostly empty. As she finished her meal Andrew entered, lifting his hand in a wave when he saw her.

"There you are," he said once he reached her. "I've been all over Base Camp looking for you."

"Sorry," she replied around a mouthful of food. "What's up?"

"We're pushing to Camp Two. Whenever everyone's ready, no big rush. I know you've kind of stepped in for James, so I wanted to check with you first, make sure you're on board. The trio is coming with us."

She knew he meant Sophie, Levi, and Penelope. "Okay."

"That won't cause any—issues?"

She blinked. "Andrew, it's alright. We're all adults here." Though she felt confident, after her conversation with Sophie, that they would be civil with each other, her stomach still churned at the thought of spending every day together.

"Okay." Andrew didn't try to hide the surprise on his face. "Well. I'm happy to hear that. Hey, meet us around the supply tent in the next forty-five minutes or so, okay?"

Evelyn nodded, frustrated that her earlier assumption had been confirmed, and doubly annoyed that James had been the one to discuss her relationship with Sophie. But it was no longer her and Sophie, a single unit, a united duo. They were separate individuals now. So she would need to push her limits, to reach the summit, to prove herself capable of scaling big mountains without her sister. She had failed on Lhotse, but Yama Parvat was a different mountain. She retreated to her tent and readied herself for the climb.

That they were climbing in the afternoon instead of waiting for the morning worried her, but it was an overcast day, which lessened the risk of sunburn and overheating. The sun could be brutal at high altitude, where the UV radiation increased, burning any exposed skin and causing climbers to overheat. At the same time, cloudy days carried the risk of snow. She knew that the forecast for today showed no snow and little wind, an unusual day in the Annapurna range. They would reach Camp Two by sunset.

Once her bag was packed and her down suit donned, she forced herself up and out to meet the others gathering by the supply tent. She was always amused by how comical they all looked from afar in their down suits and jackets, like a moon landing with more colorful attire. Her own suit was plain ma-

roon, gifted by a sponsor years ago. They offered her a new
suit every year, the latest technology, but her old suit had kept
her warm and dry through several summits now—she couldn't
bring herself to get rid of it while it was still functional.

She took her place beside her teammates. Sophie, Levi,
and Penelope stood off to the side. Once the last Canadian
climbers trickled in, Andrew clapped his hands and moved
to address the group.

"Alright, thanks for all showing up. I know it's been a
strange twenty-four hours. We're climbing this afternoon because the weather is nice. Up to Camp Two. This is a good test
of the logistics of getting such a large group up this mountain."
He glanced at the trio. "We usually go Americans first, then
us since we're a larger group. We could throw you in front or
tack you on at the end. What do you think?"

"We'll go last," Sophie replied, without hesitation. "Until
we get a sense of your speed."

"Fair enough." Andrew turned his gaze to Evelyn. "Did
I miss anything?"

Evelyn shook her head. "You're good at this. I'd just say,
'okay, let's go.'"

Andrew grinned at her. "Okay. Let's go."

Evelyn took her place, first in line, as they headed up the
mountain. It hadn't snowed in several days, so there was no
powder to fight through. Small gusts of wind sent loose bits
of snow sparkling through the air and occasionally stinging the miniscule amounts of exposed skin on Evelyn's face.
They climbed steadily, uneventfully, traversing a couple of
crevasses with ladders that were old news by now to all three
groups, who had done their share of trekking to Camp Two.
Evelyn could tell that she was acclimatizing; it was easier to

keep breathing. Occasionally she stole a glance up at the summit, the shelf of snow that loomed far above them, still more
than a mile away. She had visualized herself standing up there
several times over the last few weeks, whenever she needed
motivation to continue. Somehow it now felt farther away
than ever. The first couple of weeks had been full of excitement, arriving on the fresh slopes of an unclimbed mountain,
a new question waiting to be answered. This part of the expedition, the weeks of trudging up and down to acclimatize,
Evelyn and Sophie had always referred to as "the slog." They
weren't the only ones. It was the tedious, soul-crushing part
of climbing, massive exertions of effort only to retreat. To an
outsider, it would look like no progress was being made. But
to rush straight up without acclimatizing was an almost guar-
anteed death sentence.

They passed through the empty lower snowfield as the sun
began to slip behind some of the other massive peaks. For a
few brief minutes the surrounding mountains came alive with
alpenglow, reflecting purple, pink, and gold. The sight took
Evelyn's breath away, but still they climbed on, so she averted
her eyes to the ground in front of her, lifting her hands to
switch on her headlamp. She glanced over her shoulder for a
moment, watching the line of lights turn on behind her like
fireflies bobbing in the darkness. Seracs, huge columns of glacial ice the size of houses, rose on all sides, eerie blue and silver
shapes that resembled twisted figures erupting from the snow.

She had spent enough time at Camp Two to recognize that
the ice formations meant they were close. Another thirty minutes of walking and they arrived at the flat snowfield amid the
rising rock and ice. On a mountain like Everest, Camp One
and even Camp Two might include some Base Camp com-
forts: a mess tent, an outhouse. Since Yama Parvat had never

been climbed, the accommodations were nothing more than bare ground at higher altitude.

Evelyn stepped aside, allowing the others to trickle beyond her. Phil and Danielle stopped too, reminding Evelyn that she wasn't alone on the mountain.

"What are we doing tomorrow?" Danielle asked.

"I imagine we'll wake up early and push to Camp Three, then descend to Base Camp. I'll have to talk to Andrew, see what he thinks of the summit window." She paused. "Unless you would want to break off and climb on our own."

Phil and Danielle exchanged a look. "You heard the consensus this morning," Phil said. "Everyone thinks that larger groups are the best decision."

"Is this because of—"

"No," Evelyn said, cutting Danielle off because she knew what question was coming. "No, I just thought I'd check."

"It's up to you, Evelyn," Phil said, though she suspected he was only placating her.

"We'll stick with Andrew. Unless our schedules don't align. See you at dinner?"

She stayed still for a moment, watching her teammates disperse to find campsites, before crossing the snowfield in search of Andrew. She found him talking to a few of his teammates, but he broke off when he saw her.

"Hey. Just wanted to check logistics. What are you thinking about the summit window?"

Andrew considered her question for a moment, running a hand through his short beard. Finally, he shrugged. "I don't really know. Within the next week or ten days, maybe." He paused, as if he didn't want to continue. "Look. The avalanche last night wasn't a good sign. If conditions are getting too warm, that might happen more frequently. We didn't want to freeze our asses off by coming too early in the season, but I'm worried that we'll overstay our welcome. So, if we have a day of good weather soon, I say we go for it."

Evelyn nodded. "Thanks. That's what I wanted to hear."

"I'm not worried about you, Evelyn. But I don't want anyone else to get in over their head."

They parted ways. Evelyn headed across the snowfield to scout for a tent site, wanting to get as much quiet sleep as possible. The higher the altitude, the more difficult it was to sleep—in the death zone, above twenty-six thousand feet, she often felt like she was fighting for air while unconscious. She didn't know yet if her team would use oxygen for the summit of Yama Parvat. There were plenty of oxygen bottles stashed at Base Camp, which the guides would carry to higher elevations if the teams decided. So far, no one had climbed high enough to require extra air.

She set about pitching her tent, using the light from her headlamp to navigate the poles and stakes. She had received a new tent from her sponsor for this trip, although it was the same model as her old tent, which had survived several expeditions before wearing thin to the point of ripping on Lhotse. She had watched the small hole grow larger with each day, until she finally squeezed into a teammate's tent above Camp Three. She kept the battered tent in a box under her bed back home. She tried not to think of what was—or wasn't—waiting for her back in New York.

"Is this spot taken?"

She looked up to see Lowell, wading through the darkness. She smiled and shook her head. "All yours. I'm happy to see you."

"I'm glad to see you too. I was stuck at the ass end of the climbing train all afternoon. I get it, I'm big and slow. But talk about a depressing view, all of us climbing uphill like a bunch of ants. I much prefer being up front."

"Well, then I can't complain." She set about removing her sleeping pad and bag from her backpack and unrolling them into the tent. "Although I don't know how you can call any view on this mountain depressing. It's not commercialized like some of the others."

"That's true. But a hundred years ago, there'd be one small team trying to reach the peak, not five all going for it at once."

"And that team would have all died from frostbite or been wiped out by an avalanche." She paused. "Was that too soon?"

He shrugged. "It's reality. Wojciech seems to be handling it, though." He finished arranging his belongings inside the tent and stepped back. "Gives me more to write about, anyway."

"The way this expedition is going, you'll have enough for a book when we're done."

"Maybe." He gazed at her for a moment, then indicated his tent. "Want to sit for a minute?"

Evelyn nodded, thankful for the invitation to rest her tired legs. She paused to take off her boots as she entered and then sat back in her familiar position on the sleeping pad, across from Lowell on his sleeping bag. She glanced at his backpack, the top of which was open, overflowing with notebooks.

"How are the interviews coming?" she asked.

Lowell shook his head, a wry smile crossing his lips. "Some people here sure are cagey. Like your sister. I cornered her for five minutes the other day, and she gave one-word answers to all my questions." He looked at Evelyn and frowned. "Sorry. I shouldn't have brought her up."

"No, it's okay. That's funny. It sounds like her." Evelyn allowed herself to smile as she lied to him. It didn't sound like friendly, easygoing Sophie at all, who used to ham it up whenever she was interviewed for an article. Sophie must be under enormous stress after George's health issue—or she no longer wanted to be in the public eye.

"Yeah, but hearing about her upsets you," Lowell replied. "I can tell."

"No," she said, shaking her head. "We actually spoke the other day. It's not like we're friends again, but we had a full conversation for the first time in years."

"Oh yeah? That's great. So then, what's bothering you?"

The phone call with Miles flashed through Evelyn's mind. "Nothing important. It's just stressful, you know, standing in for James. Not that I'm doing anything but following Andrew's lead."

"Hey, if I remember correctly, you led us up here this afternoon. I didn't see Andrew holding your hand."

"Yeah, you're right." She shrugged. "It's just not how I envisioned this trip going."

"I think that's true for everyone."

Lowell's radio buzzed, a brief burst of static, and he reached down to fiddle with it. Evelyn watched him for a moment, no other distractions to draw her attention away. It was another windless night on Yama Parvat.

"I'll miss you," she said, surprising herself even though it was true.

He looked up. "What, did you just have a premonition about my death?"

"No, I meant…when this is all over."

She couldn't tell if he was smiling. "We'll see each other on another mountain, I'm sure."

Momentary courage pulsed in Evelyn's chest. The mounting dread of going back to New York, of continuing the fight with Miles, of finding another job in a career she wasn't sure she wanted was too much. She didn't even know if she had Miles to return to. It dawned on her that she had nothing left to lose. "What if we didn't have to wait that long? What if we got dinner together, in Kathmandu, before we fly home?"

He regarded her for a moment before replying. "Like a date?"

"Maybe." Yes, if she spoke to Miles again before she flew home and they decided to break up.

Lowell exhaled and looked down at his hands. "That's sweet of you, Evelyn. But I don't think my wife would like that very much."

Evelyn blinked. "Wait. You're *married*? You've never mentioned a wife."

"You're right. I don't talk about her much. But that's not for a lack of love. I don't wear my ring because, god, can you imagine losing your wedding ring in the Himalayas? I'd never hear the end of it. Not to mention the swollen fingers. But I do keep it with me." He reached for his down jacket, folded nearby, and fumbled through one of the interior pockets. Evelyn watched in silence. "Here," he said, producing the wedding band. "My wife doesn't know. She thinks I leave it with a friend each time. But I can't imagine dying without having this close to me." He stopped, as if remembering why he was showing the ring in the first place. "I'm sorry. Maybe my desire for friendship came off differently than I intended."

"That's an understatement." She shifted, uncomfortable, and looked down as images from their last couple of weeks together inundated her brain. "Why'd you spend so much time with me? Let me sleep over?" Indignation surged through her, stemming, she knew, from the embarrassment of rejection. From this small, desperate attempt to explore something new.

Lowell's expression softened. "You seemed like you needed

a friend. Especially after we talked about Sophie. And then you had to deal with James's injury. It's a lot to take on alone. I didn't want you to feel like you had no one to talk to."

"You took pity on me," Evelyn said. She leaned back, away from Lowell, drumming her fingers on the sleeping pad. "God. This always happens. I let someone in and then realize I liked them for all the wrong reasons. Even Miles. I don't understand how things turned out." Her words dissolved into a laugh as the absurdity of the situation struck her. The events of the last three years had led her to here, a practical stranger's tent, twenty-one thousand feet in the air. She'd wasted thousands of dollars on law school in return for disillusionment and un-certainty. She'd ruined her sister's marriage, to say nothing of their relationship. She'd put her mother in an impossible situ-ation. And Miles—it wasn't her fault entirely, but she hadn't seen him for who he really was. A narcissist, taking advantage of others who offered something that he wanted, or at least what he believed would improve his own life. And she'd be-lieved that he truly cared about her. How stupid she'd been.

"Who is Miles?" Lowell asked.

Had she never mentioned him either? Evelyn shook her head. "No one."

Lowell cleared his throat. "In the past, when I've been un-satisfied by my relationships, I've reexamined and found that I was the common denominator. Maybe you're doing some-thing to alienate—"

"I'm plenty aware of just what a wonderful person I've been recently," Evelyn replied. She crawled to the door—an undignified exit, how fitting for the situation—and glanced at Lowell. "I'll see you around."

He was quiet as she left. Evelyn straightened up outside, allowing the shock of cold air to pass through her. She took one step in the direction of her tent before she heard a loud banging—the dinner bell, someone hitting a pot and pan together. Tackling the next day on an empty stomach was a bad idea. So, she set off across the snowfield, quickly reaching Andrew's tent, where he doled out the noodle cups and jerky from Mingma's backpack.

"Set your alarm for 4:00," he told each climber as they took their share.

Evelyn set the alarm on her watch for 3:45 a.m. She thought that Andrew would probably rise even earlier and make plenty of noise to wake up everyone still sleeping, and he might appreciate having backup. When she looked up, she noticed that Sophie stood a few feet away. It jarred her until she remembered her new reality, that now Sophie would always be present. She approached her sister.

"Hi, Sophie. How are you?"

Sophie flinched and Evelyn realized that she must have been zoned out, or at least hadn't noticed Evelyn. She turned her head, regarding Evelyn for a moment before she replied. "I've been better."

"Oh. Tough climb up?"

She shook her head. "This new situation is strange." She looked so pointedly at Evelyn that there was no need to guess at what she meant. "You keep trying to talk to me. I don't get it."

"I just want..." Evelyn trailed off, unsure of how to proceed. "I don't want to never speak again, Sophie. I thought maybe you wanted to be in each other's lives again, too. Levi told me—"

"Leave him out of it," Sophie replied, her voice sharp. "I don't care what he said to you. He doesn't fully understand the situation and never will."

Evelyn blinked. Despite the wide-open space, she felt cornered. The others had drifted away, leaving Sophie and Evelyn alone in the darkness. She didn't know how far their voices carried. "Okay. I'm sorry. I just don't want us to go on not speaking forever."

"Sure. To make yourself feel better. You should have thought about that before..." She trailed off and took a shaky breath. Evelyn stepped closer. To her surprise, there were tears in Sophie's eyes. She lifted a hand to reach for her sister, without thinking, but Sophie stepped back, brushing away the tears before they froze on her cheeks. "I'm so tired of feeling angry." She exhaled in a burst somewhere between a laugh and a sob. "I just don't understand why you're acting like Miles doesn't exist. Why do you think that you can just gloss over him and pretend that everything is normal?"

"It's not that...this isn't about him, not entirely," Evelyn said.

"Then why did you call him?"

"Because we're still together. And while things have been better between us, I know he still cares about me. And because that's what you do—you try. You try to work things out and you try to find a way forward instead of staying stuck in the past, constantly blaming other people for the state your life is in." Evelyn's cheeks burned, partly from shame and partly from anger. "Are you happy now? Knowing that it's not working out the way I wanted?"

Sophie gave her a withering look. "I don't care about him, or about your relationship. That's not where my anger ever came from. It was a lot easier to accept that he was a horrible person than it was to accept the same about you. I knew Miles was never going to stay. He had one foot out the door after that first winter in Wyoming. But you lied to me and kept your relationship secret for almost a year. I would never have done something like that to you."

Evelyn felt the sharp sting of tears in her eyes. She forced herself to breathe and keep looking at Sophie, even though the thin sliver of moon overhead, not yet a full quarter, darkened the features of her sister's face. "Sophie," Evelyn said, her voice strangled and raw, "are you ever going to be able to forgive me?"

Sophie regarded her for a moment, still and silent. She stayed quiet for so long that Evelyn wondered if Sophie had heard her, or if her words were lost to the mountain. But then Sophie spoke.

"I don't know. I thought I could. But seeing you here—talking to you—it's so painful."

"There must be something—"

"Please, Evelyn." Sophie cut her off. "Just leave me alone. This isn't the right time. I'm so tired."

Evelyn watched Sophie turn away and retreat to her tent with slow, shuffling footsteps. The snow seemed to muffle everything, not to mention the dark blanket of night that draped itself over the mountain. So that was it. Her last chance to reestablish a friendship with Sophie, lying ruined and broken in the snow. She might never speak to Sophie again.

Evelyn trudged back across the shadowy snowfield. Approaching her tent, she heard a strange sound and looked behind her. In the barren space close to the mountain's edge, a pair of small black birds sparred, hopping close and away from each other and producing small, rippling calls. She watched in disbelief. She had seen the birds, choughs—or goraks, as the locals called them—many times before in the Himalayas, but never at nighttime and never at such high elevation. She watched for a moment longer, until the battle seemed to end. One bird lifted off in flight, swooping down into the nighttime. The other bird edged toward the cliff and seemed to debate its options before taking flight as well. She scanned the snowfield for signs of more goraks, but the mountain was deserted by all life. Except her. She retreated to her tent and did not sleep.

CHAPTER SEVENTEEN

October 2015,
Manhattan, New York

"I have a favor to ask you."

"Of course you do." Evelyn sighed, cradling her phone against her shoulder as she picked up her mug of tea. "Go on," she said, wandering over to the couch.

"This weekend," Sophie said, "Miles has a gallery show and an exhibit at a museum. I think I told you?"

"You didn't," Evelyn said, "but go on." She curled up on the couch, letting her gaze slide over to the window as the autumn evening fell, casting golden light into her apartment and deepening the shadows. She was eager for night to come; she had run errands in the city for most of the day and her body ached for stillness and quiet, which the dark always seemed to bring—nighttime didn't exactly shut out the sounds of horns honking and sirens wailing, but it softened them.

"He was supposed to stay with a friend but then the heat broke in the apartment, so that guy can't even stay at his home right now. And Miles asked around but no one else has room for him to stay. So, we—I—was wondering if—"

"You want to know if he can stay with me?" A twinge in Evelyn's stomach registered her unease before her mind did.

"Please, Evelyn," Sophie said, her voice breathless. "He really can't miss these events." Evelyn heard a faint clatter through the line, and Sophie cursed under her breath.

"Why can't he get a hotel? Also, what are you doing?"

"I'm stacking firewood," Sophie said. "And I just got a huge splinter in my finger." She paused, and Evelyn waited. "Got it," she said after a moment. "It's gotten so cold here. Last winter was brutal. I want to be prepared."

"Sophie. A hotel?"

"Oh," she said, as if she'd hoped to avoid the question. "We just...we can't really afford it right now. Money's tight from all the repairs to the cabin. We found a bunch of issues last winter that we have to fix before it snows again. It's, uh, a rapidly approaching deadline."

Evelyn wanted to ask Sophie about the money situation, but kept her mouth shut. It wasn't as if she had any to spare herself. She swallowed her concern and forced herself to sound neutral. "Okay. He can stay here."

The relief in Sophie's voice was obvious. "Oh, thank you so much. Seriously. You're a lifesaver."

"It's no problem. I've got a perfectly fine couch."

"Well, still. We really, really appreciate it."

We. It was strange to hear Sophie refer to herself and Miles as a unit, although Evelyn knew that was exactly what they were. She ran her finger over the gray fabric covering the couch's arm. "What's the exhibit?"

"I don't know all the details," Sophie said. "It's called... *Wild America.* Some new museum, I think. I guess the gallery show is related. Look, you know I've always been bad about keeping up with his art. I do know he'll be there Thursday night to Sunday, at the latest."

Evelyn grimaced. She hadn't shared her space with anyone for that long since sophomore year of college. Still, she felt an unexpected flash of pride for Miles. Maybe a little success would bring some money that he and Sophie seemed to need.

Evelyn said goodbye to Sophie and hung up. Three more days before Miles arrived. At least the apartment wasn't a mess; she cleaned religiously, three times a week, though she rarely welcomed visitors—a few friends for dinner, occasionally, but those were relaxed affairs for the sole purpose of commiseration about work. *Expect the unexpected*, her mother always said, and that translated into Evelyn having an apartment clean enough to welcome a dignitary at any given moment.

She had no idea what Miles expected but hoped she would remember to turn on the lights.

She got home late on Thursday. Miles waited in the lobby, forlorn and out of place. He wore a green shirt that had seen better days and pants that looked like they'd been on one too many river runs. She approached him, apologizing for making him wait, but he shook his head and wrapped an arm around her shoulders in a haphazard hug.

"Evelyn. It's good to see you. I can't tell you how much I appreciate you for letting me stay here."

His affection surprised her. She pulled back, appraising him up close. "You look tired. Bad trip?"

"No," he replied, gathering his bags and following her to the elevator. "Just a lot of days on no sleep. All I can say is, never buy a house."

"That bad?" she asked, pushing the button for the sixth floor.

"No. It's great, honestly. Well, you've seen the cabin. Those woods and that creek are priceless. Forty-minute drive to town, which isn't bad unless there's snow. Honestly, that property is worth a hell of a lot more than the house is. Some millionaire could buy it, raze the cabin and a few trees, and build a big old log cabin mansion. I've found they tend to prefer open land, though. Gotta let everyone else around know how rich you are by plunking down a massive house visible from the road," he said with a grin. "I like being in the woods. I don't have to look at them and they don't have to look at me. The way it should be. But—oh, right," he continued, as if just remembering her question, "it's a lot of work. Nearly every damn part of that house has had to be fixed, and as soon as I get done with a repair, something else breaks. It's like caring for an elderly parent who just isn't ready to go yet. Always sick, but full of great stories."

As they stepped out of the elevator, Evelyn thought back to the wedding and the broken pipe that had delayed Miles's arrival in Colorado. "I admit, before I visited, I was curious about where you were living, so I looked at houses for sale near there. I was shocked. Everything was over a million dollars." She fumbled with her key ring, unlocking her apartment door. "I can't complain about renting. I don't have to fix anything."

He followed her inside. "Yeah, we got lucky. That guy I used to kayak with in Washington, Ron, owned it. I'm sure Sophie told you about him. That place I had near Seattle, I rented it from him. When I got the job offer in Wyoming, he told me about a place he owned out there too. Said he hadn't visited in years, had no idea what shape it was in. But he wanted it gone and was willing to let me have it for dirt cheap. I think I was like a son he never had." He paused. "I feel like I just keep getting lucky. Meeting Sophie, the house, my art—I keep waiting for the other shoe to drop."

"Some people are just like that," Evelyn replied, circling the counter. "Lucky, I mean. Do you want coffee?" She had been up since 5:30 a.m., and now that she was home, the wave of exhaustion finally broke. If she was going to entertain a guest as talkative as Miles, she needed to stay awake.

"Sure."

"How is Sophie?"

"She's good. Busy. I think she's made friends with every single person in the park. She feels bad about missing out on some of this climbing season, but she never stops talking about your trip. She'll be guiding backcountry skiing and snowshoeing this winter. She really wants you to come out soon."

Annoyance flashed through Evelyn. She had spent all summer with Sophie, successfully summiting K2. They climbed Broad Peak after, though Evelyn felt it was a drag in comparison, with little technical climbing. The challenge of Broad Peak came in the remoteness—K2 had been fairly crowded with other teams hoping to conquer the savage mountain. But on Broad Peak there was only one other team, some French climbers who seemed determined to keep their distance from the sisters. Evelyn spent too much time worrying about the logistics of getting help in an emergency, and Sophie would remind her that their fate was in the hands of the mountain. Simple. Sophie seemed to have a better relationship with her own mortality than Evelyn could ever hope for, yet another thing she didn't struggle with. When the sisters flew back to New York, they'd gotten matching tattoos of K2, the sharp pyramid with its distinct furrows and ridges finding a place on each sister's arm, Sophie's right, Evelyn's left. She touched the tattoo often, tracing the outline of the mountain and reminding herself that she would always find a way back to climbing, even when she felt trapped by the city's claws.

And all that time—it wasn't enough? Evelyn knew she was swimming against the current, trying to maintain her relationships with friends and family and the mountains, in a place that forced her into ever-greater isolation. Not to mention work. Sophie didn't see it that way. Ever since she'd moved to Wyoming with Miles, time had seemed infinite to Sophie, a great stretch of future that involved only climbing and friends and seeing the world.

Evelyn took a steadying breath, trying to release her bitterness as she poured a cup of coffee for Miles. "I'm sorry. I really do want to visit. It's just that—"

He waved a hand, dismissive. "You're a lawyer. No one expects you to have free time."

"I still feel lucky that I got hired by my firm. But it's been pretty much nonstop since day one. A lot of stress." She shook her head. "Shocking, right? I'm complaining that work feels like work."

"I bet it's nice sometimes. Honestly. Having so much structure to your days. I miss that part of college. I mean, I wasn't the best at staying on track. But at least I had classes at scheduled times. Now it's all up to me, and I'm not the best at managing my time. It's hard, when your backyard is full of rivers."

Evelyn blinked. "You went to college?"

He grinned. "Don't look so surprised. It was art school. I'm still an idiot."

"No, it's just that Sophie never mentioned it. I assumed you had a similar lifestyle. You know, foregoing the standard path for an outdoorsy one." She paused. "I hope I don't sound pretentious. I envy Sophie sometimes."

"No, no way in hell my parents would have let me just dis-

appear to kayak. Letting me go to art school was enough of
a concession. But I got a full ride, so they couldn't say no."

Evelyn thought of how much happier her mother would
be if Sophie had finished college. "Wow. That's impressive.
No wonder you're such a good painter."

He shrugged. "I guess so. I did learn a lot. But to be fair,
I spent most of my free time in an inebriated haze. I think it
would have been worse if I hadn't gone to school, honestly.
No discipline at all, spending all day running rivers? I would
have been homeless within a few weeks." He paused, took a
sip of coffee, and glanced at her. "I have to ask. Do you always keep the lights off, or just for guests?"

Evelyn's hand flew to her mouth. "Oh, I'm so sorry. I'm
awful about turning the lights on. I didn't even notice." She
moved to pass by him, heading for the light switch near the
door, but he caught her arm. The gesture surprised her, and
she stopped.

"Don't. It's nice, honestly. I'm getting used to it."

She stepped back as he let go, still embarrassed. "It's a habit
I've picked up. The city is so overwhelming. I feel like keeping the apartment dark helps to seal in as much of the peace
and quiet as possible."

"I'd say that's a good reason. We all develop weird habits
in our private spaces anyway."

She had never thought of her apartment as a *private space*,
mostly because living in the city felt like sharing her apartment
with everyone else in the building, plus everyone walking by
on the street outside, and—why not—everyone in the apartment building across from her too. She liked to drink tea in
the evenings by the living room window, watching the city
light up as the sunlight faded. Law school had turned her partially nocturnal; all her life, she had been a morning person,

but as the assignments piled up, she found herself staying up later and later. Sometimes she wished she had Sophie's ability to compartmentalize. For Evelyn, it was all or nothing; she wouldn't rest until all her work was accomplished and as close to perfect as possible. She always felt close to burnout but hadn't tipped over the edge. Yet.

She glanced away from Miles, self-conscious of how much she had just revealed about herself. He had called it *weird*. She cleared her throat. "Would you like to grab dinner? I haven't eaten yet."

He straightened up, shaking his head. "Sorry, I can't. I gotta run down to the gallery tonight and I'm not sure how long it'll take. Then the museum in the morning, I think. Lunch tomorrow?"

"I'll be at work, and I can't bet on being able to take that long a break." She paused, then surprised herself. "But I'd like to come to the gallery opening. It's tomorrow night, right?"

He nodded. "Seven o'clock to 9:00. You don't have to come for the whole thing, obviously. But it would be nice of you to stop by."

"Of course. I can take some pictures for Sophie. Is it like…" She trailed off, searching for the word. "An expensive gallery? Should I dress nice?"

Miles grinned. "Yeah, maybe don't show up in jeans. The museum on Saturday is black tie. I'm not looking forward to that." He stretched, extending his arms above his head. "I should get going. I'll be back pretty late, so I'll try to be quiet coming in."

Evelyn pushed off the counter and opened one of the drawers. "Here's the spare key. Just tell the doorman you're staying with me if he asks. He's kind of nosy."

"Yeah, he was really staring me down earlier. I told him I was waiting for you, but he seemed suspicious."

Evelyn shrugged. "Like I said, he's nosy. It's his job. Anyway, make yourself comfortable. I'll see you sometime tomorrow."

As soon as Miles left, she exhaled. When had he become so easy to talk to? She had expected him to be dismissive and arrogant. But he seemed different now, more relaxed, with those startling green eyes always trained on her, and a willingness to listen to her, even if they'd mostly discussed his life. Often, she liked not being the center of attention, not having to dredge up some interesting information about herself to appease someone else. Beyond the mountains and her job, Evelyn considered herself a void, nothing worth noting. Luckily, those two topics were all anyone ever seemed to care about.

She set about straightening up the kitchen and then turned on one of the lights underneath the hanging cabinets, so he wouldn't come back to total darkness. She sat down at her desk and surrounded herself with work until her thoughts of Miles faded away.

The next evening, Evelyn sat on the 4 train, closing her eyes as the car swayed around her, lulled almost to sleep. She was exhausted and looking forward to sleeping in for an extra hour tomorrow and hitting the gym before another day spent glued to her desk. Or maybe she would go for a run in Central Park. The weather forecast promised a crisp day, and the leaves in the park were starting to turn now that it was October.

After returning home, Evelyn had eaten a quick dinner and stepped into a little black dress. She hadn't spoken to Miles yet that day, although he had been asleep on the couch when she woke up that morning. She had tiptoed past him into the kitchen, forcing down black coffee and heading out the door.

She got off the subway and walked a block to the gallery, housed on three floors of a bright, modern building with floor-to-ceiling windows. She checked her coat at the door and wandered in, surprised at the number of people. She took an hors d'oeuvre, a little toasted piece of bread adorned with a stuffed squash blossom, from a passing waiter. The severity of the gallery—sheer white walls and glowing white light— combined with the number of people overwhelmed her. She fell in step behind a couple, following their path through the gallery as they parted the sea of people.

She spotted Miles's paintings as soon as she rounded the corner to the last room. The two massive landscapes took up the back wall, and though she knew there was art all around her, she couldn't tear her eyes away from his. She had only seen his finished works in photos before, pictures that Sophie sent of Miles painting on the back porch in the dead of winter, bundled in a coat stained with a rainbow of colors.

It was different, seeing the paintings in person; their sheer size arrested her. A man coughed behind her and she stepped aside, still drifting forward. Painting a river was no revolutionary act, but these were different—neither of these rivers wandered through a bucolic meadow with banks choked by flowering trees. No, both of these rivers were fierce—deadly, even—cutting through gorges in winter, snow falling through the foreground in one and in the other, complete stillness, the lack of any movement in the white landscape except for the tumbling river overflowing its banks. The mountains in the distance were gray at the bottom, losing their snow. She stood for a long time in the center of the room, breathing, trying to understand why she was so awestruck. She missed the wilderness, perhaps. The starkness captured her mind the same way the world's biggest mountains did—at the core of it, she wanted to be alone, and if she could have stepped through the painting into that desolate, hostile landscape, she would have.

Eventually, she spotted Miles off to the side, engrossed in conversation with an older couple. The man was gesturing at the closest painting while the woman's eyes moved slowly over it, studying. Evelyn was thankful that he was occupied. She turned away and moved against the flow of the crowd toward the door, wondering if anyone else would have the same reaction when they got to that final room: overpowered, rendered still. She didn't like that Miles had done this to her—his brain, his hands. As she stepped into the cool air outside, she felt her phone buzz in her coat pocket. It was a text from Sophie, asking if she had gone to the gallery opening. She texted back—I'm just leaving now. It was great! Beautiful paintings. But you know that. Her phone buzzed again as she slipped it back into her pocket, but she didn't bother to read Sophie's reply. She was already beginning to feel guilty, and not just because she had forgotten to take any pictures.

Evelyn couldn't sleep that night. She stayed up reading about a case for one of the partners at her firm—some complicated assault that was *possibly* self-defense but also possibly a calculated attack. She couldn't figure out how to spin it. Whenever she opened one of the big law books, she saw rivers tumbling over the pages. Progress was slow, but she managed a page of research notes. She nearly jumped out of her skin when she heard a knock on the door.

She let out a shaky breath, realizing it must be Miles, although she hadn't heard the front door open. "Come in?"

The door opened slowly as she swiveled in her chair to face it. There was Miles, still in his suit pants and white shirt. He had turned on a light in the hall, backlit now due to the darkness in her room. "Sorry," he said, glancing over his shoulder at the light. "I didn't want to do too much fumbling."

"It's fine," Evelyn replied, reaching across her desk to switch on a rarely used lamp. She had been working by the light of her laptop screen alone. "Do you need something?"

He shook his head. "It's occurring to me now that you're probably busy. I just wanted to say thank you for coming to the gallery. I saw you, but those people I was talking to are collectors. They were interested in one of the paintings and I didn't want to let them get away." He leaned against the doorframe and Evelyn's heart sped up. "I think I'll be getting a nice check soon."

"Wow, congratulations."

He shrugged, straightening up. "It's hard not to have imposter syndrome. Like, does my art *really* belong in some rich couple's apartment? I don't know. They'll probably slap it in a cabin up north. It's not really apartment art." He took a small step back, as if conscious of overstaying his welcome. Evelyn tried to ignore how badly she wanted him to cross the threshold, to keep her company. "I'll get out of your hair. Just wanted to say thanks in case you thought I didn't see you. I did."

"Wait!" she said, immediately embarrassed by the desperation in her voice. "If you're not going to sleep yet, I was going to make coffee."

He checked his watch. It was after 11:00, and though Evelyn usually didn't drink coffee so late, she knew she wouldn't sleep much tonight anyway. "Sure," Miles replied, "why not."

Twenty minutes later they sat at opposite ends of the couch, each holding a mug of coffee and neither doing much talking. Miles's gaze drifted over the bare walls of her living room, probably wondering how someone could live in such emptiness. Evelyn wanted to apologize on behalf of her poor interior design capabilities, but she stayed quiet. She had turned on a lamp in one corner of the room, and now each object cast an unfamiliar shadow. She felt like a visitor in her own home, everything made new by his presence.

"I really do like your art," she said. "It's... I don't know how to describe it. When I walked into that gallery room, I felt like I'd stepped into a different world. Familiar and strange all at once. I wanted to walk right into those paintings and feel the rivers run."

He raised his eyebrows, a small smile on his lips. "Thank you. Rivers should be moving, right? Not meant to be still."

Evelyn didn't know how to respond. She felt she had unintentionally revealed something about herself to him. She opened her mouth to speak but found no words. The smile fell from his lips, and he turned his head to look out the window. A silence passed between them.

"Do you like living here?" he asked, without looking at her.

"Oh...the city? Most of the time I don't." She answered honestly—no reason to withhold her emotions from him the way she did from her mother and Sophie, always lying and telling them she was happy. She didn't want them to worry. "It's hard to live somewhere so—man-made. I miss the mountains every single day."

Now he looked at her directly. "I've asked Sophie about moving, but that's what she always says. That she would miss the mountains too much. But it's hard to be a struggling artist in Wyoming. There are so many more opportunities here. When I was at school, I didn't miss the wilderness."

She considered this and laughed. "I think it would be cruel to take Sophie away from nature. Like taking a wild animal from its native habitat. She complained so much in Seattle. I don't think she'll ever go back to a city." Evelyn knew that moving was a reoccurring argument between Sophie and Miles. There was no point in giving him false hope about Sophie's willingness to leave the mountains.

"You're probably right." He exhaled and glanced away. "I think that I need to come to the city for a while. I just don't know if Sophie can handle the cabin alone."

"She's more capable than you think."

"But she doesn't pay attention. If something starts to break, she doesn't notice until it's unusable. And half the time she doesn't seem to care. She always says, 'we can work around it,' or, 'we can just save up to replace it.' But that's not how it works. The whole cabin needs to be replaced. Right now, I'm trying to fix as much of it as possible."

Evelyn blinked. He seemed legitimately angry, which surprised her. She sensed a deeper undercurrent of hurt running through his words. "She can be...I hate to say it, but an airhead sometimes."

He closed his eyes, shaking his head. "We don't need to discuss her flaws."

"You're right. I just meant..." *What? Did you want to imply that you're superior to Sophie in some way, because you would notice a leaky faucet?* She chastised herself. "You're welcome to stay here again if you need to come to the city."

He seemed to consider the offer for a long time. "That's incredibly generous. I do have other friends in the city. But maybe, if they get tired of my begging, I'll come back."

She tried to hide her disappointment. The more time she spent with him, the more she liked his company. She had spent little time with him like this before, detached from Sophie. He was a different person without her around. She wondered whose fault that was.

They fell back into conversation, about kayaking and climbing and his inspirations for his paintings. When Evelyn checked the time on her phone, it was well past midnight, and she sat up with a small gasp. "Oh, my god. I didn't realize how late it was."

"Does it matter?"

"Kind of." She looked up, apologetic. "I usually get up at six on Saturdays for the gym, and then work all day. And I didn't get as far as I wanted to tonight. I mean, I figured I would be up until three anyway. But now—you get the point. I'd be up all night."

"Maybe you should just go to sleep and try tackling tomorrow fully rested. Easier said than done, I know. I'm a bit of an insomniac myself," he said with a shrug.

"Me too," she said. "If you have any issues sleeping, becoming a lawyer will steamroll you into a full-blown insomniac."

"I don't want to keep you. You should get back to work, or to sleep. But, Evelyn?"

"Yes?"

"You should come to the museum tomorrow."

"I could. I think. I have a meeting tomorrow afternoon, but it will be over by—what time?"

"Five o'clock. There's a dinner after; I'm not sure I can get away with bringing a guest. But for the exhibit, sure."

She calculated the time in her head—committee meeting at 4:00, no way she could show up in a gown. She'd have to come back across town to change, then to the museum—it wouldn't work. She would skip the meeting. Tell them she got sick. "I'll come."

"Great. We can head there together."

She stood up, feeling uneasy. "Thanks, Miles. And good night."

She took the mug from his extended hand and set it in the

kitchen sink beside her own. She could feel his eyes on her back, but when she turned around, he wasn't looking. Glass of water in hand, she retreated to her bedroom. The pile of work on her desk caught her off guard. She rarely left things in such a state of disarray—one of her favorite rituals was cleaning up before bed, to visually signify that her work for the day was finished. Now she couldn't hide from the fact that she had abandoned her work to spend time with Miles.

He was gone when she woke up the next morning. She skipped the gym and stretched instead, unrolling a yoga mat next to her bed. After breakfast she got to work, reviewing materials for her cases until her head spun. The challenge of crafting defenses still thrilled her, but the amount of work was staggering—she suspected that a lot of other people must feel the same way and emerge on the other side of law school not knowing if they even wanted to practice. She had pushed through, passed the bar, joined the firm of one of the city's best defense attorneys. Everything she had worked so hard for had fallen into place, yet sometimes she found herself staring out the window of her office or her bedroom, her mind blank, and it took enormous effort to focus again, as if her brain was protesting the task at hand. *That feeling must go away,* she thought. *Or for me it will.* Evelyn wanted to be a lawyer. She had been so certain.

By 3:00 Miles still hadn't returned. Evelyn riffled through her closet and pulled out a long black dress; she had only invested in it because once a year, the Columbia student law society had held a formal charity ball to raise money for a cause in the city. She put on the dress and looked at herself in the mirror, at her pale skin and dark brown hair falling down her back. She was tall and imposing in heels.

The front door opened and she felt a wave of embarrassment for scrutinizing herself in the mirror. She was about to change when she heard a knock on the bedroom door. "Coming," she said, and opened the door. Miles wore running shorts and a T-shirt and looked slightly disheveled.

"Wow. You look great." He glanced down at his clothes and then back up at her. "Well, I'm dressed and ready to go, too."

"I wasn't—sorry, I wasn't getting ready yet. Just trying this dress on to make sure it still fits."

"It does," he said, and then, "You apologize too much."

"I know. You'll never believe who's told me that before." She ran a hand over the dress, self-conscious. "I just didn't want you to think I was ready to leave without you."

He shrugged. "I went for a run and got very distracted. Ended up getting lunch with some old friends in Brooklyn. But here I am."

Evelyn couldn't conjure a response. He was so close, his face inches from hers, and she was aware of how easily she could reach out and touch him—worse, she suspected he wouldn't move away. Her heart was in her throat, suspended in time, waiting for something to happen. Nothing did. She swallowed hard and ran her fingers along the doorframe.

"I'll let you get back to it," he said, breaking the silence. "Whatever *it* is. Wearing a nice dress. Being impossibly smart. You know, the kind of things you do."

She realized he was gesturing to the pile of work on the desk, which hadn't changed much from the day before. "Oh. That's tomorrow's problem."

He nodded and stepped away. She closed the door and let out a breath. *What am I doing?* She couldn't deny it anymore. She was attracted to him. And unless her mind was playing tricks on her, the attraction was reciprocated. But she didn't know him well—maybe he was always like this, a little flirty, intense. That had to be why Sophie had fallen for him. *Sophie.* She remembered her sister with a jolt and felt sick. She wasn't thinking straight. She changed clothes and sat in bed, trying to meditate, to do anything to escape her thoughts, but the peace would not come.

When she emerged into the living room, Miles stared at her. It was the reaction she had secretly hoped for, as she had curled her hair and done her makeup for the first time in months. It wasn't entirely for him—she told herself—it was an important event; she didn't want to look out of place. But she also desired attention. And now she had it, his eyes traveling over her body in a way that she could feel.

"You look nice," she said, to diffuse some of the tension. He wore a black tux, and he looked the most groomed she had ever seen him—hair swept back and beard trimmed short, less the wild man of the mountains and more the dignified artist. She liked him better this way. She suspected Sophie felt the opposite, and felt superior just for a moment, for appreciating Miles in a way that Sophie did not. Besides, what harm was there in relishing her attraction to him for a moment—he would be gone tomorrow afternoon and it would be months before she saw him again. She would make a trip to Wyoming next summer, maybe, and then Sophie would be by his side. Maybe in the meantime she would dust off her dating apps and try again. But for now, no harm in noticing the man in front of her.

"You look amazing, Evelyn. I already told you that." He stood up and gestured to the door. "We should go. Might be good to be a little early."

They didn't speak much on the way to the museum. Miles

paid for an Uber that cut across the city, taking them to the Art Museum of the Americas. It was a newer museum, one she hadn't visited before, in an old, imposing brick building. People milled outside in tuxedos and evening gowns, and Evelyn felt wary as she stepped out of the car. She had attended highbrow events during law school, but this was another level.

She felt Miles's presence by her side and glanced up at him as he slipped his arm into hers. "Come on," he said, "you'll be fine," as if sensing her apprehension. She fell into step with him, aware every second of his arm brushing against hers. Together they walked up the grand staircase leading into the building. Inside, the lights were bright, the lobby crowded with people in enthusiastic conversation.

Miles cut a path through the crowd and stopped outside an exhibit room. The security guard looked at him, impassive, until Miles pulled his ID from his wallet and showed it to the guard. He took Evelyn's arm again as they stepped around the red velvet rope and into the relative silence of the exhibit room. Only a few people milled about, and she sensed that these were the most important people present, museum curators and benefactors and the other artists. Beside her, Miles let out a breath.

"It's a bit better in here, yeah? These events get so overwhelming."

She blinked. "Isn't this your first museum show?"

"Yeah. But I've done galleries before. Like last night. It's just talking, talking, talking. I get a headache."

He unlinked his arm and turned to face her, but she looked past him. "Your paintings. Wow." A series of four paintings were mounted on the wall opposite her—the same river, she realized, in four seasons, rushing wild in the spring, relatively still in summer, reflecting orange and yellow leaves in fall, and bleak in the winter, almost overpowered by the snow. Along the banks of the river, an eerie old house decomposed across the seasons. In the summertime, a fly-fisher waded through the calm water. "Do you often include people?"

He followed her gaze. "No. There usually aren't any, where I paint. But that day there was a man fly-fishing. He told me he'd hiked eighteen miles that day to reach the river and that he would camp in the area and fish all weekend. He made the trip with his dad every summer until his dad couldn't anymore, and now he makes the trip in his memory. I thought that was worth capturing." He paused, smiled. "Although I suspect the presence of humans might have helped me get into this exhibit. The curators always like a commentary on American society, no matter how small."

Before she could respond, someone spoke behind them. "Excuse me—Miles Greene?"

Miles stepped around her. "Tulliano. I'm glad to see you. Thank you, again."

Evelyn turned to see a small, elderly man. He patted Miles on the back, smiling up at him. "My pleasure. Without your art this exhibit would be incomplete." He paused, his gaze drifting to Evelyn. "Your wife?"

Evelyn opened her mouth to respond, but Miles spoke first. "Yes. Evelyn, this is Tulliano Mastel. He's one of the museum curators. We've known each other for a few years now, and Tulliano fought tooth and nail to get my paintings on display here."

Tulliano shook his head. "It didn't require much of a fight. I simply put your work on their radar." He stepped back and gave a small nod. "I must make rounds. I'll see you at dinner, if not before then."

As soon as he stepped away, Evelyn touched Miles's arm and hissed, "Your wife?"

"What?" Miles said, grinning. "He's old. I didn't want to explain that no, you're my wife's sister. It would confuse him."

"So what if he tells people that you're here with your wife?"

The smile on his face fell away. "Evelyn. It's one night. Just have fun." He paused. "If it makes you feel better, no one here has met Sophie."

She considered for a moment, then nodded, although she was feeling unsure about his idea of fun. *What if they meet Sophie in the future?* She and Sophie had only a vague sisterly resemblance—the same narrow noses and hazel eyes, but Evelyn had dark, thick hair while Sophie's was dirty blond. And Evelyn's facial features were sharp—defined cheekbones and a jaw to match. Sophie had a round, seemingly permanent baby face. The two couldn't pass for each other in a million years.

She let go of her reservations and continued around the exhibit at Miles's side. It wasn't her problem to worry about; any burden of explanation would fall on Miles. And a pleasantly warm feeling rose in her chest every time someone guessed that she was Miles's wife—it only happened a few more times, but each time she allowed herself to smile a little wider and nod a bit more enthusiastically. *Yes, we're married, yes, my husband is so talented.* She drank three glasses of champagne and let herself slip fully into the fantasy.

"You seem like you're enjoying yourself," Miles said, guiding her off to the side. The exhibit opening was winding down; a good number of people had headed off into the night, although a small crowd lingered, the people Evelyn guessed were invited to dinner.

"I haven't..." she said, and then paused, trying to find the right words. "I haven't done anything like this in a long time. Well, I've never been to an exhibit opening like this. But what

I mean is—I haven't been on anything resembling a date in a long time. Not that this is a date," she added quickly.

"You could call it that," he replied, unperturbed. "I wish I could bring you to dinner. You're good company."

She could have kissed him right there, in front of all the people. No one would have been the wiser. But she just watched him for a moment, and he seemed to be studying her, too, as if he had something to say but was afraid to ask it.

"Well," he said finally. "I think I have a dinner to catch."

"Yeah. Don't let it run away from you."

"Funny," he said. "Will you be awake when I get back?"

"Probably. I have work to do. I'm behind."

He nodded. "I hope that's not my fault." To her surprise, he leaned in and kissed her cheek. "I'll see you later. Have a safe trip home."

She went out into the cool night, the heat of his skin still lingering on hers.

She hadn't planned it, or even expected it, but when he came home around midnight she was curled up on the couch, filling out paperwork and drinking coffee to stay awake. They exchanged no words, not even a *we shouldn't*, and later, that was what Evelyn regretted the most. That she hadn't even tried to stop it. All she knew was that somehow, their bodies were drawn to each other, and then they were kissing, and then they were in her bed. The lights off, as always, nothing but darkness surrounding her.

After, lying beside each other, Evelyn tried not to have a panic attack. She measured her breathing even when tears began to stream down her face, when she realized the inevitable consequences of what she had done. She had to tell Sophie.

"You can't tell Sophie."

She shifted to look at him, bewildered by how he seemed to have read her mind. "We have to."

"No." He shook his head. "No, she doesn't need to know. This won't ever happen again, okay?"

She couldn't bring herself to respond for a long moment. He was right; Sophie didn't need to know and would never find out if they didn't tell her. "It's cruel," she said finally.

"Then why did you do it?"

She exhaled sharply, almost a laugh. "Why did you?"

"What do you want me to say? I'm attracted to you," he said. "You're charming and intelligent. Passionate."

"And Sophie isn't those things?"

"Please, don't bring her into this."

"I don't see how I can't." Evelyn paused, tension humming through her body. "You've done this before, right?"

"What?"

She had to force the words out. "Cheated on Sophie."

He stood up, tossing the blanket over where he had lain just a moment before. "I don't think this is a conversation we should have right now. Let's just get some sleep. We can talk more in the morning. But this won't happen again, so there's no need to upset Sophie." He paused. "I'll see you tomorrow."

And like that he was gone.

Alone in her bed, Evelyn wished for a crystal ball, or some other way to see the future. She kept reaching for her phone on her bedside table, and then pulling her hand away. The only person in the world she wanted to talk to was Sophie. She knew what Sophie would say, in a hypothetical situation where Evelyn had slept with some other woman's husband. *I can't believe you'd do something like that; you're not that kind of person, Evelyn. Didn't you think of the pain you would cause?* Sophie took love seriously. Evelyn felt like vomiting. She covered her

268   **LILLI SUTTON**

eyes with her hands even though it was dark and groaned. Though morning would come, she knew the night would be long. There was no escaping her own heart.

Over the next several months, Evelyn kept telling herself that the next time would be the last. That each time Miles ended up in her bed, she would feel guilty enough to put a stop to it. It never worked. She knew about the lies he carefully constructed to Sophie—that he was at a friend's apartment when he stayed with her, that he was busy with gallery events when he was taking Evelyn on extravagant dates. Sometimes the pressure nearly crushed her, and she almost picked up the phone and came clean. But all the while she was falling in love. She knew it and Miles must have, too, but still he didn't let go. They were playing a game of chicken, pushing each other closer to the edge, and Evelyn thought she would be the first to cave. But it was Miles, eight months later in early summer, who confessed.

"I think I'm going to leave Sophie."

Evelyn nearly dropped the plate she was holding. She was cleaning up after breakfast, just the two of them in her apartment. He had a flight to catch in a few hours. She opened her mouth but couldn't think of anything to say.

"Evelyn. I'm in love with you. Even if you don't feel the same, I think...I think it's time to put an end to this. I can't be with both of you."

"And you're..." Her throat was dry when she tried to swallow. "You're choosing me?"

He regarded her for a moment, as if wary of answering the question. "Yes, if you want to put it that way. It's not about you versus Sophie. She and I—we were never right for each other. We want different things, and while that didn't feel insurmountable at first, it's clear now that it's not working. She's not happy, and I wish I had met you first."

Tears filled Evelyn's eyes. "Are you going to tell her?"

"What does that mean?"

She set down the plate with a loud clatter. "Are you going to tell her that we've been seeing each other? Or just that things aren't working out?"

"I—I intend to keep seeing you."

It wasn't a direct answer to her question but she knew what it meant. She stared down at the marble countertop, tracing the dark patterns with her eyes. It was too much, and she knew it. She should say no, tell him that it was over, that he couldn't tell Sophie anything. Then she could spend the rest of her life trying to reset her karma, as Sophie would say. But there was something else in the back of her mind, a voice not unlike her own that told her that it wouldn't matter.

"Do you want to move here? Move in with me?"

It was his turn to look surprised. "I didn't think you'd want that. I know you like having your own space."

"You do too," she countered. "We're on basically opposite schedules. Were you thinking of staying in Wyoming?"

"No, no," he said, shaking his head. "I mean, I'll keep the cabin. I don't know what I thought I'd do. I hadn't really gotten that far. Couch surf for a while. I wasn't going to ask—"

"Well, you didn't have to," Evelyn said, cutting him off. Anger and sadness flooded her veins, though she couldn't pinpoint the cause. She felt out of control, as if someone else held the puppet strings of her life. Taking back the power, inviting Miles to live with her, didn't help. She wished she could look at him without seeing both the person she loved and the worst mistake she'd ever made.

Miles's expression softened, as if he sensed her surging emotions. "I know this isn't going to be easy. But I have to leave her. I can't stay in a relationship that's so clearly run its course. And I can't stay if you're in the picture."

Evelyn looked at him a moment longer and felt her brain zoom out, racing back through the years to childhood. She thought of everything Sophie had taken from her—their mother's attention, skiing, rock climbing, mountaineering—everything shared. Nothing ever hers alone. It didn't make her feel better to turn the tables, but remembering the past tempered some of the blow.

"Okay," she said. "But we should have a game plan. I'll fly out next weekend so we can tell her together, in person. It's the right thing to do."

Glass jars clunked as Evelyn set the grocery bags on the countertop. Her leg muscles ached with a vengeance and the couch beckoned to her, but she knew if she let herself sit, she'd fall asleep. She'd gone to the gym before the grocery store, set the stair-stepper to a high intensity and climbed. Anything to stop thinking about what had happened in Wyoming, the way Sophie had wailed when they told her. She had punched Evelyn, twice, before Miles had restrained her. The bruise around her eye had faded now, but for the past few days she had welcomed the physical reminder of her transgressions. As she'd driven away from the cabin, through the sad yellow grass weighed down by the lingering rain, she'd wondered if she'd ever see Sophie again.

The stove clock reminded Evelyn, with a jolt, that Miles's flight was due to land almost two hours ago. Communication had been scarce since Evelyn had flown home, but she had expected that. He'd been quiet all weekend in Wyoming; but so had she. They'd hardly spoken after telling Sophie.

The bedroom down the hallway was empty. She leaned against the doorframe, contemplating the bed, wondering if just a little nap wouldn't hurt. A knock on the front door made her flinch.

He must have lost his keys, she thought, heading to the door. She opened it to reveal her mother standing in the hallway.

"Hi, Evelyn."

Evelyn took in the sight of her mother, disheveled from traveling, a backpack on her shoulders and a small suitcase by her side. She opened her mouth, closed her mouth, swallowed. Finally, she said, "What are you doing here?"

Her mother gazed at her. "I think you already know. Don't start," she continued, as Evelyn opened her mouth again. "First, invite me in."

Evelyn stepped back so she could enter the apartment. "Are you staying here?"

"No. I booked a hotel. I knew you'd find some excuse to be busy or out of town if I told you I was coming. When was the last time you cleaned this place?"

Evelyn flushed. Everything about the apartment was orderly, but her mother had swiped a finger across the coffee table, revealing a fine layer of dust. "Before..." She couldn't call it a trip, that sounded too much like a vacation. "Before we left."

"Does he help you clean?"

"What?"

"Miles." She sighed, setting down her backpack as she lowered onto the couch. She stared at Evelyn, her mouth set in a firm line, as if Evelyn were the one who had barged into her house and brought up cleaning.

"Yeah," Evelyn replied. "Yes, of course he does, when he's here." She walked to the armchair that faced the couch, the one she never used, and sat in it, folding her feet in the chair's lap. "Mom? What did you come here to say to me?"

She shook her head and turned to look out the window. "You're always so direct. Did I raise you to be this way?" She paused. "I keep asking myself that. Did I raise you to be so cruel?"

Evelyn's stomach dropped. "Mom. There's more to the story."

"Were you ever going to tell me? When Sophie called me, I thought something horrible had happened. She'd been injured or Miles had died or god-knows-what." She exhaled, fixing her gaze back on Evelyn. "Not that this isn't horrible. What were you thinking? I mean really, Evelyn. I'd love to know what made you think having an affair—with your sister's husband—was a good idea." She paused, and Evelyn realized her mother had started to cry.

She resisted the urge to point out that technically Miles had had an affair. "Sophie and Miles were clearly having problems."

"And you made those problems worse."

"So what? Should Sophie have been trapped in an unhappy marriage forever?" Evelyn knew she shouldn't defend herself, but she couldn't help it. Her skin felt prickly, her entire body on edge. She looked out the window to her right and wished she was one of the ant-like people below, scurrying about to some inconsequential errand.

"She was thinking about their relationship a lot. She didn't tell you?"

This caught Evelyn's attention. "No. She wanted a divorce?"

Her mother waved her hand. "No. Don't start thinking you helped her in some way. She wanted counseling, but Miles said no. I wonder why." She paused, letting the information sink in. "She was thinking about asking for a break. Admitting that she rushed into the wedding."

"I tried to stop her."

"We both did. But not very hard." A silence passed between them. Evelyn's mother worried the bracelet on her wrist. "I knew Miles was bad news."

Evelyn waited a moment. "I can't tell if you're mad at him or me."

"Oh, sweetheart, I am livid at you. I don't think I've ever been so mad." She said this calmly, no longer crying, which made Evelyn's heart jump to her throat. "I've struggled with what to say to you since—since Sophie told me. On the plane I realized I probably can't do anything to convince you otherwise. You've always been stubborn." A corner of her mouth lifted in a wry smile. "Maybe that was my mistake. I let you grow up too fast but didn't teach you what being a grown-up meant."

The air in the room felt heavy. Evelyn longed to get up and open a window, but the hum of the air conditioner reminded her that it was above eighty degrees outside, July's humidity thick between the buildings. "What would you even want me to do?"

This made her laugh. "Stop seeing Miles, for one. Don't you dare let that man move in here. And apologize to Sophie. Really. Beg for her forgiveness if you have to. I don't think you realize what you've done." There were tears in her eyes again. "I had to ask my friend Lori to stay with Sophie while I came here. She hasn't gotten out of bed, has barely eaten anything. I was worried she'd...well. I worry too much sometimes."

Evelyn looked down at her hands, interlocking her fingers. Her stomach turned at the thought of Sophie crying in bed.

She wished Miles would come back, so she could remember why she'd gotten into the situation in the first place—why she was sitting in her apartment, visualizing Sophie's devastation. But she didn't need Miles to remember that it was her own fault.

"I don't want to stop seeing Miles," she said softly.

Her mother sighed, exasperated. "Then at least don't let him move in here. Not yet."

"I need help with rent," Evelyn lied.

"Then let me help you."

Evelyn's phone buzzed on the kitchen counter. She stood up, thankful for a momentary diversion from the conversation. It was Miles, telling her his plane had landed.

"Miles will be here soon," Evelyn said, leaning against the counter to face the living room.

"Are you asking me to leave?"

"I imagine you don't want to see him."

Her mother stood up, slowly. It struck Evelyn then how tired she looked, how far she had traveled to have this conversation. "I want you to think about something," she said. "I want you to think about how you would feel if Sophie had done the same thing to you."

Hasn't she already? Evelyn wanted to say. But instead, she said, "I would be devastated. I would hate her." She paused, swallowing the lump in her throat. "I know I've done a cruel thing. You didn't need to cross the country to tell me that."

Her mother shook her head and walked to the door, pausing with her hand on the knob. She half turned, as if she didn't want to say what she knew came next.

"I'm going to have a hard time moving past this, Evelyn."

A minute later Evelyn found herself staring at the shut door. It was as if her mother had disappeared, walked through the door to another plane of existence. Evelyn knew that soon enough the door would open again and Miles would appear this time. The universe as she understood it would fall back into place. But for the next hour she could be anything. A good person. A loyal sister. Someone worth loving. The thought was almost too much to bear.

CHAPTER EIGHTEEN

May 2018,
Yama Parvat, Nepal

"Only a little bit farther. You'll be fine."

Sophie watched Levi carefully. He was struggling and not doing a good job of hiding it. The entire mixed team had stopped in a barren area of snow above Camp Three, drinking some water and adjusting equipment. Strong winds buffeted the mountain, changing direction sporadically. In a short two hundred feet, they would have to climb a rickety ladder over a massive ice wall, where there would be no escape from the wind, and a strong gust could topple someone tired or inexperienced.

Levi took a last gulp of water and handed the bottle back to Sophie. "I wasn't built for this."

She took his hand, squeezed it through her thick gloves. "If you want to turn around, just say the word."

"I wouldn't make you go back with me. Besides, we came here to summit this mountain. We're doing it."

Sophie couldn't manage a smile even though his words were meant to reassure her. All day his breathing had been labored, and they'd trailed the mixed team. "I don't want you to risk your life for the summit. I'd rather have you safe and alive back in Switzerland."

"I'm far from life-risking territory. We've got, what, fifteen hundred more feet? Easy."

Sophie frowned, knowing how difficult it was to gauge "life-risking territory." A person could go from tired to incapacitated in a matter of minutes. Still, when Andrew strode by to gauge their readiness to continue, she gave him a thumbs-up. Levi was an adult and could make his own decisions. Maybe he felt better than he looked.

When it was Sophie's turn at the ladder, she didn't allow herself to look down. For all her adventurous spirit, she wasn't a huge fan of heights; the vertical ladders were her least favorite part of climbing. She could deal with exposure on a glacier, where she could self-arrest if she fell, but the thought of a straight-down free fall made her head spin. She clipped onto the rope anchored to the rock next to the ladder—meant to prevent the free fall she feared—and grabbed the first rung.

The wind shook the ladder as she climbed, and every few steps she paused to breathe and flex her fingers. Tensing up didn't help. The distance to the top of the ice wall gradually shortened and a few minutes later she reached it. She unclipped, unzipped her down suit partway for ventilation, and stepped back beside Penelope and a few others. Evelyn was still below. Sophie was keenly aware of her whereabouts. After their conversation a week ago, she was determined to avoid Evelyn, to underline that she had meant it—no more conversations. No more trying to fix what was broken.

She stepped back to the edge, looking down at the rock

face as Levi began his climb. He was probably less afraid of the ladder than she was—he had much more experience with ice climbing, and in less extreme conditions he might tackle a similar wall without a ladder or a fixed rope. He climbed slowly, pausing every few rungs as she had done, but for longer, as if struggling to catch his breath. When he reached the top, she resisted the urge to wrap her arms around him out of relief. He approached her, grinning, and pulled the sunglasses away from his eyes for a moment.

"I told you. Easy."

"Sure," she replied, drifting away from the edge. "And now we have hours of slogging to do." She stepped closer to Penelope, who turned to face them.

"I don't like the look of those clouds," Penelope said, pointing. Sophie followed her gaze to a low point between two distant peaks. Clouds had gathered, thick and gray.

"They're not close. It could just be fog," Sophie said, but her voice caught in her throat, betraying her uncertainty. Himalayan weather was notoriously fickle. They were supposed to summit tomorrow. If the weather turned, they would be forced back down until they could make another exhausting push for the top. It was too dangerous to spend multiple nights at Camp Four, which, at 24,500 feet of elevation, was close to the death zone.

"Right. Fog." Penelope shook her head. "You are too optimistic, Sophie. I have a bad feeling about this mountain. She has teeth."

Sophie knew what Penelope meant. Since the avalanche, everyone had been subdued, no longer speaking of the summit but instead focusing on each day. But now they were so close, a little more than twenty-four hours from standing on the peak. She offered Penelope a small smile.

"So do we. We'll manage." She glanced at Levi. "Feeling okay?"

"Better than ever."

She allowed herself to appreciate his enthusiasm. A short distance away, climbers continued to reach the top of the ladder. Andrew was the last to appear above the cliff edge. Sophie zipped her suit and touched Levi's arm.

"If you need to stop, let me know."

"I'm fine. I promise. Stop worrying about me." Even though his tone was gentle, she knew she was bothering him. She nodded and fell into line behind Penelope. There was nothing she could do except keep moving forward. Levi would find his way behind her, or he would falter. She could only help him if he let her.

They reached Camp Four a few hours later, exhausted but in good spirits. Unlike the lower camps, all of which were situated on snowfields, here there were no wide stretches of flat ground, and tent sites had to be cut in and stomped down to ensure enough ground to sleep on. It was tedious work, some of which had already been done by the combined Polish and Japanese team, who had reached Camp Four the night before. They had left their tents standing, and Andrew made quick work of checking them.

"They're not here," Andrew reported as he returned to the group. "They must have made their summit attempt."

Evelyn checked her watch. "Then they should be there now, or close. They've had good weather so far. I guess we'll know soon if they made it."

The group dispersed. At this elevation, everyone slept in pairs, for safety and convenience. There simply wasn't enough room for that many individual tents on the narrow slope. The team before them had left six.

"It's weird that they didn't pack out their camp, right?" Levi said as they set about establishing a site from the cliffside. The wind made it difficult, blowing snow back over the packed ground. Sophie gazed over her shoulder for a moment, at the peaks below them. At this elevation, the world looked small, topographic features no more than hints of light and shadow. A few false steps would be deadly; it was impossible to even stand upright on the steep slope.

"A little," Sophie replied. "But I think they probably wanted to be as light as possible for the summit. And maybe they wanted an established camp in case they come back exhausted. Or maybe they left the tents for us." She laughed. "Probably not. I guess we'll know their plan soon enough." She couldn't resist looking up, although large rocks blocked the view. It was impossible to see the actual peak from this angle, and she suspected it would be difficult to see anyone descending. Still, her stomach did small flips. Even if Yakumo and Wojciech succeeded, taking away the chance of a first ascent, it would be fascinating to hear their account.

They spent most of the afternoon inside the tent, away from the sun's dangerous light. There was nothing to do but play cards and snack to pass the time. After a few hours, Levi dozed off, but Sophie stayed awake, unable to stop thinking about tomorrow. If she didn't make it, her sponsorships would likely drop. They could easily find a younger, more talented face. New climbers were always emerging on the scene. She had been one, once, and now a few years later she worried if Yama Parvat might be her last big mountain. She would have to go back to guiding in the States to make enough money to continue climbing, and that meant leaving Levi.

★ ★ ★

The thoughts were enough to keep her awake until evening, when she heard someone banging two pots together, the group's sign for a meeting. She shook Levi awake, both impressed and concerned that he had slept so well for so long. He had to be exhausted.

He looked up at her through bleary eyes. "Is it time?"

"For dinner, maybe. But no, we're not climbing now." She reached over and ran a hand through his hair, watched the smile form on his lips. "Come on. I think there's a meeting."

To her surprise, she saw snow falling when she opened the door. The howling winds had masked the sound of it hitting the tent, or maybe she'd been too deep in thought to notice. Either way, it wasn't a good sign. She brushed the thick, wet flakes off her sleeves and waited for Levi to emerge.

The others huddled together, pressing in for warmth and to hear Andrew, who stood at the head of the group, his face creased with worry. Evelyn stood by his side, shielding her face from the snow with her left arm. Sophie and Levi had ended up in the middle of the group—the warmest place to be, but claustrophobic. Sophie had trouble reaching her arm up to brush snow off her head without bumping into someone else.

"Everyone here?" Andrew called, shouting to make his voice heard. A small, affirmative chorus returned his call. "Okay. I'll keep it short. Weather's turning. I got this damn radio working, and Base Camp said satellite looks bad overnight. No summit tomorrow."

A few groans rippled through the crowd. Sophie kept quiet but felt the disappointment just as deeply. They had come so far and would have to do it all again. She felt Levi squeeze her left hand and another thought raced through her brain. *He's too weak to climb to Camp Four again, let alone the summit.*

"Base Camp has heard nothing from Yakumo or Wojciech. We're to keep an eye out for them overnight. But we can't search in this weather. We'll descend in the early morning if things clear. That's all. Get some rest."

The crowd dispersed quickly, eager to leave the bitter cold for the relative warmth of their shelters. Sophie let go of Levi's hand and followed him back to the tent, her mind racing with each step.

"You need to be honest with me," she said, as soon as they were settled. "Can you make another trip up here?"

He didn't meet her gaze. He studied the thin wall as it moved in the wind, seeming to consider her question. She normally liked his thoughtfulness, but now it made her impatient. She curled her hands into fists and then relaxed them, trying to keep the circulation going in her fingers.

"I don't know," he admitted. "This experience has been harder than anything I've ever done in my life. But I want to make it. If we get another chance, I don't want to be sitting at Base Camp, waiting to hear if you made it. I want to be there."

She nodded slowly. "I understand that. But knowing when to call it quits is important. Of course, you know that," she added, seeing the look on his face. "But it's ten times more important on a mountain like this, so remote, where help might be days away. You have to see dangerous situations before they happen and avoid putting yourself in them."

He took her hand. "I know. Let's just get through tonight, and we'll cross that bridge when we come to it, okay?"

She nodded again, out of useful words to say. She leaned back against the sleeping bag, took a long breath of thin air, and settled in for a sleepless night.

★ ★ ★

Sophie blinked and sat up. She had fallen asleep sometime during the fitful evening—the raging storm hadn't made for good sleeping conditions. Now it was eerily quiet.

"Sophie. Levi."

She flinched. Someone had said their names outside. She unzipped the door and gazed up at Andrew's face, framed by a clear, star-filled night sky.

"Hi. Conditions changed. I've been radioing back and forth with Base Camp. They say the system fizzled out and the weather should stay clear. They gave us the okay and want us to look for the missing team. It's midnight. Can you be ready in an hour?"

Sophie nodded, absorbing the fact that Yakumo and Wojciech hadn't returned. "Yeah. Yeah, we'll be up and ready."

"Good." He grinned. "We're doing this. We're summiting."

He stepped away into the darkness to wake the next pair. Sophie glanced over at Levi, who sat up, half-awake. "Did you hear?"

"Some of it. We're going?"

"Yes. If you're ready."

"Readier than ever," he said with a yawn.

She bit her tongue. He looked exhausted and disoriented, but he had just woken up in the middle of the night at high altitude. She had to give him some grace. She set about readying her supplies—packing up her stove and any scattered snacks, making sure that any necessary gear like carabiners and supplemental oxygen were close at hand. She didn't plan on using the oxygen unless she had to; her biggest fear was adjusting to a high level of oxygen and then running out. She had only used oxygen on Everest; since then, she climbed without it.

She went through the long process of redressing herself.

She had stripped to just her base layers to sleep in; her high-altitude sleeping bag was rated for -40 degrees Fahrenheit and kept her plenty warm. At the end of the tedious layering ordeal she once again donned the down suit, already sweating as she wriggled into the final layer. Levi had been completing the same process, albeit slower, so she partially unzipped the door while he finished dressing, trying to cool off.

"I'm ready," Levi said. Sophie glanced at the oxygen bottles attached to his backpack.

"I thought—"

"I will if I need to," he said, laying a gloved hand on her arm. "But I'm going to start without."

Sophie nodded and crawled outside, switching on her headlamp as she went, although it was hardly necessary given that the night was clear and the moon was nearly full. Any lingering clouds from the snowstorm had disappeared. They walked up the narrow slope in silence, gathering with the rest by Andrew's tent.

Once everyone had arrived, Andrew stopped fiddling with the radio to address them. "Alright. I've checked in with Base Camp again, they've confirmed we're good to climb. As I mentioned already, we're going to the summit and we're going to keep an eye out for anyone from the Japanese or Polish teams. This is not a rescue mission. If we find anyone in less-than-optimal condition, we're going to radio Base Camp and they will send guides up from Camp Three. Got it?" The group murmured in agreement. "Good. Now let's not waste time. We've got about two thousand feet to climb, and it's steep as hell. I think we'll go Canadians, mixed team, Americans for our order. Sound good?" When no one protested, he grinned. "Alright. Let's go."

Sophie glanced at Levi as the others began to move, getting into order. "How would you feel about switching places with the Americans?"

"You're too worried about me."

"I just don't want them to rush you if you want to go slower."

"Sophie. Please. I'm fine. Leave it alone."

She sensed his patience was wearing thin. "Okay. I'm sorry."

The line had quickly assembled around them. Sophie fell in behind Kathryn, one of the Canadians. Levi moved behind her, and when Sophie glanced over her shoulder, Penelope grinned and pumped her fist. A rush of adrenaline ripped through Sophie as she remembered—this was not just another day of slogging up and down. If everything went well, she would stand on the peak of a formerly unclimbed giant in just a few grueling hours.

The first hour was uneventful. The only sound was the crunching of snow and heavy breathing. Sophie fought the urge to glance back at Levi frequently; whenever she did, his head was down, focusing on each step that he took. As the slope steepened, Sophie too kept her head down, fighting through exhaustion as the mountain became almost vertical, the exposure dizzying whenever Sophie looked back, but the view overwhelmingly beautiful. Soon the pace slowed, each step requiring multiple breaths of effort. A snail's pace march into the unknown.

They approached a massive ice wall. There was no ladder affixed here, but someone had attached ropes using spikes and carabiners—the missing team. They had at least made it this far. Sophie's stomach lurched as she watched Andrew clip onto the fixed ropes and begin the ascent. The exposure, already sheer, became extreme high up on the wall. She shuddered to think of descending it later today, even more fatigued. She pushed the thought away. There were no bodies lying beneath the ice wall; no one had fallen to their death here. The line shuffled forward, and she reminded herself to breathe and utilize the moment of rest.

When it was her turn, she moved carefully, using her ice axe and crampons to establish grips and footholds before moving upward. The fixed line offered some security, but the precarious position made Sophie's stomach lurch. At least it wasn't windy. Every time a chunk of ice came loose from her axe or crampons, her heart skipped a beat, but she made it to the top of the wall. The slope above was only slightly less steep, still nearly vertical, but now Sophie's chest pressed against deep snow rather than ice. The others had continued ahead. She took one glance back to Levi; he was moving at a fine pace. She resumed the exhausting process of navigating the footholds. With each step they inched closer to the death zone.

An hour passed, maybe two. Sophie lost track and forgot to check her watch. The only hint of dawn was a light band of blue on the eastern horizon. Somewhere in between, Levi had stopped to put on an oxygen mask, holding up the line while those ahead shuffled on. For a short time, Sophie had worried that the leaders would lose them entirely. But now, she realized that the group before her had stopped. *Probably just a break*, she thought. Someone brushed past her, breaking the line. Sophie saw the familiar maroon of Evelyn's suit, just before she disappeared beyond those in front. A few seconds later, Andrew's voice carried on the wind.

"No way. It cliffs out."

"But that's the route," Evelyn's voice replied. "We'll have to climb that ice wall."

"It's not a wall. It's a serac. You can go look for yourself."

The rest of the climbers shuffled closer as Andrew and Evelyn argued. Sophie unclipped from the line and stepped forward. "What's going on?" she asked, now a few feet away.

Andrew turned to look at her. "Having some trouble with the route. That," he said, pointing to an area of the mountain that sloped up gradually before them, "cliffs out. I know it doesn't look like it would. Which means," he continued, turning to point at the sharp ridge that rose above the slope, "that the ridge is the only way up."

Sophie drew a breath. "I thought we knew that."

"We suspected it. But," he said, gesturing, "that alternate route looked promising. If it was an easier option, I wouldn't want to ignore it."

"Can I go look? I trust your opinion. But I want to see it for myself."

"Be my guest," he replied, turning back to Evelyn.

Sophie glanced back at Levi. "I'll be quick, okay?"

He nodded, unable to respond verbally because of the oxygen mask.

The mountain had gradually leveled out; Sophie could walk mostly upright now, without staring straight into snow. She felt relatively safe, even without the fixed line. She followed what looked like the route, straight ahead past Evelyn and the others, stamping through knee-deep snow. A serac rose to her right, hanging on beneath the mass of sharp rock that composed the ridge. The correct way, according to Andrew.

The cliff appeared so suddenly that it surprised her. She stopped dead, caught off guard by how the ground a few feet before her disappeared. She looked to the right and confirmed Andrew's statement; there was no way to climb the serac. She dropped to a crouch and crept forward, curiosity compelling her to look over the edge. When she saw what lay below, she gasped.

The bodies of two climbers in dark attire stood out against the pristine white snow, just a few feet apart from each other. They weren't moving. Sophie's stomach lurched. They must have fallen hours or even a full day ago, perhaps tricked by the false route while climbing in the darkness. She cupped her hands around her mouth and called out, asking if they needed help, but the distance was too great. Besides, she knew the truth. If the fall hadn't killed them, they had frozen to death by now. Their bodies were stuck in strange, contorted positions.

She scooted clumsily backward until she was a safe distance from the edge and stood up shakily. She retraced her steps, using her headlamp to carefully scan the way, aware of the steep drop that was now to her right. When she returned to the group several minutes later, they looked at her expectantly.

"Did you look over the edge?" she asked Andrew.

He shook his head; his eyes flooded with concern.

"Two climbers fell. They must have gone over the cliff. Or tried to climb the serac."

"God. Was there a way down?"

"Not that I saw."

He pressed his hands over his face for a moment. Sophie wished she had some way to comfort him, but there was nothing she could do. She folded her arms across her chest and waited, trying to ignore the biting cold that was setting in.

"Could you recognize them?" Evelyn asked. Sophie glanced at her but it was difficult to discern her sister's expression.

She nodded slowly. "Their suits were navy. They must have been Japanese."

"Okay. Thank you for looking. I'll radio Base Camp and we'll carry on," Andrew replied.

Sophie turned away, making brief eye contact with Evelyn, whose face was still stony. She stumbled past, toward Levi, wanting to relay the news herself before Andrew or someone else announced it. She found him standing by Penelope, his oxygen mask off. It brightened her spirits ever so slightly to see his full face again, though she knew from his expression that he sensed something was off. She told Levi and Penelope what she had seen before they had time to ask. Penelope cursed softly under her breath. Levi touched Sophie's arm.

"Are you okay?"

She nodded. "They're not the first bodies I've seen. I'm more concerned about where the rest of them ended up. Or are," she added, trying to sound less pessimistic. The rest of the Polish and Japanese climbers could be anywhere—maybe they had already descended to one of the lower camps. Maybe they were still alive.

Moments later, Andrew's grim face lowered her hopes. "I've spoken to Base Camp," he announced as the climbers gathered closer. "No word from Yakumo, Wojciech, or anyone else for that matter. I gave them a rough idea of where the bodies are located, but it's out of our hands for now. They gave us the okay to continue. So, without further ado."

Evelyn broke off from the group, followed by her two teammates. "Phil and Danielle are turning back. Neither of them feels up to it."

Andrew nodded, peering around her at the two climbers. "I respect that decision. Can you descend on your own?" They both nodded, but Andrew stayed quiet for a moment, seeming to deliberate. His gaze shifted to one of the American team guides. "Mingma, will you descend with them? Reaching Camp Three by this afternoon would be a good plan."

Mingma nodded and circled around to Phil and Danielle.

Sophie watched them go, wondering how Evelyn felt. In an instant, she'd become the only American climber left. Their group had now shrunk to ten—a more manageable size, but fewer people to help if an emergency struck. She tried again to read Evelyn's face, but she had turned away, her shoulders square and her arms still at her sides. Whatever Evelyn was feeling, she wasn't going to show it.

Now they ascended the ridge, an ugly affair of jagged rock covered in fresh, powdery snow. The sun had made its appearance in the east, casting golden light over the horizon's edge. Sophie reached into one of her suit's pockets and pulled out her sunglasses, slipping them on and turning off her headlamp in a fluid motion as she climbed. The last thing she wanted was to be visually impaired while on the ridge, especially with the steep exposure on both sides. One mistake would send her plummeting. There were no fixed ropes on the ridge, and probably not any on the rest of the route. Each step was a life-or-death endeavor.

Gradually the ridge flattened out into a shelf of snow. The group trickled down to the right, curving around another rock wall before the snow shelf moved upward, promising the finish line after a few hundred more feet of steady walking through snow that now reached Sophie's thighs. Her muscles alternatively ached and screamed with fatigue, never painless. Her head pounded, her throat was raw and dry, and the exposed skin on her face had chafed from windburn hours ago. But with the top now in sight, her spirits lifted. Another hour of climbing—two, if the ascent was steeper than it looked— and they would make it.

She bumped into Kathryn. "Sorry," she mumbled, stepping back. She hadn't realized that the woman in front of her had stopped, but as she sidestepped to look around her, she saw that the others in front had stopped as well. They were looking at a body.

Sophie's stomach sank. The body wore a navy down suit with the Japanese flag sewn on the right sleeve. She looked at the face. Yakumo. He had died curled in a fetal position, trying to keep warm. His ice axe rested in the snow beside his body. Evelyn said something quietly under her breath, and Andrew put his hand on her shoulder.

"He didn't try to bivouac," Sophie said quietly, more to herself than to Kathryn or Levi.

Beside her, Levi muttered under his breath as he tugged away his oxygen mask. "God, this isn't good."

"I'll radio Base Camp," Andrew said, addressing the group.

Sophie turned to Levi, desperate for whatever small comfort she could find right now. The oxygen mask had created harsh indents in his face, and the angry red lines made him look much older. She moved closer to him and took his hand.

"I'm worried."

"Me too," he replied. "But I feel okay. Physically, I mean. We're so close."

"I know." She removed her sunglasses for a moment and looked at him. The others fell away until it was just the two of them.

She must have stared for a moment too long; Levi gave her a puzzled look. "What?"

"Nothing. I can't wait to get off this mountain."

"I agree."

"The radio isn't working well," Andrew announced, returning from where he had strayed, searching for a signal. "I only hear static on their end. Maybe I got through. No use in worrying about it now."

Evelyn gestured for them to resume the line. The climbers shuffled into place, even more somber than before. Levi squeezed Sophie's hand and then repositioned his oxygen mask. The line moved forward; each climber's head bowed as they passed Yakumo. Some stole sideways glances at his curled body, unable to look away from the bleak message about the dangers of the mountain. Others looked straight ahead. Sophie kept her gaze focused on Kathryn's back. She would say a prayer for Yakumo that night, she told herself, when they were back safe at Camp Four. For now, she couldn't let her focus drift to the dead, lest she join them.

The summit revealed itself slowly as the climbers pushed on, struggling against the gusting wind and sheer exhaustion. Sophie lifted her head and noticed clouds rolling in, turning the western horizon a bleak gray. She thought about saying something but kept her mouth shut. Surely everyone had seen the clouds. The weather was not supposed to turn. Her mind couldn't stay occupied with worrying for more than a few moments. Wading through the snow was too grueling. Fatigue rippled through her body with each step. So close— she lost track of all time. She heard a shout and looked ahead. Andrew stood with his fist raised not far in front of her. She glanced back at Levi to offer him a final dose of encouragement, but his head was down.

When Sophie set foot on the summit, she felt nothing, no congratulatory pat on the back. She stepped aside to make way for the others and turned back to Levi, saw him stumble and struggle to stay upright. She went to him immediately.

"Hey. You're okay. We made it."

Levi nodded weakly, clinging to her for support. She glanced around at the others celebrating, oblivious to Levi's condition. When she looked back at him, he had removed his oxygen mask. Light flurries had begun to fall, melting instantly against his exposed skin.

"You should keep that on," she said, as fear ran through her body. If symptoms of altitude sickness set in now, such as thinking he was fine without supplemental oxygen, it would be a difficult—or impossible—task to bring him down the mountain. She shuddered to think of the ridge and the ice wall between the summit and Camp Four.

"It's...okay. I'll put it...back on...before we descend." He labored for breath between words, but he was smiling, his eyes bright as he slipped off his sunglasses. "Want some of that...summit air."

Sophie nodded. "Of course." Someone touched her back and she turned to see Andrew.

"A picture?" He held a small digital camera. He waited for them to pose, arms around each other's shoulders, and snapped the photo. "We made it," he said, high fiving each of them. "Congratulations."

Sophie scanned the group behind him for a moment, taking it all in. She noticed a pile of boxy black objects near the center of the summit. "Are those..."

"Summit registers. Yakumo and Wojciech must have made it." She could hear both the pain and the admiration in Andrew's voice, the respect he held for his fellow mountaineers. Each team had brought its own register since no one had been to the top of Yama Parvat before. If only one team made it, there would still be a marker left for future groups. But it seemed that each team who reached the peak would leave its own. She touched Andrew's arm for a moment.

"Hey. We don't know where Wojciech is. He might still be out there, along with several others."

"I know. Can't give up hope yet and all that." He looked up

at the sky, at the heavy gray clouds that dispensed the snow. "I don't like the look of that. We'll take a minute or two more and then descend."

Sophie nodded. She took Levi's hand and wandered the shelf's edge, staring out at the other monstrous peaks that soared toward the sky—some taller, like the infamous Annapurna I, and others smaller, like the other Annapurnas and Tilicho. She remembered standing at Sarangkot in the bright sunshine a lifetime ago, when George had pointed out these very peaks. She turned to Levi, feeling impossibly small beneath the yawning gray sky. In a few short days they would leave Base Camp and trek back to Pokhara where their journey had begun more than a month ago.

Something below caught her eye. "Look," she said to Levi. "Pemba and Dawa stayed behind." The two men stood side by side a few feet below. She realized, with enormous respect, how much they had sacrificed, the physical effort they had displayed, to come so far and not set foot on the summit. Above all, they respected Yama Parvat.

Levi was struggling to put on his oxygen mask. It took her a moment to see it, absorbed in her thoughts as she was, but his hands shook violently as he attempted to move the strap over the back of his head.

"I'll help you," she said quickly, feeling guilty for getting distracted. She slipped the mask over his head and paused. "Are you okay? Please be honest. I want you to get down safely."

He hesitated and then shook his head. "I can…manage, I think, but…I'm so. tired."

Sophie focused on turning her fear into attentiveness. She positioned the oxygen mask on his face and took his sunglasses from his other trembling hand, although the clouds solved part of the snow blindness threat. She didn't want to take any risks.

"You're going to be fine," she said, slipping the sunglasses onto his face. She pulled the hood of his jacket over the back of his head, brushing the accumulated snowflakes off it. "We'll be back in our tent drinking broth in no time."

While she had been focused on helping Levi, the others had begun to descend. There seemed to be no order to the line now; with the snow picking up and the cold wind blowing, everyone wanted to return as quickly as possible. Sophie gestured for Levi to follow her and fell in behind one of the Canadians. They shuffled off the shelf, walking along the exposed ridge of snow as the jagged rock began to take shape to their right.

Sophie heard the distinct sound of a body hitting the snow behind her and turned as quickly as she could. Levi sat in the snow, his legs tangled, breathing hard. She went to him without thinking. There was no one behind them. She looked back at the line of climbers, already disappearing into the flurrying snow. She cupped her hands around her mouth and shouted, certain that the wind would steal her words again.

One paused and turned back.

Andrew trudged toward them, his cheeks red enough to match his hair. He stopped a few feet away, taking in the sight of Levi on the ground, of Sophie standing over him.

"What's wrong?" Andrew asked.

Sophie tore her gaze from Andrew. Levi tugged weakly at his oxygen mask. She removed it for him.

"Bottle's out," he said in one breath.

Sophie looked back at Andrew. "You can go," she said. "We'll just be a minute."

Andrew hesitated. She saw on his face the code of the

mountains, his unwillingness to leave behind a weakened member of the team. But Sophie felt strong as ever, and she thought—hoped, prayed—that Levi would too with a fresh bottle of oxygen.

"Please go," Sophie said, raising her voice over a gust of wind that sprayed snow across her face. "If you wait any longer, you'll be separated from the rest. We'll be just a minute. Right behind you."

Andrew opened his mouth, then closed it and nodded. "If you're sure."

"Certain," Sophie said, though she was nowhere near it. But separating Andrew from his team would surely put more people in trouble. Though the Tetons were nothing like the Himalayas, her emergency preparedness training came flooding back. Remain calm. Check for injuries. Protect the weakened climber from the elements.

Andrew turned away, and Sophie focused her attention on Levi.

She quickly removed the empty bottle from his backpack, tossing it in the snow. She allowed herself to ignore the usual guilt she felt for littering. Levi didn't have the strength to carry down the empty bottle, and she had no room for it in her pack. She pulled out the other bottle and adjusted the dial for a moderate flow rate. She didn't want to risk running out before they reached Camp Four, where more oxygen was stashed.

"Here. Breathe," she said, fitting the new mask over his face.

He pointed at the bottle on her backpack, a question.

"I don't need it yet," she told him. She was wary now of taking any oxygen for herself. "I'm going to clip you to me," she told him. "We'll figure out a way to get you down the ridge." And then the ice wall. "Can you walk?"

He nodded, and she stood to help him up. She forced her

freezing hands to work quickly, fastening a system of two carabiners and a short rope that ran from her harness to Levi's. When she was done, she looked in the direction of the route. Visibility had dropped because of the storm, but she saw no one ahead of them. Andrew must have already caught up to his team. The weight of their aloneness sank in. She reminded herself to breathe, to get as much oxygen as possible so that her brain didn't stop working on the descent. Reluctantly, she let go of Levi. He stood braced in the wind, as if just standing took all his strength.

She took one step. Something made her stop and look back toward the summit. Through the whirling snow, she squinted. Someone was there. Another person, a dark shape moving. She turned Levi around, pulled his snow-dusted sunglasses off, and pointed.

"Do you see it?" she half whispered, hoping that it was an illusion, a trick of her imagination.

Beside her, Levi nodded.

CHAPTER NINETEEN

May 2018,
Yama Parvat Summit, Nepal

Evelyn hadn't meant to stay behind. She had played along on the summit, smiling and embracing the Canadian climbers, the closest thing she had to teammates. Lowell had hugged her, and she knew it meant *no hard feelings*—but lately, all of Evelyn's feelings had been hard. Then the snow started and everyone rushed to ready themselves for the descent. She decided to let them go, didn't want to be bumped off the mountain by someone in a hurry. How quickly they had all left her behind. Now that the storm had arrived, they weren't wasting any time looking over their shoulders.

She had never stood alone on top of the world before. There were always cameras snapping and flags pushed into the snow and elated teammates. Or at least Sophie. Now, her only company was the wind, screaming past her ears at dizzying speed. She felt an acute exhaustion, not just from the physical exertion, but from everything—her final conver-

sation with Sophie and her pathetic attempt at romantic re-
demption with Lowell. She hadn't spoken to either of them
in the last week, which left her a lot of time to think. Then
Phil and Danielle had turned back before reaching the summit. She had failed them, failed to inspire them to push on,
failed to instill in them the confidence that the journey's end
was within their reach. She could see their faces, their ex-
pressions of defeat and resignation, and Danielle leaning in
to ask, *Are you sure you want to go on?*

Danielle's question had surprising accuracy, because Evelyn had reached the conclusion that returning to a normal
life after this trip was impossible. Her teammates' failure to
summit had reinforced that she was incapable of assisting anyone up a mountain. There was nothing waiting for her back
in New York—no career, probably no Miles. She thought
again of radical change, of reinventing herself. Her thoughts
seemed filtered through a layer of fog, each idea coming to
her like a whispered secret. She didn't have to stay in New
York. She didn't have to win Sophie's forgiveness. She didn't
have to remain a lawyer. The world unfolded before her in
sparkling glory, or maybe it was only the snow and the un-
ending white sky.

Evelyn gazed up and walked in small circles. Already, she
felt the lack of oxygen; her movements slow and uncoordi-
nated, as if she were gradually losing control of her body. She
observed her physical changes from afar, removed from the
sensations. A small part of her brain screamed at her to descend, told her how difficult it would be the longer she waited.
But another, louder voice told her that she was on the cusp
of understanding her own path. She just needed to hold on.

She heard a sound and stopped, turning slowly to look for
the source. It had sounded almost—human? She waited; the

sound did not come again. Probably another figment of her overexerted brain. Auditory hallucinations commonly occurred while freezing to death, but she didn't think her body temperature was low enough.

No—there it was again. The sound. Evelyn brushed snowflakes from her eyelashes and walked away from the summit shelf, toward where the other climbers had descended. She stayed silent, a creature of the snow. Seconds later, a body nearly collided with hers.

"You—Evelyn?"

It took her a moment to register Sophie's face, which was lobster red. She hadn't realized the visibility was so poor, that her sister could simply emerge from the snow without warning.

"What are you doing here?"

"What are *you* doing here?" Sophie replied, her tone accusatory, her voice hoarse. "We got separated from the others and I turned around and saw someone up here. I didn't expect it to be you."

How? Evelyn wanted to ask. She didn't understand how Sophie had seen her when Evelyn couldn't see a few feet in front of her own face. Evelyn glanced from Sophie to Levi, who looked as if he was barely managing to stay upright.

"What's wrong with him?"

"I don't know," Sophie said. "Hypoxia or altitude sickness. I don't have time to diagnose him."

"We need to go," Evelyn said. In mere seconds, her thoughts had sharpened and crystallized like the snowflakes falling all around them. The future could wait: in the meantime, Sophie had to get Levi down the mountain.

"Come on," she shouted over her shoulder as she brushed past them both, uncertain if the wind would snatch her words away. After a few more feet she stopped to look back; Sophie and Levi were following, although Sophie paused to steady him every couple of steps.

God, Evelyn thought. *At this rate we'll all die on this mountain.* There was no way the two of them were descending without her. While her sister inched forward, Evelyn maneuvered a bottle of oxygen from her backpack and strapped the mask to her face, setting the dial for a low flow. The fresh air helped immensely. Sophie seemed to have gotten Levi moving forward at a better pace, and the trio made its way off the summit. They remained silent, the wind too loud to speak above unless they were inches apart and shouting. Besides, both Levi and Evelyn now wore oxygen masks. Evelyn wondered if she should stop and suggest the same to Sophie, but the force of the storm kept her forging ahead. She took careful steps, moving as quickly as she could, tracing the rock that rose to the right, the route so narrow that one false step could be fatal. She felt the weight of her responsibility—to safely deliver Levi and Sophie into someone else's hands. It occurred to her that perhaps this was what she had been waiting for, why she'd stayed behind. Some intangible part of her being had sensed Sophie was in trouble. With fresh oxygen drawing down into her lungs, reinvigorating her brain, Evelyn could bring Sophie and Levi to safety. No small task, but in a way one she'd been preparing for her entire life.

The power of the weather on a mountain always astounded Evelyn. How quickly the wind rose and gusted, even in May, when the risk of avalanches should have been higher than the risk of blizzards. But mountains were never predictable. Evelyn estimated that the gusts were close to seventy miles an hour. She had been in similar winds on K2, but tucked safely in a tent beside Sophie. Descending through these conditions was entirely new territory. The oxygen mask did a decent job at shielding her cheeks from the elements, but her eyes were exposed to the full force of the wind and stinging snowflakes. She lifted an arm to shield her face and kept going. At least it wasn't night. Somewhere far above the clouds, a weak sun did its best to shed light on their path.

Evelyn checked her watch. Almost an hour had passed already, and they had made little progress. The snow relented and then picked up again as the wind screamed like a banshee over the rock wall. Evelyn stopped, blinking against the snow, though it was a futile game. She knew, without seeing, that they had reached the ridge.

She turned around, laying her eyes on Sophie and Levi for the first time since they had begun walking. She had resisted looking back, knowing there was little she could do to save either of them if disaster struck. Either Sophie and Levi would descend the mountain, or they wouldn't. Somewhere nearby, Yakumo's body lay in a shallow snow-covered grave. She held her breath until she saw them emerge from the clouds, a few short steps behind her. Levi was weaving, unable to walk straight, but doing his best to keep up with Sophie's shuffling pace. The line between them was pulled tight.

Evelyn yanked her mask down and moved close to Sophie, shouting to make herself heard. "The ridge. Can he make it down?"

Sophie's wide hazel eyes stared back at her. She looked so terrified that Evelyn wanted to comfort her, but there was nothing to do or say. Nothing would improve until they reached the relative safety of Camp Four.

"The ridge, Sophie," she repeated.

Sophie blinked, as if hearing her for the first time. "I don't know," she shouted back.

"Should we bivouac?" Evelyn didn't want to suggest it, but

Sophie's dazed state left her no choice. If her sister wasn't en-thusiastically willing to attempt the ridge, they would have to hunker down and wait for the storm to pass. Bivouacking was risky, but when death lurked around every corner, some-times staying still was the safest option.

Her suggestion seemed to snap Sophie out of her fog. "No way. He won't survive. We have to keep going."

Evelyn gazed at Levi, who stood with his head down, look-ing like a long sleep would do him wonders. She knew that he was probably exhausted, but Sophie was right—in a weakened state it was all too easy to give up fighting and accept death.

"Okay. But once we're on the ridge, we can't stop."

"I know."

Evelyn nodded once and slipped the oxygen mask back over her face. She went to Levi and lifted his head, forcing him to look at her. She took off his sunglasses and searched his eyes—for what, she didn't know, but she saw it, some spark still there, a willingness to survive. She let go of him and stepped back, shoving his sunglasses into her pocket. He had no use for them now. Sophie looked at Evelyn as she passed, her open mouth ready to ask a question, but Evelyn kept mov-ing forward, gesturing for them to follow.

The ridge proved a different beast in bad weather. The storm helped hide the exposure on either side, although if Ev-elyn looked down, she saw an endless gray abyss below. The wind was the true enemy, gusting relentlessly and doing its best to push them off the rocky ridge. Evelyn squatted low, using her ice axe with each step. She couldn't remember how long the ridge went on for. Each breath of bottled oxygen burned her sore throat. She was desperate for water.

She heard a cry, followed by the awful sound of an ice axe

striking rock. She twisted, gripping the rock for support, and saw nothing. Sophie and Levi were gone.

Evelyn yanked off her oxygen mask and screamed Sophie's name. It was like she said nothing at all. The wind surged around her, continuing its deathly howl. She inched back in the direction they had come, still shouting, her lungs fighting for every inch of air as she tried to out-scream the wind. Pain bloomed in her chest. She needed oxygen, but she needed her voice even more.

She heard something. Another cry. She stopped and yelled her sister's name again. Another faint cry in return. She looked down the right side of the ridge and saw something—a spot of color amid the white. She didn't think twice.

Evelyn quickly secured a rope to one of the small spires of exposed rock. She had no idea if it would hold her weight. She tugged the rope as hard as she could; the rock held. She clipped on and rappelled down the side of the ridge.

Sophie had self-arrested with her ice axe about fifty feet down the ridge. Every muscle in her upper body held on for dear life. Evelyn saw right away why Sophie was unable to pull herself farther up. Levi hung from her sister like deadweight, lying unmoving on his side.

She used her own ice axe to anchor herself and look down at Sophie, her mind racing. They could try to climb back up using the ropes, although it was risky. Her tie had been fast and it wasn't even a proper rappel system, just the quickest job she'd been able to do. Sophie could make it, maybe, but there was no way Levi would. The other option was down the mountain, into the abyss. Evelyn bit her cheek so hard she tasted blood. She knew what she had to do.

"Don't panic," she shouted to Sophie.

Her sister's eyes filled with alarm. "You can't leave us here."

"I'm not going to."

Evelyn rappelled lower, carefully making her way around Sophie. Her hand shook so hard that she almost lost her grip on the rope. She felt Sophie's eyes on her as she reached her sister's waist. She had no time to hesitate, no time to say anything else. She reached over and unclipped Levi.

He cried out as he began to fall. That was the worst part. In the seconds beforehand, Evelyn had convinced herself that he was unconscious already, that he would feel nothing as he fell. But now she realized that he had been awake the whole time. If the fall didn't kill him, he would freeze to death, injured and alone, somewhere far below on the mountain.

But she couldn't think about that now. Sophie's unintelligible screams filled the air, piercing her ears. Evelyn grabbed her instantly, afraid that she would let go of the ice axe. But Sophie's grip remained tight as she howled, her cries joining the wind in a chorus of unnatural agony.

"Sophie," Evelyn shouted. "We have to climb back up."

It felt futile. Sophie wasn't looking at her. She knew Sophie would run out of oxygen eventually, and so she clung to the rope with one hand and her ice axe with the other, her arm muscles burning in protest, until Sophie's screams fizzled to choking sobs, and then she was gasping for air.

"Climb. Grab the rope. You're going ahead of me."

It was a miracle that Sophie listened. Maybe she was too exhausted to object, or in shock, or maybe a tiny part of her understood why Evelyn had done it. The necessity of ending one life to save another. Whatever the reason, Sophie took hold of the rope, pulled her axe free, and climbed.

It was no easy task to return to the ridge. Every part of Evelyn's body burned with fatigue by the time they reached the top. A strong gust of wind almost sent her over the other side and she clung to the rock, desperate to reach a part of the mountain where they were shielded from the power of the wind.

Sophie stared down the side of the ridge, where they had come from. Evelyn grabbed her shoulder, afraid that Sophie would plummet down the side if given half a chance.

"Put on an oxygen mask," Evelyn said, reaching around to grab a bottle from her sister's pack. Sophie nodded dumbly and strapped the mask to her windburned, puffy face. With horror, Evelyn noticed that Sophie's nose was turning gray. Frostbite. She hadn't used any protection on her face for the last several hours, not even a face mask. Evelyn quickly reapplied her own oxygen mask. The surge of fresh air helped to dull the ache in her chest, but only mildly.

The sisters pushed into the wind, each shuffling step forward a new battle. The universe answered, allowing them to progress down the ridge. Sophie had always been the believer, but now Evelyn muttered quiet prayers into the wind—anything to keep her mind focused.

They made it to the end of the ridge. Both sisters collapsed for a moment, hunkering down on their knees to catch their breath and, for a moment, stop fighting the wind, which still swirled around them, pulling at their suits and flinging bits of stinging snow onto exposed skin. Evelyn stared at Sophie, whose eyes were blank. She wanted some sign from her sister, some indication that she still had a will to live, but Sophie gave her none.

Evelyn stood up, a slow, graceless process. She extended a hand to Sophie, who stared at her blankly. She grabbed her sister's arm and hauled her upward, steadying her as she rose. She didn't have the energy to remove her mask again to tell Sophie to follow her. Pain radiated from her chest in rhythmic bursts, a constant reminder of overexertion. Evelyn turned away and began walking again. The slope was almost level at this part of the mountain. She had forgotten what the scenery looked like; she used the rock wall to the right to navigate. She knew that the false route was somewhere along the other side of the massive rocks, where two climbers had fallen to their deaths. Each step brought them closer to the ice wall.

Hours passed and still the wind roared. Evelyn couldn't make sense of the numbers on her watch. It felt like days since the summit. An eternity of leaning into the wind, plowing forward, shielding her eyes from the snow, stealing glances back at Sophie. Her sister plodded on behind her. Evelyn stumbled as she looked forward again, falling to her knees. She was exhausted and could no longer ignore it. *Why haven't we reached the ice wall yet?* She squeezed her eyes shut, desperate for relief from the relentless snow. A hand touched her back.

Without looking up, Evelyn pulled down her oxygen mask. "We have to sleep here. I can't keep going." Just shouting the words took all her energy.

Sophie stepped in front of Evelyn, forcing her to look, and pointed at the rock wall. Though jagged, it provided some crevices. Evelyn understood Sophie's intention: they could dig out a small shelter and bivouac. Evelyn thought of sleep, of rest, and managed to push back to her feet. The sisters walked beside each other to the rock wall. Where it curved and rose in jagged spires toward the sky, they found a narrow cranny and began digging, using both hands to shovel the snow away from the rock.

Evelyn heard something. A grunt. Maybe just the wind groaning over the rocks. Then it came again. She stopped and looked skyward, terrified of seeing a serac overhead that they had ignored, a shelf of ice coming loose. But the rock above was either bare or only dusted with snow. She looked at Sophie, who had also stopped digging.

Evelyn reached to pull down her mask, but Sophie had already turned away and was brushing snow from the ground left and right, as if searching for a lost item. Evelyn joined her. It was only a few minutes before her hand struck something solid. A body.

She dug as quickly as her lethargic body would allow, sweeping the snow away to reveal a body wrapped in a black bivy sack. The top of the sack was partially unzipped, a bad sign. Evelyn fumbled with the zipper and revealed the body's face. Lowell.

Now she did pull down her mask as she placed a gloved hand against his face, which was nearly encased in ice. She hoped the warmth of her hand would melt the ice, but her glove was cold and did little to help. She brushed away the icicles sealing his eyes shut and they fluttered open. He grunted again, an attempt to communicate, and she realized that his lips were frozen shut. She rested her hand over his mouth and blew her breath over his lips, amazed that he was alive, and terrified, too, because it hadn't occurred to her that perhaps others had not made it to Camp Four. She thought of her teammates, wondered if they had turned around with enough time.

Lowell grunted again and she withdrew her hand. He worked his jaw slowly, as if it caused him great pain. His cheeks and nose were scarred with frostbite.

"Evelyn," he said weakly.

She moved her face closer to his to hear him above the wind. "What happened?"

He blinked up at her. "The storm." His dry sense of humor was still intact. "I'm with," he said, motioning his head the

tiniest bit. Evelyn glanced back at Sophie. She had also uncovered a body beneath the snow. "Eddie. We went slow.
We made it to the ice wall but the snow kicked up and—"
he paused to take several labored breaths "—turned around.
Came here, thought we'd sleep until it's over. Two hours ago,
maybe. I don't know."

Evelyn made the effort of rolling up her sleeve to check
her watch. "It's just after 3:00."

"Perfect for a nap."

"You need oxygen," Evelyn said. "Do you have any?"

The smallest shake of his head. "No. Gave it all to Eddie.
Used my bottle on the way up, gave my second to him. He's
really struggling."

"Why are you so far apart?"

"Didn't want to use another man for body heat. Isn't that
funny. He'd rather die."

"He's alive."

Evelyn flinched and glanced over her shoulder. She hadn't
noticed Sophie move closer, but she was just behind Evelyn's
left shoulder, listening in. The first words she had spoken
since Levi had died. Since Evelyn had killed him.

"Sophie," Lowell said. "You're here too. What about—"

Evelyn shook her head quickly. He couldn't mention Levi;
his name might send Sophie spiraling again.

Something changed in Lowell's eyes as he seemed to understand.

"I have an extra bottle of O2," Evelyn said.

"I can't use it. You'll run out."

"And you'll get hypoxia. Sophie, can you grab it?" She felt
Sophie's hands on her backpack, pulling the cylinder of oxygen free. "Take this." Evelyn handed it to Lowell. "We're
staying here. None of us are getting down the ice wall."

Evelyn shrugged off her backpack and forced her numb fingers to undo the buckles and straps. She pulled her bivy sack from the backpack and unrolled it, glancing up occasionally to make sure Sophie was doing the same. Evelyn removed her crampons and slipped inside, shivering, and settled in, checking on her sister once more before making sure to close the zipper completely around her own head. She was encased in darkness and had no idea when the storm would end. The rocks overhead provided little shelter from the snow, and Evelyn soon understood why both Lowell and Eddie had been covered. She flung an arm over her face and squeezed her eyes shut, willing herself to go inward, to ignore the prickling, burning sensation in her toes that soon faded to numbness. The afternoon was wearing thin. Perhaps, like yesterday, the storm would end with the onset of night. She could only hope.

Strange things came to her in dreams. Miles, emptying their apartment and painting rivers on the walls before he left. Her father, headless, transparent, walking behind her as she entered the courtroom for a case. He was the accused, but she could not interrogate him; he had no mouth with which to speak. A vision of her mother sitting alone in the dark, crying. Evelyn and Sophie sat at her feet, just children, reaching out for her, calling her name, but she couldn't hear or see them. Then Evelyn was climbing. She reached up to touch her face and great pieces of skin came away in her hand, rubbery and pale like chicken flesh. She touched her face again and felt bone. She looked back and saw Sophie falling away down the mountain, her mouth open in a silent scream. Someone yanked her hand and pulled her forward. Levi. Had she—

Evelyn woke up breathless. Her oxygen had run out. She couldn't move her arms and for an agonizing moment she struggled, almost paralyzed by the fallen snow. Finally, she wriggled an arm free and pawed at the mask. Her fingers weren't working. She couldn't feel them at all. She managed to push the mask aside and gasped for air. She reached up and managed to wedge a hand between the two zippers and open the top part of the bag.

Evelyn stared straight up at the most impossibly dark sky. The moon had been swallowed by thick clouds. A few snowflakes floated down, melting as soon as they touched Evelyn's cheeks. She marveled at that—how her frozen body was still warm enough to melt the snow. The wind had stopped almost entirely. She wondered if she should try to stand up, to rouse the others. It might be their only window to descend. But her body felt so heavy. Each breath brought her closer to sleep; she wanted nothing more than to rest. She closed her eyes and drifted again.

Someone was saying her name. The same person held her wrist and pulled her forward. She could only see their back, leading her into the perpetual darkness, across a field of snow. Ahead were mountains, tall and white, fog rolling around the peaks. *No. I don't want to climb again.*

She pulled her arm back and opened her eyes. She was still alive—how? Her face felt like a thousand hawks had dug their talons into her skin. It was light out. Someone was looming over her; it took her too long to recognize the face. Sophie. She looked like a child's drawing come to life, sketched in red and black crayon. She looked like she shouldn't be alive.

"Evelyn," Sophie said, and that single word seemed to take all her strength. Her lips were cracked and bleeding.

Evelyn opened her mouth to speak and felt the sharp pain of her own lips splitting, felt the warm blood roll down her chin. Sophie reached forward, slowly, to wipe it away. Evelyn's throat screamed for water. Every part of her felt dried out and numb. She couldn't feel her fingers or toes and knew they were probably gone, lost to frostbite. Judging by Sophie's face, all that awaited them if they made it off the mountain was reconstructive surgery. She pulled her straying thoughts in, wondering if it was the oxygen deprivation that caused her mind to wander. Every moment counted. She didn't have time to think about the future.

"Eddie's dead," Sophie said.

Evelyn absorbed the news silently. Another death on a mountain that had taken so many lives already.

She tried to say "Lowell," but words failed to escape her raw throat. Her lips bled again and she shut her mouth quickly, moving her left forearm to cover the searing pain. Sophie seemed to understand anyway. She moved around Evelyn and began sweeping the snow away from his face and torso. Summoning all her strength, Evelyn sat up and joined in.

It was a clear morning; the sky overhead was a gentle blue, lit by a generous sun rising in the east. No wind blew. Evelyn was struck by how beautiful the morning was, how quiet, how soft the colors. A breathtaking moment of perpetual winter. She looked at her watch; the screen had gone dark. She pushed at it for a moment, pressing the buttons clumsily, but nothing happened. She judged that it was early, maybe 6:00 a.m. She wondered if anyone would come looking for them and knew they couldn't wait around to find out.

She uncovered Lowell's right arm and took his pulse, counting out the seconds in her head and wishing, for the millionth time, that she'd brought a spare battery for her watch.

"Pulse?" Sophie asked. She must have been counting the seconds too.

Evelyn nodded.

"Okay. I'll try to wake him." Evelyn didn't know how Sophie managed to speak. She watched her sister say Lowell's name and shake him gently. Evelyn swallowed spit, trying to relieve her burning throat, and joined in.

After a long minute, Lowell's eyes blinked open. He turned his head incrementally, taking in both Evelyn and Sophie. He still wore the oxygen mask; Sophie reached over to gently pull it from his face.

His breath came in a wheeze. Evelyn and Sophie shared a look, and she knew they were both thinking of George. If Lowell was suffering from an embolism, they had no way of getting him down the mountain.

Lowell grunted and sat up, like a bear coming out of hibernation. He looked stronger than she had anticipated. He blinked rapidly in the bright light and looked between the sisters again.

"Eddie didn't make it," Sophie said, anticipating the question he would ask.

Lowell drew a sharp breath.

"We have to try," Evelyn managed to say. She wasn't sure what she meant, but both Sophie and Lowell seemed to understand. Try to do what the others couldn't, through luck or circumstance: survive.

A few minutes later, by sheer will and effort, they were all standing, backpacks shouldered, crampons attached to their boots. Evelyn swayed under the weight of the pack but found her balance. They left their bivy sacks behind; it went unspoken that none of them would survive another night in the open. Silently, Evelyn took the first step forward.

The calm weather made the descent significantly easier, but each step tested Evelyn's willpower. She hadn't eaten in a day, her brain seemed to work at half-speed, and the numbness had spread into the lower part of her legs, though bursts of pain occasionally radiated up from her feet and ankles. Each excruciating step also brought her closer to safety, and she tried to remember that as they approached the ice wall, pausing to breathe several times between each stride.

The trio stood at the edge, looking down. No ladder, just ropes. It wasn't an extremely difficult wall to climb—Evelyn had managed fine on the way up—but descending the wall in her current condition was a different game. She assessed for a moment longer and made her decision.

"I'm going to try rappelling," she managed to say. No one scoffed at her idea. The short sentence left her gasping for breath, and she stood for a moment, imagining the bottles of oxygen that awaited them below. She swung off her pack and tried to open it and dig through for ropes. Her numb fingers made the task nearly impossible. Sophie crouched to help, then Lowell, and together they managed to pull out the ropes.

"This isn't going to work," Sophie said, and Evelyn knew she was right.

Evelyn lifted her right hand to her mouth and gripped her glove with her teeth, turning her head to yank it off. The sight made her gag. The fingers were discolored and gnarled, almost like a claw, frozen into shape. Sophie stared at the hand, wide-eyed, probably imagining what her own looked like.

"It has to work." Evelyn maneuvered her ungloved hand around one of the ropes and lifted it toward her chest harness. It took a few tries, but with Sophie's help she managed to clip on the carabiner. She looped her backpack back over her shoulders, worried about the extra weight but reluctant to leave all the essential supplies behind. She stood and moved to the edge, holding the other end of the rope in her hand.

She clipped onto the fixed rope at the top of the wall on the first try, bracing it against the ice. Sophie and Lowell peered uncertainly over the edge.

"Don't wait until I'm at the bottom. Start as soon as you can." At least she could speak again, though it still took more air than seemed worthwhile. Evelyn used her teeth to pull her glove back on. Holding her ice axe in her left hand, she dropped her gaze down and set about descending, carefully feeling for footholds. Finding handholds was out of the question; she used her forearms to press against the ice, relying on her upper-body strength to descend. It worked. By some miracle, she made progress down the wall. When she was about a third of the way down, she looked up to see Sophie clipping on.

Then Evelyn slipped. She felt the ice splinter beneath her boot a split second before she fell. She swung wildly with the ice axe and finally made contact, driving the point deep enough to hold her weight. She kicked with both feet and found footholds. The fall hadn't been long, but her heart contracted in painful beats and her whole body shook as she looked down. She didn't have much farther to go. Sophie and Lowell were yelling her name above. She shouted back that she was okay and set about trying to unclip herself from the rope. When the carabiner released, she fell backward again, this time into the snow below. The impact knocked the remaining breath from her body and she lay there for a moment, staring up at the sky and feeling the pain explode through her chest and head, burning white-hot before fizzling out only slightly. Then she stood up.

Sophie and Lowell made their way down. Evelyn paced back and forth, marveling at the cold, at her exhaustion, at the miracle of making it down the wall. They regrouped at

the bottom, shoving ropes back into backpacks with uncoop-
erative hands. Another thousand feet until Camp Four. She
had no idea if anyone waited for them there.

The descent came and went in fragmented pieces. Evelyn
remembered the brilliant white shine of the snow whenever
she lifted her sunglasses, and the blue dome of the sky overhead. She remembered the other Himalayan giants scraping
the sky like outstretched hands with mangled fingers. Like
her own. She remembered the sound of labored breath and
the crunch of ice and snow beneath boots. A gorak soared
across the sky but Evelyn said nothing, convinced the bird appeared only to her, some premonition from a distant dream.
Like after her argument with Sophie. She hadn't figured out
yet if the goraks were an omen of fortune or misery.

Camp Four revealed itself suddenly, the small cluster of
tents nestled into the mountain taking them all by surprise.
Of course. They'd never seen it from the opposite side before.

Lowell called out for help, his roaring voice echoing off the
rocks. No call returned. He tried again as they moved closer,
and this time, something stirred. A person emerged from
one of the tents and then another, until a quartet approached
them. Andrew and several of the guides, Mingma included.
He must have returned to Camp Four after descending with
Phil and Danielle. Evelyn forced herself to keep walking, although her pace was slow compared to Andrew's approaching party. Her chest felt like it was on fire.

"Holy shit," he said as they drew closer. "You're alive.
Good god."

He pulled each of them into a hug, thumping their backs,
as if he were an uncle at a family reunion. Evelyn could only
think of sleeping. Her vision began to blur.

Andrew looked between them. "Is Levi—"

Evelyn looked at Sophie. To her surprise, Sophie stared back, and she saw something in her sister's eyes, a kind of dissolving. She saw through the front Sophie had managed for the last day—shock and trauma had allowed her to forget. Pushing the pain aside was the only way to survive. But she had not really forgotten, and she would certainly never forgive. Evelyn knew that she would have rather died with Levi than done nothing to save him. Despite what she said, Sophie might have, one day, forgiven her for Miles. But Levi's death was something different. She saw all this, and understood, before Sophie looked back at Andrew.

"Levi is gone."

The words hung in the air for a long moment before Lowell said, "Eddie too."

Andrew shook his head. Silence lingered for another moment. "Well, you're all alive. And thank god for that."

He said something else, about waiting for them all night, guides coming up from Base Camp to search, how they had looked that morning but not far enough. Something about food and oxygen. Evelyn heard it all as if trapped in a nearby room, listening through the wall. The others all turned their backs and moved away, toward the tents, toward warmth and safety. Evelyn tried to take a step and sank to her knees in the snow. The flame inside her chest grew higher, licking up to her throat, spreading from her heart to her lungs and her shoulders. Burning her alive from the inside. She tried to call out but the ground was there to catch her. She felt the cold snow brush against her cheek, closing her eyes as she returned to the darkness that had always kept her safe. She thought she heard someone saying her name, but she was too tired to open her eyes. She had delivered Sophie safely to Camp Four. There was nothing more to be done. Someone slipped their hand into hers. Without looking she knew it was Sophie. She breathed the thin air, felt it meet the fire in her chest, and went still.

CHAPTER TWENTY

No one returned to Yama Parvat for ten years.

As soon as the last climbers left that spring, Nepal decreed it illegal to trek to or around the mountain, at the price of a fine no rulebreaker was willing to pay. All permits were discontinued. The government would not even allow search parties to recover the remaining bodies, citing the dangers of the mountain. It always struck Sophie as strange. The mountain itself was not dangerous; all the teams had summited. They were subject to bad luck—the avalanche, the storm—but death was not unheard-of on an unclimbed mountain. She hated to think that way—of course, she hadn't wanted anyone to die. In hindsight, the survivors agreed that so many people attempting to climb the mountain at once had probably not helped. They had all gotten caught up in the excitement, the prospect of fame and glory, without foreseeing the consequences of so many mountaineers trying to make a first ascent.

The news reports had focused more on the deaths than
the successful summits. After the first week in the hospital
in Kathmandu, spent in a haze of grafting surgeries and pain
medication, she had befriended one of the nurses and asked
for articles about the climb. Reading them, seeing Evelyn's
and Levi's names listed among the dead in print, didn't make
her feel better, but it did take her mind off the searing pain in
her hands, face, and feet. The one she didn't read was Lowell's article for *Summit* magazine. It had been picked up by the
New York Times, accompanied by a series of film photographs
he had taken. But she knew what the article contained, unlike the others—quotes, not just from survivors, but from the
dead. Sophie knew Lowell had interviewed both Evelyn and
Levi, and she wasn't yet ready to hear their voices again. She
didn't know if she ever would be.

In the meantime, Sophie adjusted to her new body. The
doctors had amputated some toes on each foot, but miraculously they had saved all her fingers, though they remained a
little bent and had lost some sensation. She tried to grip a plastic cup of water and couldn't tell how much pressure she used
until the flexible sides caved inward and the water spilled out.

She spent a month in the hospital, swaddled in bandages,
afraid to imagine what her face looked like beneath the white
gauze. She had never overvalued her physical appearance, but
now she worried that she resembled a monster, that friends
would no longer be able to look at her. Her thoughts bounced
back and forth between her injuries and Levi. What had she last
said to him? Something about hanging on, while she fought
with all her strength to keep his deadweight afloat on that exposed mountainside. She couldn't see anything past that; the
moment of his death was blank. Mercifully. She knew that his
parents had already held his funeral; she didn't mind missing it.

Whenever the thoughts overwhelmed her, she used the clunky bedside phone to call her mother, who always answered, no matter the time difference. They talked for as long as Sophie needed, racking up the international call fees. She joked that Sophie was talking her out of house and home, but she cried on the phone, too, about Evelyn. Sophie tried not to imagine what would have happened if both her daughters had died.

The doctors released Sophie with instructions for her recovering injuries, along with salves and bandages and pain medication. She felt more like a burn victim than anything else, and avoided looking at herself in mirrors, at the wrinkled, discolored skin that stretched across her cheeks and forehead. Only her eyes were unchanged.

She stayed for two nights at a cheap hotel in Kathmandu, gorging herself on momos to make up for a month of bland hospital food. At the airport she felt like a creature that had crawled up from the depths of the earth, aware of the stares from other passengers. She wanted to yank a paper bag over her face or hole up in the condo and never step into public again. But there was something she needed to do first.

Sophie flew back to Switzerland to box up the apartment she had shared with Levi. His parents drove in from Basel— the second time she had ever met them—and stayed for a week, helping her to clean and organize the remnants of their life together. Each moment felt like a dream, as if any second Levi would walk around the corner and begin helping her pack. In the beginning she told herself that she was packing up so they could move to Wyoming together, but the fantasy quickly wore thin.

She found the wrapped gift box beneath their bed on the third day. She had been sleeping in the apartment while Levi's parents went to a hotel every night, and that morning she woke up, got out of bed, and sank to the floor, overwhelmed by the task of cleaning up a life she had known for such a short time, but so deeply. With her face pressed against the hardwood floor, she blinked through blurry eyes until they focused on the colorful box. She knew immediately—her birthday present. Her stomach turned and she forced herself to sit up, to drag the box from underneath the bed with shaking hands. She didn't want to open it, hardly wanted to look at it, but Levi was right—it was too big to bring on the plane.

Sophie unwrapped it slowly, carefully, and when she lifted the lid from the box, she couldn't stop the tears that flowed down her cheeks. It was a wooden carving of Yama Parvat, large, the entire massif captured in minute detail—every col, every ridge, even crevasses were etched into the mountain. On the very top were two tiny figures—impossibly small, so small that she didn't notice them for several minutes. She set the mountain down on the bed and lay beside it, still crying, gazing in awe at the mountain that had followed her here, to Switzerland, and would follow her home. When Levi's parents arrived, an hour later, and found Sophie still in bed, still studying the carving, they offered to mail it to Colorado for her. Weeks later, when the package arrived at her mother's doorstep, she would repeat the process, crawling into bed beside the mountain and observing it for hours.

On her last full day in Switzerland, Andrew texted her a photo—Sophie and Levi on the summit of Yama Parvat, arms around each other, grinning. Sophie did not look worried and Levi did not look weak. She had three copies printed at the nearest office store. She framed one and gave it to Levi's parents at their last lunch together. She tucked one copy into her luggage. And she left the last on the kitchen counter of their apartment, at her final walk-through, before she locked the apartment for the last time. Someone would find it soon, a cleaning crew or the landlord, and throw it away. But until then, an image of them, happy, existed in the apartment, as they had a few months ago. Before Yama Parvat.

Sophie said goodbye to Zoe and a few of Levi's friends. She spent the night in a hotel and flew back to Colorado the next day. Her mother greeted her at the airport, weeping so openly that other people stopped and stared. Sophie held her and let her cry right there at baggage claim, watching the minutes tick by on the nearest screen.

Finally, she let go and said, "You're home. I thought I'd never see you again."

Her mother talked a lot on the drive to the condo. Sophie stayed silent and studied her. She had lost weight, and her hands shook whenever she let go of the steering wheel. But she got them home safely, talking all the while about how difficult it had been to keep hearing the news that poured out from Nepal, each new death and disaster. How she had sat in shock the night that James had called from Base Camp to tell her that Levi and Evelyn were dead, but Sophie was alive.

Sophie wandered the house like a ghost for a few days, looking at the pictures of Evelyn—everywhere, the walls, the mantel, the refrigerator. She did not have the sensation, as with Levi, that Evelyn would appear at any moment. She had watched her sister die, held her hand as her heart gave out and she took her last breath against the cold, dry snow. A coroner had confirmed the cause of death, after the guides carried her body back to Base Camp, a painstaking two-day process: heart attack.

The funeral was held on the Sunday after Sophie arrived home, to allow for Sophie's presence, though Sophie herself was uncertain how much she wanted to be present. Worse, Miles showed up—she hadn't given him a moment's thought until she walked into the funeral home and saw him standing against the back wall. She blinked twice, unwilling to believe her eyes, and glanced at her mother, who simply brushed past, heading off to greet extended family.

Sophie knew Miles probably saw her, but they never made eye contact. She stayed silent at the funeral and didn't give a speech. There was nothing she could possibly say to summarize Evelyn. She still didn't know if she hated or loved her sister, and that wasn't what their grandparents wanted to hear. So, she listened to her mother's tearful speech, to a cousin recounting Evelyn's intelligence and passion, and to an uncle talk about how Evelyn died doing what she loved. Sophie ducked out as soon as the ceremony ended, breathing in the fresh air as twilight fell over the Colorado mountains.

She mailed the divorce papers to Miles a week after the funeral and he signed them without protest. They hadn't owned much of value together. All the furniture in the cabin had either come with the house or from a thrift store. The cabin itself belonged to Miles. The artwork that hung on the walls was his. What did she own? Some cooking equipment, maybe, but most of that belonged to Miles, too, always the one to prepare their meals. She had almost nothing to her name.

Sophie came home from work exhausted, her muscles protesting after a particularly difficult day. She stopped at the sight of a large package at her doorstep, addressed to Sophie Wright.

She couldn't remember ordering anything but stooped to lift the package in her arms and pushed the front door open. Her hands still gave her difficulty sometimes, but after ten years, she had adjusted to maneuvering her way through everyday tasks. She had returned to guiding in the Tetons, too, welcomed back to her old job after she'd proven her ability to make ascents even with the changes to her body. She found her clients were often curious about the damage to her face and hands and asked questions, eager to hear a story of overcoming the wrath of the mountains. The ones who knew who she was never asked. She told the inquisitive ones to search for Yama Parvat when they returned home, to read her story then.

She set the package on the table and looked about for scissors, distractedly reaching over to pet her black cat, Momo, who meowed incessantly until he received attention. She cut the box open and drew a breath. Inside were two large, heavy plaques. One had Evelyn's name, the other Levi's, with their birth and death dates. Below the dates, a quote: *If adventure has a final and all-embracing motive, it is surely this: we go out because it is our nature to go out, to climb mountains, and to paddle rivers, to fly to the planets and plunge into the depths of the oceans... When man ceases to do these things, he is no longer man.* Sophie recognized it—written by Wilfrid Noyce, one of the members of the expedition that made the first ascent of Everest.

She had heard about the project from James a few weeks ago. The Nepal mountaineering organization wanted the surviving climbers to return to Yama Parvat's Base Camp—whoever was willing—to place plaques for the deceased climbers, a monument to the fateful expedition. She had agreed without really thinking. Now that she stood with the plaques before her on the table, she had no idea if she could legitimately repeat the journey.

That evening, sitting cross-legged on the couch across from a roaring fire, she called home.

"Do you think Evelyn would want this?"

Her mother paused, a long echo of silence on the phone. They were close again. So much could change in ten years. On the surface, her mother was the same, just older, still managing the lodge at the ski resort. But she had gone through chemo four summers ago, defeated the cancer that had arisen mysteriously in her lungs. Sophie had made trips from her small house in Wyoming back to Breckenridge whenever she had a day off.

Sophie's gaze drifted up to the mantel over the fireplace, where she had long ago placed the wooden carving of Yama Parvat. Beside it rested Levi's climbing sunglasses, folded, which she had retrieved from Evelyn's jacket pocket after her death, and a copy of Lowell's book, *Ghosts on the Mountain*, which she had never read, let alone opened. The book was published two years after the climb, on the anniversary of their summit day. Lowell had mailed her a copy with a note—*you don't have to read this, but I want you to have it.*

Weeks after the funeral, she had gone through Evelyn's things with her mother, brought back by Miles from New York. She had ended up taking nothing, left it all in boxes at the condo—climbing equipment, clothes, journals, and books. She had no use for any of it and besides, none of it would bring Evelyn back. Memories of her sister followed her like the clouds of a gathering storm, ready to unleash a torrent of regret and pain. A physical reminder would only concentrate that sorrow.

"I think Evelyn would want to know that she didn't die for nothing," her mother said, breaking the silence.

Sophie knew what she meant. Evelyn would want some degree of forgiveness.

She booked a plane ticket that night.

A month later she stood in Pokhara with the handful of others who had come—James, Phil, Danielle, Penelope, Andrew, Lowell, Charlie, Kathryn, Wojciech, Haruki, and Aoki. Sophie had heard, in the hospital after the climb, how the last three had turned up at Camp Three, somehow descending past Camp Four in the early morning while the storm raged. They had suffered less frostbite than Sophie and Lowell had, but still told of a desperate afternoon and night spent bivouacking on the mountain after their successful summit. Nina and Oskar had also slipped from the ridge, which gave Sophie a twisted comfort—perhaps their bodies lay with Levi's. Perhaps he wasn't alone.

The two bodies that Sophie had seen past the cliff on the false route were Shiro and Yasuhiko. And the last climber, Takashi, had wandered off from Haruki and Aoki and was never heard from again.

George was in poor health and couldn't make the journey. Ruslan and Ivan—who hadn't made the summit, who had been at Camp Three during the storm—had never responded to the original invitation.

Some of the others had brought along a significant other—Lowell's wife, Anne, seemed the most excited to be in Nepal, in awe of every inch of the country. She seemed to sense Sophie's apprehension and dutifully showed up at the door of her hotel room every morning with tea and breakfast.

The group shouldered their packs and set out. It felt markedly different from trekking to Base Camp before an actual climb. There were no ice axes or crampons in Sophie's pack, just a sleeping bag and sturdy tent in case any of the teahouse accommodations fell through. And the two plaques—they were responsible for most of the weight. No porters trailed behind them. Much of the route took them along the Annapurna circuit, which was crowded with backpackers in high spirits. Each day, rain or shine, they rose and marched on, through valleys and mountains and rainforest. Each day, they drew closer to Yama Parvat.

★ ★ ★

Sophie stood outside on the porch of a teahouse the evening before they were due to reach Base Camp. The forest had given way to icy peaks that towered overhead. The teahouse itself was hard to see from a distance, built from rock, nestled into rock. They were off the main Annapurna circuit now, so the accommodations were quieter, less sophisticated. Twilight turned the ridges purple and orange.

"Beautiful evening."

She flinched at the voice and twisted to see Lowell. His face, too, had been reconstructed, the skin of a thigh stretched over a cheekbone. It made him look older, more weathered. "Yes. We've been lucky."

"Have you been…" He trailed off, as if trying to find the words. "Anxious this entire trip? An increasing sense of dread?"

She tilted her head, considering. "Yes. No. Somewhere in between."

He shrugged and leaned against the stone porch railing. "Maybe I'm being too sensitive. But that mountain wanted no part of us ten years ago. Who's to say that will change tomorrow?"

"I think we'd be very unlucky to die at Base Camp."

Lowell waved a hand. "You know what I mean."

"What does Anne think?"

"She's just happy to be here, away from her job." He looked down at his gnarled hands.

Sophie found herself looking at his hands, too, and then at her own. Strange, to share a mark of survival with someone she hardly knew. "I know you still write. Do you still climb?"

He shook his head. "Can't. Not after what happened. I used to climb in the memory of a friend who died. I've known other people who have passed away over the years, of course, but nothing like this. Not so many in one season on one mountain. Besides," he said, lifting his hands, displaying them in the evening light, "I just didn't think I could. Physically or mentally. Anne is convinced I had PTSD. Saw a therapist, had me on all kinds of medication. Nothing worked. I couldn't sleep through the night. We moved back to Anne's hometown near Montréal and now I walk the dogs in the woods and occasionally travel to write about an exciting expedition. It's changed the quality of my work, not climbing. But I can't give up both things I love." He cleared his throat. "And that's my story."

Sophie could tell he was self-conscious about speaking so much; she waved him off. "It's okay. I didn't really stay in touch with anyone else who was there, and I feel bad about that. We all went off to live such different lives. I still climb. I guide. I tried to stay away from it but I couldn't. Nothing else satisfied me. It took a lot of practice and frustration to figure out what I could and couldn't do. I don't think I'll ever climb a giant again, but I'm happy in the Tetons."

He looked at her sideways, a smile on his face. "Maybe there's a lesson in this for some of us. We only ever needed small lives to be happy."

"Honey? Dinner is about to be served." They both turned to see Anne standing in the doorway. She waved to Sophie, grinning.

"We'll be inside in a minute," Lowell replied, and Anne ducked back through the door. He turned back to Sophie. "I don't know if you know this, but I got pretty close to Evelyn. She seemed—how do I put this—tormented by the state of your relationship. She loved you so much, Sophie. I hope you never doubt that. People make complicated, senseless mistakes all the time. It's part of life. You can love someone and still want to hurt them. But I don't think she wanted that, either. She just wanted to find her place in the world. Maybe she didn't in this lifetime, maybe she did. But she loved you. I have no doubt of that."

Tears sprung to Sophie's eyes as she listened. Before she could reply, Lowell continued.

"I have something for you." He reached into his back pocket and extended his hand toward her, a flash drive cradled in his palm. "I debated giving this to you. I don't know you that well. I don't know how you're doing now. So, if you don't want this, my feelings won't be hurt."

Sophie didn't have to ask what it was. She knew.

"I recorded all my interviews. There were a lot with Evelyn and a few with Levi. Yours are here, too, although if you're like me and cringe at the sound of your own voice, you'll want to skip those. There are some pictures, too. They're in the book, but—"

Sophie blinked back more tears, still looking at the flash drive. "I never opened the book," she said, her voice a soft squeak.

"I figured. But this is different. It's—it's hearing their voices. I listen to the interviews every year, on the anniversary of—you know. Of everyone who passed. A sort of memorial." He paused, tilting his hands toward her. "So?"

She opened her hand to accept it, the tiny object that contained Evelyn's and Levi's ghosts, and slipped it into her pocket. "Thank you. Just having it means so much."

He touched her shoulder gently. "Don't mention it," he said, nodding toward the door. "Let's not leave dinner too long or we won't get a plate."

That evening, Sophie set the flash drive on the bed beside her laptop. Another ten minutes passed before she worked up the courage to insert the small device. It was neatly organized: four folders, labeled Evelyn, Levi, Sophie, Pictures. Out of context, it could have been a family reunion.

It's not often you're given the choice between hearing two ghosts. Sophie's mouse lingered over the Evelyn folder for a long minute before she clicked. A dozen audio files, each labeled with Evelyn's name, the date, and the time. Twelve pieces of information about her sister's life in the weeks before she died. It was almost too much to bear.

There was a photograph, too, misplaced from the Pictures file. Evelyn, at Base Camp, her brown hair caught in a gust of wind. Her mouth was open in a smile, her cheeks ruddy to match her maroon suit and her eyes bright. She was bent forward a little, in laughter, and despite what Lowell had just said about her emotional state, she looked happy. Sophie studied the photograph for as long as she could bear, trying to sear this version of Evelyn into her brain. She closed the picture.

Sophie opened the first audio file, dated April 2, 6:15 p.m. It played automatically, a moment of rustling before Lowell's voice rumbled through her laptop speakers, asking Evelyn to introduce herself. And then Evelyn's voice. Clear and bright, and alive, and Sophie wished to crawl through the screen and into the file itself and back onto the snow-covered mountain. If only she had marched up to Evelyn that first day, turned her around so that they faced each other, and told Evelyn that it didn't matter. That she was forgiven, and that Sophie couldn't summit without her, not really. That she couldn't go through life without Evelyn, that a piece of herself would always be missing.

When Sophie's name left Evelyn's lips, Sophie knew, in some intrinsic way, that it had been the same way for Evelyn. In those last few weeks, perhaps even as she died, Sophie had been the person on Evelyn's mind. It gave Sophie little comfort to think that with more words and more time, perhaps they could have both lived to grow old together, as sisters, as friends. She knew it wasn't a rational thought—the storm hadn't been a manifestation of their inability to reconcile. It was simply nature, acting in response to a thousand unseen variables of atmospheric and environmental cues. A storm, a falling rock, a coyote moving through a darkened field—it all meant nothing. But still.

Sophie paused the recording before it ended, shut her laptop, and turned off the light.

The thing about mountains is that they never change. On a geologic timescale, of course, snow falls and melts away. Rivers overflow and change course, forests burn in fires, but the physical structure of a mountain is largely unchanging in the scale of a human life. So, when Sophie set foot on the rocky tumble of Base Camp the next day, her heart caught in her throat. It looked the same as it had ten years ago, minus the dotting of bright tents. Prayer flags were still affixed to poles, crisscrossing overhead, nothing more than little tatters of colored fabric after enduring years of harsh conditions. They approached the undecorated Chorten in silence, listening to the wind ripple through the prayer flags.

Finally, Haruki slung off his pack, pulled out the plaque for Yakumo, and stepped forward to place it at the base of the Chorten. He bowed his head and said something quietly in Japanese, before stepping back.

The others who had been given plaques repeated the process, setting the plaques down to encircle the base of the Chorten and saying a quick word to pay their respects. Sophie stood frozen, unable to move, until she felt someone's hand on her shoulder and realized that she was the last one left. She glanced over; the hand belonged to Penelope, who studied her with a faint smile and sadness in her eyes.

"I will help you," Penelope said, and Sophie had never been more grateful.

Together, they carried the plaques to the Chorten, Sophie with Levi's and Penelope with Evelyn's. Sophie knelt on the rocks and laid Levi's plaque amid the others. "I love you," she whispered. "I'll never stop loving you and I'll never, ever forget you."

She reached up to wipe away a tear, smearing dirt across her face, and reached up to take Evelyn's plaque from Penelope, avoiding her gaze. She shifted across the rocks, nestling Evelyn's marker between Eddie's and Levi's.

She drew a breath, the familiar feeling from Evelyn's funeral returning. She could think of nothing to say. "All my life I've wanted to be just like you. I'm glad I'm not, because I could never fill your footsteps. I love you. I'll see you again soon."

Sophie rose and stepped back; her face flushed. She had whispered but didn't know if Penelope had heard her private communion. She'd had more trouble believing in anything spiritual since Levi's and Evelyn's deaths; she had looked for signs of them everywhere and seen nothing. She gave Penelope a tight smile and mouthed *thank you* before walking back to the others. At James's suggestion, they bowed their heads in a moment of silence.

Sophie tried to keep her eyes closed, but something told her to open them. She looked up, blinking against the brilliant midday sun, to the peak of Yama Parvat. A dark blur of movement caught her attention. Far overhead, against the dramatic backdrop of the white mountain, a pair of black birds soared. Goraks, they were called. In tumbling flight, the birds dipped and rose, riding the wind. She watched as they turned to specks and then disappeared, finding someplace safe to land on the mountainside.

"What are you looking at?"

Penelope's question made Sophie flinch. She realized that everyone had opened their eyes and were moving, discussing the hike back to the teahouse.

"Just the mountain," Sophie said. Penelope squeezed her hand, a kind gesture, and stepped away to shoulder her backpack. Sophie picked up her own, much lighter now, and felt the comforting weight settle against her back.

As the group began to trickle out of Base Camp, beginning the long journey home, Sophie paused to look over her shoulder, shielding her eyes against the sun. She saw no birds, no signs of life, only Yama Parvat, solid and imposing against the blue sky. She listened for a moment but heard only the wind. It was over. The mountain had nothing left to say.

★ ★ ★ ★ ★

Acknowledgments

Many people shaped this book over several years. I'm grateful for this moment to express my thanks to everyone who touched these pages, both directly and indirectly.

To Jessica Faust, my wonderful agent, for believing in this story, and for your enthusiasm and wisdom throughout this experience. Meredith Clark, my incredible editor, for guiding this story to its best and brightest version. Endless thanks to you both. To production, cover design, marketing, sales, publicity, and everyone else at MIRA, thank you for bringing this book to life.

To David, Jordan, Judith, and Teresa. I couldn't ask for a better writing group and I am equally thankful for your feedback and friendship. This book would not exist in its current form without each of you. I appreciate every single one of the countless hours we've spent on Zoom, laughing, commiserating, and telling our stories.

To my early readers, including Nicole, Tanya, and others who kindly read drafts: thank you for taking the leap of faith in reading a stranger's work, for sharing your ideas, and for motivating me to keep going.

To Dr. Heidi Hanrahan, Dr. Carrie Messenger, Dr. James Pate, and the rest of the Shepherd University English department—thank you for giving me the courage to pursue my creative dreams.

To Greg, thank you for making my author photo process painless and fun.

To Dana. We're nothing like the sisters in this book—we're not nearly as dramatic—but I can't imagine a world without a sister like you. Thank you for being older, wiser, and cooler than me.

To Atlas, thank you for the many hours spent curled up at my side as I wrote this book. I wouldn't have taken so many writer's-block-curing walks without you.

To Adam. My first reader, always. You've never gotten tired of my stories—or if you have, you've hid it well. Thank you for treating my characters as if they are real people, for the many long drives where we talked through ideas, for listening to every single thought that goes through my head, and, most of all, for believing in me. I love you.